A PICTURE OF MURDER

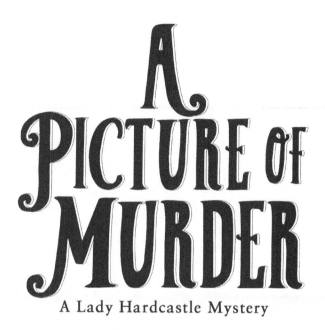

A PICTURE OF MURDER

A Lady Hardcastle Mystery

T E KINSEY

THOMAS & MERCER

Text copyright © 2018 by T E Kinsey
All rights reserved.

Published by Thomas & Mercer, Seattle

www.apub.com

Amazon, the Amazon logo, and Thomas & Mercer are trademarks of Amazon.com, Inc., or its affiliates.

ISBN-13: 9781542046022
ISBN-10: 1542046025

Cover design by Lisa Horton

Printed in the United States of America

A PICTURE OF MURDER

Chapter One

'Just hold it steady and try to keep your hand out of the shot,' said Lady Hardcastle with only the tiniest hint of exasperation.

I had been summoned to the studio in the orangery at eight o'clock that morning. It was half-past eleven now and we were both becoming only the tiniest bit impatient with each other.

'Perhaps we should take a break, my lady,' I said. 'I'll get Miss Jones to make us a nice pot of coffee. I think she had some biscuits on the go, too.'

'Just . . . one . . . more . . . shot . . .' she said, reaching across to the camera to flick the shutter release. 'There. All done, I think. I just need to make up some nice title cards and then *Town Mouse and Country Mouse* will be ready for the viewing public. Or the villagers, at any rate. I'm not sure the wider public could give a fig one way or the other. But Gertie assures me that the village is abuzz – she really did say "abuzz", you know – the village is abuzz with excited talk about "Lady Hardcastle's moving picture".'

'Daisy speaks of little else,' I said. 'I was in the Dog and Duck at lunchtime yesterday while you were fussing about in here and she was holding court behind the bar. "That Lady Hardcastle," she said, "she's some sort of genius or sommat making them moving pictures and that."

A genius, my lady. And she's actually met you. Your artistic endeavours may yet be the salvation of your shaky reputation.'

'They may yet,' she said distractedly as she continued to fiddle with the camera. 'Did you say something about coffee?'

'And biscuits. I'll pop up to the kitchen and see what I can find.'

'Bless you. I'll just tidy up here and I'll meet you in the morning room.'

I left the orangery and walked the short distance to the back door. The house had been built a few years earlier in the modern style – all red brick and white-painted window frames. One concession to earlier fashion had been the inclusion of the orangery. Lady Hardcastle rented the house from her old friend Jasper Laxley. He had designed it with the intention of moving into it when he and his family returned from India. Events had conspired to keep them on the beautiful subcontinent for longer than expected and he was delighted to be able to rent the newly built home to a trusted pal. It seems Mr Laxley had anticipated bringing exotic plant specimens back from India and had created the orangery to accommodate them. When we moved in, Lady Hardcastle had immediately reappointed it for use as a photographic studio. It was not at all what Mr Laxley had in mind, of course, but the light really was rather splendid.

I was only out of doors for a few moments but autumn was making its presence felt and I was glad to get in out of the chill.

I found Miss Jones, the young cook, hard at work in the kitchen. She seemed to be preparing a rack of lamb for our Sunday lunch.

Lady Hardcastle had employed her when we first moved to Littleton Cotterell. She was terribly young to be a cook. So young, in fact, that none of us could bring ourselves to call her Mrs Jones as tradition dictated. It seemed wrong, somehow. Despite her youth and inexperience, her cooking skills were a revelation. I've always thought myself a bit of a dab hand in the kitchen, but Blodwen Jones made me look like the worst sort of bumbling bungler by comparison.

'Oh, hello, Miss Armstrong,' she said as I stood by the range, warming my hands. 'Edna's been askin' where you was. Somethin' about her thinkin' we needs new table linen for the dinin' room. And she's run out of beeswax. And her duster has worn out. Nothin's going right for her today. I think you've been lucky keepin' out of her way, to be honest.'

I tried not to sigh. 'I'd better go and have a word,' I said instead. 'Can you conjure up a pot of coffee while I'm gone, please? Lady Hardcastle will take it in the morning room.'

'Of course,' she said with a smile. 'I made some shortbread this morning as well if you think she'd fancy that.'

'You read my mind,' I said.

I set off to find the housemaid.

'How stands the Empire, Edna?' I said when I finally found her in one of the bedrooms.

'I've been better, Miss Armstrong,' she said wearily.

'Oh dear,' I said. 'What's the matter?'

'Everythin' seems to be goin' wrong. I've run out of polish, this blimmin' duster's seen better days' – she held up a limp collection of ostrich feathers at the end of a battered handle – 'I can't get the table linen to come up nice . . . I'n't nothin' workin' as it should. And I can't tell you how many times I've put things down and can't find 'em again.'

'That'll be the house ghost. It's the time of year for it, after all.'

'Oh, don't say that,' she said. 'I knows you and the mistress don't go in for things like that, but I takes it very serious. I've seen a ghost at our grandma's house. I a'n't never felt a chill like it. And the barrier between their world and ours is weakest at Halloween.'

'I was teasing,' I said. 'I think we're safe. This house is less than ten years old – it's not been here long enough to acquire any ghosts.'

'You shouldn't make fun of them,' she said earnestly. 'You never know what went on here in days gone by.'

'I'm sorry, I was just trying to lighten the mood. It's not like you to be so downhearted over a few minor setbacks. Is there something else wrong?'

She looked up from making the bed. 'Oh, it's sommat and nothin', m'dear,' she said with a fleeting smile. 'My Dan was hurt t'other day at work. He'll mend, but it's a worry, though.'

'Oh no, I'm so sorry. I had no idea. Is it serious? Should you be looking after him?'

'He's fine. It's just a broken leg. But we'll miss his wages – Dr Fitzsimmons reckons he'll be off work for six weeks or more.'

'What does he do?'

'Farm work for Toby Thompson, at the moment. Him with the dairy herd. He usually works for Noah Lock up the hill, but he goes where the work is. A few odd jobs here and there, you know. Dan-of-all-trades, I calls him.'

'He'll be scuppered with a gammy leg, then,' I said. 'Would it help to do a few more hours here? I can have a word with Lady Hardcastle.'

She looked up from her bed-making. 'I must admit it would be a boon, my lover,' she said. 'But only if it's real work, mind. I don't want no charity.'

'Of course not. Nothing was further from my thoughts. I'm sure we could find plenty to keep you busy.'

'Then it would be much appreciated, I'm sure.'

'And Dan can do without you?'

'As long as he's got his pipe and a couple of bottles of cider, he can see hisself through a couple of afternoons without me waitin' on him.'

'I shall see what I can do, then,' I said.

'Proper work, mind. Don't forget.'

'I give you my solemn word that we shall work you like a navvy, Edna. Don't you worry about that.'

Reassured that there was nothing too much amiss, I returned to the kitchen. Miss Jones was just putting the pot and cups on the tray as I walked in.

'Thank you,' I said. 'Did you know about Dan?'

'And his broken leg?' She sighed. 'I haven't heard about nothin' else. Is that why she's all of a pother about every little thing?'

'It seems so.'

'They'll miss his wages,' she said. 'He can't work with a broken leg.'

'No, that's what she said. So I've offered to talk to Lady Hardcastle about doing a few more hours here.'

'That's very kind of you.'

'You don't mind?'

'Why ever should I mind?' she said, sounding rather bemused.

'Well, I'm not sure we can offer you any more hours. To tell the truth, I've no real idea what we're going to find for Edna to do. But don't tell her that. She's determined not to accept charity.'

'Mum's the word,' she said. 'She's a proud one, our Edna. But don't you worry about me. I'm happy with my mornin's. Suits me fine. I still needs to get back to our ma.'

'Of course, of course. How is your mother?'

'Ups and downs, you know,' she said. 'She has her good days and her bad. But we gets by.'

'It must be hard. But don't be like Edna. If you need help, you will say, won't you?'

'You're very kind, miss. Do you want me to take this tray through?'

As usual, she had set the tray for two – both she and Edna had quickly accepted the idea of Lady Hardcastle and her lady's maid eating and drinking together.

'No, don't worry,' I said. 'I'll take it. You get back to working your arcane magic on that lamb. Tell Lady Hardcastle she said she'd meet me in the morning room if it seems as though she might have forgotten.'

'Can you smell smoke?' asked Lady Hardcastle as she breezed into the morning room, still in her overalls.

'I asked Edna to light the fires,' I said. 'I thought we'd already been sufficiently stoic and hardy. It's gone beyond "a bit chilly" and we're well on the way to "brass monkeys". Warmth was called for.'

'You're quite right, of course,' she said, sitting down. 'A stiff upper lip is much less impressive when its stiffness is caused by its being frozen solid. But I meant outside. There seemed to be quite a whiff in the air when we went out into the garden this morning, didn't you think?'

'Perhaps everyone lit their fires today?'

'No, it smelled more . . . messy. Not like logs or coal.'

'Bonfires?' I suggested. 'Burning the leaves and other garden detritus? One last tidy-up before winter?'

'It's bucketing down now, dear,' she said. 'Who would light a bonfire in the rain? Are you sure you didn't smell anything?'

'Not that I noticed,' I said. I poured her a cup of coffee and offered her one of Miss Jones's shortbreads. 'I hope the weather cheers up for Friday. I love Bonfire Night.'

'Me too. Father used to take us all to a big fireworks display on Guy Fawkes Night. There would be stalls selling food and drink. I had the most vivid memory of a Yorkshireman selling "bonfire toffee" – brittle black stuff that could break your teeth. But that was all right because you could also use it to stick them back together. I insisted that we had visited him every year and that I absolutely adored bonfire toffee. When I was older, Mother told me that we'd only seen him once and that I'd taken one splintered bite and then spat it out on to the grass, declaring it to be "the horridest thing in the whole Empire". The fireworks were magical, though. Always.'

'Guy Fawkes Night was our last show before we packed up the circus for the winter,' I said. 'We'd do the show and then lead the crowd out to the field. We'd put on fireworks like they'd never seen while the fire eater did his act by the light of a massive bonfire. I was quite disappointed when we moved back to Aberdare so Ma could look after Mamgu. The town couldn't afford anything like what we'd seen growing up.'

'Do you remember the fireworks in Shanghai? We ought to get those chaps to come over here and show us how it's done. Still, they always make an effort in the village, even without Chinese expertise. I have high hopes.'

'If Lady Farley-Stroud is organizing the moving picture show, though, who's in charge of Bonfire Night?' I asked. 'Sir Hector?'

Sir Hector and Lady Farley-Stroud were the local landowners. Lady Hardcastle had once described them as 'the most charming old buffers ever to draw breath', and over the past year or so they had all become firm friends.

'Hector? Really? I love him dearly, but he couldn't organize a bun fight in a bakery, bless him. No, I think there's a committee of some sort with Gertie still at the helm. She can run the moving picture show and still keep a firm hand on the Guy Fawkes Night tiller. She's a steam-driven marvel of capability, that woman.'

'And a half,' I said. 'With ornamental brass knobs on.'

She glanced at her wristwatch. 'I say, it's nearly lunchtime. Why did you let me eat biscuits? We should be pestering Miss Jones for pie.'

'I wanted elevenses at eleven, but you wanted to get "just . . . one . . . more . . . shot . . .",' I said. 'I'm a good girl, me. I always do as I'm told.'

This earned me a harrumph, but I was spared anything more stinging by the ringing of the telephone.

'Who on earth can that be?' she said.

'I shall find out,' I said.

I went to the hall and took the telephone earpiece from its cradle on the side of the wooden box screwed to the wall.

'Hello,' I said. 'Chipping Bevington two-three.'

7

'Armstrong?' said a familiar lady's voice. Talk of the Devil and all that. 'Armstrong? Is that you, m'dear?'

'It is, Lady Farley-Stroud,' I said. 'Would you like me to fetch Lady Hardcastle for you?'

'No, m'dear, there's no need for that. Just fetch Lady Hardcastle for me, would you?'

'Right you are, my lady,' I said. 'Hold the line, please.'

We had a similar conversation nearly every time she called. I was beginning to wonder if it was me.

'Who was it, dear?' said Lady Hardcastle when I went back into the morning room.

'Lady Farley-Stroud,' I said. 'I think she'd like a word.'

She was gone for a fair few minutes. I could hear only snippets of her side of the conversation but there were sufficient 'oh my goodness'-es and 'I say, you poor things'-es for me to be able to surmise that all was not well at The Grange.

'All is not well at The Grange,' said Lady Hardcastle as she returned.

'I surmised as much,' I said. 'What's the matter?'

'That smell of smoke I remarked upon when I came in was from their kitchen.'

'Mrs Brown has ruined their Sunday lunch?'

'Much worse,' she said. 'The whole kitchen has gone up in flames. Someone forgot a candle, they think. It caught a cloth and, well, one tragic thing followed another.'

'Heavens,' I said. 'Was anyone hurt?'

'Thankfully, no,' she said. 'Nor was the rest of the house affected. They're just without a kitchen.'

'Is there anything we can do to help?'

'That was the reason for her call. They were supposed to be hosting the visiting kinematograph people – Colonel Something-or-other and three actors.'

'Colonel Cheetham,' I said. 'Nolan Cheetham.'

'That's the chap. She asked if we could put them up.'

'You agreed, I hope.'

'In a flash. They can have a room each – it's not like we're short of space. The only thing I worried about was whether you'd be able to cope.'

'Not on my own,' I said. 'But it happens that Edna wants to work a few more hours while her husband is on the sick list. I'm not so sure about Miss Jones, but she might be persuaded. She's very eager to please, but she likes to be at home to look after her mother.'

'I think Gertie Farley-Stroud knows her mother – I believe they're on a couple of village committees together – she might be able to persuade her to encourage young Blodwen to get out a bit more and get on in the world. And Gertie has offered us the use of Dora and Dewi for the duration.'

Dora Kendrick was one of the housemaids at The Grange. We didn't get on. Dewi Rees was the footman. He was a plodder and was given to swearing at people in Welsh when he was under pressure, but he was a good sort.

'I think we'll be fine,' I said. 'When is everyone arriving?'

'The servants will be here tomorrow morning, the guests tomorrow afternoon.'

'Oh. Edna and Miss Jones have already gone for the day. I'll have to tell them tomorrow.'

'Did Miss Jones leave us any lunch?'

'Rack of lamb,' I said. 'I'll just put on the finishing touches.'

Later that evening, Lady Hardcastle and I were drinking brandy together by the fire in the sitting room.

'I do love village life,' she said, shifting a little in the armchair to make herself comfortable. 'But it does seem to involve a great deal more commitment and effort than living in the city.'

I laughed. 'It's not like they've asked us to do much. You're always saying we should have houseguests.'

'Oh, I know. I'm not complaining. I was just musing on the idea that when Lady Whosit throws a party in London, she doesn't expect all her neighbours to pitch in. We just turn up in our best frocks and frolic the night away. When it's time to go home, carriages are summoned and we all depart, leaving her household to clean up the mess. Out here, though . . .'

'Out here they ask ever so nicely if you wouldn't mind helping them out of a spot of bother. Then they offer you the use of their own servants to make sure that they're putting you to as little trouble as possible. I'm not sure I don't prefer the country way.'

'When you put it like that, young Flo, I'm not sure I disagree with you.' She took another sip of her brandy. 'Does village tittle-tattle have anything to say on the subject of our houseguests? Gertie has been very unforthcoming.'

'Daisy is my main source of gossip, as always,' I said. Daisy was the butcher's daughter who spent her mornings in her father's shop and her afternoons and evenings behind the bar in the local pub, the Dog and Duck. She was giddy and foolish, and quite the best friend I had in the village. 'She says that the Cheetham fellow has a bit of a reputation as a charismatic showman, but his – how did she put it – "his star is on the wane".'

'Unusually poetic for dear Daisy.'

'She read it in one of her magazines. She lent me her copy.' I indicated the magazine on the table between us. 'They have a "kinematograph" section sometimes. He was widely regarded as the Great Panjandrum of the English moving picture world, she says. There are others snapping at his heels, but by all accounts his new picture is set to reassert his supremacy.'

'And he's bringing it here?' she said with some surprise. 'How exciting.'

10

'"Bringing the kinematograph back to everyday folk", or some such. Daisy said something about him thinking that his fellow producers concentrate too much on the big cities and not enough on rural communities, so he's going to continue the premiere tour of his new production right here in Littleton Cotterell. I'm sure you can cross-examine him closely while he's here.'

'There's usually no need – showmen do love to talk about themselves. And what of his cast? Does Daisy know anything of them?'

'Two actresses and an actor,' I said. 'She told me their names, and rambled at length about the ups and downs of their careers, but I'm afraid my attention wandered. I can't remember a thing she said.'

'Then it shall be part of the fun to meet them and find out all about them,' she said. She poured us both another measure of brandy. 'Now then, what do you say to a little music before bed? That poor piano looks like it could do with a bit of exercise. What do you fancy?'

'Do you have something spooky, my lady?' I said.

'"Spooky"? Why "spooky"?'

'It's All Hallows' Eve,' I said. 'The night when the spirits are abroad. Edna is convinced they've been stealing her dusters.'

'We'll have to nip that nonsense in the bud,' she said. 'Gertie informed me in hushed tones – well, as hushed as she could manage while she was bellowing into her telephone – that her own servants have been muttering about supernatural forces being responsible for the kitchen fire.'

'You city folk forget how seriously your country cousins take this sort of thing.'

'Ghoulies and ghosties. And long-leggedy beasties?'

'The very same. And witches and monsters. *Nos Galan Gaeaf*, my mother used to call it. The night before the first day of winter. She taught us all the old customs. When we moved back to Aberdare some of the families there still observed them. They were good chapel folk all year round, but the old ways came out one night a year.'

11

'How exciting. Were there ceremonies? Rituals?'

'There was *Coelcerth*,' I said, shamelessly adopting the hushed tones of a storyteller at the most chilling part of the tale. 'The women and children would dance around a huge bonfire. Each of them in turn would write their name on a stone and place it in the fire. As the fire burned down, everyone would scatter and run for home. The last one out in the dark risked being caught by *Yr Hwch Ddu Gwta* – a fearful black sow with no tail – and the headless woman that walked with her.'

'Gracious me,' she said with a smile. 'And I thought Wales was a cheerfully friendly land of poetry and song.'

'That's not all, my lady. In the morning, they would check the stones in the fire to make sure that they were all still there. If anyone's name was missing, that person would die before another year had passed.'

She laughed. 'That all makes Nanny's jack-o'-lantern seem rather tame. A clumsily carved turnip with a candle inside and a dire warning not to have anything to do with witches pales by comparison.'

'You Londoners with your city ways,' I said, still in the role of ghostly storyteller. 'You don't know the half of it.'

She laughed again. 'Saint-Saëns, perhaps?' she said. '"Danse Macabre" should fit the bill nicely. Or Mussorgsky? I'm sure I have "Night on Bald Mountain" somewhere. Or perhaps both. Or neither. They're both quite tricky.'

I settled back into my armchair and closed my eyes, losing myself in the music. They were, indeed, both rather tricky, but she managed them with her usual accomplished ease.

It was midnight by the time we retired and I took two lighted candles with me as I went to bed. One can never be too careful on *Nos Galan Gaeaf.*

Chapter Two

As is so often the way after a late night, I was awake at a disappointingly early hour. By the time Edna and Miss Jones let themselves in by the side door, I already had the range lit and the kettle on. I was setting the copper laundry tub to boil as they came in to the kitchen.

'Mornin', Miss Armstrong,' said Edna cheerfully. 'Y'ere, that's kind of you, thank you. There's not many lady's maids as would get the washing goin'. Much appreciated, my lover, I'm sure.'

'It's no bother,' I said. 'But I confess I do have an ulterior motive for wanting to get in both your good books.'

She raised a quizzical eyebrow.

'You remember our conversation yesterday?' I continued. 'You were saying you wouldn't mind a little extra work.'

'So long as it's proper work,' she reminded me. 'I i'n't no charity case.'

'Quite so,' I said. 'Would four houseguests count as proper work, do you think?'

'Four?' said Edna and Miss Jones in unison.

'I'm afraid so,' I said. 'Lady Farley-Stroud was going to be putting up the visiting kinematograph people, but after the fire—'

'Oh, goodness, yes. The fire. Our ma told us about that,' interrupted Miss Jones, quite uncharacteristically. 'In the kitchens. I've always been terrified I might accidentally start a fire in a kitchen.'

'They says it was the spirit of a cook from the 1600s,' said Edna.

'Do they, indeed?' I said.

'Yes. Cruelly treated by the son of the lord, she was. Died givin' birth to his illegitimate son. Local story says she comes back this time of year to warn the servants to watch out and to take her revenge.'

'On whom?' I asked, fascinated in spite of myself.

'The family what done her wrong,' said Edna firmly.

'But they're long gone. The Farley-Strouds bought the place in the eighties.'

'No one ever said ghosts had access to the Land Registry,' she said. 'All she knows is that she died in her kitchen and someone needs to pay.'

'I see,' I said. 'Well, fortunately, no one had to pay. Although Mrs Brown was a little shaken.'

'That lazy old trout,' said Edna. 'I heard as how she took one look at the damage and did a bunk to her sister's.'

The village gossip network was as efficient as ever, it seemed.

'At Gloucester, apparently,' I said. 'But the lack of a fully working kitchen and the inconvenient absence of an experienced cook has left Lady Farley-Stroud feeling that she can't entertain her guests. She's asked if they can be billeted with us. Two gentlemen and two ladies, I understand. One of the gentlemen runs the company, the others are his actors.'

'Actors?' said Edna. 'Can't trust 'em. Our Dan's sister used to work in the Theatre Royal down at Bristol. She could tell you some stories about actors.'

'I'm sure they'll be no trouble,' I said. 'And Lady Farley-Stroud has offered to send us Dora and Dewi to help out—'

'That pair of useless articles?' exclaimed Edna. 'Tryin' to get 'em out from under her feet, more like.'

'She's offered to send us Dora and Dewi to help out,' I said again, trying desperately to regain control of the conversation. 'We shan't be shorthanded, but it will disrupt our usual routine.'

'Well, I did ask for proper work,' said Edna with a chuckle. 'I suppose I should be careful what I wishes for.'

'What about food?' asked Miss Jones anxiously. 'We've not got enough in – I never thought to order more. And I can't work all day. I'm really sorry, but I've got our ma to think about.'

'Don't worry about that,' I said. 'I can order extra groceries and we can work something out between us. I'm not a complete duffer in the kitchen, you know.'

'Oh, I know, miss. I didn't mean . . . But it's not part of your duties. You've got enough to be getting on with, lookin' after the mistress.'

'It was just her and me for quite a while before we moved here. We were never in one place long enough for her to employ other servants so I ended up doing most things.'

'I'd love to hear some of your stories some day,' she said. 'Never mind no gossip about actors. I reckon you've had some adventures.'

I laughed. 'More than a few. And there's more than a few of those I can never tell. State secrets and all that.'

She goggled at me.

'Take no notice, my lover,' said Edna. 'She's teasin' you.'

It was my turn to raise an eyebrow.

'No, Edna, I believes her,' said Miss Jones. 'She and Lady Hardcastle has got stories to tell.'

'If you like, dear,' said Edna. 'But stories'll have to wait. When are these actors arrivin'?'

I smiled sheepishly. 'Bert is picking them up from the station in Chipping Bevington . . . at lunchtime,' I said.

'Today?' they said in unison.

I told Edna that I'd be asking her to take charge of Dewi and Dora while the three of them readied the house for our visitors. She seemed pleased. She had been in service for a long while and had been house-keeper in a medium-sized house in her younger days. She enjoyed the easier life of part-time work for Lady Hardcastle, but I got the impression that she was looking forward to showing what she was capable of. I left her to make her plans.

Meanwhile, Miss Jones and I discussed some menu ideas for the rest of the week and reviewed the state of the larder.

It belatedly occurred to me that we had never asked how long our houseguests would be staying, but I estimated that we'd have to feed them until at least breakfast-time on Saturday. The 'Travelling Picture Extravaganza', as Lady Farley-Stroud's committee had enthusiastically named it, was due to end on Thursday, with the visitors being invited as guests of honour at the village's Bonfire Night celebrations on Friday. It seemed likely that they'd want a night's rest before they got on their way to their next engagement, so we would need to provide food for four extra mouths for up to fifteen meals. The local shopkeepers were going to be pleased to see me.

I heard a knock at the side door. Edna was nearby and answered it. It was probably a delivery. I thought briefly about catching whichever lad it was and sending him back to his employer with our revised order but I decided that a personal appearance would be better. I paid no further attention until I heard my own name and realized that the voices I could hear were not those of Edna and a young butcher's boy, but of Edna and another adult.

Edna was speaking. '. . . and Miss Armstrong has asked that you two—'

'Stuck-up little madam,' said Dora.

'I beg your pardon?' said Edna.

'Your "Miss Armstrong". Thinks she's better than the rest of us because she pals around with that batty old gimmer Lady Hardcastle. Comes in the front door at The Grange, she does. The front bloomin' door! And all because her soft-headed mistress managed to solve a couple of puzzles.'

'Watch your tongue, girl. That's no way to talk about anyone, most especially not women like them two. They's worth two dozen of you. Each.'

Dora, it seemed, was undaunted. 'And don't think we're gonna be takin' none of your old nonsense, neither,' she said. 'We works for the Farley-Strouds and you a'n't got no business bossin' us about. We gots our instructions. We knows what to do.'

I'm not usually given to looming. Obviously my diminutive stature precludes a properly intimidating physical loom, but, even so, I'm not fond of it as a leadership technique. In my early days as a scullery maid in Cardiff, the other girls and I were letting off steam one day, grumbling about the way one of the more senior housemaids treated us, when one by one, the others all fell silent. I turned to see Mrs Llewellyn, the housekeeper, looming over me. We were all scolded for our insolence, but it was the stomach-crampingly awful moment when I looked up and saw her angry face that stayed with me. If I were ever in her position, I vowed, I would never loom. It's an awful thing to do.

Dora, though, had never been one of my favourite people in the village and was, I thought, in dire need of a bit of looming. I signalled Miss Jones to stay quiet and tiptoed to the door of the 'boot room' – our rather grand name for the little cubby where the conversation was taking place. Edna had her back to me, standing between the newcomers and the kitchen. For once, my size might make for a more effective loom.

I approached stealthily, getting up as close as I could behind Edna and using her to shield me from Dora's view. She was still in full flood, listing my and Lady Hardcastle's inadequacies and our general unsuitability for life among decent country folk.

I peered slowly round from behind Edna's shoulder.

It took Dora a couple of seconds to notice me before her voice trailed off with an unconvincingly defiant, 'Yes . . . well . . .' She blushed a shade of red I'd last seen on a lobster served at a banquet hosted by the Italian ambassador in Paris.

'Hello, Dora, *fach*. How lovely to see you again,' I said. 'Has Edna explained the arrangements?'

She glared at me for a moment, but she couldn't hold it for long and was soon staring at her own boots.

'There's a lot to be done over the coming week,' I continued, 'but I suggest that you pay close attention to Edna's instructions and things will run as smooth as clockwork.'

Throughout all this, Dewi hadn't said a word. To his credit, though, the lanky Welsh lad looked embarrassed at the way his fellow Grange servant was conducting herself. He nodded his assent while Dora continued her close inspection of her boots.

'And, Dora,' I said to the top of her head, 'if I ever hear even the vaguest rumour that you've spoken like that about Lady Hardcastle again, I will spend the rest of my life making the rest of *your* life more miserable than you can possibly imagine. You can say what you like about me and the worst it will get you is a smack in the chops if I can be bothered. But one word against her – one word, Dora Kendrick – and you'll wish your mother had never taught you to speak. Do I make myself abundantly clear?'

'Yes, miss,' she mumbled.

'Splendid. I shall leave you to it, Edna,' I said. 'I need to get into the village to order a few things. See you all in a little while.'

I put on my overcoat and slipped out through the back door. By a colossal effort of will, I managed not to slam it.

I had calmed down a little by the time I reached Weakley's greengrocers – 'Visit Weakley's Daily for the Best Fresh Veg'. I gave Mr Weakley our order and he all but squealed for joy when he saw how much extra we wanted. 'Is your mistress hosting a banquet, Miss Armstrong?' he asked.

'She has unexpected houseguests for the week,' I said.

'I hope it's not too much bother for you, but I can't pretend I'm not glad of the extra business. Oh, is it the people who were going to be staying with Lady Farley-Stroud? We heard about the fire. Terrible business. They say no one knows how it started, but Mrs Weakley says one of the scullery maids reckons they regularly sees a ghostly figure with a lantern walking the halls that night. The lantern glows blue, she said. There i'n't no natural lantern flame as glows blue – none as I've ever heard of, leastways.'

'Maybe not,' I said. 'But being a scullery maid can be terribly boring sometimes. They make things up to help the days pass more quickly. One girl I worked with in Cardiff when I was young swore blind that the ghost of the master's dog flew in through her bedroom window in the night and performed the Dance of the Seven Veils, polished her Sunday boots, and gave her a tip for the next day's race meeting at Chepstow.'

'Did it win?' he asked.

'It was called Aunt Jemima and it finished fourth. It was later disqualified following a stewards' enquiry. But my point is that she made it all up. And I'm sure the girls at The Grange are making things up, too.'

'But Mrs Weakley i'n't gullible. She reckons—'

My own grandmother had 'the sight', as she called it, and I always thought of myself as having an open mind when it came to the supernatural, but this was getting out of hand. A ghost at The Grange? I decided to derail this particular train of thought.

'Still,' I said, 'at least no one was hurt in the fire. But we do have some extra houseguests.'

'They're the ones from the moving picture show?' asked Mr Weakley, seemingly unfazed by the sudden change back to the original topic.

'That's them, yes,' I said. 'Lady Hardcastle stepped into the breach and they're staying at . . .' I was once again struck by the fact that the house had no name. '. . . at the house,' I concluded limply.

'Well, you just leave this with me, miss, and I'll get the boy to deliver it as soon as possible.'

I left him clucking over his good fortune and wondering if he had enough potatoes and carrots.

Mr Holman, the baker, was similarly chuffed with the extra business and offered me a deal on his famous pork pies. I accepted, of course, and he wrapped them for me while making promises about the early delivery of all our other needs.

Mrs Pantry, the general grocer, was as sour as ever and managed to make the sale of many shillings' worth of goods (which she otherwise would definitely not have sold) seem like the most dreadful inconvenience.

It was with some relief, then, that I made my final call of the morning. I was always afforded a reassuringly warm welcome at the sawdust-strewn shop of F Spratt, Butcher.

Even the bell above the door – which I'm sure came from exactly the same factory in the Midlands as Mrs Pantry's – seemed to give a more cheerful tinkle as I entered.

The Spratt family were in full attendance.

Mr Spratt looked every inch the butcher in his blood-stained apron, and most of those inches were round his middle. His face lit up when he saw me. I like to imagine that it was just for me, but I rather suspected that he was pleased to see everyone.

'Good mornin', m'dear,' he said as he put down his huge knife and wiped his hands on the cloth that hung from his apron string. 'How lovely to see you.'

'Good morning, Mr Spratt,' I said. 'It's lovely to see you, too.'

Mrs Spratt was tying a package for delivery. Her chubby fingers were surprisingly nimble and she had the meat wrapped more quickly than I could ever have managed. 'Call 'im Fred, my lover,' she said as she put the package to one side. 'Everyone does. "Mr Spratt" sounds far too grand for a great lummox like him.'

'I calls him "our dad",' said Daisy. 'So does Wilf.' Wilf was Daisy's older brother. He was a junior rating in the Royal Navy and I'd never met him but the whole family was proud of him.

'But Miss Armstrong can't call him "our dad" because he's not her dad,' said Mrs Spratt. 'Anyway, ignore Daisy, she's all of a tizzy because this Cheetham fella and his – what did you call 'em, Dais? His troupe? – they's all coming to the village.'

'Is that right, Daisy?' I said. 'Then you're going to love my news.'

Daisy looked up from the ledger where she was carefully totting up her father's takings.

'They're staying with us,' I said.

'They's never!' she said. 'That's so excitin'. I don't suppose you needs an extra maid? I could do the books. Or sommat. I won't get in the way. I'd love to meet 'em. Introduce me.'

I laughed. 'Of course,' I said. 'Do you want me to put in a good word for you? I might be able to get you a part in his next picture.'

She all but swooned. 'Wouldn't that be the best thing that ever was, though? Me . . . in a picture . . .'

'You've been in a picture before, my love,' said Mrs Spratt.

'What, that bloke down at Weston?' said Daisy.

''S right.' Mrs Spratt turned to me. 'Few years ago it was, mind. We all went down to Weston-super-Mare on the train. A proper village outin' it was. And while we was there, we saw this bloke with one o' they cameras, like. You know . . .' She mimed cranking the handle on the side of a moving picture camera. 'We larked about when he pointed it at us – dancin' and that. Then his assistant comes over and gives us these

21

flyers sayin' that if we comes along to a church hall off the promenade at four in the afternoon, we could see ourselves.'

'Course,' said Mr Spratt, 'we could'a seen ourselves anyway, just by lookin'. Not like we was difficult to spot, all paradin' up and down in our Sunday Best.'

'So anyway,' continued Mrs Spratt, undeterred, 'a few of us troops along to this church hall they was on about, pays our ha'penny each, and sits down. Afore long, in comes the bloke we seen with the camera. He sets up this magic lantern thing and starts turnin' the handle. And there we are, larger than life on this huge white sheet he's got stretched on the wall.'

'How exciting,' I said.

'Course, it weren't nothin' we'd not seen before, mind. But it's a bit more fun when it's you what's on the screen, i'n't it?'

'I imagine it is,' I said. In truth, I'd seen myself captured in moving pictures when a friend of Lady Hardcastle's in London had brought a camera to a party a few years before, but I wanted Mrs Spratt to have her moment.

'I reckon folk round here would get a thrill from it. You think your Colonel Cheetham could do sommat like that for us?' she said.

'We can lose nothing by asking him. What do you reckon, Daisy? We could get you in one of his pictures that way.'

She tutted. ''T i'n't the same, is it? I fancies bein' one o' they actresses. All glamorous, like. I reckon movin' pictures is gonna see the music hall off.'

'Rubbish,' said Mr Spratt with a laugh. 'Can't no flickerin' shadows on a wall replace proper performers. Where's the songs? Where's the jokes? Can't walk out of a kinematograph show hummin' the tunes. It's a fad. Nothin' more.'

'You're such an old fogey, Dad,' said Daisy.

'I might well be,' he said good-naturedly. 'But I'm right. You mark my words. Now, then, enough of all this chatter. We're keepin' Miss

Armstrong from her business. You've got things to be gettin' on with, I'll be bound. Can't be standin' here jabberin'.'

'Believe me,' I said, 'after visiting Mrs Pantry's, it's a relief to find myself welcome in a village shop.'

'I don't know how she gets away with it,' he said. 'I s'pose there i'n't nowhere else for folk to go. But what can we get you now you've escaped her? I got some lovely pork chops.'

'I have a list,' I said, and handed over the last of my scraps of paper.

He took it and looked at it for a moment before laughing explosively. 'Well, blow me down. How many did you say you've got comin'?'

'Just four,' I said. 'But Lady Hardcastle is keen that we should present them with a groaning board.'

'It'll groan, all right,' he said, still chuckling. 'It'll take me a little while to get this little lot together. I'll send the lad over later.'

'No rush,' I said. 'We've enough for tonight.'

'Between these kinematograph people and Mr Hughes and his merry men and women . . .' began Mrs Spratt.

'Mr Hughes?' I asked.

'The leader of that motley bunch outside the village hall with their placards,' she said. 'With one lot here to promote their kinematograph show, and this Hughes bloke rollin' into the village to preach the evils of the kinematograph show, I'd say we was goin' to 'ave a profitable week. Mr Holman has already ordered more meat to make pies for them all.'

'I'm glad to be the bearer of glad tidings, then,' I said with a smile. 'And meat orders.'

I left another Littleton Cotterell shopkeeper to contemplate the unexpected benefits of a visit from the moving picture people.

◆ ◆ ◆

Back at the house, all was calm. Edna was bustling about, and chattered inconsequentially when I arrived as though nothing were amiss. She was very much inclined towards inconsequential chatter and I should have thought nothing of it, but it was also obvious that Dora was keeping out of my way, so I suspected that all was not fully resolved.

Dewi, bless his little cotton socks, did his best to be polite and friendly. When I first met him at The Grange, he was lazy and surly. One day he had sworn colourfully at our friend Inspector Sunderland in Welsh and I took him by surprise when I admonished him in the same language. As I got to know him, I found that his cantankerousness was born of a dismaying lack of self-confidence. He wasn't always quick to understand what was going on and had managed to convince himself – no doubt with plenty of unkind prompting from others – that he was 'just a stupid mutton-head'.

He dealt with his imagined inadequacies in the traditional way by adopting an aggressive and antagonistic manner. It kept people at arm's length, which helped to protect him from further mockery, but also prevented all but the most determined from offering him friendship. For some reason, though, he was never quite as brusque with me and we always got along passably well. Perhaps it was a Celtic thing.

'I think I've done all I can for now, Miss Armstrong,' he said as he came into the kitchen a little while later.

I was making a pot of tea while Miss Jones carried on quietly and efficiently preparing the brace of pheasants we were planning to cook for dinner.

'The gentlemen's rooms are ready, then?' I asked.

'I've checked the wash stands and put out fresh towels,' he said. 'Dora made the beds. The wardrobes is cleaned out and we've opened the windows to give the rooms a bit of an airing. I'll close them up in a bit, I reckon, and one of us can light the fires if they needs it, like.'

'Splendid. Then you're just in time for a cuppa and a sit-down. Miss Jones has made some scones, too, if you fancy one.'

'Don't mind if I do,' he said, sitting down at the new table. We'd spent more than a year without a kitchen table because, apparently, we didn't need one. Except, of course, that they really are terribly useful. After I'd put up with altogether too much grumbling from Edna, I had finally persuaded Lady Hardcastle to buy one.

I put the teapot on the table and sat opposite him.

'How are things up at The Grange after the fire?' I said as I poured three cups.

'Not so bad,' he said. 'I reckon they was all more shocked than anythin'. When you get in there, there's not really that much damage. Could have been much worse.'

'They could have lost the whole house,' I said.

'I suppose they could,' he said slowly, as though this were the first time the thought had occurred to him. 'I suppose that's why the mistress is so shook up about it. And Mrs Brown, too.'

I had my own thoughts about Mrs Brown using the fire as an excuse to take some time off, but I wasn't about to disparage her, no matter how much of a lazy, bullying old trout I thought her.

Miss Jones put down the second freshly plucked pheasant with a satisfied sigh and wiped her hands on her apron.

'Come and join us, Miss Jones,' I said. 'I'll butter you a scone.'

'That would be most welcome,' she said. 'I loves pheasant, but I hates pluckin' the little perishers.'

I was about to tuck into my own scone when the front doorbell rang. According to the large clock on the kitchen wall it was just past twelve.

'I think that might be our guests,' I said, standing up and straightening my uniform. 'As we used to say in the circus, "It's show time."'

I opened the door.

Arrayed before me on the doorstep were two men and two women. I had only a moment to take in their appearances before deciding who to greet first. As leader of the group, I thought Colonel Cheetham should receive the welcome on their behalf, but which one was he?

He wasn't either of the women, obviously. The older of the two looked to be in her early fifties. She had lost none of the beauty of her youth, though it had been softened somewhat by the passing years. Her days as a leading lady were behind her, and I would have said that she was what our theatre friends called a 'character actress'. But not a dowdy one. Her light-brown hair was greying slightly where it peeped out from beneath her fashionable hat, but her blue eyes still held a twinkle that must have broken many young men's hearts along the way.

The younger was in her twenties and was a beauty by any standard. Her hair was jet-black and her eyes seemed almost black, too. Helen's face might have launched a thousand ships, but this girl's face could launch a thousand more and persuade them to fetch her a ha'p'orth of chips on their way back.

So it obviously wasn't either of them. But the two men . . .

The younger of the two wore a dapper suit and a well-brushed bowler hat. He had a boyish face and could have been anywhere between thirty and fifty years of age. He must be the actor, I thought.

So presumably it was the older gentleman in the unfashionable overcoat and top hat. He had the lined face of a man who had spent years in the sun, and a moustache of impressively military proportions. This must be Colonel Cheetham.

All these thoughts passed through my head in a couple of seconds and I was about to greet the older gentleman when the younger one tipped his hat and said, 'Hello there. I'm Nolan Cheetham. Is Lady Hardcastle at home? I believe she's expecting us.'

He had a northern accent. I was never particularly good at judging which side of the Pennines accents came from. I know they get terribly cross when you get it wrong, as though the Wars of the Roses really were fought between their two counties and not between two Plantagenet families bearing their names, but I was going to plump for Lancashire. Manchester, probably. We'd employed a safe-cracker in 1902 to get some papers for us from a certain European embassy in London. He was the best in the business, and he sounded just like this Cheetham fellow. 'Of course, sir,' I said with a little curtsey. 'She is, as you say, expecting you. Please come in.' I stepped aside to let them pass.

They each muttered their thanks and waited patiently while I took their hats and coats and hung them beside the door.

Dewi knew his duties well and had slipped out through the side door to give his colleague Bert a hand with the bags. As the motor car burbled off back down the lane, Dewi was hefting the bags into the hall. With the front door finally shut, he set about carrying them upstairs.

I was about to go and fetch Lady Hardcastle, but she emerged from her study and saved me the trip.

'Ah, you've arrived safely,' she said. 'I'm so glad. Welcome to our home. I'm Emily, Lady Hardcastle. You've met Miss Armstrong, I see.'

'Thank you, my lady,' said Colonel Cheetham. 'We weren't introduced, but her reputation precedes her. Nolan Cheetham at your service.'

This was happening more and more lately. I wasn't sure I liked having a reputation, favourable or otherwise.

'How do you do, Colonel Cheetham?'

'Please, my lady, it's more by way of an honorary rank. I volunteered in the Lancashire Militia, man and boy, and eventually found myself a colonel, but I've not mustered these past few years. And certainly not since they became the Special Reserve. Makes them sound like a vintage port. Call me Nolan.'

Lady Hardcastle smiled, and inclined her head in acknowledgement. 'And your companions?' she prompted.

'Oh, I do beg your pardon,' he said. He indicated the older of the two women. 'Allow me to present Zelda Drayton, one of England's finest actresses and the beautiful but wicked villain in my latest moving picture.'

Zelda smiled.

Cheetham continued. 'Then we have Miss Euphemia Selwood, a rising star in the moving picture world. Our ravishing leading lady.'

The younger woman blushed a little, but seemed pleased with her introduction.

'And this old reprobate is Basil Newhouse. He's been acting on England's theatre stages since before any of us were born, but he has chosen to share his gifts with moving picture audiences as our noble hero.'

Newhouse bowed deeply.

'How delightful,' said Lady Hardcastle. 'Welcome all. Now, if we can find . . .'

Dewi chose exactly the right moment to begin clumping down the stairs.

'Ah, there you are, Dewi,' said Lady Hardcastle. 'Perfect timing. Dewi will show you to your rooms, gentlemen. And Dora . . . ?'

'She's up here, my lady,' said Dewi.

'Splendid. Dora will help to make you ladies comfortable. They'll take care of anything you need. If we get you settled in, you can rest a moment and shake the dust of your travels from your boots. Shall we say one o'clock in the dining room for lunch? We have so much to talk about.'

I left them to find their rooms while I returned to the kitchen to help Miss Jones with the preparations for lunch.

Chapter Three

The new arrivals came downstairs together. They'd clearly gathered somewhere – probably in Mr Cheetham's room – to save arriving in dribs and drabs.

Lady Hardcastle was waiting for them in the dining room.

'Do come in and make yourselves at home,' she said as Zelda poked her head tentatively round the door. 'I'm afraid it's all rather informal here. I do apologize if you were hoping for the full upper-class experience. Lady Farley-Stroud does that so well, but I find that with just me and Armstrong here most of the time, it's altogether far too much fuss.'

The four guests filed in.

'Please sit anywhere,' said Lady Hardcastle, indicating the places that had been set around the table. 'Edna will be just a moment. I sent her to fetch some wine. Do you take wine with lunch? Don't feel obliged, but I do like a glass with company.'

There were non-committal mumblings as the four of them shuffled around the dining table and found themselves a chair each.

I, meanwhile, was standing quietly by the sideboard.

'Now,' said Lady Hardcastle, 'I do have to mention this one because it bothers some people. Miss Armstrong here has been working for me since ninety-four and for a lot of that time it's just been the two of us, so we're in the habit of eating together. I've asked her to join us.'

There were more self-conscious mumblings from the assembled actors. None of them, I felt sure, had the first idea where a lady's maid ought to be eating and were probably more uncomfortable now than they would have been if I'd simply joined them without comment. I decided it wasn't really my problem and just sat down at the last remaining place.

Edna arrived with the wine, closely followed by Miss Jones with the first platters of food. We had agreed that Mr Holman's pork pies would be just the ticket but I had been disappointed that salad season was long gone. Miss Jones, though, was not daunted. She had some 'winter salad' ideas involving cabbage and other raw vegetables. With bread and a selection of her delicious chutneys, it made a splendid autumn lunch. Even with Edna's help, it took three trips to bring it all through.

'This looks gradely,' said Mr Cheetham. 'But I hope you've not gone to too much trouble on our behalf.'

'Nonsense,' said Lady Hardcastle. 'It's no trouble at all. And you're doing our little village a great service by bringing your moving pictures to us. I remember seeing travelling shows everywhere a few years ago, but they seem to have rather fallen from favour. One has to go to the big towns now. It's a rare treat for us to have such wonderful entertainment.'

'Then I hope we shan't disappoint,' he said. 'We gave a few private screenings of our new show to people in "the business" and it was quite well received. We're hoping that the public will take to it just as enthusiastically. To tell the truth, we're rather depending on it. It's an expensive business, making moving pictures. We need to attract the paying public. But we have high hopes – it's quite appropriate for the time of year.'

'Oh? The coming of winter?'

'No, my lady – witchcraft,' he said, with a mischievous grin.

'Oh, I say,' said Lady Hardcastle. 'How wonderful. And you others are the stars?'

'Yes, my lady,' said Zelda. 'I play the witch, young Phemie here plays the village girl, and dear old Basil is the Witchfinder General.'

'Perfect time of year for it,' said Basil Newhouse. 'Halloween and all that. And the mysterious fire up at Lady Farley-Stroud's place—'

Zelda reached out and grabbed a pinch of salt, which she threw over her left shoulder.

'—we should be able to get quite an audience, I'd have thought,' he continued.

Euphemia gave him an oddly disapproving look.

'I can hardly wait,' said Lady Hardcastle.

'Lady Farley-Stroud tells me that you've made a moving picture of your own,' said Cheetham.

'Oh, just a little experimental piece,' she said. 'We met Monsieur Méliès in Paris a few years ago at a special presentation of his *A Trip to the Moon*. I was quite taken with it and asked him about his techniques. Ever since then I've been dabbling. Just as an enthusiastic amateur, you understand.'

'Nonetheless, I look forward to seeing it. We've left a spot for you in the show.'

'Thank you.'

'You have your own equipment, I take it?' he said.

'I keep a little studio in the garden,' she said. 'It was originally intended as an orangery, but the light is excellent and it serves me well.'

'I should like to take a look before we leave. If you don't mind, of course.'

'It will be a pleasure to show it off to a professional.' She turned to Euphemia Selwood. 'Have you been acting long, Miss Selwood?' she said.

'Since I were a nipper,' said Euphemia. 'My old ma works the music halls. I was born to it, you might say.'

Whereas Zelda had the well-modulated tones of a classically trained actress, Euphemia's voice was that of a stall holder from one of London's less salubrious markets.

'Your mother is Millie Selwood?' I said with some surprise.

'That's right, miss,' she replied. 'You've heard of her, then?'

'We've met her,' I said.

Lady Hardcastle raised a querying eyebrow.

'At the Hackney Empire, my lady,' I said. '1903. The Portuguese Affair.'

Lady Hardcastle nodded. 'Ah, yes,' she said.

Euphemia's mouth fell open in surprise. 'I knew I'd seen you two before,' she said. 'You come backstage, didn't you? Oh my stars, that was the night Jimmy Brownlow got shot. I was there visitin' me mother.'

'I fear that was us, dear, yes,' said Lady Hardcastle. 'Though to be fair, it was only a matter of time before someone shot Brownlow.'

'They said he was a spy. It was in the papers,' said Euphemia.

'He was quite a good comedian, as I recall, but not an especially talented spy,' said Lady Hardcastle dismissively. 'More of a weaselly chancer, really. The stupid little man imagined he could make himself wealthy by playing both sides against each other in a game of international intrigue. He was in way over his head. Sooner or later someone was going to tumble to him – it just happened that we got to him first.'

'And you shot him?' said Basil, his astonishment making him drop a forkful of food. 'I say.'

'He left me no choice, I'm afraid. Armstrong had relieved him of his pistol but he had a derringer concealed in his sock, of all places. He levelled it at her. One simply doesn't do that sort of thing and expect to get away with it.'

'Oh my stars!' said Zelda, fanning her face with her hand. 'You didn't really?'

'Course they did, Zel,' said Euphemia. 'Saw it with my own eyes.'

'In the theatre?'

'You make such a fuss, Zel. You act like you've lived in a convent all your life, but you've seen more than all of us put together.'

Zelda harrumphed but said nothing further. I confess I tended to agree with Euphemia to some extent – Zelda's reaction did seem a little . . . actressy.

'There's more to you than meets the eye,' said Cheetham. 'I thought we were the storytellers, but I'd wager you have a few tales of your own. I wouldn't wish ill upon Lady Farley-Stroud and her household, but I can't say as I'm disappointed to have ended up billeted with you, my lady.'

He steered us back to calmer conversational waters, and we all shared lighter anecdotes and memories as we demolished Miss Jones's 'winter salads'. By the time Edna brought in the coffee, things were wrapping up and Lady Hardcastle was offering Cheetham a tour of her orangery studio.

'You're all welcome, of course,' she said. 'Although I don't suppose it will be particularly impressive after some of the places you must have worked.'

The actors politely accepted, though the glances they shared seemed – to me, at least – to indicate that she might be overestimating the glamour of the world of the kinematograph.

'I think we'd all like that,' said Cheetham. 'I think it's grand that people are getting interested in moving pictures again. It used to thrill everyone so. But not so much any more. Time was when I used to do shows up and down the country where I'd photograph folk going about their daily business in the morning, then I'd process the film in the afternoon and show it to them in the evening. It used to go down a storm. Not so much these days. Folk have got a bit blasé about it, I reckon.'

'Oh,' I said. 'I'm glad you mentioned that – I'd been wondering how to broach the subject. I was talking to the butcher's wife this morning and she was reminiscing about a chap doing exactly that in

Weston-super-Mare a few years ago. I did wonder if we might be able to persuade you to do it for us.'

'No need to be shy when it comes to asking me to show off, Miss Armstrong,' he said. 'I can certainly get my equipment sent down if you think they'd like it. I'm sure we could find the time to make the film, but . . .'

'If time is a worry,' said Lady Hardcastle, 'perhaps I could do some of the work for you? I can certainly process the film here and, if you were to show me how to use your camera, I could capture some of the images for you.'

'That would make it very possible. Very possible indeed. I do love watching people's reactions when they see themselves on the screen. I just didn't think anyone was interested any more so I've not allowed any time for it.'

'That's settled, then,' she said. 'I'm so glad you mentioned it, Armstrong. What fun.'

I smiled.

'Right,' she said decisively. 'Let's take a look at the orangery before it starts to rain, and then we can leave you good people to rest. A long journey and a hearty meal should be enough to knock anyone out. Dinner shan't be until eight, so there's plenty of time to recuperate.'

We all rose to leave.

I left them to their tour while I returned to the kitchen to offer my help there.

◆ ◆ ◆

A short while later, having had my offer of help politely declined, I was upstairs on the landing. I was on my way to fetch a dress from Lady Hardcastle's wardrobe whose lace collar was in need of repair.

I had my hand on the bedroom doorknob but the sound of a heated conversation from one of the guest rooms made me stop. I was unable to make out the details of the exchange, but it seemed to be coming from Basil Newhouse's room further along the landing. Mr Newhouse was arguing with a woman.

Mr Newhouse's door opened and I hurriedly stepped into Lady Hardcastle's room. Before I closed the door behind me, I very clearly heard Euphemia Selwood's voice saying, 'You want to watch out, Basil. You could find yourself dead.'

She slammed the door and stomped to her own room, where she slammed that door as well. I had no idea what it could all be about, but whatever it was I judged Euphemia's reaction to have been as melodramatically actressy as Zelda's had been earlier. Still, they livened up the place.

◆ ◆ ◆

With the dinner preparations well in hand and the collar repairs done, I sneaked off to hide out for a few moments in the sitting room with a cup of tea and a book. I curled up on one of the comfortable armchairs and quickly lost myself in a copy of E Lynn Linton's *Witch Stories* that I found lurking on the bookshelf.

I was skimming through the account of 'Elspeth Cursetter and Her Friends' when I heard light footsteps in the hallway. With a rattle of the doorknob, the door opened and Mr Newhouse peered tentatively round it.

'Ah,' he said. 'Sorry to disturb you, my dear.'

'Not at all, Mr Newhouse,' I said. 'Please come in. I'm just taking a little break. I'm not sure the tea will be up to much, but it's no trouble to make a fresh pot.'

'Very kind. The truth is, I'm actually looking for somewhere to enjoy a cigar. Would here be all right?'

'I'm so sorry, sir,' I said, 'but Lady Hardcastle isn't terribly fond of cigar smoke.'

'No matter, no matter,' he said affably. 'Often the way in ladies' houses. Quite understand. I'll nip out into the garden.'

'Oh,' I said, feeling guilty that we were such unaccommodating hosts. I was also mindful of his recent falling out with Euphemia and wondered if he might be in need of a chance to settle himself a little. 'But it's raining. I'll tell you what, how do you fancy a stroll to the village pub? I could do with having a word with my pal who works there and you can puff away on your cigar with no one to complain. I can introduce you to some of the villagers, too – I'm sure they'll be excited to meet an actor.'

He laughed. 'Always happy to meet my public,' he said. 'Though I doubt anyone will be too impressed. And' – he paused for a moment – 'won't we get just as wet walking into the village as I would in your garden?'

'True,' I said. 'But in the garden you just stand in the mud on your own. If we do it my way, I get to show you off to my pal Daisy.'

'You make a good case, Miss Armstrong,' he said. 'Will you not be missed?'

'Terribly,' I said. 'The place would grind to a shuddering halt were I away too long. But under the circumstances, I feel it's also my duty to act as guide to the local sights and attractions.'

'Aha, a "bear-leader" they used to be called,' he said with a nod. 'The Grand Tour comes to Gloucestershire. And the villagers shan't be aghast at the sight of a young lady accompanying a disreputable old actor unchaperoned?'

'Much of what I do and say leaves folk aghast,' I said. 'I tend not to take any notice these days.'

'Good for you,' he said. 'Now if you can help a chap find his hat . . .'

I got up from the armchair and led him back into the hall. I was helping him into his overcoat when the telephone rang.

I answered it. 'Hello,' I said. 'Chipping Bevington two-three.'

'Hello?' said a certain, familiar, loud, female voice. 'Armstrong? Is that you again?' It was Lady Farley-Stroud.

'Yes, my lady,' I said. 'If you'll wait one moment, I'll fetch Lady Hardcastle for you.'

'Right you are, m'dear,' she shouted. 'Thank you.'

Her hearing seemed to be improving.

Lady Hardcastle, meanwhile, had already emerged from her study.

'Gertie?' she said.

I nodded as she took the earpiece from me.

'My own coat is still in the boot room,' I said to Mr Newhouse. 'I shan't be a moment.'

I returned a minute or two later in hat and raincoat. I grabbed two umbrellas from the stand by the door and turned to catch Lady Hardcastle's attention. She was reassuring Lady Farley-Stroud that Mr Cheetham and his associates were settling in nicely. She had to hold the earpiece away from her head to avoid being deafened by the reply.

'Good show,' shouted the crackly voice. 'Might drop in later. Show my face. Will that be acceptable?'

While she was talking, I mouthed the word 'Pub' to Lady Hardcastle, who gestured her understanding and sent us on our way with a cheery wave. We heard her offer an open invitation to both of the Farley-Strouds as we left.

◆ ◆ ◆

The Dog and Duck was a lively village pub. The landlord was 'Old' Joe Arnold, whose family had owned the inn for several generations. He was a generous soul with a heart uncluttered by malice and a mouth uncluttered by teeth. Lady Hardcastle and I had lived in the village of Littleton Cotterell for over a year and had yet to set eyes upon the woman whom Joe referred to as 'our ma'. We presumed she was his wife, and that the honorific indicated that there might be junior Arnolds somewhere in the world, but we knew nothing of them, either.

We passed the door to the public bar and entered the snug. Through the open door between the two sections of the pub we could see the usual collection of local farmhands crowding the tables in the public bar. They filled the room with loud chatter, raucous laughter, and a thick fug of tobacco smoke. Old Joe was chatting to a couple of his regulars in one corner.

The snug, by contrast, was almost deserted. Mrs Grove, the vicar's housekeeper, was sipping a small sherry while she listened with rapt concentration to her friend's account of her own tribulations. I thought I recognized her companion but I didn't know her name. I had a vague inkling that she was a farmer's wife from the other side of the village, and her frustrated description of the travails of milking time seemed to confirm my assumption.

The only other occupants of the room were a man and a woman whom I didn't know at all. She was young, slender, blonde and dressed in a very expensive-looking, dark jacket with a matching skirt. It was tailored from fine wool in a cut so fashionable that it labelled her instantly as a city girl. Her companion was a gentleman who looked to me to be in his mid-forties. Like the young woman, he was conspicuously not a country dweller. But whereas she had the look of a well-to-do socialite dressed up as a professional person of business or commerce, he was more bohemian in appearance and was dressed up very much as an artist. His greying hair was wild and unkempt. His van Dyke beard was long, with the moustache flamboyantly twirled. His velvet jacket was of a rich emerald green, and a silk cravat in a garish Paisley pattern seemed to bubble up from the collar of his shirt. These were not locals.

'Great merciful heavens,' muttered Mr Newhouse under his breath. 'That's all we need.'

I didn't get a chance to ask him what he meant before Daisy appeared behind the bar.

'Flo!' she squealed. 'I was wonderin' when you'd come in.'

'*Prynhawn Da*, Daisy, *fach*,' I said.

She and Mr Newhouse looked at me quizzically. 'Good afternoon, Daisy, dear,' I translated. 'Honestly, if you stand on the church tower you can spit on Wales from here, but not one of you speaks Welsh. Even Blodwen Jones doesn't understand half of what I say. *Blodwen*. How much more Welsh can you get without actually having a dragon tattooed on your forearm?'

'It's all sing-song gibberish and throat-clearing to me, my lover,' said Daisy.

I harrumphed. 'It's lucky for you that you're so pretty, you heathen. There'd be no hope for you otherwise.'

She flashed me an insolent grin and bobbed a curtsey. 'And what brings you to Joe's fine establishment on this rainy afternoon?' she said.

'Mr Newhouse,' I said by way of reply, 'please allow me to introduce my good friend Daisy Spratt. Daisy, this is the celebrated actor Mr Basil Newhouse.'

'How do you do, my dear?' said Mr Newhouse with a gracious bow.

'Oh my stars,' said Daisy. 'It's really you, i'n't it?'

There was a loud and very obvious 'tut' from the gentleman at the table.

'I am certainly he,' said Mr Newhouse. 'Am I to take it from your response that you've heard of me?'

'Everyone's heard of you, you ridiculous old ham,' muttered the bohemian. 'Your thieving master has seen to that.'

I turned towards the table. 'Good afternoon, sir,' I said. 'My name is Florence Armstrong. I gather you know my mistress's guest, but you are . . . ?'

'Aaron Orum,' he said with a sneer. 'At your service.'

'It's a pleasure to meet you, Mr Orum, I'm sure,' I said, and returned my attention to Daisy.

'I most certainly have heard of you, Mr Newhouse,' she said. 'I reads all the magazines and I knows all about you.'

There was another loud tut from Mr Orum.

'Is it busy in the public, Daisy?' I said.

'Quite,' she replied. 'But there's a table over by the window, I think.'

'Shall we?' I said to Mr Newhouse, gesturing towards the open door that led to the public bar.

He cast a glance towards Mr Orum, who was still sneering at us.

'Why not, my dear?' he said cheerfully. 'Let's leave these two to their conversation.'

I followed him through to the other room, closing the door behind me as I went.

'Can I get you a drink?' he said as I was sitting down.

'A brandy would be most welcome,' I said.

'A woman after my own heart.'

He made his way purposefully to the bar, ignoring the curious looks of the villagers and farmhands as he passed them. Daisy appeared behind the bar again as though by magic. She collared poor Mr Newhouse and seemed to be subjecting him to an enthusiastic interrogation as she poured the drinks. I couldn't hear them above the hubbub but I gathered from his chuckles that she was gushing. At length he seemed to gain control of the conversation and managed to ask a few questions of his own.

He eventually returned to the table and set down two glasses of brandy.

'She's quite a gel, your pal,' he said as he sat down. 'Cheers.' He held out his glass and we clinked.

'She's very excited to meet you, that's all.'

'She's certainly very well informed.'

'She does love the gossip in the magazines,' I said. 'In fact she seems to love reading about moving pictures more than actually seeing them. I offered to take her into the city in the summer to see *Too Much Lobster* and a couple of other comedies but she wasn't interested.'

He laughed. 'Not surprised,' he said. 'Dreadful picture.'

'Excellent title, though.'

'I'll grant you that,' he said.

'So what's the story with you and Orum?' I said. Subtlety and discretion are all very well in their place, but sometimes one has to be direct. 'And who's the woman with him?'

'He's . . .' he began. 'Well, let's say that he's a fellow practitioner of the performing arts. Give a chap a moment to light his cigar and I'll tell you all about him.'

As he fussed with his cutter and then a match, I looked over at the bar. Daisy was engaged in conversation with one of the young farmhands, but as she caught my eye she gave me a grin and a wink. It seemed that bringing our actor guest to the pub had been a popular decision with one person, at least.

'Ah, that's the ticket,' said Mr Newhouse as he took his first puff. 'Been looking forward to that since lunch.'

I allowed him to luxuriate in a few more satisfied mouthfuls of the sweet-smelling smoke.

'Now then,' he said at length. 'Where were we?'

'Mr Orum,' I prompted.

'Ah, yes, the sad tale of Aaron Orum and Nolan Cheetham. I'm surprised you don't know it.'

'I'm afraid I don't keep up with the world of popular entertainment quite as much as I should like to,' I said. 'There was a time when I knew about everyone and everything, but no more.'

'Did you, indeed? You come from a theatrical background, perhaps?'

'My father was a circus knife thrower. The Great Coltello.'

'Goodness me!' he said. 'How very exotic. My father was a gentleman's valet in north London. Our lives seem to be reverse images of each other.'

'I'd not swap mine for a thousand pounds,' I said. 'I loved the circus – I still love the circus – but I've had so many more adventures working for Lady Hardcastle.'

'I can only imagine,' he said. 'That story you told at luncheon raised more questions than it answered, but it certainly hints at a life of intrigue.'

I smiled. I could see I was going to struggle to keep him on track. Like many active minds, it seemed his was apt to wander. 'You were going to tell me about Messrs Cheetham and Orum.'

'So I was, my dear, so I was.' He took a contemplative puff on his cigar. 'We are in Manchester,' he said, theatrically. 'In the 1860s, two young lads are growing up on the streets of one of the Empire's greatest industrial cities. Born about a week apart on the same street, Aaron and Nolan are the best of pals. Inseparable. Like brothers, they say. If there were games to be played, they were playing them. If there were plans to be laid, they were laying them. If there was mischief to be made, they were making it.

'Both sets of parents were mill workers. Poor, but respectable. They didn't have much, but they got by. One year, they saved up to take the two boys to a theatre show in the city as a joint birthday treat. They were utterly captivated. The songs, the jokes, the reaction from the audience. They knew then and there what they wanted to do when they grew up.'

'I know that feeling,' I said. 'I worked day and night to learn my father's skills. I wanted to be out there where he was. It wasn't so much that I wanted them to adore me – I wanted them to admire my skill, the way I admired his.'

'I'm much shallower than that,' he said with a self-deprecatory chuckle. 'I just wanted to be loved and adored. But it takes us all differently, the entertainment bug, and so it was with our two heroes. Neither of them wanted to be actors, or singers, or comics. They were imaginative, inventive boys, and they were fascinated by the artistry of it. Young Aaron felt the magic of the dialogue, the patter. He wanted to write the words the actors spoke. While Nolan was transfixed by the technical aspects – the scenery, the sound effects, the flash pots and trapdoors. He wanted to make the magic.

'They followed their mothers and fathers into the mill, but they clung to their dreams. They put on shows for their friends in the back rooms of pubs, in village halls – anywhere there was a space big enough. They gathered a troupe of actors and slowly began to attract the attention of the press. Soon they were offered the chance to stage one of their shows in a small theatre in the city. Acclaim was showered upon them. They had the world at their feet. And then . . .'

'They fell out?' I suggested.

'More than that, my dear,' he said. 'To this day no one but they themselves knows what cast those two lifelong friends asunder, but cast they were. A bitter enmity arose between them and they never spoke again. And since then, their careers have proceeded along entirely separate lines. Aaron Orum continued to work in the theatre and, for a time, so did Nolan Cheetham. But something new came along and he discovered a technical art to eclipse anything that could be done on the stage: moving pictures.'

'I see,' I said. 'But why would Orum come all this way now? It doesn't seem from Orum's attitude just now that any sort of reconciliation is on the cards.'

'Alas, no,' he said. 'One of the last things the two were working on together was a play about an eighteenth-century witch of great power who was undone by her own petty jealousy. They fell out before production began. They never staged the play.'

'Aha,' I said as I twigged. 'And that's the story of Cheetham's new film. Which explains what Orum meant when he described Cheetham as a thief just now.'

'In a nutshell,' he said. 'He's been sending menacingly quasi-legal letters to Cheetham for a few months, threatening to sue him into perdition if he doesn't cough up for the royalties and credit Orum thinks he's owed. It would seem that he's grown tired of that, and that a physical confrontation of some sort is on the cards.'

'We shall just have to make sure it doesn't ruin the shows this week,' I said. 'Lady Farley-Stroud has worked hard to organize everything. I should hate it all to be spoiled by an old spat between former friends.'

'We shall have to warn Cheetham, of course. There's not much else we can do, though.'

'I suppose not. Do we know who the woman is?'

'Not the foggiest, my dear.'

As I took another sip of my brandy, the door to the snug was flung ostentatiously open. It banged loudly against the wall and everyone fell silent for a moment as they watched Aaron Orum stride through the door with the unknown woman on his arm. She was laughing, presumably at something devastatingly witty he had just said, as she gazed up adoringly at him. He caught me looking at them and favoured me with a sneering smile.

He opened the outer door and they stepped out together into the gathering gloom. He struggled briefly with an umbrella and then they were gone.

◆　◆　◆

By the time we got back, there were sounds of life and activity in the house. It seemed the other guests might also have ventured from their rooms.

We found the two women, Zelda and 'Phemie', in the sitting room drinking tea and chatting amiably. I left Mr Newhouse with them and went off in search of Lady Hardcastle.

She was in the dining room with Mr Cheetham. They had spread an array of papers across the table and were standing up, poring over them. They looked up as I knocked on the door.

'Ah, Armstrong,' said Lady Hardcastle. 'There you are. Thank you for looking after Mr Newhouse. Is he all right?'

'Quite well, my lady,' I said. 'He wanted to smoke a cigar so I took him to the Dog and Duck.'

'Where you could introduce him to Daisy,' she said.

'Exactly so. It seemed like a two-birds-one-stone sort of a thing.'

'Splendid. Mr Cheetham has been showing me some of the notes and sketches he makes before he starts work on one of his moving pictures. I must say I'm beginning to feel more and more like the dabbling amateur I am. I don't do nearly this much preparation.' She waved her hand across the jumble of papers. 'Look here. A detailed breakdown of the plot, ideas for how to frame the shots . . . even a diagram of a wonderful little special effects device. Ingenious.'

Cheetham assumed a suitably bashful expression, but it was obvious that he was also basking in her admiration.

'We bumped into an old . . . "friend" of yours in the pub, Mr Cheetham,' I said. 'Mr Orum.'

He scowled. 'Oh heck,' he said. 'Did he say anything? I hope he wasn't rude.'

'Rude enough,' I said, 'but nothing too unpleasant. Just some sniping.'

'He does that,' he said sadly. 'Always has. I suppose he's here to cause trouble.'

'He didn't say so, but Mr Newhouse told me your story so I can only presume that he intends to try.'

Lady Hardcastle raised an enquiring eyebrow, but I raised one of my own and inclined my head towards the door, our customary signal for 'I'll tell you later when we're on our own.'

'I'm so sorry,' said Mr Cheetham. 'I'd hoped we'd be able to settle everything in private. It seems he has other ideas.'

'He wasn't alone,' I said. 'He was in the company of an elegant young lady – slim, blonde, strikingly attractive, expensively dressed. His sweetheart? Wife?'

'Sounds like his type. She could be his latest paramour, I suppose. He always liked to portray himself as something of a rake. A girl in every port, like. You're sure they were together?'

'Thick as thieves when we arrived,' I said. 'Though she kept quiet while he was putting in his snide little digs.'

'Ah, yes. He likes them vapid and docile. The sort to hang on his every word.'

'She didn't have an air of vapidity. To tell the truth, there was more of a look of shrewd contemplation about her as she sat there weighing us up.'

'Then I am at a loss,' said Cheetham.

'I'm sure we'll find out in due course,' said Lady Hardcastle. 'Daisy will know.'

'She will,' I said. 'I'd have asked her already if I'd had the chance, but she was busy and Mr Newhouse was such entertaining company that I didn't feel an especial need to abandon him for the sake of a little tittle nor, indeed, tattle.'

'Quite right, too,' she said. 'Sufficient unto the day is the busybodying thereof.'

Mr Cheetham chuckled. 'Our Basil can be quite the raconteur when he puts his mind to it. I should take most of what he says with at least a pinch of salt, though, if I were you. And perhaps a little vinegar. And some Worcestershire sauce.'

'Duly noted,' I said. 'If I might be excused, my lady, I ought to make sure that everything is in hand for dinner.'

'Of course, dear,' she said. 'Gertie will be joining us.'

'And Sir Hector?'

'She seemed uncertain. Best to make sure we can feed him if needs be, but don't let anyone else go short. I'm sure he won't mind mucking in.'

'There's plenty to go round,' I said. 'Pheasant always goes further than one expects.'

I took my leave and went through to the kitchen, where Miss Jones had left everything in splendid order. There were even notes to indicate our next steps. Edna joined me, and between us we put a wonderful meal together.

Chapter Four

''Ere, lady, are we really gonna be in a kinemono . . . a kinematamo . . . a movin' picture?'

I had been pestered into driving the little Rover over to Chipping Bevington at the crack of dawn to fetch the camera and its attendant impedimenta. Having enlisted the help of the station master's son, 'Young' Roberts, in packing the gear into and on to the tiny motor car, there was precious little room for me to get into it myself.

After breakfast and a quick lesson from Mr Cheetham on the correct operation of the camera, we had carted the camera and a mighty wooden tripod into the village, where we had set up on the green.

The aim had been to capture the shopkeepers opening up, the villagers going about their business, the children on their way to the little village school.

'I should love a candid record of life in the village,' said Lady Hardcastle. 'Something that historians can look back on in a hundred years.'

After an hour, I began to hope that her hypothetical future historians were patient people with an interest in watching people self-consciously mugging for the camera. Our latest irritant was a small boy who ought, I was certain, to be sitting at a desk reciting his times tables or learning the kings and queens of England. He should not be on the village green asking foolish questions.

Lady Hardcastle, to her eternal credit, was a good deal more patient than I. 'Yes, dear,' she said indulgently. 'But if you stand too close to the camera, it won't be able to see you properly.'

'That don't make no sense,' said the urchin. 'The closer you gets, the easier it is. Any fool knows that.'

'Sadly, however, the camera is so much worse than a common or garden fool. It knows only that it can see you better if you toddle over yonder, towards the church. Perhaps it's the divine light filtering through the sacred stained glass, perhaps it's the mere effect of the feet and inches betwixt you and the lens, but I assure you that you have a better chance of being seen on the screen if you perambulate in the general direction of the Lord's house.'

'You talks funny,' he said.

'I do, dear,' she replied.

I was about to say something about pots and kettles and the relative levels of blackness thereof, but I held my tongue.

The child regarded her appraisingly for a moment, clearly uncertain what to make of the mad upper-crust lady. He began, though, to do as he'd been bidden and strolled off towards the church.

'This is much harder than I was expecting,' she said. 'I was hoping to capture a few candid moments of village life for posterity. Instead, I seem to have many, many feet of rather expensive film devoted to a permanent record of people waving.'

'We need some sort of hide,' I said. 'Like hunters use.'

'I fear that might be just as conspicuous in the middle of a village green, dear,' she said.

'You might be right,' I conceded. 'Do you have anything useable at all?'

'I'm not sure. We'll have to see when we get home. I'll keep crank-ing, though – you never know what we might capture. I've plenty of spare film back in the orangery.'

'You'd better focus on that lad for a bit,' I said. 'He's stuck to his side of the bargain and left us alone.'

'You're right, of course. Where's he got to . . . ? Oh, I see him. Hold on . . . Let me just . . . Oh, I say, who on earth is that?'

As she spoke, a charabanc clattered around the corner from the Bristol Road and chugged its way towards the church. Even above the clanking of the engine we could hear a rousing chorus of 'Onward, Christian Soldiers' coming from the occupants.

'A church outing?' I suggested.

'On a Tuesday?' she said. 'Aren't church outings more of a weekend thing? Shouldn't the men be at work?'

They made such a fascinating sight that she trained the camera on them instead of the young lad. His obedient – if reluctant – compliance with her instructions might not be rewarded after all.

The open-topped charabanc drew to a rattling halt in front of the church. A man and woman sitting at the front rose immediately to their feet and turned to face their fellow passengers. Their voices were muffled by distance and would have been masked by the raucous din of the vehicle's engine in any case, but from the loud cheer that greeted their words, it was apparent that theirs had been a rousing speech to rival King Harry's.

The leaders disembarked first and directed the driver to help them with a number of items stored in the luggage compartment. As their travelling companions clambered down on to the pavement, they were each handed a placard on a stick.

'How exciting,' said Lady Hardcastle. 'I do believe it's some man-ner of protest.'

Once everyone had alighted from the charabanc, the driver took his seat once more and, with a loud grinding of gears, conducted his cacophonous vehicle around the green and back towards the Bristol Road.

His passengers moved along the path slightly and formed a ragged line in front of the doors of the village hall. They raised their placards and began a spirited rendition of 'Rock of Ages'. They shook their placards in time with the old hymn and seemed very much to be enjoying themselves.

'Your eyes are so much sharper than mine, dear,' said Lady Hardcastle. 'Can you make out what's exercising them so?'

I had already been squinting at the signs but I couldn't quite see them clearly enough.

'There's something about "the Devil's work" and "Thou shalt not suffer a witch to . . ." something or other.'

'To live, I expect,' she said, still cranking the camera. 'I do believe they're displeased with our Mr Cheetham's moving picture.'

As we watched, the vicar – Reverend James Bland – emerged from the church door. He walked briskly along the pathway and out through the lych gate towards the assembled protesters. Clearly he wanted to know what was going on as much as we did.

There was a muttered and very un-churchlike oath from Lady Hardcastle. Another roll of film was required, it seemed, and she was singularly unimpressed by the timing of this interruption to her filming.

We swapped the rolls of film. This was, in my humble opinion, an unnecessarily complex and tedious procedure. Surely it wasn't beyond the wit of man to devise a simpler way of carrying out such a necessary, and regular, part of the moving picture process. By the time we were done, Mr Bland's conversation was over and he was hurrying towards us across the grass.

Lady Hardcastle took a moment to snatch a few feet of film of the urchin pulling faces at the protesters before the vicar arrived.

He was panting as he drew up in front of us.

'Good morning, Lady Hardcastle,' he wheezed. 'I do hope our visitors haven't ruined your efforts. I gather you're making a portrait of the village for the moving picture show.'

'I am, Vicar,' she said. 'News travels fast.'

'A murmur here, a whisper there,' he said. 'It doesn't take long for interesting news to spread. Fortunately, the Good Book proscribes only damaging indiscretions and the spreading of falsehoods or I'd never hear anything.'

'We've had cause to remark more than once on the reliability of the village news network. It has helped us a lot.'

'Sadly, though, it has let us all down this time. No one knew anything about Mr and Mrs Hughes and their band of spoilsports.'

'Spoilsports?' I said. 'Do you disapprove, sir?'

'I most certainly do, Miss Armstrong. Mine is a loving God who takes delight in the achievements of His creation. He's sophisticated and wise and understands the subtleties of Man's ingenious inventions. Mr Cheetham is a respectful and godly man. He sent me a thorough description of his moving picture to make certain that I should have no objection to its being shown in the church hall. I pointed out that it's the "village hall" but that I would have no objections even if it were under my direct control. The picture is modern, it's even a bit racy, but it doesn't go against the teachings of our Lord.'

Lady Hardcastle frowned. 'But these . . . these . . .'

'Hughes, my lady,' I said.

'Thank you, dear. These Hughes people think it does?'

'Such is their claim,' said Mr Bland. 'I'm not certain whether they believe it to be unchristian or whether they've manufactured a plausible religious objection to bolster their complaint. I do very much get the impression that Mr Hughes has managed to turn complaining into his life's work, you see. I don't mind so much – heaven knows there is much in the modern world that I should like to complain about had I the time to devote to it – but I do wish people like Hughes wouldn't involve the Lord quite so recklessly in their endeavours. One has to admire the resourcefulness they exhibit in their careful selection of scriptural texts to support their small-mindedness, but it doesn't always sit well with the Christianity I preach.'

'Can they be stopped?' I asked. 'Lady Farley-Stroud will be terribly disappointed if they spoil her "festival". Not to mention the other villagers. Daisy will be devastated if it doesn't go ahead.'

'There's not a great deal I can do, I don't think,' he said. 'I should have something to say if they were on Church land, but they're on the public highway. Perhaps Sergeant Dobson can give some advice on the matter, but I fear that among the many freedoms we enjoy as citizens of the Empire is the freedom to be a blessed nuisance.'

'I could rough them up a bit if you like,' I offered with a wink. 'There's only, what, a dozen and a half of them? They all look a bit flabby. They wouldn't stand a chance.'

He frowned quizzically. 'I'm sure we can resolve matters without resorting to fisticuffs, Miss Armstrong,' he said. He leaned in more closely to us both and continued conspiratorially: 'To tell the truth, I did wonder about setting my wife's dog on them.'

Lady Hardcastle laughed. 'Hamlet?' she said. 'He's a big softy. They might die laughing at his antics, mind you.'

'Ah, yes,' said the vicar, smiling for the first time. 'But they wouldn't know that. Until you've met him properly, he seems like a fearsome hound.'

'He's huge,' said Lady Hardcastle, 'I'll give you that. Perhaps you should get Mrs Bland to bring him for a walk and see how they react.'

'I might well do. In the meantime, though, might I prevail upon you to contact Lady Farley-Stroud by telephone? We still haven't managed to persuade the bishop to have one installed at the vicarage and I should like her to know well in advance so that she's not too discomfited when she arrives and sees them all standing here.'

'Leave it to me, Vicar,' she said. 'And don't worry too much about Gertie – she's made of the sternest stuff.'

◆　◆　◆

Back at the house, Lady Hardcastle telephoned Lady Farley-Stroud, who reacted, as I was told after the call had ended, 'with a "pfft" and a "silly ass" and an assurance that she will be carrying her heavy-handled umbrella when she arrives for the show tonight.'

Mr Cheetham, on the other hand, seemed altogether more anxious.

'This is just exactly the sort of palaver we don't need,' he said when Lady Hardcastle had recounted the arrival of the Hugheses and their followers. 'They've been dogging my every move for months. At first it was calmly reasoned letters to parish councils describing the evil nature of my picture. When that had no effect, they took to writing directly to the local vicar. Still they were ignored so they went to the bishops. It so happens that I'm on very good terms with the Bishop of Rochdale – he was an army chaplain as a lad and I got to know him in my militia days. He got one of Hughes's letters. Delivered by hand, it were. And written in green ink. It started out nice and calm, like, but as it went on, detailing the blasphemies I was committing, listing in detail the hellish torments that would be visited upon all who saw the work, it became increasingly rambling and incoherent.'

'What did the bishop do?' asked Lady Hardcastle.

'He wrote back that he had seen the picture himself and that there were nothing in it that constituted blasphemy of any sort. He said it portrayed magic and superstition, but in a way so as to tell an extremely moral tale. He pretty much told Hughes to get lost.'

'Which presumably didn't amuse Hughes.'

'He were livid. Wrote to the archbishop. When nothing came of that, he went quiet for a few weeks, but it seems he were keeping his powder dry for one last attack. He's come here to cause trouble.'

'There's not really very much they can actually do, though,' Lady Hardcastle reassured him.

'Standing there with their banners, and their hymns, and their shouting? They'll put people off. Intimidate them.'

'I think you underestimate the fine people of Littleton Cotterell, Mr Cheetham. It takes a good deal more than a few hymns and a bit of pseudo-religious chanting to stop them from having a good time. My worry would be that some of the local lads might find sport in roughing them up a little. The Hugheses clearly believe they have right on their side, but I know who my money would be on in a scuffle. And then it would be the village boys who would end up in chokey.'

'Aye, that would be a shame. But I can't pretend there's not a part of me as wouldn't be tempted to join 'em if they decided to give the old prudes what for.'

'I'm sure it shan't come to that,' said Lady Hardcastle. 'There may be a little argy-bargy and some name-calling, but it won't spoil anyone's fun. And with the vicar on our side, no one's going to be swayed by all their misquoted bible verses and threats of eternal damnation.'

''Appen you're right, Lady 'ardcastle, 'appen you're right.' Mr Cheetham's accent had become less and less refined as he became more and more distracted by his troubles. 'But it's not going to be quite the carefree evening of thrills and excitement we planned for them.'

Lady Hardcastle returned to her study to catch up with some urgent correspondence while Mr Cheetham and his actors gathered in the morning room, presumably to finalize their plans for the evening. I decided to check that all was well 'below stairs', or 'behind the stairs', since the house wasn't large enough to have a subterranean servants' area. And it was a good thing, too; all was not cheerfulness and contentment in the kitchen.

'I haven't touched your bloomin' polish,' said Miss Jones. 'What would I want with polish? To give my pie crust a nice shine? You've run out. You was tellin' everyone as would listen this mornin'.'

There was a brief pause while Edna reviewed her memories of the day. The antagonistic mood seemed to evaporate before my eyes.

'I'm so sorry, m'dear,' she said. 'I don't know what's gettin' into me lately. Of course I've run out. I'd best get into the village and get some more.'

I scuffed my feet as I walked in, a technique I'd learned from a butler I once worked with. I found it a better way to announce my arrival than clearing my throat.

'Anything I can do to help?' I asked. 'I can pick up some polish from Mrs Pantry.'

'Are you sure, m'dear? It's not the sort of thing you ought to be doin'.'

'Nonsense,' I said. 'We all pitch in together here. And, besides, I'm at a bit of a loose end so another stroll into the village might be rather nice. If I stay here I'll only be repairing yet another rip in one of Lady Hardcastle's skirts.'

'Well, if you're sure it's no trouble,' said Edna, 'that would be grand. I can get on with cleanin' the fireplaces while you're gone.'

'It's no trouble at all,' I said. 'Do you need anything, Miss Jones?'

'No, ta,' she said. 'Oh, unless you gets a chance to pop into the greengrocer's. I needs another marrow. That one he sent over t'other day was rotted through when I cut it up this mornin'.'

'Polish and marrow,' I said. 'Righto. I'll not be long.'

I put on my coat and left by the side door.

◆ ◆ ◆

As I walked around the village green I saw that the protesters appeared to be settling in for a long innings. A couple of hampers stood open on the path and several of the group were sipping something from tin cups. Something warm, I hoped – it was a bitterly cold day.

I was so intent on getting to Mrs Pantry's before I froze to death that I was almost bowled over by a man exiting the small tobacconist's shop next door. He was moving at some speed and it was only my own lightning reflexes that kept me from being knocked into the road. At least that's how it would be when I recounted the incident later. In reality I was saved from the ignominy of being knocked on my bum by the fact that he barely brushed my shoulder as he crossed my path. Nevertheless, he stopped to apologize.

'I do beg your pardon, miss,' he said. 'I hope you're all right.'

'Right as rain, sir, thank you,' I said. He wasn't a villager, but he seemed familiar. He was a man of unremarkable appearance. His eyes were the colour of dishwater and were separated by a long, narrow nose. His thin lips were topped by an equally thin, wispy moustache. He looked like the sort of downtrodden schoolmaster who never wins the respect of his pupils and maintains order by the liberal use of spiteful comments and unfair punishments.

'Are you with the group who arrived earlier?' I asked, nodding towards the cluster of protesters outside the village hall.

'My wife and I are privileged to call ourselves its leaders,' he said. 'Hughes is the name.' He tipped his hat. 'Noel Hughes.'

'How do you do, Mr Hughes?' I said. 'Florence Armstrong. I work for Lady Hardcastle.'

'I've seen her name somewhere,' he said thoughtfully.

'She has been mentioned in the newspapers,' I said. 'Perhaps there?'

'No . . . no . . . something more recent.' His face darkened into a scowl as the memory came back to him. 'She has a moving picture in that wicked abomination of a "show" that Nolan Cheetham is attempting to pass off as entertainment.'

'Oh, yes,' I said with a smile. 'It's about mice.'

He harrumphed. 'There's no need for you to sink to their level, you know. You're an employee, not a slave. You don't have to condemn yourself to eternal damnation out of a misguided sense of loyalty.'

'I beg your pardon?' I said.

'Join our protest,' he continued. 'Show them that this ungodly so-called "entertainment" will not be tolerated in our Christian country.'

'Thank you, sir,' I said. 'But to tell you the truth, I'm really rather looking forward to the show.'

He shook his head and set off briskly to rejoin his fellows. After a few steps he stopped and turned back towards me. 'This will all end badly, you know,' he said. 'No good can possibly come of meddling with demonic forces like this.'

He set off again before I could respond.

◆ ◆ ◆

I mentioned the encounter to Lady Hardcastle when I arrived home with the supplies. She was amused more than perturbed, and we returned to our respective tasks before reconvening shortly before six o'clock for our trip into the village.

We arrived at the village hall early. Lady Farley-Stroud had asked that we be there to help with the final arrangements, but both Lady Hardcastle and I suspected that she rather wanted to have a friend on hand for moral support.

We passed through the picket line without any difficulty. A dour-looking woman of late middle age delivered a brief homily on the evils of modern popular entertainment as we approached. I rather hoped we might simply brush past her and carry on into the hall, but Lady Hardcastle stopped and listened. At the end of her address – which had included one or two surprisingly inventive reinterpretations of scriptural texts to make them more appropriate for the new century – she held out a pamphlet. Once again, my own inclination was to ignore it and walk on, but Lady Hardcastle smiled warmly and took the proffered leaflet.

'Thank you, dear,' she said. 'I do hope you don't get too cold standing out here. It's not really the weather for it, is it?'

Indeed it wasn't. The rain had cleared, but so had the skies, and there was a definite chill in the air without the warming blanket of cloud.

The woman regarded us coldly. 'Will you turn from the path of the ungodly? Will you join us in our vigil?' she asked.

'Oh, my word, no,' said Lady Hardcastle, still in the friendliest of tones. 'I'm rather looking forward to this. I do love a scary story, don't you, dear?' She turned to me as she said these last words.

'Very much so, my lady,' I said.

'Perhaps you'd like to come in and join us,' she said to the stern-faced woman. 'I'll happily treat you and your friends to the price of a ticket each if you fancy some fun.'

The woman might have looked less scandalized if Lady Hardcastle had invited her to attend a human sacrifice in the name of Beelzebub.

'No, thank you,' she said primly. 'We place a much higher value on our immortal souls than you seem to. We shall pray for you.'

'How very kind,' said Lady Hardcastle with yet another warm smile. 'Well, come along, Armstrong, we need to get inside. Good evening, madam. Don't get too cold.'

We left the scowling woman to her picket duties and entered the hall.

The village hall was filled with the sound of chairs being scraped across the floor. The stacks of bentwood chairs that usually stood along the rear wall had been hefted into position so that they could be set out in rows facing the large white sheet that had been stretched taut at the other end of the room.

Daisy was in charge of the seating. This seemed to involve nothing more than standing with her arms folded, wearing a sternly authoritarian expression and directing a couple of young men I recognized from the rugby club to do the actual fetching and carrying. She returned my wave, but not my cheery hello. I didn't mind – she was clearly trying to cultivate a reputation as an uncompromising martinet, and something as frivolous and casual as greeting a friend would do nothing for her image. I smiled and left her to it.

Mr Cheetham was standing in the centre of the room with Lady Farley-Stroud and Dewi the footman. He and Dora had been given the evening off to enjoy the show, but it seemed he had been roped in to help and that his time was not really his own.

'Have you got it, son?' asked Mr Cheetham.

'I think so,' said Dewi slowly. 'I light this lamp by here, then I crank this handle.'

'That's it. Do you know "Daisy Bell"?'

'I know Daisy Spratt,' said Dewi uncertainly. 'She's over by there, look.' He pointed to where Daisy stood, arms still folded, marshalling the rugby players in their chair-setting endeavours.

Mr Cheetham laughed. 'No, the song. "Bicycle Built for Two"?'

'Oh, yes, I know that.'

'Good. Sing that in your head as you turn the handle – it'll help you keep a steady speed.'

'Right you are, sir.' Dewi was becoming more confident.

'But keep your eye on the screen. You want it to look natural. If they look like they're running through treacle, you need to sing a little faster. If they're jittering about the place like they've got St Vitus's Dance, slow it down a little.'

'I understand.'

'Good lad.'

'Well done, Dewi,' said Lady Farley-Stroud, who had also been paying rapt attention. 'Knew we could count on you.'

'He's a very reliable fellow,' said Lady Hardcastle as we approached. She addressed Dewi directly. 'Your help has been greatly appreciated. Thank you.'

He looked pleased. 'My pleasure, my lady,' he said.

'Are we all set, then, Mr Cheetham?' she said.

'Ready as we'll ever be,' he said. 'All things considered.'

'What things?'

He glanced nervously at the door. 'That lot out there, for one.'

'Don't give them a moment's thought. They'll soon grow bored of standing out there in the cold and being ignored. It's all going to be simply marvellous. And you, Gertie? Is there anything you need from us?'

'No, m'dear,' said Lady Farley-Stroud. 'It's all in hand. Blessing in disguise, this wretched kitchen business. Servants unexpectedly free. Got Dora helping with the refreshments.'

I felt a moment's churlish glee at the news that Dora didn't have the night off after all. The feeling was accompanied by a tiny amount of guilt, but not enough to taint the pleasure.

The Ladies Hardcastle and Farley-Stroud drifted off towards the kitchen at the side of the hall, deep in conversation. Dewi was engrossed in the workings of the projector. Daisy was in her element, lording it over the two muscular lads.

I was left, contrary to custom, with nothing to do.

I read the parish notices on the board. Users of the hall were reminded that it was their duty to leave the premises in the condition in which they would hope to find them. Mr Easton was desirous of starting a chess club and asked that anyone interested call on him at home. Mrs Butler had dropped a sixpence at last week's embroidery class and asked that the finder return it to her at once as she needed it to pay for medicine for her beloved cat, Alphonse.

Time passed slowly.

The lamps in the hall were dimmed. On the lectern in front of Mr Cheetham, an oil lamp flared. The assembled villagers fell silent.

'Good evening, ladies and gentlemen,' said Mr Cheetham, his voice now refined and his words meticulously enunciated. 'Welcome to Nolan Cheetham's Moving Picture Theatre. I'm so glad that so many of you were able to join us on this exciting night where we shall be presenting, for the first time anywhere in Gloucestershire, our thrilling new moving picture, *The Witch's Downfall*.'

He extinguished the lamp on the lectern, plunging the hall into what felt like complete darkness. There were gasps from one or two of the more sensitive souls in the audience.

This sudden darkness was evidently Dewi's cue to bring up the lamp on the projector and begin cranking.

A title glowed on the screen, white letters against a black background: THE WITCH'S DOWNFALL. A rumbling bass chord rolled from the piano in the corner of the hall where Lady Hardcastle had been persuaded to sit to provide a musical accompaniment to the picture.

Mr Cheetham's voice rose above the sound of the piano. 'The witch is a dastardly creature,' he said. 'Harnessing the forces of black magic to serve their own evil ends . . .'

It seemed he was intending to narrate the story. I'd seen, or rather heard, the same sort of thing at a picture show a few years earlier, but I got the impression that the practice had fallen out of fashion. Mr Cheetham was clearly too much of a natural performer to let something as trivial as fashion stop him from being part of the show.

The scene cut to an image of Zelda Drayton, almost unrecognizable in her makeup, standing over a bubbling cauldron in her witch's hovel. She cast a few sprigs of herbs into the pot, which smoked menacingly. All the while, Mr Cheetham kept up his commentary, telling us about the witch and her bitter jealousy of Phoebe, the beautiful young village girl.

The scene shifted to an image of a young girl in seventeenth-century clothes, pouring a tankard of ale for a handsome young man in a tavern. The girl was played by Euphemia Selwood, who was made up to look as innocent and comely as Zelda had been made to look evil and haggard. The young man was handsome, if a little vapid-looking, and from the love-struck glances he was getting from Phoebe, it was clear that he was everything the simple tavern wench had ever dreamed of. He returned her affectionate gaze as Mr Cheetham told us that the witch, too, was in love with this insipid man, whose name turned out to be George.

Back at the hovel, the witch produced an apple from the smoking cauldron, and cackled maniacally in close-up.

The next shot was of Phoebe tucking in to the delicious, shiny apple, and we didn't really need Mr Cheetham's melodramatic narration to warn us of the dire consequences of her actions. Clutching her throat, Phoebe collapsed.

Things were falling into place for the evil old crone, who now had only to feed George her love potion for her plans to be complete.

But wait. An investigation was underway. The Witchfinder – played by Basil Newhouse in an enormously wide-brimmed hat – condemned the witch to death.

She was arrested and clapped in irons, but as she was led away, a tiny doll fell from her hand. It was wearing a huge hat and had a pin through its heart.

Inevitably, the next shot was of the Witchfinder clutching his heart and falling down dead.

The next scene was slightly less easy to predict and did actually benefit from Mr Cheetham's explanation. George, it seems, was so overcome with grief at the death of beloved Phoebe that his wits deserted him. In a fit of madness, he threw himself from the church tower. I confess I didn't really understand the point of this scene and I might have advised Mr Cheetham to cut it if he were to ask, but it was dramatic enough as George wrestled with his inner demons before rushing towards the low parapet and jumping over it. Naturally we had to imagine the fatal consequences of the fall, but to judge from the gasps from the audience, the scene certainly proved thrilling, no matter how pointless I felt it to be.

The closing shot was of the witch, lashed to a stake atop a pile of firewood, with villagers moving menacingly towards it brandishing burning torches.

A final title card appeared, declaring that this was THE END.

The whole thing had lasted less than ten minutes, but it brought the house down. There was applause, a few whistles, and one or two shouts of 'Bravo!' The lamps came up to reveal Mr Cheetham, now standing in front of the screen and grinning broadly. He was flanked by Zelda and Euphemia on one side, and Mr Newhouse on the other. He introduced them each by name and they took their bows. Lady Hardcastle, whose improvised piano part had added so much to the experience, was also encouraged to stand and take a bow of her own.

As the tumult subsided, Mr Cheetham stepped forwards.

'Thank you, ladies and gentlemen, thank you. Ordinarily, we would screen this particular picture at the end of our week's stay, but we were so excited to show it to you that we couldn't wait.'

There were a few cheers, and one young woman shouted, 'Thank you!'

Mr Cheetham beamed. 'Since you've enjoyed it so much, perhaps we can screen it again at the end of the week as well.'

More cheering followed this announcement.

'And, in the meantime, we have a packed programme of thrills and comedy to fill your evenings with the most magical modern entertainment known to Man.'

He went on to list almost a dozen other titles that would be screened during the rest of the week. The next picture, by way of light relief, was to be *Town Mouse and Country Mouse*, by 'your very own Lady Hardcastle'.

Once again, the small crowd went wild as the gaslights dimmed and Dewi began cranking the projector. Lady Hardcastle started to play once more as the title appeared in her own strong, neat hand:

Town Mouse and Country Mouse – a moving picture fantasy by Emily Hardcastle.

The rest of the evening was an unqualified success. Lady Hardcastle's film caused almost as much of a stir in its own way as had *The Witch's Downfall*. There were 'ooh's and 'ahh's as the little toy figures played out the well-known story, and she received just as warm a reaction when it was over.

At the interval, while everyone was enjoying the tea and biscuits laid on by the Village Hall Committee, several people approached Lady Hardcastle to ask her what magic she had used to make the toys move in such a lifelike way. She enthusiastically explained the technique of stop-motion animation, but their expressions of goggling incomprehension meant that she may as well have been describing how to build a suspension bridge with hockey sticks, clotted cream, and a mermaid's tears.

By ten o'clock, the hall was empty once more and Ladies Hardcastle and Farley-Stroud were congratulating each other on the part each had played in making it such a wonderful evening.

Most of the audience, as well as Mr Cheetham and his cast members, had decamped to the pub. We debated joining them.

'It might be fun,' said Lady Hardcastle, 'but I'm absolutely done in. You go if you want to, though – I'd hate to spoil the fun.'

'It's all right,' I said. 'I could do with an early night myself. And I can't let a poor, bewildered old lady like you go wandering abroad on her own. It's still close to All Hallows' Eve – there might be witches about.'

'There might, indeed,' she said. 'Not to mention Mr and Mrs Hughes and their miserable band of prudes.'

'I don't think we have anything to fear from them. I'm pretty certain I could handle them all on my own if it came to a barney. And Daisy said she saw Mr Hughes sneaking into the hall as the show started, so there's even a possibility that he might have realized there's nothing to protest against and slung his hook back to whatever dreary rock he crawled out from under.'

'We can but hope, dear,' she said, and we left the hall together.

'Did you enjoy Mr Cheetham's picture?' she asked.

'I did,' I said. 'The stuff with handsome George was a bit on the superfluous side but other than that and the witch burning, it was great fun.'

'What was wrong with the witch burning?'

'In England, convicted witches were hanged, not burned at the stake,' I said.

'Were they? Were they, indeed? I am, as so often, in awe of your historical knowledge, dear. I wonder where we got the idea they were burned.'

'They burned a few in Scotland,' I said. 'And on the Continent. Never in England.'

'I shall recommend you as historical consultant to Mr Cheetham's next project.'

'And you shall advise him on matters scientific,' I said. 'It can be our new business venture.'

'Certainly a lot safer than most of our previous joint ventures,' she said.

We walked on.

The protesters were long gone so we were spared the tedium of a further encounter.

We could hear the sounds of laughter and merriment from the Dog and Duck as we passed the pub on our way around the green.

'Are you sure you don't want to go in for a quick one?' asked Lady Hardcastle as she caught sight of me looking in through the window.

'Quite sure,' I said. 'I'm done in, too, to be honest.'

'Although I might fancy a quick brandy back at the house before we turn in.'

'I thought you might,' I said.

We carried on around the green and up the lane to our home.

Chapter Five

I was awoken the next morning by the ringing of the front doorbell, accompanied by insistent hammering on the door itself. I stumbled blearily downstairs, tying my dressing gown as I went.

It was Sergeant Dobson from the village police station.

'Good mornin', Miss Armstrong,' he said, knuckling the brim of his helmet. 'I'm sorry to waken you so early, but these days you're my first port of call when somethin' untoward 'appens. Doubly so under the present circumstances.'

'Think nothing of it, Sergeant,' I said, stifling a yawn. I had no idea what time it was, but it was still dark outside. 'Would you care to come in out of the cold and tell me all about it? I think I'm the only one up. I'm not even certain whether Edna and Miss Jones have arrived yet, but I'm sure I haven't forgotten how to put the kettle on.'

'Thank you, miss, that would be most welcome,' he said.

The sturdy little sergeant settled at the kitchen table. He sat ramrod straight in his chair, yet another military man in our midst.

Meanwhile, I set about lighting the range and making a pot of tea. The kitchen clock proclaimed it to be half-past five.

'I've got some very bad news, I'm afraid,' he began. 'One of your houseguests has been found dead over by the rowan tree in the churchyard.'

I turned away from teapot-related activities to give him my full attention. A dozen questions swirled in my mind, but I said simply, 'Who?'

He consulted his notebook. 'Mr Basil Newhouse,' he said. 'One of the actors from the moving picture.'

'Oh,' I said, feeling rather shocked. I sat down. 'I liked him. I liked him a lot. But am I to assume from the urgency of your visit that it wasn't natural causes?'

'We thought so at first, but, on closer inspection, it seems not.'

We heard footsteps on the stairs and a moment later Lady Hardcastle arrived, yawning.

'Make one for me, too, dear, would you?' she said, indicating the teapot.

The sergeant had stood when she entered, but she waved him back to his seat. 'I'm sorry to disturb you so early, m'lady,' he said.

'It sounds quite justified,' she said, sitting next to him. 'I overheard much of what you said as I came down the stairs. Poor Mr Newhouse. Quite a charming fellow. Would you mind starting from the beginning for me?'

'Of course, m'lady. Young Hancock was out on routine patrol first thing when he spots somethin' odd over by the old rowan tree. He thought at first it might be as someone had dumped some rubbish there, but as he got closer, he sees it's a man. His next thought was that it might be a tramp sleepin' out. We has 'em passin' through here sometimes on their way between Bristol and Gloucester.'

I was glad I was facing away from them while I saw to the tea. My involuntary smile at the news that Constable Hancock undertook a 'routine patrol' wouldn't have been appropriate. But then I suppose that 'Young Hancock was sneakin' back to the cottage in the small hours after a night on the ale with his mates' wouldn't have been entirely appropriate, either.

'Anyway,' continued Sergeant Dobson, 'he goes over to rouse the hedge-bird and move him on. Fella doesn't respond so Hancock checks his vitals and it turns out he's dead as a doornail.'

'He thought it was natural causes, you say?' said Lady Hardcastle.

'No signs of violence as far as he could tell in the dark. But when he does one last check, feelin' under the bloke's jacket to check his heart, his hand comes away slightly wet. Sticky, like. He knew it was blood straight off.'

'Oh dear.'

'So he comes and gets me, and I checks an' all. He was dead, all right, and there was blood under his jacket.'

'But not on it?'

'Still too dark to tell for certain,' said the sergeant. 'Even with my lantern. But it didn't even feel damp.'

'And you're certain it was Mr Newhouse? Even in the darkness?'

'Sure as eggs. I saw him yesterday with Miss Armstrong, and again last night at the picture show. It was Newhouse, all right.'

'What a terrible shame. I don't think there's much to be gained by waking his friends. We shall tell them in due time. I presume you've informed the Gloucester CID, though?'

'It was my first call,' said the sergeant. 'They gets right uppity when we talks to Bristol. Didn't do me no good, though. Duty sergeant up there says they're too busy and I should call Bristol after all. They's sendin' someone up.'

'Good show,' said Lady Hardcastle. 'Have you moved the body?'

'Bristol asked us to leave it where it was for their detective. Clues and whatnot. I left young Hancock on guard.'

'Right you are,' she said. 'And is there anything you'd like from us?'

'Tell the truth, m'lady, I'm not sure. I s'pose I just wanted to talk to someone afore the detective shows up. See if there's anythin' I might have missed, if you knows what I means. They city detectives looks down on us, see? I'd like to look like we knows what we're doin'.'

'I've always found you to be more than competent, Sergeant,' she said. 'I'm not at all sure I'd have anything to add at all. When is the detective expected?'

'They said they'd get someone to come up as soon as they could, but that there weren't no point in him gettin' here till after first light.'

'We have a little while, then,' she said. 'How would it be if we were to get ourselves dressed and come over to have a quick look before he gets here?'

'That would be most welcome, m'lady.'

'We shan't find anything you've not already thought of, of course.'

'It'll put my mind at ease, though,' said the sergeant gratefully. 'I'd be obliged to you.'

By the time we were dressed and had made our way across the green to the church, it was half-past six. Dawn was still about half an hour away, but a dishwater light was beginning to rob the darkness of its power.

We found the two village policemen just inside the lych gate, at the edge of the churchyard, close to what I knew from our conversation with the sergeant to be 'the old rowan tree'. Sadly, and despite Lady Hardcastle's patient instruction on the noble art of arboreal identification, without this clue I should still have been unable to tell a rowan tree from any other.

The sergeant acknowledged us with a polite nod.

Lady Hardcastle smiled in return (though I doubt he saw it in the gloom). She turned to the younger policeman. 'Good morning, Constable,' she said warmly.

'Mornin', m'lady,' said Constable Hancock.

We approached the tree, and the two policemen stepped aside to give us our first glimpse of Mr Newhouse's body. He was sitting upright, with his back against the rowan's trunk. His head lolled on his chest and he could easily be mistaken for a drunken vagrant.

'He'd not be easily visible in the dark, Constable,' said Lady Hardcastle. 'How did you come to notice him from the road?'

'I was cuttin' through the churchyard, m'lady, on my w—'

'On his regular patrol,' Sergeant Dobson interrupted. He clearly saw no need to introduce distracting details of Constable Hancock's off-duty activities.

'I see. But you had no lantern?'

'Beg pardon, m'lady?' said Hancock.

'The sergeant told us that it was he who brought a lantern. I'm not trying to catch you out, dear, but the detective will. If you don't want to let on that you were cutting through the churchyard on your way back from . . .' She paused for a moment. 'Maude Holman's house?'

Even in the pre-dawn gloom I could see the tall constable blush. It was well known that he was walking out with the baker's daughter, but perhaps not how long he lingered at the house once the rest of the family had gone to bed.

'. . . then perhaps the two of you need to sort out a consistent story. But that's by the by. There was the lightest frost but the ground is still soft from the recent rain. You'll be looking for footprints before the detective gets here, I'm sure.'

'Naturally, m'lady,' said the sergeant.

'Good man,' she said. 'And you'll almost certainly examine his clothes to see if there's any clue as to what sort of instrument caused his fatal wound.'

'We shall, yes.'

'And you'll search the vicinity for other signs of activity, of course.'

'Of course,' said the sergeant.

'Then you seem to have everything in hand. I can't think what you were worried about. Would you think it awfully improper if we were to take a look ourselves? I promise not to disturb anything too much.'

'That's rather why I invited you over, m'lady,' said the sergeant. 'You might not have the trainin', but you've shown us before that you have a keen eye.'

'Thank you,' she said, and stepped delicately across the soft ground to the base of the tree, where she crouched down beside Mr Newhouse's body.

Careful not to disarrange his clothing too much, she examined his jacket. She seemed reluctant to unbutton his waistcoat but felt across its surface with her fingertips, inside and out. At length, she stood and made her way back to where we waited.

'There are no holes in his jacket, his waistcoat, or his shirt,' she said. 'But there's blood on the shirt and the lining of the waistcoat. Not as much as one might expect, but it seems to indicate that there's a wound of some sort under there. So whatever pierced his chest managed to do so without disturbing his clothing.'

'Just as we thought in the dark,' said the constable.

'There's something else odd, too,' she said.

The two policemen looked blankly at her.

'It was perishing cold out last night, and Mr Newhouse is without his overcoat. We know he possessed one – he was wearing it when he arrived at the house on Monday. He wasn't dressed for outdoors.'

''Pon my word, you're right,' said Sergeant Dobson. 'When you comes upon a corpse, the thing you notices is that the poor blighter's dead. You don't always see all the other irregularities.'

'I think you're right, Sergeant,' she said. 'Whereas I was expecting him to be dead, so I was able to concentrate on other details. Now, for all that we've been careful not to disturb the ground too much, it seems it was to no avail. You see how the ground is all churned up? I fear there's precious little to be learned from any marks there.'

'You're sure that's not us, though, m'lady?' said Constable Hancock. 'I wasn't none too careful 'fore I realized as how he was dead.'

'Quite sure, Constable,' she said. 'We've left our tracks in the frost. Do you see? The other muddle is all frosted over – the marks were left before the frost settled. I don't think it will tell us much.'

The sergeant diligently noted all these observations so that he could present them as his own.

The light was growing by the moment and there was already a definite glow to the east as dawn approached. While our policeman friends made their notes and agreed upon how they would present things to the Bristol detective, Lady Hardcastle and I took advantage of the increased visibility and conducted a little search of our own.

We circled the tree, and didn't have to go far before we found something the others definitely needed to see.

'I say, Sergeant,' I said. 'You might want to make a note of this.'

Dobson walked over and looked at the spot I indicated.

On the other side of the tree, nestled among the roots, was a small doll. It was dressed in a neat, grey suit and wore a large, military-style moustache. A long pin, topped with a blood-red bead, pierced the doll's heart.

◆ ◆ ◆

Very soon after the sun had first begun to peek through the gaps between the houses to the east of the village, we heard the sputtering progress of a motor vehicle coming from the Bristol Road. It wasn't long before it turned on to the road around the village green and began making its way towards the pair of little cottages that served double duty as both police station and accommodation for our two policemen. Constable Hancock was despatched on to the road to direct the driver to the scene of the crime instead.

The motor van was painted black, and the driver and his mate were sombrely dressed. As the van pulled up, they both stepped smartly out and presented themselves to Sergeant Dobson. There seemed to be some disagreement over what was to happen next. I couldn't quite hear all of the conversation but when the immortal phrase 'We got our orders, a'n't we?' drifted across the frosty grass, I knew that the sergeant was on a hiding to nothing.

The driver's mate returned to the van and took a stretcher from the back. Within moments, Basil Newhouse's body had been placed on the stretcher, covered with a sheet, and carried to the back of the van. There was nothing the two village policemen could do but watch as the van spluttered round the green and headed back towards the city.

Ten minutes later, we heard the sound of another vehicle coming from the Bristol Road. A smart new motor car took the same route around the green, heading for almost exactly the spot so recently vacated by the van.

I nudged Lady Hardcastle as I recognized both the occupants of the motor car.

'Inspector Sunderland, my lady,' I said. 'And your friend Dr Gosling.'

We had met Inspector Oliver Sunderland shortly after first moving to the village eighteen months earlier. We had 'assisted' (or 'interfered', depending upon one's point of view) in the investigation of a couple of 'minor unpleasantnesses' (as Lady Hardcastle subsequently termed them), and we and the inspector had eventually formed a friendship born of mutual respect.

Dr Simeon Gosling was an old friend of Lady Hardcastle's. He worked at the Bristol Royal Infirmary and had provided valuable information on naturally occurring poisons.

'Goodness, so it is,' said Lady Hardcastle. 'How lovely. Let's go and say hello.'

Dr Gosling parked the motor car neatly at the curb and the two men climbed out.

'Inspector Sunderland,' called Lady Hardcastle. 'How wonderful to see you.'

The inspector smiled ruefully. 'Good morning, my lady,' he said. 'I might have known you'd be here.' He turned to his travelling companion. 'Gosling, may I introduce Lady Har—'

'Emily and I are old pals,' interrupted Dr Gosling. 'What ho, old girl. Interfering again?'

'You know me,' she said.

'Only too well, old thing, only too well.' He bounded over and hugged his friend. 'I say, I knew you were living in the middle of nowhere, but I hadn't realized you were quite this remote. It's taken us an absolute age to get here.'

'It's only fifteen miles, Sim, dear. Are you sure it's not just because you drive like my grandmama?'

The inspector confirmed her guess with a frustrated nod, which Dr Gosling caught out of the corner of his eye.

'You're welcome to take the train next time, Sunderland, old boy,' he said cheerfully. 'Just say the word. Don't mind my own company on a long drive.'

The village policemen had joined us by now and Inspector Sunderland attempted his introductions again.

'Good to see you, Sergeant Dobson,' he said. 'And Constable Hancock?'

'Hancock, sir, that's right,' said the constable.

'This is Dr Gosling, our new police surgeon.'

'How do you do, sir?' said the sergeant.

'Police surgeon?' said Lady Hardcastle. 'You never mentioned your new job, Sim, dear.'

'Spur-of-the-moment thing. Job came up and I thought, "Dash it all, Simeon, do you want a life of adventure, or do you want to calcify in the dingy corridors of the BRI?" I gave it a moment's careful consideration and here I am.'

'I keep telling him not to hold out too much hope for a life of adventure,' said the inspector. 'But it's refreshing to have an enthusiastic man on the job for a change. Dr McDermott was a fine physician but you'd never describe him as being overbrimming with joy and wonderment. Even "cynical" and "jaded" didn't really do him justice.'

'I'll start to grate on you in the end, Sunderland,' said Dr Gosling. 'I do try, but I've been told more than once that I'm better in small doses.'

'I'll bear it in mind,' said Inspector Sunderland. 'But to business. Sergeant? Constable? I believe you have a body to show us.'

Two conflicting expressions were fighting for control of the sergeant's face. Somehow, contrition got the upper hand and anger was forced into temporary retreat as he said, 'I'm sorry, sir, but the mortuary men just took him.'

'They what?' said Inspector Sunderland furiously.

'Just afore you arrived, sir. They turns up in their wagon and insists they got their orders to take 'e away. Nothin' I could do. I'm so sorry.'

'Not your fault, Sergeant,' sighed the inspector. 'They did have orders to pick up the body and I didn't say anything to the mortuary about waiting for us. I didn't think I'd have to – I thought we'd be here first.' He looked at Dr Gosling, who smiled sheepishly.

'Sorry, Sunderland,' he said. 'I honestly had no idea we were in a race.'

'Nothing to be done about it now,' said the inspector. 'Let's have a look at where the body would have been if it were still here.'

'Right you are, sir,' said Sergeant Dobson. 'He was over y'ere.'

While the four men examined the ground around where the corpse had lain, Lady Hardcastle and I loitered by Dr Gosling's motor car.

'What do you think?' I asked. 'It was carefully staged to look like witchcraft, wasn't it?'

'Artfully, one might say,' she replied. 'And we know from the business with the séance a few months ago that there are plenty hereabouts who will swallow that one hook, line, and whatnot.'

'It's the way his character died in the moving picture,' I said.

'I know.'

'Wouldn't it be super,' I said wistfully, 'if just once we could have a little fun without finding ourselves up to our knees in corpses?'

'I'm not certain we should mention our knees in public, dear,' she said. 'This isn't quite as permissive a place as London, you know. They's afraid of ladies' knees out y'ere.'

'Duly noted,' I said. 'But you know what I mean. Every time we think we've got the chance to enjoy ourselves, someone comes along and dies. Quite aside from anything else, it's so . . . what's that phrase you use? "Statistically anomalous"?'

'The high incidence of murders in the area certainly doesn't match the national trend,' she said absently. 'The inspector remarked upon it when we first met him.'

'It's not just this area, though, is it?' I persisted. 'We went away for a week's motor racing in Rutland and were scraping bodies off the tarmac before I even had a chance to get behind the wheel.'

'Do you think perhaps we've been hexed?'

'Well, you did insist on turning away that old woman in Bucharest a couple of years ago. I was sure she was a witch.'

'Whereas I was sure she was a chancer who thought she could tap a rich lady for a few bob if she muttered some threatening-sounding curses in broken English.'

'We've certainly had more than our fair share of bad luck ever since,' I said.

'On the contrary, I'd say we've had splendidly good luck. Look how many people have come to a sticky end while we continue to thrive.'

I harrumphed.

'Don't do that, dear. It makes you sound like a distressed water buffalo.'

I scowled instead. She ignored me.

'Look out,' she said. 'Here come the boys.'

Inspector Sunderland and Dr Gosling walked out of the church-yard, leaving the local men in charge of the scene of the crime.

'Still hanging around, Emily?' said Dr Gosling. 'I thought you'd have beetled off for some breakfast while the boring stuff was going on.'

'We're hungry for news,' she said.

'There's not much to tell you beyond what you – I beg your pardon – beyond what Dobson and Hancock have already discovered,' said Inspector Sunderland.

Dr Gosling smiled at this. He looked to the inspector for confirmation that it was all right to speak. The latter nodded his assent.

'I'll know more once I've got him on the slab,' said Dr Gosling. 'I agree with . . . with "Dobson" that it was staged to look like a super-natural killing – the witch's doll and whatnot. From the evidence on the ground, and from what Dobson has said about his examination of the body, there wasn't a great amount of blood. The chances are that he was stabbed after he was already dead, although he might have been cleaned up before he was moved. But, as I say, that's for the autopsy.'

'You definitely think he was moved?' I asked.

'Yes, but not by witchcraft,' said Dr Gosling.

I scowled at him, too.

'From "Dobson's" excellent observation about the lack of an over-coat,' said the inspector, 'we're presuming the murder was committed elsewhere and the body brought here for maximum effect.'

'You know about the moving picture, then?' said Lady Hardcastle.

'Hancock gave us the gist,' he said.

'More than just the gist,' said Dr Gosling. 'We practically had to stop him from acting the whole thing out.'

'So we're definitely working on the basis that the death and the moving picture are connected?' said Lady Hardcastle.

'"We", my lady?' said the inspector with a smile.

'Oh, come now, Inspector,' she said. 'You can't possibly imagine that we could be dragged out here before dawn to look at a corpse and then not involve ourselves in the case. You know us better than that.'

He gave his familiar throaty chuckle. 'I do,' he said. 'Anyone else would be sent off with a flea in their ear for interfering, but you two . . . Well, you two are an altogether different kettle of fish. It happens that I have another couple of cases to be getting on with back in the city so I'm sure I should be most grateful to have a pair of competent amateurs such as yourselves poking about here in the village on my behalf. Sergeant Dobson already has cause to be most grateful to you – you've done much to make him look extremely competent this morning.'

'One does one's best,' she said.

'Just tread carefully,' he said. 'A staged corpse with a witch's doll beside it means a planned murder, not a crime of passion. This is what the more sensational members of the press would call a "cold-blooded killer".'

'I'll look after her,' I said.

He looked at me for a long moment. 'Of that, Miss Armstrong,' he said at length, 'I have always been quite certain.'

'Is there anything in particular you'd like us to do?' asked Lady Hardcastle.

'Since the body has already been picked up, I shall need to return to Bristol with Dr Gosling,' he said. 'I'll not be back until later this afternoon. If you could let me have a list of everyone involved with this moving picture business, I'll have somewhere to start.'

'Consider it done,' she said. 'Call for me at the house. We shall supply you with tea, cake, and a comprehensive list of suspects. I may even prepare my famous—'

'Crime board?' he interrupted.

'The very thing,' she said.

'What the devil's a "crime board"?' asked Dr Gosling.

'I'll tell you on the drive home,' said the inspector. He turned back to Lady Hardcastle. 'One last thing before we go: I don't suppose you know who Mr Newhouse's next of kin might be?'

'I'm afraid not,' she said. 'His friends are all staying at our house, though, so I could easily find out. I'm not certain of the protocol. Should we tell them of his passing or is that something you need to do?'

'It ought to be one of us,' he said. 'But I'm sure they'll take the news better from you. Just be sure to watch their reactions, though.'

'Surely you don't think . . .'

'It's early days yet, my lady. I don't think anything at all yet. Just keep your eyes open, that's all.'

With a nod of farewell, we set off back towards the house, leaving them to their slow drive back to Bristol.

Edna and Miss Jones had arrived for work by the time we returned to the house.

Miss Jones rather excitedly told me that her mother had insisted she work longer hours to feed the 'famous actors', and began outlining her plans for more elaborately impressive evening meals. I let her babble on for a bit – there seemed little profit in spoiling her mood with the sad news from the churchyard.

Misses Drayton and Selwood were already in the morning room, sharing a pot of tea and chattering excitedly about the reaction of the villagers to their moving picture. I followed Lady Hardcastle into the room and closed the door behind me.

'Good morning, ladies,' she said calmly and quietly.

Perhaps their acting skills had taught them to read emotions, or perhaps Lady Hardcastle had about her such an air of impending bad news that all but the most closed of minds would have spotted that all was not well. Whatever the case, the two actresses stopped talking at once and the smiles tumbled from their faces.

'You look like something dreadful's happened, dear,' said Zelda.

'I'm afraid it has,' said Lady Hardcastle. 'It would have been more proper to tell you all together, but I don't think it should wait.'

'We can get the others,' said Euphemia, standing up.

Lady Hardcastle waved her back to her chair.

'No, dear, stay where you are. I understand you were both quite close to Basil Newhouse.'

'"Were", dear?' said Zelda. 'Oh my goodness. What's happened?'

'I'm so terribly sorry to be the bearer of bad news, but he was found in the churchyard this morning by the village constable. I'm afraid he was dead.'

The actresses looked as though they'd been physically struck. Euphemia began to cry, her body shaking with silent sobs. Her friend put a comforting arm around her shoulder.

'Was it his heart?' said Zelda. 'He was starting to have trouble with the stairs, you know. But he was fine when we left him at the pub last night. Drinking and yarning with the locals, he was. Right as ninepence.'

Lady Hardcastle sat in silence for a moment. Eventually she seemed to make up her mind that there was no gentle way to break the news. 'He was murdered,' she said.

Euphemia stopped sobbing at once and stared at Lady Hardcastle with her mouth hanging open. Zelda was similarly stunned.

'There must be some sort of mistake,' said Zelda. 'It was his heart. He wasn't well. No one would have wanted to kill him.'

As unsensationally as she could, Lady Hardcastle told the two women how Mr Newhouse had been found.

Predictably, perhaps, the two women were aghast when they learned of the connection with their moving picture.

'Who could possibly have done such a horrid thing?' said Euphemia. 'Basil was such a lovely man. He looked after me. After us all. Especially Zel. He was like her dad.'

Zelda hugged her closer. 'He was, my dear,' she said. 'No decent person could have done it.'

'He didn't seem like the sort of man who would have any enemies,' said Lady Hardcastle.

I could see what she was doing, and it was a gamble. One of the best ways of getting people to tell you things that they might otherwise prefer to keep hidden is to make a false statement and give them the chance to disagree with you. Even the most reticent of people love to contradict you when they think they know something you don't, and they love explaining exactly why you're wrong. In this case, though, it probably wasn't a falsehood – Basil Newhouse had seemed to me to be a perfectly charming man who would have made few enemies in his cheerfully gregarious life.

'I've never met a soul who didn't think the world of old Basil,' said Zelda. 'He was kind, generous, and easy-going. He wouldn't hurt a fly, and he wouldn't stand by and let anyone else hurt one, either. He was a true gentleman.'

It was much as I suspected, then – Basil Newhouse had been well liked by one and all. It made the argument I'd overheard between him and Euphemia seem all the more incongruous, but I didn't think this was the moment to ask about it.

'I'm so terribly sorry to be the bearer of such terrible news,' said Lady Hardcastle. 'You have our deepest sympathy. We shall leave you to yourselves for now, but don't feel that we're abandoning you to your grief. If you need anything at all, we'll do whatever we can.'

'Thank you, my lady,' sniffed Euphemia, who had begun to cry again.

'Would you like to tell Mr Cheetham?' asked Lady Hardcastle as we stood to leave. 'I can pass on the news if you can't bear to do it, but it's up to you. Perhaps it would be better coming from his friends?'

Zelda thought for a moment. 'No, dear, would you do it, please? I don't think I could get the words out.'

We left them to assimilate the terrible news in private.

◆ ◆ ◆

Lady Hardcastle took coffee alone in the dining room while I hovered in the hall waiting to intercept Mr Cheetham as he came downstairs. Dora glared daggers at me as she passed but said nothing. On another occasion I might have given her a piece of my mind for being so rude, but I didn't have any to spare. My mind was otherwise engaged.

Dewi was more cheerful. Despite his reputation for being a little surly, he was always pleasant to me.

'Mornin', Miss Armstrong,' he said as he reached the bottom of the stairs. 'I've seen to Mr Cheetham but I can't get no answer from Mr Newhouse's room. I could just go in, I suppose, and I would if it were Sir Hector – he don't mind, see? – but you never know with folk who aren't born to it, like. Some of 'em are a bit embarrassed at havin' servants about the place.'

'Don't worry about it,' I said. 'You did the right thing. Go and see Edna – I'm sure she'll have a few things that need doing.'

He smiled. 'Usually fetchin' things off high shelves,' he said. '"Y'ere, I wishes I 'ad longer arms," she goes. Sometimes I'm no more use than a pair of steps.'

His impression of Edna was uncannily accurate and I laughed in spite of myself.

'I'm sure you come in handy for lifting heavy packages, too,' I said.

Mr Cheetham appeared at the top of the stairs.

'Off you trot, Dewi,' I said. 'I need to nab Mr Cheetham.'

Dewi duly trotted off.

'Did I hear my name?' said Mr Cheetham as he stepped off the last stair.

'Yes, sir,' I said. 'I was just telling Dewi I needed to catch you before you went into breakfast.'

'Sounds ominous,' he said.

'I'll let Lady Hardcastle explain. She's waiting for you in the dining room.'

'Right you are. He's a good lad, that Dewi.'

'He is, yes.'

'One thing's been puzzling me, though. His name. How do you spell it?'

'D-E-W-I,' I said.

He looked blankly at me. 'But he calls himself "Duh-wee",' he said incredulously. 'How on earth . . . ?'

'It's a Welsh name, sir,' I said as I led him to the dining room door and ushered him in. 'We have our own way of spelling things.'

'Well I never. Good morning, my lady,' he said. 'Miss Armstrong here tells me you want to see me.'

'I do, yes,' she said. 'Come on in, Armstrong, and close the door.'

'I was just saying it sounded ominous. It's not sounding any better.'

'No, I'm afraid it's not good at all. Sergeant Dobson, one of our local policemen, called on us this morning to tell us that your friend Mr Newhouse was found dead in the churchyard.'

Mr Cheetham was as stunned as his actresses had been.

'A detective and a police surgeon from Bristol were summoned after a preliminary examination of the body by the local men. I'm sorry to have to tell you it was murder.'

'But how . . . why . . . who . . . ?'

'The why and the who elude us for the moment, but as for how . . . He was stabbed through the heart. A witch's doll was nearby, dressed as Mr Newhouse, with a pin through its own heart.'

'My moving picture,' he said. 'They're trying to ruin me. He was killed just like the Witchfinder. Oh, poor Basil. This is all my fault. I should never . . .'

'It's not your fault, Mr Cheetham,' said Lady Hardcastle kindly. 'But what makes you say so? Why would anyone have it in for you? And why would they attack Mr Newhouse if you were the object of their hatred?'

'There's a number of people with a grudge against me,' he said. 'Aaron Orum, for one – he insists I stole his idea, you know. And those Hughes creatures. They've been trying to close me down for months. It could be one of their acolytes.'

'But what good would killing Mr Newhouse do any of them?'

'Bad publicity, my lady,' he said forcefully. 'They want to close me down, to stop me from bringing my art to the world. What better way than to start a scandal around the picture. Questions will be asked in the press. "A man has died. How many more will die as a result of this evil picture?" I'll be ruined.' He sat heavily in one of the dining chairs. 'Ruined.'

I slipped discreetly out to fetch a pot of tea. Ruined or not, he was going to feel less despondent about it with a nice cup of tea inside him.

Chapter Six

The three remaining 'film folk', as Lady Hardcastle had dubbed them, were closeted together in the morning room for a couple of hours. We left them to it, but after they had been in there for some time, Lady Hardcastle urged me to try to find out what was going on.

I had often cursed Jasper Laxley, the man whose house we rented, for having such deep pockets and high standards. If only he had skimped a little on the building then the walls might have been thinner and earwigging on guests considerably easier. As it was, I had to use the old servants' trick of lingering by the door with a tray so that I could appear to be on some important serving errand if they should open the door suddenly and find me walking away. Despite this none too subtle subterfuge, I was still unable to hear what was going on.

For the most part I could make out only the general hum of conversation but I did hear Euphemia exclaim, 'Well, I think it's too dangerous!' before the sound of approaching footsteps forced me to step away and pretend to be about my business.

They emerged into the hall, with Mr Cheetham looking a good deal less comfortable and confident than we were used to.

'We've had a chat,' he said, 'and we've decided that, as the old circus phrase has it, "The show must go on". We'll be opening up the village hall again this evening with our planned second programme. We'll be showing *The Witch's Downfall* as well, in honour of Basil.'

My own opinion was that the villagers would be horrified by Mr Newhouse's death and would think a rescreening of the moving picture a most disrespectful act. I could well imagine that some of them would be terrified by the idea of a murderer on the loose and wouldn't want anything further to do with *The Witch's Downfall* or with anyone involved in it, lest a similar fate befall them.

Lady Hardcastle, too, frowned momentarily, but said, 'I'm sure it's the right thing to do. He wouldn't have wanted the actions of some madman to spoil your collective achievement.'

Mr Cheetham looked pleased at this, although the two ladies seemed less certain.

'Thank you, my lady,' he said. 'I'll say a few words, you know – make it into a proper tribute.'

'That would be fitting,' said Lady Hardcastle. 'And perhaps—'

But her next suggestion was cut off by the insistent ringing of the doorbell.

I answered it to find the well-dressed young woman we had previously seen in the pub in the company of Aaron Orum. She was alone this time, but as impeccably turned out as before in another exquisitely cut suit. Her hat was especially daring. It appeared to be a gentleman's bowler, with a broad ribbon around the crown, tied in an exuberantly large bow and holding a peacock feather in place. This was a woman who liked to make an impression.

She presented her card. 'Good day,' she said. 'I understand Mr Nolan Cheetham is staying here. I should like to see him, please.'

I looked at the card. Miss Dinah Caudle, it told me, was employed by the *Bristol News*.

'Shall I tell him what it's about?' I asked with as much innocence as I could muster.

'The murder of one of his company,' she said bluntly.

I checked the weather. It was shaping up to be a bright enough day, if a chilly one. 'Just a moment, please, miss,' I said. 'I'll see if he's available.'

I closed the door. Journalists, I thought, can wait outside, especially journalists who palled around with people who were so obviously antagonistic towards our guests.

I turned back to the little knot of people who had been standing behind me during the brief exchange at the door. It seemed unlikely that Miss Caudle wouldn't have been able to see them all. I handed Mr Cheetham the card. He examined it briefly.

'Do you know her?' he said.

'I saw her in the pub on Monday afternoon,' I said. 'She was the woman I told you about, the one with Mr Orum. But we weren't introduced so I had no idea that she was a journalist.'

'A journalist,' he said. 'That puts a different slant on things altogether. If he's walking out with a journalist . . . well, one or other of them must be up to something.'

He didn't seem at all comfortable with this conclusion.

'It could just be a coincidence,' I suggested. 'That she's a journalist, I mean. She is extremely attractive. He might just be with her because she looks good on his arm.'

'Aye, maybe you're right,' he said uncertainly. 'It's certainly part of his bohemian image, is that – hanging around with pretty young girls. Pretty, young, rich girls if he can manage it. They're always good for a few bob to fund his latest project.'

'She certainly gives every appearance of being rich,' I said. 'It must have taken a procession of wagons to bring her wardrobe.'

He seemed to relax a little. 'She might not be up to anything, eh? I suppose I'd better see her. Set her straight. I don't reckon as how I can stop her from writing whatever sort of sensational nonsense she wants about poor Basil's death, but I can give our side of the story, at least.'

'The drawing room would suit you best, I think,' said Lady Hardcastle. 'We'll keep out of your way unless you want . . .'

'Want what, my lady?' he said.

'I was going to say "a witness",' she said. 'But it suddenly sounded so melodramatic. I'm sure she's utterly trustworthy, but I wondered if it might be reassuring to have a third party present who could verify the details of your conversation in the event of any dispute.'

He looked thoughtful for a moment. ''Appen you're right at that,' he said. 'If it's not too much trouble, like.'

'I was thinking Armstrong might fit the bill. Neither of us has any real reason to be there, but she'll be more inclined to ignore Armstrong. She'd have to make polite conversation with me.'

'Right you are, then,' he said, and made his way towards the drawing room.

I reopened the front door. Being left on the doorstep, even in the watery November sunshine, hadn't lifted Miss Caudle's spirits at all. She glared at me as I said, 'Please come in, Miss Caudle. Mr Cheetham will see you in the drawing room.'

She said nothing as she followed me through the hall and into the drawing room. I waited inside for her to pass and then closed the door. She looked as though she was about to say something to me – ask me to leave, perhaps – but she was distracted by Mr Cheetham's warm greeting.

'Good afternoon, Miss Caudle,' he said genially. 'How wonderful of you to come round to express your sympathy. My colleagues and I greatly appreciate it.'

Her eyes narrowed. She clearly didn't appreciate this attempt to catch her off balance. 'It must be a terrible time for you,' she said. 'It's devastating enough to lose a friend, but to have your moving picture blamed for it . . . well. One can only try to imagine how awful you must feel.'

'Shall we sit?' he asked.

As they made themselves comfortable in two of the armchairs, Miss Caudle gave me an impatient look. It was obvious that she would prefer that I wasn't there, but she knew she had no real power to expel me while she was in someone else's house, especially not when one of the houseguests apparently wanted me there. I ignored her stare and stationed myself in the corner of the room by the bookcase.

'Are they blaming my picture?' asked Mr Cheetham mildly.

'It's only a matter of time before they do,' she said. She opened her handbag and took out a leather-bound notebook, embossed in gold leaf with her initials. She rummaged in the bag for a short while longer and produced a black pen with a red-topped cap. She removed the cap and looked up at Mr Cheetham, poised to begin writing.

'Why would they "blame" my picture?' asked Mr Cheetham. 'I produced a work of entertaining fiction, not a manual for murder.'

'Come now, Mr Cheetham,' she said as she began to take notes. 'Everyone will soon know that Basil Newhouse died in exactly the same way as his character in your picture.'

'*Exactly* the same way, Miss Caudle? Are you suggesting that he was killed by witchcraft?'

She frowned again. Or continued to frown, at any rate. It seemed that disdainful disapproval was her default expression. 'You know very well what I mean,' she said. 'And you know very well what people will say. There will be a small constituency who genuinely believes that supernatural forces were at work. But there will be a larger and more vocal group who will see your work as a corrupting influence that inspired a madman to act in this terrible way.'

'But you'll be setting them straight, I'm sure,' said Mr Cheetham with a smile. 'The *Bristol News* doesn't go in for sensationalism.'

'We report the news, Mr Cheetham. And we shall also report such opinions as are expressed by our readers and the population at large.'

Hmm, I thought, snooty *and* pompous. What a winning combination.

'You're a news reporter, then?' asked Mr Cheetham. Somehow he seemed to be the one conducting the interview.

'Well, no,' she said, seeming slightly flustered for the first time since I'd encountered her. 'Not exactly. I write mainly for the society pages. And for our women readers. But I also report on the arts, and I believe that moving pictures are going to be frightfully important. I intend to make sure that they get all the coverage they deserve.'

'Including stirring up fear and prejudice against them? Against me?'

She hadn't anticipated being put on the defensive, and she didn't seem pleased about it. She changed the subject abruptly. 'You must be used to having people turned against you,' she said. 'There was an outcry after you stole Aaron Orum's story, for instance.'

'Ah, yes,' he said coolly. 'Miss Armstrong told us you'd been keeping company with Aaron. How is he? Well, I trust? I do hope your . . . "relationship" hasn't compromised your – what do they call it? – "journalistic integrity". The people of Bristol have a right to expect honest objectivity from the press.'

Miss Caudle blushed crimson but chose to ignore his barb.

'But you don't deny that you stole his story and that public opinion turned against you,' she said.

'I deny both of those things. *The Witch's Downfall* is entirely my own work and the only opinion turned against me was that of my former friend Aaron Orum.'

'Will you be withdrawing your stolen picture now that it has inspired murder?' she said.

He appraised her silently for a moment. 'I don't think we have very much of any use to say to each other, Miss Caudle. Thank you for calling. Miss Armstrong, would you show her out, please?'

I opened the door while Miss Caudle hurriedly stuffed her notebook and pen back into her handbag. She left without another word.

Mr Cheetham had nodded his thanks and taken himself back off to the morning room with the two ladies. Lady Hardcastle felt that she ought to be doing something useful, so I was sent to the attic to fetch the blackboard and easel – her infamous 'crime board'.

We set it up in the dining room as usual and she started work on her sketches.

'From what we know already,' she said as she put the finishing touches to her drawing of the victim, 'Newhouse was killed by someone who was familiar with Mr Cheetham's moving picture. The murder was carefully planned and neatly staged to leave no doubt about the connection to the story.'

'Last night was the first public showing in the whole of Gloucestershire,' I said, 'so we can safely rule out our friends and neighbours – they would never have had time to plan and carry out such an elaborate crime.'

'Just so.' She began scribbling notes on a piece of scrap paper as she talked. 'Let's see, then . . . We have Cheetham himself, of course.'

'An ambitious man,' I said. 'He likes to be in control, I think. And he likes to put on a show. But why would he kill one of his own cast? It's not quite killing the goose that laid the golden egg, but it's just making work for yourself to kill your own staff.'

'I know,' she said. 'The same thought has saved your life more than once. There may be circumstances of which we know nothing, though. They might have quarrelled. There might be some long-standing grudge. Or debts. There could be any number of reasons for wanting to bump someone off. We'll put him on the list. The two actresses?'

'For completeness, yes. It's not like we've not met our fair share of murderesses lately, so we can't rule them out simply because they're women. And there was something I overheard on Monday afternoon. I forgot to tell you.'

'Oh?'

'Euphemia Selwood was arguing with Mr Newhouse. I couldn't hear clearly, but her parting shot was something like, "You want to watch out, Basil. You could find yourself dead." It could be construed as a threat. And then there was her comment about "danger" just before they all came out of the morning room.'

'They very well could be threats,' she said thoughtfully. 'But she's such a charming, lovely young woman. It's difficult to imagine her wanting to kill anyone, much less a man she regarded so fondly.'

'She's an actress, though,' I said. 'You can't trust them.'

She laughed as she jotted down their names. 'Very well. There would be others involved in the production, of course. Backstage chaps or whatever they call them in the moving picture business. And the young actor who played George.'

'I suppose we should consider them. But we've seen no sign of any of them yet, so perhaps we ought to stick to people that we know are here.'

'Very well. Aaron Orum.'

'He comes across as a thoroughly obnoxious egomaniac,' I said. 'He seems to have a very high opinion of himself and a correspondingly low opinion of everyone else. He was extremely unpleasant when we encountered him in the pub.'

'Unpleasant enough to commit murder?'

'Unpleasant and flamboyant enough, yes. I shouldn't let my prejudices get the better of me, but even the way he was dressed made him look like the sort of person who would murder someone like this.'

'But why?' she asked as she jotted down his name. 'What would he gain by killing Newhouse?'

'He hates Cheetham. You should have heard him.'

'Yes, but if he hates Cheetham, why kill Newhouse?'

'To ruin him?' I suggested. 'By linking the death to the new moving picture, he could kill the project before it properly set sail. He mentioned how expensive it all is. Losing the audience might bankrupt him.'

'It's possible,' she said. 'But it's a bit indirect.'

'I've never quite understood the idea of killing someone who upsets you. They can't be sorry once they're dead. And even at the moment of their death they might not know it was you who killed them, or why. Far better to ruin them, to make their lives a misery.'

'Remind me never to upset you,' she said.

'I'd be without a billet and a salary if I were to ruin you, my lady,' I said. 'You've been saved more than once by that knowledge.'

'Touché. So how about this journalist character? Deborah Crundel?'

'Dinah Caudle. She seems clever in a superficial way, but she's not . . . wily. She came in with a half-baked plan to unnerve Mr Cheetham and get her story, but she let him run rings around her. She's not a strategic thinker. I don't know if she could plan a murder.'

'But she had a plan of sorts when she came here. She only stumbled when things didn't go as she thought they would. If everything went the way she imagined it, she'd be capable?'

'I suppose so,' I said.

'It would help to make her name in the newspaper world if she were the one to break a big murder story. And what better way to be the first to report on a murder than to commit the murder yourself? You don't really need to get any sensational quotes if you already know the whole story, so maybe her interview wasn't planned at all. Perhaps she just needed to speak to him so she could say she had.'

'Hmm,' I said. 'Perhaps.'

'I'm putting her on the list. Inspector Sunderland wants as complete a roll call as we can muster. Which leaves us with the Hugheses.'

'Wet blankets and spoilsports,' I said. 'But very competent ones if the vicar is to be believed.'

'Mr Bland is a man of principle and honour. I think we can take him at his word on most matters.'

'In that case, it would appear that they are professional troublemakers. I wouldn't put it past them to murder someone to stir up a little controversy and further their cause.'

'It's a big step,' she said.

'If they feel strongly enough about their cause, who knows how big a step they might be prepared to take? He seemed quite the zealot when I bumped into him outside the tobacconist's.'

'Well, quite. Of course, if we're including everyone who knew about the plot of the moving picture, the vicar needs to be on the list, too, you know.'

'A wise old woman once told me that Mr Bland was a man of principle and honour and that I could take him at his word on most matters. I think that might extend to assuming that he's not a deranged murderer.'

'I'm forty-one.'

'Forty-two on Sunday,' I said. 'See? Old.'

'Cheeky wench. I've a good mind to—'

I was saved from whatever her good mind had conjured up by the ringing of the telephone.

'I'll just answer that, my lady,' I said, and scooted from the room.

'Take a message, would you?' she called. 'I'll get on with these sketches.'

'Righto,' I said.

'Unless it's Gertie.'

'Of course,' I said.

'Or anything particularly urgent.'

I sighed and picked up the telephone. 'Chipping Bevington two-three,' I said loudly and clearly. 'Hello?'

'Flo?' said a man's voice. 'Blimey, is that really you?'

'As far as I can make out,' I said.

'Yeah, it's you.'

'I'm glad we've got that sorted out. But you have the better of me, Mr . . . ?'

'It's me,' said the voice.

I said nothing. This could go on for days.

'It's me,' he said again. 'Skins. Remember?'

Ivor 'Skins' Maloney was the drummer in the ragtime band that had been mixed up in the business at The Grange when we had first arrived in the village. He and his bass-playing friend Barty Dunn had stayed with us briefly when everything had been settled and we had spent an entertainingly musical evening together. Of course I remembered him.

'Of course I remember you, Mr Skins,' I said. 'How wonderful to hear from you.'

'You might not think so when you find out why I'm callin',' he said.

'You've done bloody murder and you're looking for a place to lie low until the rozzers lose the scent?'

'More like we're on our way to Gloucester and the train's broken down at Chipping Bevington. But we do need a place to lie low. Or lie down at any rate. Any chance of us kippin' down at your gaff?'

'Us?' I said. 'The whole band?'

He laughed. 'No, just me and Barty. Best rhythm section in London. We're in demand. Sittin' in with some bunch of yokels up Gloucester way. What do you say?'

'It's not my place to say anything, I'm afraid. Can you hold the line while I speak to Lady Hardcastle?'

'Certainly can, my little Welsh cake,' he said. 'But be quick. There's an old dear here wants to use the telephone and I'm not sure I can fight her off for long.'

I placed the earpiece on the hall table and scooted back into the dining room. I recounted Skins's request.

'Oh,' said Lady Hardcastle. 'How delightful. I don't see why not. We've got the room. More so now that Mr Newhouse is no longer with us. And if the film folk are out tonight, it would be fun to have company.'

'We're not going to the picture show?'

'You can if you like,' she said. 'But they're going to be showing *The Witch's Downfall* again and I'm afraid I really do still think it's in terribly poor taste. It feels less like a tribute to Newhouse's talents as an actor and more like a ghoulish celebration of his murder. I was planning an early night, but an evening with our musical friends would be quite refreshing.'

'I'll tell him the good news,' I said, and returned to the telephone.

◆ ◆ ◆

A few minutes later, we received another telephone call, this time from Inspector Sunderland. He was tied up with work on his two other cases and wouldn't be able to return to Littleton Cotterell that afternoon, but he was grateful for our list of possible suspects. Lady Hardcastle held the earpiece so that we could both hear.

'Just keep an eye on things for me,' he said. 'Dobson and Hancock are decent chaps if they've got someone around to nudge them in the right direction, so just do whatever nudging is required and I'll come up to the village as soon as I can.'

'Did Simeon do his autopsy?' asked Lady Hardcastle.

'No, the mortuary van broke down on the way back to town. He was called out on another case so he missed them. He's planning to spend the day tomorrow catching up with his "slicing and rummaging", as he calls it.'

'That sounds like Sim,' she said. 'Solemn and respectful.'

'I'm sure it doesn't bother his patients, not in their present state, but I do hope he manages to rein it in if he ever has to deal with relatives and loved ones.'

'I don't think you have anything to worry about there – he's not quite the idiot he likes to pretend to be. We look forward to seeing you tomorrow, Inspector.'

'I shall call on you before I do anything else.'

The call ended with the usual exchange of goodbyes.

'How long do we have before the boys get here?' asked Lady Hardcastle once she had replaced the earpiece on its hook.

'It depends how quickly they can arrange transport from Chipping,' I said. 'Skins expressed an intention to "have a swift half" in the pub while they waited, though, so I'd not expect them within the hour. Longer if halves turn to pints.'

'Plenty of time, then,' she said.

'For . . . ?'

'For popping into the village and kicking some wasps' nests.'

'Splendid,' I said. 'I fancy doing a little kicking.'

'Then button up your boots and let's go,' she said. 'You fetch hats and coats and I'll tell the film folk we'll be back in time for tea.'

Mr and Mrs Hughes and their devoted acolytes were chanting half-heard slogans outside the village hall. The placards were familiar from the previous day, all save one. It read: 'Romans 6:23 "For the wages of sin is death . . ."'

'Well, really!' said Lady Hardcastle. 'I think we need to have a word with these Hugheses.'

'It does seem a little crass,' I said. 'The poor man's not been gone more than a day and they're busy blaming him for his own demise.'

'Come then, tiny one. Let's go and see what they've got to say for themselves.'

We were halfway across the green when the vicar emerged from the great oaken doors of St Arild's, accompanied by his diminutive wife. And her dog.

James and Jagruti Bland had met while he was serving as a missionary in India. She had worked as a teacher in the small village school he helped to set up, and as the years passed pleasantly by they fell in love and were eventually married. When the time came for Mr Bland to return to England, Mrs Bland, of course, came with him.

They met with a certain amount of mockery – the tall, gangly priest and his tiny wife did, to be perfectly honest, present an endearingly comical image. But they also encountered an unpleasant amount of hostility – the English priest and his Indian wife made a lot of small-minded people extremely angry. They had served many parishes around the country before the villagers of Littleton Cotterell took them to their hearts and they found a place where they were finally accepted.

More or less.

Mrs Bland ('Jag' to her friends, of whom there were many) was a woman possessed of many fine qualities. She was intelligent and witty, kind and generous. She played the harmonium. Without fanfare or folderol, she fed and clothed her husband's parishioners when they fell on hard times. But she had one failing. She was utterly devoted to the world's most preposterous dog.

Hamlet was a Great Dane. At the very least, as Prince of Denmark, he was an important Dane. But in this instance, Hamlet was one of those improbably large dogs formerly known as the German Boarhound and which we now know as the Great Dane. He was blueish-grey in colour, with white socks on his forelegs, and stood just shy of three feet tall at the shoulder. He weighed in on the heavy side of twelve stone. This meant that the top of his head was roughly level with Mrs Bland's armpit and that he weighed about twice as much as she did. He was friendly, playful, inquisitive, and was possessed of that most terrifying of animal attributes: a mind of his own.

Hamlet was often to be seen taking Mrs Bland for a walk around the village and, unless you took the trouble to engage her in conversation, you might imagine that the only English words she knew were 'Hamlet! No!' He was generally genial and well meaning, but his size, exuberance, and wilfulness, coupled with his mistress's inability to curb his more boisterous excesses, meant that he spent a lot of time tied to fences and gate posts – he was no longer welcome in many of the homes and shops of Littleton Cotterell.

Sometimes, though, a colossal, disruptively ill-disciplined dog is just what the doctor ordered, and this was precisely one of those times. As Mr Hughes, the leader of the protesters, spotted the Blands, he gave a sneeringly self-satisfied smile. This was their chance to act. He signalled to his cohorts and, as one, they rounded on the vicar and his wife. The chanting, which until this moment had been reasonably good-natured – one might even have called it 'jolly' – took on a sinisterly aggressive tone. Things seemed to be getting ugly.

Mr and Mrs Bland seemed inclined to ignore the small crowd and stepped out into the road in order to get round them rather than trying to push their way past. Unfortunately, there's a mystical force that takes control of crowds and turns a collection of perfectly reasonable individuals into an intimidating mob, no matter how benign the intentions of those individuals might be. One of the women took a step towards the Blands. It looked to me as though she was merely trying to regain her balance after leaning over too far, but the mystical mob force took her step as its cue to impel the rest of the group to also take one step forwards. For no readily discernible reason, the volume of the anti-cinema chanting increased as they did so.

Whether he saw it as an opportunity for play, or for mischief, or whether he perceived the movement as a threat to his own beloved humans, Hamlet was certain that something was afoot – or a-paw, at least. He barked. A loud, sonorous bark. The sort of bark that would make even an enterprising burglar stop a-burgling and abandon his felonious little plans. The woman whose stumble had precipitated the crowd's collective step screamed in fright. The man next to her took another solo step and brandished his placard at the dog, yelling something unintelligible as he did so.

Now Hamlet knew for certain that the game was on. He gave another full-throated bark and lurched forwards, yanking the lead from Mrs Bland's tiny hand. He caromed exuberantly into the man who had stepped towards him, knocking him flying into the woman who had started it all. Both protesters fell to the ground but Hamlet carried on, bounding through the group and barking gleefully all the while. Within seconds he had knocked everyone on to their backsides and was still bouncing around the fallen, barking and wagging his tail.

Mr Hughes began shouting angrily at the dog and its human companions. He tried to get to his feet, more effectively to remonstrate with them, but Hamlet interpreted the shouting – which must have just seemed like barking to him – and the sudden movement as an invitation to continue the game. He bounced over to the lead protester and knocked him flat on his back once more.

'I think Mr Hughes might be a little busy,' said Lady Hardcastle. 'Perhaps we should confine ourselves to visiting Mr Orum at the Dog and Duck.'

'It might be best,' I said. 'Hughes seems to have quite a lot to deal with at the moment.'

As we turned away, Mr Hughes was still supine, with Hamlet's forepaws on his chest. The happy hound stood with his head bent towards his unwitting playmate's face, barking and drooling and, as always, completely oblivious to the chaos he had caused.

Chapter Seven

I hadn't been entirely certain that the trip to the pub would be a productive one. Lady Hardcastle had wanted to speak to Mr Orum, and although we knew he was staying in one of the two rooms that Old Joe let out to paying guests, we neither of us had any idea where he would actually be. He might have been sitting in his room, reading an improving book. He might just as easily have been braving the November chill and striding manfully across the Gloucestershire fields, trying to further cultivate his image as a windswept romantic artist. That seemed the most likely possibility to me, actually. Anyone who wore that paisley cravat definitely had an image to cultivate.

He was sitting in the snug with a pint of Old Joe's best cider, and a newspaper. He peered over the newspaper as we entered, but flicked it ostentatiously back up in front of his face as soon as he realized who we were.

Lady Hardcastle ignored him and proceeded to the bar. There was no one there to serve us, and so, in her finest schoolroom voice, she called out, 'Mr Arnold? Are you there?'

Answer came there none.

'He's in the cellar, fetching . . . something or other,' said Mr Orum, still concealed behind his newspaper.

'Thank you,' said Lady Hardcastle. 'Mr Orum, isn't it?'

'It is,' he said, finally lowering the paper. 'You have the advantage of me, Mrs . . . ?'

'Lady Hardcastle,' she said. 'How do you do?'

'How do you do . . . my lady?' he said.

'You're here for the moving picture shows?'

'That's right. Nolan Cheetham's Travelling Whatnot.'

'Indeed,' she said. 'He's staying at the house. I gather you used to be friends.'

'Used to be, yes. What poison has he been spreading?'

'He's said very little, actually. We heard your story from the late Mr Newhouse.'

'That old buffoon? I might have known. He couldn't keep his mouth shut in a slurry pit, that one. He . . .' But he seemed to catch himself before he said anything further. 'Shouldn't speak ill of the recently deceased, though, eh?'

'Especially not when one has provided the inspiration for their murder.'

His drink stopped on the way to his mouth. 'I beg your pardon?' he said.

'My understanding was that you maintain *The Witch's Downfall* was your idea. If you wrote the picture, then you devised the means of murdering Mr Newhouse.'

'I didn't invent the idea of witches killing their victims using spells cast on dolls.'

'No, of course not. But you included it in your story, and it was acted out in gory detail in the churchyard in the wee small hours exactly as you scripted it.'

'Unless a witch did it,' he said.

'We shouldn't rule it out, I suppose. Although one might think it more than a little suspicious that you turn up out of the blue after falling out with your old friend and then one of his company is murdered.'

He looked momentarily alarmed, but was soon back to his sardonic self. 'I wouldn't put it past Euphemia Selwood to do away with him over some imagined slight. They're very touchy people, actresses. They have enormous egos, but they're built on fragile foundations. One little tap, and . . .' He mimed knocking something over with a gentle touch from his finger. 'Or Zelda Drayton, perhaps? She was always trouble, that one.'

'I got the impression that they were all the best of friends,' she said.

'Oh, yes, indeed,' he said, archly. 'The absolute very, very closest and best of friends. Never a cross word between them. Not one.'

Joe arrived at that moment and said, 'Good afternoon, m'lady. What can I get you?'

'Ah, good afternoon, Mr Arnold, how lovely to see you.'

'I keeps tellin' you t'call me Joe, m'lady. Everyone does.'

'Of course, Joe, I'm so sorry. I think it's a bit early for brandy. I wonder, do you have any lime cordial?'

'Sorry, m'lady, we ran out t'other month and I a'n't ordered no more,' he said. 'I got some sarsaparilla, but it's a bit old, mind – we don't get much call for it. Tastes like medicine. Ginger beer? How about a nice glass of ginger beer?'

'That would do splendidly. One for you, Armstrong?'

I nodded.

'Make it two, please, Joe. Mr Orum? Would you allow me to treat you?'

He held up his pewter tankard. 'Don't mind if I do,' he said.

We took our drinks to his table.

'And do you mind if we join you?' said Lady Hardcastle.

'It would be churlish to turn you away now that you've been generous enough to buy me a drink,' he said, and folded his newspaper. He took a sip of his fresh tankard of cider. 'Your very good health, my lady.'

Lady Hardcastle and I raised our own glasses.

'Were you here last evening?' she said. 'After the show, I mean.'

'Most of the village was in here,' he said.

'Well, quite. But were you?'

'I was. Why?'

'I'm interested to know when Basil Newhouse was last seen, that's all.'

'Ah, yes,' he said. 'I'd heard you fancy yourself as a bit of an amateur sleuth. Yes, I was here. I saw Cheetham and his eager minions in the other bar. Or, rather, I heard them. Full of themselves, as usual, and eagerly claiming all the credit for my work.'

'Did you speak to them?'

'I was going to go and give them a piece of my mind – I'd have set those fawning villagers straight about a few things while I was at it – but I was persuaded to keep my own counsel.'

'By whom?' I asked.

'Miss Caudle of the *Bristol News*. She's staying here. You saw her here on Monday, Miss . . . Armstrong.'

'I did,' I said.

'And we both saw her again today,' said Lady Hardcastle. 'She bearded him this morning.'

'In his lair,' he said.

'In *my* lair,' she said. 'She doesn't want for impudence, that one.'

He laughed. 'I'll let her know. She'll be delighted.'

'You do that,' she said. 'You might also do me the service of telling her that she should make an appointment if she wishes to badger my guests any further.'

He laughed again. 'She'll be further delighted to know that she engendered such vexation, I'm sure.'

'I'm sure,' said Lady Hardcastle. 'Did you see when Mr Newhouse left?'

'I'm afraid not. I heard the others leave shortly after midnight – lots of hearty congratulations from the assembled sheep, and beseechments that they should give another performance of my moving picture. I was so sickened by the whole experience that I went upstairs to my bed and left them to it.'

'And Mr Newhouse remained?'

'To the best of my knowledge. He was never one to turn down an opportunity to be adored and admired. Especially not if there were free drinks on offer.'

I don't know if Lady Hardcastle had any further questions – I certainly did – but at that moment we were interrupted by the arrival of a panting Edna.

'Beggin' your pardon, my lady,' she wheezed. 'But there's a couple of . . . gentlemen at the house. Says they's expected. Musicians by the looks of 'em.'

'Oh, how wonderful,' said Lady Hardcastle. 'Thank you.' She turned back to our less-than-willing companion. 'I'm afraid we shall have to abandon you once more to your solitude, Mr Orum – we should return to greet our guests. Are you recovered sufficiently to return, Edna? There's a couple of half-finished ginger beers there if you'd like a few more minutes. I'm sure Mr Orum won't mind.'

Mr Orum had already picked up his newspaper. Edna paused a moment, then poured what was left of my ginger beer into Lady Hardcastle's glass.

'If you don't mind, my lady,' she said, 'I could do with a quick sit-down.'

Without waiting for approval, she carried her full drink into the public bar, leaving us to return home on our own.

◆ ◆ ◆

Back at the house, we found a pile of familiar musical instrument cases on the front path.

'That's definitely our boys,' said Lady Hardcastle. 'Who else would dump a drum set and a double bass outside a lady's front door?'

I opened the door and stood aside to let her in.

Barty and Skins were standing in the hall, looking slightly bewildered.

'Good afternoon, gentlemen,' said Lady Hardcastle. 'How absolutely delightful to see you.'

'Afternoon, Lady H,' said Skins, holding out his hand. 'You're sure it's no trouble? Your housemaid seemed a bit put out.'

'No trouble whatsoever,' she said. 'I neglected to tell her you were coming, that's all. Now, if I can leave you in Flo's capable hands for just a few moments, I shall go and tell the film folk what's what, and then we can get you settled.'

'Wotcha, Flo,' said Skins, grinning broadly. 'Got anywhere we can stow our gear?'

'Mr Skins,' I said. 'How lovely of you to drop by. And Mr Dunn. Good afternoon to you, too.'

'Miss Armstrong,' said the charming bass player.

'Give me your hats and I'll pop them over here on the hatstand for you, out of the way. Then we can get someone to see to your traps.'

'"Someone"?' said Skins. 'You've got more someones now?'

'We'll tell you the tale later, I'm sure, but we have Dewi – you remember Dewi, the footman from The Grange? We have him on loan for a week.'

'People on loan like library books, eh?' said Skins. 'How the other half lives, eh, Barty?'

Where Skins was a small, wiry bundle of energy, Barty was tall and loose-limbed, and had an altogether more relaxed and easy-going manner. He also had charm by the wagonload and I remembered his dalliance with a certain housemaid.

'Dora is here as well,' I said.

Barty looked blank.

'Dora Kendrick,' I said. 'The housemaid from The Grange.'

He continued to look baffled.

'Don't worry about him,' said Skins. 'He has so many kitties on the go, he can't keep up.' He turned to his pal. 'Dora, mate. Flighty bit. You "comforted" her when we played the party.'

The recollection slowly surfaced. Or stirred in the murky depths of his memories of amorous adventures past, at any rate. 'Dora, yes,' he said slowly. 'Tall, blonde girl with a limp?'

I sighed. 'No. You'll see her later, I'm sure,' I said. 'She might not want to be remembered, but if she says anything, do at least pretend you know who she is.'

'Right you are,' he said with a cheery grin. 'Will do.'

I sent them to the drawing room while I enjoined Dewi to put the double bass and the drum set in the orangery, and their suitcases in their rooms. Miss Jones put the kettle on and I asked Edna to bring a tray through when it was done. Dora, as always, was nowhere to be seen, but for once I thought this was probably a good thing. She was aggravating enough as it was, without stirring up whatever passions – or resentment – might result from the presence of the handsome bass player.

◆ ◆ ◆

What with all the train shenanigans, the musicians hadn't eaten since breakfast. The film folk, for their part, were keen to eat before another evening of entertaining the villagers. Lady Hardcastle and I had some-how missed lunch, too, and so we agreed that serving a hybrid dinner-lunch-supper at teatime would probably suit all our needs.

I worked with Miss Jones to put together a meal fit for artists. Her supper preparations were already well advanced by the time I sprung the change of plans on her, but the main dish – a venison pie – wouldn't be ready in time. I managed to persuade her that this could be turned to her advantage since we could serve it on Thursday with most of the work already done.

'I still a'n't got nothin' to give 'em right now, mind,' she said.

'What were you planning to serve for lunch?' I asked. 'Could we put it in a smart frock and turn it into something more elegant and dinner-ish?'

'I was just goin' to do cheese sandwiches,' she said disconsolately.

'Bung them under the grill and you've got Welsh rabbit,' I said. 'If we serve it with some vegetable soup and give it a fancy name, everyone will be impressed by your inventiveness.'

'Cheese on toast?' she said. 'For dinner?'

'With mustard. And pop a fried egg on top. We'll call it . . . *Lapin au pays de Galles.*'

'What does that mean?'

'Welsh rabbit,' I said.

She laughed. 'I'll get a soup on, and you take care of the cheese on toast. You're Welsh, after all.'

'True,' I said. 'But then so are you. Although I don't think the dish is especially Welsh.'

'It don't 'ave no rabbits in it, neither.'

'Touché.'

'I i'n't Welsh, though, mind.'

I goggled. 'Not Welsh?' I said. 'You're called Blodwen Jones. You couldn't be more Welsh if you were wearing a tall hat and singing "*Sospan Fach*" while you make laver bread.'

'Our dad was Welsh. I was born in Littleton Cotterell,' she said proudly.

'I stand corrected.'

We were seven for lunch-dinner-supper-tea. I had been anticipating a sober mood, perhaps even sombre, but with the two musicians present things had taken a more buoyant turn. Showing a level of sensitivity I hadn't expected from either of them, both Barty and Skins had encouraged the three film folk to talk about their old friend. Almost in spite of themselves, they had been coaxed from damp-eyed declarations of sadness at the passing of their dear friend to sharing stories of adventures, pranks, and triumphant stage performances. Laughter filled the room. No one mentioned the Welsh rabbit.

With the room nicely warmed up, Barty Dunn had turned up the wick on his legendary charm and focused the beam upon Euphemia Selwood. She basked in the warmth of its flirtatiously complimentary glow.

He noticed that the conversations around him had stopped and that we were all listening to him.

'Don't stop, Barty, mate,' said Skins, resting his chin on his hand. 'You carry on with what you're doin'. We're all just lookin' for tips, like. We come seekin' wooing wisdom.'

The look on Barty's face suggested that, in other company, his pal might get a smack in the chops rather than a class in the art of courting, but when both Lady Hardcastle and Zelda copied Skins's attentive posture and looked raptly at him, he laughed and held his hands up in surrender.

'You can't blame a bloke for trying,' he said.

Euphemia blushed and took a spoonful of soup, but she was smiling, too.

Despite the teasing, Barty clearly didn't want to have to stop talking to Euphemia. 'It must be peculiar, though,' he said, 'just performing for a camera. I can't play my best without an audience.'

'You get used to it,' she said. 'I done a bit of work in the music halls with me mum when I was little, and a few plays when I started out on me own. So you know where the reactions is gonna be. You just sort of play it as natural as you can, but imagine the audience in your head.'

'We tried something similar,' he said. He turned to Skins. 'You remember that time we tried to make a gramophone record with Roland Richman?'

Skins laughed. 'Disaster. There were more blokes in overalls carryin' spanners than there were musicians. And we only 'ad one go at it. So we spent all mornin' rehearsin' the blessed thing. It was rubbish by the time they started the machine up. No life in it at all. No spark.'

Barty nodded.

'But double back a bit,' said Skins. 'Did you say your mum was in the music halls?'

'That's right,' she said.

'She's Millie Selwood,' I said.

'Millie . . . ?' said Skins. 'Straight up? We worked with her. We was in the pit orchestra at the Alhambra for a couple of months a few years back. Remember that one, Barty? Classy gaff. Best bib and tucker, even in the pit. She was fantastic, your mum. Sang like an angel. Mouth like a docker off stage, mind you. Well I never.'

'That was her,' said Euphemia proudly. 'Even the stage hands is terrified of her.'

'She's still working, then?' said Skins.

'Not so much as she used to, but she keeps her hand in.'

'But you didn't fancy followin' in 'er footsteps?'

'She wanted me to,' she said. 'Me dad did, too – he's her manager – but I inherited her looks and his ear for music. And he's tone deaf, love him. Can't sing a note. So I had to turn to proper actin'.'

'The music hall's loss is cinema's gain,' said Mr Cheetham.

'"Cinema"?' said Lady Hardcastle. 'Oh, I say, what a splendid name for it. We've been stumbling around "moving pictures" and "kinemato-graph" and who knows what else for weeks. "Cinema" has a ring to it. I do hope it catches on.'

Mr Cheetham smiled and inclined his head in acknowledgement. I'd have been willing to wager a substantial sum that it wasn't his own idea, but it seemed churlish to challenge him.

Once the soup and Welsh rabbit had been consumed, Edna and Dora cleared the table and brought in tea and cake in lieu of pudding.

Dora, as always, said nothing and reacted with only a curt nod when the film folk thanked her. She studiously ignored Barty Dunn, and the bass player returned the favour. But I had seen her look of surprised recognition when she had brought in the main course, so I knew it was merely an act.

The cake and tea didn't last long, and the conversation wound down as the film folk made their excuses and headed back to their base in the morning room to finalize their plans for the evening. Once they were gone, Lady Hardcastle addressed the musicians.

'Well, gentlemen,' she said, 'what say we adjourn for now and reconvene at half-past seven for cocktails and reminiscences? We've put your instruments safely away, but I'm sure we can amuse ourselves. A few hands of cards, perhaps?'

'Sounds grand, m'lady,' said Skins. 'Tell the truth, I'd welcome an adjournment. And maybe forty winks. I'm wagged out. Not sure what it is, but travellin' always does for me.'

'For us all, dear. You go and have a rest. We need you bright-eyed and bushy-tailed, or it won't be fair when we thrash you at cards.'

He laughed. 'Right you are,' he said.

'We've got some interesting news for you as well,' said Barty as he opened the door to leave. 'From your brother.'

'Oh?' said Lady Hardcastle. 'How intriguing. Can you not tell us now?'

'It can wait,' he called from the hall.

At half-past seven we were in the drawing room. Lady Hardcastle had acquired a card table and four surprisingly comfortable chairs from B Maggs & Co in Bristol. She wasn't ordinarily given to shopping in 'department stores', but we had popped in on a whim during a trip to Clifton, where, still driven by impulse, she had bought these few items of furniture. We had used the table for our regular two-handed evening card games, but this was its first test as a table for four. It performed rather well, and the comfortableness of the chairs attracted compliments from both musicians.

'You'll not distract us from your awful play by talking about the furniture, Mr Skins,' I said. 'I make it ten tricks to three . . . So that's four points – and the game – to us.' I marked down the score on the little notepad with a triumphant flourish.

'Course, if we was playin' a proper game,' said Skins, 'we'd 'ave thrashed you. You'd be signin' over your whole fortune before the eve-nin' was out.'

'And what do you consider to be a "proper" game?' asked Lady Hardcastle.

'Poker, Lady H. You wouldn't stand a chance.'

Lady Hardcastle gave a half-smile and turned to me. 'Do you remember playing poker in that club in Berlin?' she said. 'How much did we win from Herr Armbrüster?'

'Ten thousand marks, my lady,' I said. 'Which would be about five hundred pounds, I think.'

Skins's jaw dropped. 'A monkey? At cards?'

'Well, that and the free use of his brothel, but we politely declined that charming offer.'

The two men laughed.

'That reminds me,' said Barty. 'I have some news, and a message from your brother.'

'Oh dear,' said Lady Hardcastle. 'I do hope he's not setting up a brothel. I had rather hoped Lavinia was going to be a calming influence on the silly boy.'

Barty frowned. 'No, my lady, nothing like that. It was you men-tioning Berlin that reminded me.'

'Aha,' she said. 'Our good friends in the German Empire are up to no good again, eh?'

'I don't know about that,' he said. 'But he's looking into the doings of one German in particular. Some bloke called—'

'Burlingham,' interrupted Skins.

'No,' said Barty. 'Günther Ehrlichmann.'

This time, it was our jaws that dropped.

'I think someone might be making mischief,' said Lady Hardcastle.

'That's as may be,' said Barty. 'But that's who the bloke we met in the Rag-a-Muffin a few nights ago said he was,' said Barty.

'A nightclub?'

'Ragtime nightclub, yes,' he said. 'West End of London. It's written out like Rag-a-Muffin to emphasize the "rag" bit.'

'And you met a fellow there who claimed to be Günther Ehrlichmann?' she asked. 'He introduced himself to you? Did he say why?'

'He did, and he did. He got up after our set and sidled over to us.'

'Slithered, more like,' said Skins. 'Nasty piece of work.'

'Yeah, he wasn't the pleasantest bloke we've ever met,' said Barty. 'So he slithers up and says, "I have been looking for you two fellows for some time. I have frequented a lot of these . . . 'nightclubs' in search of two particular 'musicians'. You know Lady Hardcastle, yes?" So I says, "Yes, what of it? How do you know us?" And he says, "I have read about you in the newspapers. You were involved in an affair at a country house last year. Murders and jewels, I believe." He was German. Really thick accent. So I says, "That's right." Wasn't any point in lying. So he says, "When you see Lady Hardcastle next, tell her Günther Ehrlichmann sends his regards." And then he slithers off.'

'What did he look like?' I said.

'Tall, thin, blue eyes, white hair, hooked nose.'

'He sounds similar, my lady,' I said.

'Yes, but . . .' she said.

'We didn't think nothin' of it,' said Skins. 'But the next night, in comes this tall English bloke with a sort of familiar look about him. He hands us 'is card and introduces himself as Harry Featherstonhaugh. He says, "Good evening, gentlemen. I believe you know my sister." And I thinks to meself, "Aye, aye, here's Barty about to get his comeuppance. Some aggrieved brother come to settle old Barty's hash for dallyin' with 'is dear sister." But he seems to see where my mind's goin' and he smiles and says, "Lady Hardcastle." So we let him buy us a drink and sat down with him.'

'He bought you a drink?' said Lady Hardcastle. 'Did you check his card thoroughly? You're sure he wasn't an impostor?'

Barty laughed. 'No, he was the real thing. We had quite a chat about you and Miss Armstrong later on.'

Lady Hardcastle raised an enquiring eyebrow.

'Nuffin' indiscreet, like,' said Skins hastily. 'Just a few reminiscences about the emerald thing. And then he filled us in on the stuff about the racing driver – you know, all the juicy bits what didn't make the papers.'

'I'm sure he embellished wildly,' she said.

'It sounded just like the sort of thing you'd get up to,' said Barty. 'Anyway, before we got to all that, he said he was with the Foreign Office and that his men had been following this German bloke for a few days. They'd told him that the German had been seen talking to us the night before.'

'He asked us what he'd said. So we told him,' said Skins.

'I'd have liked to have seen his reaction,' said Lady Hardcastle.

'He was quite calm, actually,' said Barty. 'He just said that if we could contrive to find a way to drop in on you in the next couple of days, we should pass on this Ehrlichmann's message. We should also tell you that he was handling things and you shouldn't worry.'

'So your train didn't really break down?' I said.

'It did, as a matter of fact,' said Skins. 'Harry – he told us to call him Harry—'

'He does that a lot,' I said.

'Well, Harry seemed to reckon it wasn't all that urgent, so we was going to drop in on our way back from Gloucester. When we had a bit more time, like. When the train broke down, we thought we could kill two birds.'

'And you're absolutely certain that the man who came up to you, the man my brother was following, was called Günther Ehrlichmann?' said Lady Hardcastle. 'There can be no confusion? No misunderstanding? Nothing misheard or misremembered?'

'No, my lady,' said Barty, seeming slightly unsettled by her sudden intensity. 'That's the name, all right.'

'I see,' she said. 'The trouble is, Günther Ehrlichmann is dead.'

'Dead?' said Skins. 'Are you sure?'

'Quite sure, dear,' she said. 'I shot him myself.'

For a few moments, the only sound I could hear was the ticking of the hall clock. Eventually, Skins spoke up again.

'You never did!' he said. He turned to me. 'She never did, did she?'

'I'm afraid so,' I said. 'Surely you must have some inkling of who we used to be?'

'You told a few tall tales when you put us up for the night after Wally died,' he said. 'But I just thought you was layin' it on a bit thick. Playin' to the gallery, like.'

Lady Hardcastle looked at our guests appraisingly for a short while. 'I confess I do play to the gallery most of the time,' she said at length. 'It amuses me no end to offer oblique hints about our past deeds – or "misdeeds" as we often like to characterize them. But I seldom speak about them directly. I can usually invoke "state secrets" or "discretion is the better part or whatnot" if people become too curious, but, for the most part, I just don't want to.'

'Then we should leave it at that,' said Barty. 'We don't want to pry.'

Skins nodded his agreement.

'Ah, but I fear you might have become . . . how shall we say . . . "embroiled" in matters you might have preferred to have left well alone.'

'We ain't afraid of some sly-lookin' German in a club,' said Skins.

'If he really is Günther Ehrlichmann,' said Lady Hardcastle, 'or even if he's just associated with him in some way, then you really, *really*, don't want to have anything to do with him. And now that whoever he is knows who you are, and has connected you to me, I'm afraid "embroiled" rather sums it up. I think it's only fair that you know the tale.'

'Only if you want to,' said Skins.

'We owe it to you. I might leave the telling of it to Flo, though. She has a knack for the telling of tales. It's her Welsh blood, I think.'

'Strictly speaking, I'm only half Welsh,' I said. 'But I'm happy to take on tale-telling duties if you'll agree to another round of brandies.'

'When have you ever known me to turn down a brandy?'

I pretended to think for a moment. 'Do you know,' I said, 'I'm not certain you ever have. Do you think you might have a drinking problem?'

'A dipsomaniac? Me?' She, too, pretended to contemplate this possibility. 'It would explain a lot, wouldn't it? But I think not. I just like a glass of brandy now and again.'

'. . . and again . . . and again . . . and again,' I said.

'If you insist, dear,' she said, holding out her glass. 'Now shut up and tell our tale.'

'Shut up *and* tell our tale?'

'Did we ever properly research the modern legalities of beating obstreperous servants?'

'I think we decided you were going to try not to embarrass our guests too much,' I said. 'Does everyone have a drink? Shall I begin?'

Chapter Eight

'I was seventeen years old when I first met Lady Hardcastle,' I began. 'I'd been working for a family in London as a housemaid when she stole me from them.'

'I thought you was a circus kid,' interrupted Skins.

'Born and raised,' I confirmed. 'But Mam wanted to go back to Aberdare when Mamgu – my grandma – was ill. Actually, she lived in Cwmdare, but no one's ever heard of that.'

'I've never heard of Aberdare, neither,' said Skins.

'Well, now you have, haven't you? She took me and my twin sister Gwenith with her, but our dad and our brothers stayed with the circus for a few years more. We went to the local school until we were thirteen, and then we had to make our way in the world. Gwenith took to life in the town and started helping at the grocer's shop where our mam worked. But I wanted to see more. We grew up on the road, and I couldn't imagine settling in one tiny town for the rest of my life, even if it were somewhere as wonderful as the Welsh valleys.'

'So you moved to London?' suggested Skins.

'Not at first,' I said. 'I worked in Cardiff for a couple of years, for a family called Williams. I learned a lot there. It was tough, mind you. I'd been used to doing as I pleased, and here I was in a strict routine with drudgery as far as the eye could see. It's not a barrel of laughs being a scullery maid. But they had a library.'

'Where you could skive?' said Skins.

'Where I could read. I loved the big towns when we were on the road. We'd turn up and set up in a park or a field. Next morning, I'd cadge a ride into town and try to find the library. I'd stay there all day until someone from the circus came to turf me out. They always knew where to find me. I missed that when we settled. There was a library in Merthyr Tydfil but it was a bit of a trek. In the Williams's house, all I needed was a bit of time to myself. It was easiest when the family was away, but I took my chances. I got away with a lot.'

'Until you got caught,' said Lady Hardcastle.

'That just made it easier,' I said. 'I became Mr Williams's little project.'

'Saw himself as a bit of a whatchamacallit, did he? A philanthropologist?' said Skins.

I laughed but decided not to correct him. 'Something like that,' I said. 'He came home and found me sitting on a cushion on the floor by the fire, completely lost in *Emma*. I thought I was going to get the sack, but he sat down with me and talked to me about Jane Austen. From then on, I was encouraged to read whatever I wanted. Books, magazines, newspapers – whatever he had. He talked to me about what I'd read. As I said, I was his project. But it worked against him in the end. I saw an advertisement in the newspaper one day. An agency in London was looking for reliable staff.'

'Sounds like you'd been there a while, though,' said Barty.

'A couple of years,' I said. 'I still have the clipping from the newspaper. It was the 12th of July 1892, so I was fifteen. I replied to the advertisement, and within a month I'd packed my bags and my very lovely reference, said my tearful goodbyes and was on a train to Paddington.'

'Where you were immediately engaged by Lady H,' said Skins, apparently keen to get the narrative moving.

'Not immediately, no. I said we met when I was seventeen, remember? I spent two years working for Sir Clive and Lady Tetherington—'

'Very good friends of mine and Roddy's,' interrupted Lady Hardcastle.

'Such good friends that when you were short of a lady's maid, you swanned in and pinched one of their maids,' I said.

'It was worse than that,' she said. 'I pinched the very best maid they had.'

'You're too kind,' I said. 'But the upshot was that by 1894 I was working for Lady Hardcastle as her lady's maid.'

'Quite a jump, that,' said Skins. 'Housemaid to lady's maid, and all at seventeen. I always said you was remarkable.'

'Remarkably useless,' I said. 'I had absolutely no idea what I was doing. I had Sir Roderick's valet to help lead me in the right direction, but mostly I just fumbled my way through it all and hoped for the best. He was a kind man. Jabez Otterthwaite. Yorkshireman—'

'I should hope so, with an 'andle like that,' said Skins.

'I wonder what became of him,' I said.

'He didn't want to come with us when we were posted to China,' said Lady Hardcastle. 'So Roddy gave him a splendid reference and sent him on his way.'

'"Posted"? Sounds like we're getting to the meat of the story,' said Barty. 'Not that I mind hearing about you,' he added swiftly. 'It's just . . . you know . . .'

'I know,' I said. 'But I thought that if I were going to tell the tale at all, I might as well tell the whole tale.'

'Fair enough,' he said. 'Carry on.'

'Actually,' said Lady Hardcastle, 'I think she's right. If we're going to tell this tale, I ought to tell you my story, too. Do you mind, dear?'

'No,' I said. 'You carry on. I'll slice some more cheese.'

'Splendid idea,' she said. 'Is there any Stilton left? I do love Stilton.'

I went to the kitchen to fetch more biscuits and to hunt for the blue cheese.

◆ ◆ ◆

'Now then, where were we?' said Lady Hardcastle when I returned. 'Ah, yes. Me. I grew up in London, as you might have guessed. Papa was Permanent Secretary to the Treasury and Mama was . . . Well, she was Mama. And a jolly fine job of it she did, too. Harry is my older brother – by two years. He took an unremarkable degree at King's College, Cambridge and then followed our father, Sir Percival Featherstonhaugh, into the civil service. I was supposed to finish my education at home, attend some ghastly finishing school in Switzerland, and then marry someone exactly like Papa or Harry so that I could be a devoted wife and mother just like Mama. But I was so terribly jealous of Harry. He went away to school while I was stuck at home with a succession of increasingly out-of-their-depth tutors. When it was announced that he was going up to Cambridge, I managed such a spectacular sulk that they eventually relented and agreed that I could apply to Girton College. It's a women's college in Cambridge, but it's not part of the university. I usually play that down. I studied for the natural sciences tripos and did passably well.'

'Extremely well, in fact,' I said. 'If they awarded women the same degrees they award to the men, she'd be fêted throughout the land as a scientific genius. The things she knows would make your head swim.'

'Hardly,' she said with a laugh. 'But I grant that we worked just as hard as the men for none of the acclaim. But still. While I was there, I saw quite a bit of dear old Harry, and that meant I also met his pals. And one of his pals was Roderick Hardcastle. I'd like to say it was love at first sight, but the truth is we just sort of grew towards each other. By the time he went down and joined the Foreign Office, we were engaged to be married.'

'She hasn't mentioned what a handsome man he was,' I said. 'They made a striking couple.'

'It's true – he was extraordinarily handsome. But, despite his desirability, I stayed up to finish my studies, and that's when the story really began.'

'At long last,' I said.

'You were the one who insisted on starting your story when you were still in the cradle.'

'A splendid point and excellently well made, my lady. Please proceed.'

'Thank you. One spring day in my final year, I'd gone into town with one of my pals. We finished our business at the bookshop and decided to walk along the Backs. We were trying to appear as though we were just two studious young women out for a stroll, but really we were only there so that she could "accidentally" bump into a chap from Trinity whom she was sweet on. To be honest, I hadn't really thought that part through – I had no idea what I was going to do when we met him, as meet him we surely did. I just sort of ambled away towards the river while they gazed into each other's eyes and talked gibberish.'

'"Murmured sweet nothings"?' I offered.

'It would be much more romantic to think so,' she said. 'But they were both such top-notch idiots – it was mostly gibberish. I watched the mallards and kicked idly at the daisies for a while, and then a be-gowned don huffed towards me from the south. "Miss Featherstonhaugh?" he said. I treated him to my severest quizzical frown. "I do beg your pardon," he said. "I knew your brother. Henry."

'"Harry," I corrected him reflexively. We always called him Harry. Henry Alfred Percival Featherstonhaugh was such a cumbersome name. I suppose Emily Charlotte Ariadne wasn't much better, though, eh? Where was I? Oh, yes, the mysterious don. He prattled at me for a while about what a splendid fellow Harry was and how he'd heard about my engagement to Roddy. I thought I should be stuck there forever, enduring endless small talk about the Featherstonhaugh heir, but after a while his prattling became altogether more serious. He was still hesitant and slightly bumbling, but I started to think that the absent-minded-don persona was just a costume he wore. There was a shrewd old man behind the grimy spectacles.

'He asked me about my studies and my plans after Girton, and then made the most extraordinary proposal. He wondered if I might like to work for Her Majesty's government. "Not in a conventional sense, you understand. Can't have women in the civil service. Wouldn't be seemly. But we . . . ah . . . we need young men and women of your calibre to . . . ah . . . to do certain . . . ah . . . certain discreet jobs for us. A little bit of nosing around. That sort of thing. Nothing too dangerous, you understand, but . . . ah . . . well . . . you see, if you were to marry young Hardcastle . . . well, I know that he's already considered to be something of a rising star in the Foreign Office and . . . ah . . . yes . . . you'd be well placed to gather certain . . . information . . . from Her Majesty's friends abroad . . . and her enemies, naturally."'

'A spy, like?' said Skins.

'Just so,' said Lady Hardcastle. 'I made no commitment then, but by the time Roddy and I were married, I had made up my mind. If I were to make a career of being a diplomat's wife, I might as well put my position to some practical purpose. We made quite the team, Roddy and I. We were young, we were fun, and we threw quite the loveliest parties. We knew all the right people. And we were entirely above suspicion. Who would ever have thought that the Hardcastles were up to no good? Actually, Roddy was genuinely above suspicion – it was yours truly who did all the snooping. Encouraging the great and the good into a little indiscretion here, an overheard conversation there, the tiniest bit of breaking and entering now and again. I loved it. And we made a name for ourselves in the right circles.'

'Breaking and entering?' said Barty.

'Just a little. Here and there. Locks can be picked, windows can be jemmied. I was never especially good with safes, but I knew a chap. So, there we were, the darlings of the *corps diplomatique*, and, of course, the exotic postings started to come our way. Assorted European capitals, the United States, India – you name it. Roddy was awarded his knighthood and life was grand. Really rather splendid. We were back in London for a while when I engaged young Armstrong here. So it's over to you, I think, dear.'

I helped myself to a slice of cheddar and a glob of quince cheese. 'Does anyone know why it's called quince "cheese"?' I asked. 'It's not exactly cheesy, is it?'

'The Spanish call it *membrillo*, if that's any help,' said Lady Hardcastle.

'None whatsoever,' I said.

'Marmalade used to be made from quinces,' she said. 'Portuguese word, I think. *Marmelada*, or some such. I think a quince is a *marmelo*.'

'Fascinating, of course,' I said. 'But still no help. We're no nearer to "cheese", are we?'

'Lemon curd?' she offered. 'That doesn't involve curds. Perhaps we just like cheesy names for fruity things.'

'That'll have to do,' I said, and munched on my cheese and biscuit for a bit. 'Back to the tale, though. The Hardcastles are living in London and I'm making a bit of a hash of being a lady's maid, but we're all muddling along.'

'I can't get over the fact that you was only seventeen,' said Skins. 'All the lady's maids I've ever known was in their thirties at least.'

'All the ones you've ever known?' said Barty. 'You've know a lot, then?'

'A fair few. I've been around.'

'No one was more surprised than I,' I said. 'But I had plenty of time to puzzle things out – Lady Hardcastle had a tendency to disappear for days on end, leaving me to my own devices. I learned to sew and mend, how to get mysterious stains from lace and silk – all the things a proper lady's maid needed to know. Some of the stains – mud, blood, and axle grease were among the more common – would have been a good deal less mysterious if I'd known what my new employer was up to when she vanished, but I was too busy trying to follow Mr Otterthwaite's patient lessons in their removal to give it very much thought.'

'I came very close to telling you a few times,' said Lady Hardcastle. 'I had to weigh the need to keep the government's secrets against the need to explain why the cuff of my jacket was soaked in someone else's blood and there was mud splattered up the back of my skirt. I could have said, "I came upon my snitch in an alley with a knife in his belly and had to run for my life before the foreign spies who did for him did for me, too." Somehow, though, that didn't seem like the sort of thing I could comfortably say to the bookish little Welsh girl I'd brought into our home as my maid.'

'For my part, I suspected nothing,' I said. 'If I hadn't seen how much the Hardcastles adored each other, I might have thought her frequent absences meant she was having an affair, but that still wouldn't have explained the damage to her clothes. Well, it might, but it would have been a very wild affair. So I just got on with it and, though I'm reluctant to admit it in her presence, she was a model employer. We got along splendidly and my first year in the job passed extremely agreeably. Sir Roderick was getting itchy feet, though, I could tell. He had been angling for another posting for a few months, and in the summer of 1895, he got his wish. He was to be posted to Shanghai.'

'I've always wanted to go to China,' said Barty. 'I walked out with this Chinese girl in Limehouse once. Lovely, she was. I might have married her, but her family was having none of it.'

'You?' said Skins. 'Marry? Pull the other one. Closest you ever got to marryin' was that bit in Shoreditch with the wonky eye. And that was only because her brother threatened to do you in if you didn't.'

'Hair like silk, she had,' said Barty obliviously. 'And the gentlest hands . . .'

I decided to press on and leave him to his reminiscences. 'Mr Otterthwaite declined to accompany his master,' I said, 'but for reasons I'll never quite understand, Lady Hardcastle was really rather insistent that I made the trip.'

'How could I possibly get by without my semi-competent maid?' said Lady Hardcastle. 'There was certain to be much more mud, blood, and axle grease. Whom else could I entrust with their removal?'

'When you put it like that . . .' I said. 'So I wrote to my mother and my sister, I packed up my meagre possessions, and I boarded a P&O steamer at the Royal Docks, bound for the mystic East. Three weeks, it took. Three weeks. I'd seen enough atlases and read enough travel memoirs to know that China was a dickens of a long way away . . . but three weeks. I used to think it was a long way from Mamgu's house to the grocer's shop.'

'It's a long way from our gaff to the grocer's, an' all,' said Skins.

'Well, quite,' I said with a frown. 'Sir Rodney was posted to the British Consulate in Shanghai, and we were billeted in a little house in the British Settlement. It was like living in London, only warmer, if I'm honest. The place had been carved up by the European powers and you'd have to look closely to tell the difference between there and Kensington. Herself was still prone to disappearing at odd hours, more so than in London, I'd say, but I still suspected nothing.'

'So you saw nothing of proper China?' said Barty with some disappointment. 'Shu-chun was going to show me wonders, she said.'

'I showed her wonders,' said Lady Hardcastle. 'I engaged a local woman as a housemaid and she taught us Mandarin and Shanghainese. And then she took us into the Chinese area of the city, where we would shop and eat and meet the locals. I bought us some clothes, too, didn't I?'

'You certainly did. I wish I still had that dress.'

'Me too. We should go back one day. I'm afraid I rather scandalized the genteel ladies of the consulate, though – they thought I was "going native". Not the done thing at all.'

'They'd have been even more scandalized if they knew what you were really up to. I was quite shocked myself the night I found out.'

The musicians were both listening attentively now.

'It was just after dawn, actually,' I said. 'I heard the front door closing and I thought it must be Sir Roderick coming back from one of his all-night card games. But then I remembered that he'd arrived home shortly before I retired for the night. So, obviously, I had to go and look.'

'Well, you can look after yourself,' said Skins. 'We know that. I remember what you did to old Haddock.'

'Not then, I couldn't,' I said. 'I was just a frightened eighteen-year-old girl with less sense than the Good Lord gave a cabbage. But look I did. And there, in the hall, with his back to me, was a plump Chinese man. I must have gasped in surprise because he turned round and revealed himself to be none other than Emily, Lady Hardcastle, wearing several layers of padding and a Chinese tunic.'

'Of course, the cat was out of the bag then, so I had to tell her everything,' said Lady Hardcastle. 'It was that or make up some story about overnight rehearsals with the consulate ladies for a production of *The Mikado*.'

'I might have believed that, actually,' I said. 'I was still only eighteen. Or perhaps I was nineteen by then, I can't quite place the date of it – I'm certain it was early '96, but I don't recall precisely when. Anyway, I was young, and although I might have seemed worldly, what with growing up in the circus and all, I still knew little of the lives of the rich and powerful. For all I knew, everyone rehearsed Gilbert and Sullivan in the small hours.'

'Oh, we do,' she said. 'But never *The Mikado*. Ghastly load of patronizing old nonsense. We much prefer *The Pirates of Penzance*. I always wanted to play Major-General Stanley. It happens that I actually am the very model of a modern Major-General, you know. I'm reasonably certain I did once write a washing bill in Babylonic cuneiform—'

I coughed. 'Finished, my lady?'

'Quite finished, thank you, dear,' she said, and took another sip of her brandy.

'While I drew her a bath, she told me everything I've just told you, and more,' I said. 'The Cambridge don, the spying, the days away from home, the murdered informers . . . everything. I thought I had been astonished enough for one evening, but there was just one more astonishing thing to come. She offered me another job.'

'I was so tired,' said Lady Hardcastle. 'It's not easy being a beagle at the best of times, but a woman spy has it doubly hard. It's the corsets, you know. Roddy couldn't help – either with the spying or the corsets – our modus operandi really rather depended upon his being the highly visible man about town while I got on with the skulduggery unnoticed and unsuspected. I needed an assistant, a trusted ally. Someone bright and energetic. Someone who could do as she was told and still think for herself. Someone who could pass unnoticed in the world of servants and working people. Someone, in short, exactly like Florence Armstrong.'

'Any port in a storm,' I said.

'Well, there's that, too, but it turns out that I made a splendid choice. She agreed, as you might have guessed, and I began to teach her what few tricks I'd managed to learn from the arcane and poorly recorded world of the modern spy. Most of the work simply involves keeping one's ears open, though, to be perfectly honest. That was why Roddy and I cultivated our reputation as party-givers and merry young things. We tried our damnedest to be quite the utterest utter. Anyone who was anyone wanted to be seen at our little gatherings and there was never a shortage of vain young men in the foreign diplomatic missions. They couldn't resist showing off to the dizzy wife of one of their rivals about how powerful and influential they were, about how many little secrets they knew. And the ones who managed to keep their gobs shut around me could always be relied upon to try to impress the clerk's wives and the businessmen's wives – that was where Flo came in handy. I could just shove a tray of drinks in her dainty paws and send her off round the room, where she could earwig on anyone's conversation without arousing even the slightest suspicion.'

'There was a certain amount of burglary, too. And one or two clandestine meetings in the dead of night,' I said. I'm ashamed to admit that I was slightly miffed at my part in the success of the Shanghai mission being reduced to that of champagne-carrying earwigger.

'There was,' she said. 'And that, I'm afraid, proved to be our undoing. And is what has possibly placed you two lovely gentlemen in danger.'

'At long last,' I said. 'More cheese, anyone?'

'Crumpets,' said Lady Hardcastle.

'And the same to you,' I said.

'No, we need crumpets. And something warming to drink. This last part requires a comfortable seat by the fire and something comfortingly warm in our bellies.'

'Hot chocolate?' I said.

'With a tot of brandy in it,' she agreed.

'I'll be back presently.' I went back to the kitchen.

◆ ◆ ◆

By the time I returned to the drawing room, our four armchairs had been arranged around the freshly logged fire. They'd placed a low table in the middle of the arc of chairs and I set the tray on it. I poured the hot chocolate, Lady Hardcastle poured the brandy, and Barty speared a crumpet with the toasting fork before holding it near the flames.

'Three years passed,' I said as I sat down. 'By 1899 I was twenty-two. I had learned more and more of Lady Hardcastle's skulduggerous methods, we had both learned a good deal more Mandarin and Shanghainese, and Her Majesty's government had learned a great many things to its political, strategic, and commercial advantage. We were the Foreign Office's first choice when it came to snooping, prying, and generally minding other people's business.'

'Perhaps I should mention,' said Lady Hardcastle, 'that the previous year had been something of an important year in China. Treaties and whatnot. The British had control of Hong Kong, the Germans had Tsingtao. The whole of the coast was being grabbed by the Europeans. And by '99, as you probably know, Imperial Germany was starting to get a tiny bit bellicose. Muscles were being flexed. Sabres rattled. And so, of course, the other Great Powers wanted to know at all times what the blighters were up to. Which meant that Roddy and I, with Flo in attendance, were sent north to Tsingtao. The story was that we were there as Her Britannic Majesty's representatives to wish our German friends continuing good fortune with their new port, but, naturally, we were really there to have a good old nose round.'

'It was going to be a good opportunity to practise our Mandarin, if nothing else,' I said.

'I sometimes wish that was all we'd done,' said Lady Hardcastle wistfully. 'But it wasn't. Word reached us that the Imperial German Navy was testing a new vessel in the Pacific, imagining themselves to be well away from prying eyes. So we set our eyes to prying. We used a plan we'd used before: Roddy got himself invited to a card game, a billiards evening, or some other men-only activity and then, pleading a headache or similarly non-specific malady, I would regretfully decline the corresponding ladies-only event and take to my bed. Once the evening was well under way, Flo and I would slip out and see what we could see.'

'Must have been difficult,' said Barty. 'Two English ladies would stick out like a couple of sore thumbs over there. Especially you, Lady H – you must be a foot taller than some of the Chinese women.'

'It wasn't so hard,' I said. 'In our Chinese garb, and with a little stage makeup, we could pass casual scrutiny. At night. In the shadows. From a distance. As long as nobody was actually looking at us.'

'But you're right, Barty,' said Lady Hardcastle, 'we had to be circumspect. Fortune smiled on us, though. The German dockyard was a busy place, but everyone had work to do so they had no time for looking into the shadows. Over the course of the night we managed to worm our way close enough to the secret pens to see what the Kaiser's navy was up to.'

'And what was that?' asked Skins.

'A submarine,' I said.

'What's one of them when it's at home?' he said.

'The Germans call it an *Unterseeboot* – an under-the-lake boat. Or under the sea, at any rate.'

'You're havin' us on,' said Skins. 'A boat underwater? Who'd sail it? Mermaids?'

'You can be such an idiot sometimes, mate,' said Barty. 'You should pay more attention to what's going on in the world. They're watertight. No one gets wet.'

'What's the point of that, then?'

'You can't see them coming,' said Barty. 'One of them could sneak up on your ship and sink you before you even knew they was there.'

Skins digested this for a moment. 'And the Germans have got one?' he said at length.

'Many more than one by now,' I said. 'And even more deadly than the one we saw. Remember, this was ten years ago.'

'Blimey,' said Skins. 'I ought to pick up a newspaper once in a while.'

'We found ourselves a place to hide among some wooden crates and metal drums,' I said. 'Lady Hardcastle sketched the boat and the dockyard while I made notes about all the personnel and equipment we'd seen. Then we sneaked out the way we came and were back in bed with no one the wiser.'

'Not even the other servants knew we'd been out,' confirmed Lady Hardcastle. 'All that remained was for me to add a covering letter to my drawings and Flo's notes and slip the whole lot into the diplomatic bag for onward transmission to London. A couple of days later we were on our way back to Shanghai.'

'It should have been just another job,' I said. 'We'd done dozens like it over the years, but this time it all went horribly wrong.'

'We should probably have left China there and then,' said Lady Hardcastle. 'The Boxer Rebellion had started. The violence was mostly confined to remote rural districts, but it was beginning to spread to the cities on the coast. It wasn't a safe time to be a European in China. But we stayed. We were safe. Of course we were – we were British. Who would dare . . . ?'

'Not the Chinese rebels, as it turned out,' I said. 'We'd been back for a couple of weeks and one day Lady Hardcastle went for lunch with a friend while Sir Roderick stayed at home to finish some work in his study. I went along to the club to keep Lady Hardcastle's friend's maid company. It was great fun, as I recall. When it was all over, we went back to the house, but there was something wrong. Neither of us could put our fingers on exactly what had spooked us, but all was not quite right. Then we saw that the front door had been forced. Lady Hardcastle put her finger to her lips and we stepped in as silently as we could.'

'That was when we saw our lovely Chinese maid lying in a pool of her own blood on the tiles,' she said. 'She was still breathing, but she was out cold. I think that angered me as much as anything else that horrible day. One accepts that one is placing oneself in danger, but Mrs Lee was a non-combatant. How dare someone wallop her round the head and leave her for dead? We might have left at that moment and gone to seek help, but my blood was up. We kept a revolver in a drawer in the hall table "just in case" and I'm afraid I took it out.'

'Meanwhile,' I said, 'I could hear voices in Sir Roderick's study. A German voice said something like, "We cannot tolerate your spying any longer, Hardcastle." Then Sir Roderick said, "I'm sure I have absolutely no idea what you're talking about, Herr Ehrlichmann. I am a representative of Her Majesty's government here in China. The very suggestion that I have been involved in 'spying' is impertinent in the extreme. I should go so far as to say that it is slanderous." He could be very imperious when he chose to be.

'The German man carried on: "I would find your indignant denials much more convincing and much less amusing had we not intercepted your report. We know you were in our naval dockyard, 'Diamond Rook'. Not the most impenetrable of code names. And now you must pay the price for your meddling. You have been a . . . What is the expression you use . . . ? A 'thorn in our side'? Yes, you've been a thorn in our side for far too long. It is time we plucked you out."'

Lady Hardcastle's eyes were moist with tears as I spoke. She took a sip of her hot chocolate and used the movement to try to disguise the fact that she was wiping them away.

'There was a gunshot,' I continued. 'Somehow it was all the more shocking for being so quiet. We heard the sound of a body slumping to the floor and then the German man burst out of the room. He skidded to a halt when he saw us there, with Lady Hardcastle pointing the revolver at him. His own weapon was a tiny single-shot pistol. He laughed. He said, "Ah, the good lady wife. And with a gun. How charming. It is a pleasure to meet you, Lady Hardcastle, but get out of the way. I have no quarrel with you." Cool as you please, she just cocked the revolver and said, "You have the advantage of me, Mr . . . ?" His smile was fading a little by this point. He clicked his heels and with a little bow, he said, "Herr Günther Ehrlichmann of the Imperial German Embassy, at your service." Lady Hardcastle hadn't taken her eyes off him. She said, "Well, Herr Ehrlichmann, I think you've made one or two rather silly mistakes."'

'He was such an arrogant piece of work,' said Lady Hardcastle. 'Just standing there, smirking at me, with Roddy lying, shot, in the next room.'

'He was,' I agreed. 'He said, "I don't think so, your ladyship. I am not the sort to make mistakes. Now get out of my way and I might forget how foolish you are being. I have said that I have no quarrel with you but you do not, I think, wish to join your husband." He took a step towards her, reaching for the gun. And she pulled the trigger.'

'I wanted him alive,' said Lady Hardcastle. 'I wanted him to answer for what he'd done, so I took him in the shoulder. The shock of it made him flinch away and he stumbled back against the doorframe.'

'She told me to go and check on Sir Roderick,' I said. 'He'd been shot through the eye and I returned to the hall, shaking my head. Lady Hardcastle said, "More than two mistakes, actually, you Teutonic nitwit. In the first place, Roddy was not a spy. I am Diamond Rook, you dunderhead. Second, you came armed only for a single shot. What kind of inept assassin are you?" There was a flash of movement and suddenly Ehrlichmann was holding a knife in his uninjured hand. He threw it at her, but from his position slumped on the floor, there was no power or accuracy in the throw and she dodged it easily. "Third," she said, "you allowed yourself to be goaded into disarming yourself. If you're the best weapon Imperial Germany has at its disposal, the world is safe. Fourth, you killed my darling husband." He was still defiant. He said, "And why was that *Kartoffelkopf*'s death a mistake?" And then she said, "Because of mistake number five. For reasons I can't fathom, you still don't actually believe that I'm about to kill you." He did, indeed, look genuinely shocked as she pulled the trigger again and ended his life.'

The two musicians sat in stunned silence.

'Then how . . . ?' said Skins.

'How did he turn up in your club in the West End?' said Lady Hardcastle. 'That's what I'd like to know. Harry said nothing else?'

'Nothin',' said Skins.

'Well, I think you can understand my scepticism,' she said.

'After all that, I reckon we can,' he said.

'I'd still like to know what happened next,' said Barty.

'I think we need to save that for another time,' I said. 'The short version is that we saw to Mrs Lee and called the consulate. Or tried to. It was under attack, you see. A group of Boxer rebels had taken it upon themselves to strike at European targets in Shanghai.'

'I managed to speak briefly to the duty officer at the consulate,' said Lady Hardcastle. 'He just told me to get out of the city as fast as I could. "Take a boat to anywhere," he said. But we couldn't, you see. We spent the rest of the day trying, but it was hellishly difficult to get to the docks. And we soon learned that the Germans were looking for their missing assassin. For the reasons you now know, and which they were slowly fathoming out, Ehrlichmann wasn't going to be reporting in. They had a pretty good idea who to blame and so they were watching the docks and every shipping agent in town. We had no choice but to pack light and head inland.'

'But China's huge,' said Skins. 'I've seen it in an atlas.'

'Huge, indeed,' she said. 'That's why the rest of the story will have to wait. It took us two years to get across China and another two to get home from India. There's a lot more to tell. But for now, I'm declaring it bedtime.'

Chapter Nine

Once again, despite the excesses of the night before, I didn't manage to sleep in and I was up with the lark on Thursday morning as usual. Significantly before the lark at that time of year, in fact. I still knew nothing of the matutinal habits of larks, but I'd lay a hefty wager they were still slumbering in their larkish nests while I was stumbling into our darkish kitchen.

The kitchen lantern hung from a pulley in the centre of the ceiling. I untied the cord from the cleat on the wall and lowered the lamp on to the new kitchen table. A good maid always has a box of matches in her apron pocket and I used one to light the lamp before hauling it back up to the ceiling and tying off the cord.

It wasn't until I crossed the room to light the range that I noticed something terribly amiss. Lying on the flagstone floor, a half-eaten apple in her outstretched hand, was our young actress guest, Euphemia Selwood.

'Oh, for the love of . . .' I said, more exasperated than shocked. 'Not again.'

I checked for a pulse in her neck, and again at her wrist just to be certain; she was definitely dead. As undetective-like as it might seem, my first thought was not of waking Lady Hardcastle before summoning the police, but of shielding Edna and Miss Jones from the sight of a dead body in their place of work. They both had a latchkey for the side door, so I threw the bolt to make sure they couldn't come in without my also being there to keep them away from the corpse.

I hastened upstairs and shook Lady Hardcastle awake, trying to rouse her quietly so as not to disturb our guests.

'What on earth is the matter?' she said blearily. 'I thought we'd discussed this need of yours to waken me before dawn. I'm not one of Nature's early risers, dear, I'm really not.'

'I know, my lady,' I said. 'And I think you have to agree that I've been very good about that lately, but an emergency has arisen and I really do need your full, fully-conscious attention.'

She struggled into a sitting position and looked about in the gloom. 'It's still dark,' she said. 'And you've brought no tea.'

'Both these things are true, and I apologize. But the situation is somewhat urgent and there was no time to light the range and brew tea.'

She yawned extravagantly. 'Well?' she said. 'What's the matter?'

'Euphemia Selwood is dead.'

'She's what? Oh, for the love of . . .' she said. 'Not another one.'

'My sentiments almost to the word. I found her on the kitchen floor with an apple in her hand.'

'Another *Witch's Downfall* death, then. That's the way her character died, is it not? A poisoned apple.'

'Just so,' I said. 'We need to tell Sergeant Dobson and Inspector Sunderland. If I go into the village and try to knock up the sergeant, can you take care of the phone call to the Bristol CID?'

'Of course, dear. We'd better get cracking.'

So I got cracking. I hastened to fetch my hat and coat and to put on some outdoor boots. By the time I was ready to scoot out of the front door, Lady Hardcastle was already in the middle of her telephone call.

'. . . Yes, I'm aware it's early . . . No, I didn't expect the inspector to be there at this hour . . . No, nor the police surgeon . . . Quite so, that's why I wish you to take a message . . . No, Sergeant, you're not a hotel porter, I understand that. If you were a hotel porter you'd be a good deal more helpful . . . I shall take whatever tone I please, Sergeant, you're getting in the way of one of Inspector Sunderland's cases . . . Very droll. All I ask is that you tell the inspector that Lady Hardcastle has informed you that there's been another death, that it looks like murder, and that it is almost certainly connected to the first . . . I didn't say so before because you chose to spend so long lecturing me on the inspector's working hours . . . Very well, I'm most grateful to you, and I'm sure the inspector shall be, too . . . And good morning to you, Sergeant.'

She returned the earpiece to its hook on the side of the telephone. I feared for a moment that the wooden box might fall from the wall with the force of it, but it was made of sterner stuff.

'All done, my lady?' I said.

'Of all the impudent . . .'

'I'll go and speak to our own sergeant.'

'Dear old Sergeant Dobson,' she said. 'That other fellow is the sort that gives our police force a bad name.'

I let myself out and went to summon our own 'dear sergeant'.

For reasons long since lost in the mists of bureaucratic inscrutability, Littleton Cotterell was the hub of the local police network. As Sergeant Dobson and Constable Hancock were always quick to point out, they served not only the village in which they were stationed, but also villages and hamlets for miles around. It was for this reason that their accommodation was so generous – the two officers had a small cottage each, adjoining the police station itself – and their bicycles were so well maintained.

As I crossed the green, I noticed that there was a light in the police station window. I felt the tiniest twinge of relief that I wasn't going to have to spend the first five minutes of my errand hammering on the sergeant's front door. Someone was already awake.

My relief was short-lived. I found the front office, with its lamp burning brightly, completely deserted. They kept a little brass bell on the counter so that visitors might summon one of the officers if they were working in the back office or attending to a prisoner in the cell. I didn't have time for that. I lifted the flap in the counter and made my own way through to the office. There was no one there. I ventured further and eventually found Constable Hancock, fast asleep on the cot in the cell.

It seemed I wasn't to be spared from hammering on doors, after all, but at least this way I would be able to gauge the effects of my efforts. I beat the side of my fist three times on the open door of the cell and the effect was not only easy to gauge, but also extremely pleasing.

The constable jolted instantly awake and tried to stand to attention.

'I weren't asleep, Sarge, I swears,' he mumbled as his knees betrayed him and he flopped back on to the iron-framed cot. 'I was just . . .' He noticed me. 'Oh, Miss Armstrong, it's you. How did you . . . ?'

'Good morning, Constable,' I said brightly. 'I'm sorry to awaken you so early, but there's been . . . an incident at the house, and we need you to attend as quickly as you can.'

His senses were returning as he fumbled with his tunic buttons. 'What sort of incident?' he asked.

'I'm rather afraid it might be another murder,' I said, and explained the circumstances of my grim discovery.

''Pon my word,' he said. 'We'd better get the sergeant. He won't want to be left out of this, not with the inspector from Bristol placin' so much trust in him yesterday.'

We heard someone moving about in the front office.

'Hancock!' It was Sergeant Dobson. 'Where the dickens are you, boy?' Heavy boots on the flagstones. 'If you's asleep in that blasted cell again, I swear, I'll . . . Oh. Good mornin', Miss Armstrong.' He knuckled his forehead.

'Good morning, Sergeant,' I said. 'I hope you don't mind my being back here. We need urgent help up at the house and I found the station open but no one at home. Constable Hancock was out here checking the cell so he didn't hear when I rang the bell.'

There was doubt in Dobson's eyes – from his earlier remark it was apparent that Hancock had often been caught sleeping his way through night duty – but he seemed to decide that my concerns were more pressing.

'What sort of help, miss?' he said, favouring Constable Hancock with a sidelong I'll-deal-with-you-later glance.

Once again, I recounted the events of the morning so far.

The sergeant scribbled a few details in his notebook. 'We needs to . . . What was that phrase the inspector used, Hancock? Secure the . . . ?'

'Preserve the scene of the crime, Sarge,' said the constable.

'That's it, we need to preserve it. Hancock, get yourself over to Lady Hardcastle's house and don't let no one interfere with nothin'.'

'Right you are, Sarge.'

'I'll join you both presently. I'd like to telephone Bristol myself, just so's they knows we's dealin' with it, like.'

The constable and I hurried out.

'Thank you,' he said as we retraced my frosty footprints across the green.

'What for?'

'For not snitchin' on I,' he said earnestly. 'Ol' Sergeant Dobson's been on my back these past few weeks. I can't seem to do nothin' right.'

'I'm sure he just wants you to do well,' I said. 'It's his job to encourage the careers of junior officers.'

'I s'pose,' he said. 'But I appreciates it anyway. It weren't the first time I kipped down in that cell. 'T i'n't too comfy in there, but sometimes you just has to. They late nights is killin' I.'

'That's no good at all. Perhaps we can take your mind off it by trying to fathom what – or, rather, who – is killing our houseguests.'

◆ ◆ ◆

Back at the house, Lady Hardcastle was dressed (after a fashion – we would definitely need to make some adjustments if she were to have to venture out in public). She greeted us both and apologized for the lack of tea.

I directed the constable into the kitchen, where he made a great show of minutely examining the body and its surroundings while scribbling in his notebook. Meanwhile, I lit the range and set a kettle to boil.

The telephone rang, so I left the constable to his investigations and went to answer it.

'Hello,' I said. 'Chipping Bevington two-three.'

'Ah, Miss Armstrong,' said the familiar voice of Inspector Sunderland. 'Good morning to you.'

'And good morning to you, Inspector,' I said. 'Would you like to speak to Lady Hardcastle?'

'I'd be delighted to, as always, but there's no need if she's busy. I'm quite confident that you can tell me what's going on just as well as she.'

'Thank you kindly,' I said. I curtseyed sarcastically (if a curtsey can be sarcastic) but realized he couldn't see me.

'Hmm,' he said. Perhaps he could see me, after all. 'The message I got from the desk sergeant here was that there'd been another death.'

Not for the first time that morning, I recounted the events surrounding – and following – my discovery of Euphemia Selwood's body.

The inspector listened attentively and then said, 'It sounds as though you have everything in hand. I can't get there until this afternoon so

I'm relying on you and Lady Hardcastle to . . . to help the local bobbies gather as much evidence as possible. Dr Gosling is busy with another case so he'll not be able to come out to you at all. Can you get Sergeant Dobson to arrange for the van to pick up the body?'

'Of course,' I said. 'Is there anything in particular you want us – I mean the local police – to look out for?'

'I'm sure they'll think of everything,' he said with a chuckle. 'Just make certain not to lose the apple. If it's in her hand, the mortuary boys might take it away with them and then there's a fair chance we'll never see it again. Prise it free and wrap it in brown paper. But handle it with extreme care – if it's poisoned like the one in the moving picture, it could still be dangerous. I'll collect it when I call and then I can make sure that it gets to Dr Gosling for analysis.'

'Right you are, Inspector,' I said.

'And make sure you bag up the rest of the apples, too, if there are any. If there's a possibility that the one she was eating was poisoned, there's no reason to suppose that the rest weren't. Again, handle them with care.'

'Of course. Anything else?'

'No, that should do it. I'll leave everything else up to you and I'll be with you after lunch.'

We said our goodbyes and I returned the earpiece to its hook. I liked to imagine that it was grateful for the gentler way I treated it.

I returned to the kitchen to find that Lady Hardcastle was already hard at work supervising the constable's investigative efforts. The kettle was boiling.

'Did neither of you think to take the kettle off the stove?' I said.

'It's only just come to the boil, dear,' said Lady Hardcastle. 'We knew you would return soon enough.'

I harrumphed and set about making some tea for us all.

'I think you ought to make sure that the apple is properly examined,' she said to Constable Hancock. 'If our suppositions are correct and these deaths are linked to the moving picture, then that should turn out to be the murder weapon.'

'That was the inspector on the telephone, my lady,' I said. 'He asked that we wrap the apple in brown paper so that he can take it back to Dr Gosling.'

'Great minds and all that, eh?' she said.

'Apparently,' I said. 'Although I'm also given to understand that fools seldom differ.'

'That, too. Could you pass me a couple of spoons, please? I should be able to get it free without touching it.'

I hurried to the dining room and grabbed two soup spoons from the sideboard. On my way back, I searched Lady Hardcastle's study for some brown paper.

'I thought soup spoons would be better,' I said upon my return. 'They're flatter so they should do less damage to the fruit.'

'Smart as a whip, that girl,' said Lady Hardcastle. 'Wouldn't you agree, Constable?'

'I always said you was both the cleverest people I ever met.'

'Oh, you are a poppet,' she said. 'But we stumble through as best we can, just like everyone else does.'

'You speak for yourself, my lady,' I said.

'Quite right,' she said. 'I stumble through, but Armstrong here is a towering genius. I don't know what I'd do without her.'

'That little chap with the garrotte in that alley off St Martin's Lane would have seen you off, for a start,' I said.

'Gracious, yes,' she said. 'I'd forgotten him. What on earth were we doing there?'

'Looking for a way to break into the Garrick Theatre.'

'Oh, yes, we were, weren't we? We never did get to the bottom of why that Prussian chap bought tickets for that one particular box every night for a month.'

'If it wasn't an elaborate plan for an assassination, I still say he was just sweet on one of the players.'

'There were some very pretty boys and girls in the company, weren't there?'

'There were. But the lad with the garrotte wasn't so handsome.'

'Especially not after his encounter with you, dear,' she said. 'You sorted him out good and proper. There you are, Constable, without young Florence here, I'd be dead in an alley between Charing Cross Road and St Martin's Lane. She's a . . . marvel.'

This last pause was occasioned by the effort required to free the murder weapon from the victim's rigor mortis grip.

'There,' she said. 'Now, let's wrap that up for Simeon and we can have a cup of tea. You'll join us, Constable?'

'Don't mind if I do, m'lady. Although, I'd prefer it if we could drink it somewhere else.' He nodded towards the body on the floor.

'Of course, of course. There's nothing else for us to do here.'

A key rattled in the servants' door, followed by a few polite but firm knocks.

'That'll be Edna or Miss Jones,' I said. 'The other two aren't due for another hour and they don't have a key.'

'I think we ought to declare the kitchen out of bounds for the morning,' said Lady Hardcastle. 'But Edna and the Grange contingent will have plenty to do elsewhere.'

I drew the bolt and let Edna in.

'Is the lock broke?' she said as she bustled in and took off her coat.

'I don't understand,' I said, trying to block her way through to the kitchen before I'd had a chance to tell her what was going on.

'I put the key in the lock – habit, like – but it didn't turn. Then when I tried the door I found you'd thrown the bolt. So I wondered if the lock were broke.'

'Not as far as I know,' I said. 'I assumed it had been locked as usual. I never checked.'

'Then why was it bolted? You never leaves it bolted, else we wouldn't be able to get in.'

Yet again, I explained what had happened.

We withdrew to the dining room. Ordinarily we would have been in the morning room, what with it still being morning, but the crime board was in the dining room as usual and Lady Hardcastle wanted to show the constable how we were getting on. While she was going through the runners and riders, I popped back to the kitchen to fetch the tea tray.

On my way back, I stopped in the drawing room to offer a cup to Edna, who was, quite understandably, rather shaken by the morning's events. I put an extra couple of lumps of sugar in her cup and told her to sit for a while – she looked ashen.

'I'll be all right, my lover,' she said. 'Just 'ad a bit of a shock is all. I found our ma when she died, but she was old and frail. It was her heart. I a'n't never seen nothin' like that, though. That poor girl. So young. So beautiful. Poisoned just the same as Phoebe in that movin' picture. They says they's evil, and I'm startin' to reckon they might be right. I reckon they might even have conjured up evil spirits with it. What if they've come to possess someone? What if the Devil hisself has taken hold of that Zelda woman and made her into a real witch? She could be actin' all this out without even knowin' it.'

I let her ramble on. There wasn't much I could say yet to counter her fears apart from, 'Oh, for goodness' sake, don't be so stupid,' but I knew that wouldn't really help. Instead, I said, 'Are you certain you wouldn't prefer to go home? Dewi and Dora will be here soon. I'm sure we can manage without you for one day.'

'You're very kind, but I can't leave you with they. That Dora child will go to pieces soon as she finds out what's happened. And if she don't, she'll pretend to, just to try to skive for the day. You'll be even more shorthanded.'

I remembered how Dora had laid it on with a trowel when there had been a murder at The Grange. Edna was right – she would make every effort to turn the tragedy into a day off.

'I can't say I disagree with you,' I said. 'So, thank you. But if it all gets too much, just let me know.'

'Right you are, m'dear. Just let I sit here with a cuppa for ten minutes and I'll be right as ninepence. You go and do what you needs to do.'

I was about to say something encouraging and uplifting when the doorbell rang. With a sigh and an it-never-ends raise of the eyebrows to Edna, I went to answer it.

It was the two mortuary men.

'Mornin', missus. Got a body for us?' said the driver's mate.

I briefly considered chiding him to be a bit more respectful but, again, I thought it would probably be unhelpful. Instead, I said, 'Bring your stretcher round to the side entrance. I'll let you in.' I pointed to my left, indicating the path that ran around the outside of the house.

Constable Hancock supervised the removal of the body and returned to the dining room. His tea had gone cold.

'I reckon I ought to be gettin' along now,' he said. 'Sergeant Dobson will be expectin' me back now the body's gone. Thank you for keepin' me posted with your whatsitsname . . . crime thingummy. Most instructive. I shall let the sergeant know. He loves to hear how you civilians is thinkin' about these things.'

'Give him my regards, won't you?' said Lady Hardcastle. 'And please let him know that Inspector Sunderland is intending to visit the village this afternoon. I'm sure he already knows, but it doesn't hurt to make sure.'

'Right you are, my lady,' he said. 'I'll bid you both good day. Cheerio now.'

I showed him out.

'Any sign of the film folk?' said Lady Hardcastle when I returned to the dining room. '"Film folk". I'm going to have to drop that moniker – there's only two of them left. I don't quite know how we're going to break this one to them.'

'It'll be a blow,' I said. 'They both loved Euphemia. We need to find out who's doing this before anyone else gets hurt.'

'We do. Leave me to ponder a while, would you? I'd like to spend some time with the crime board – perhaps something will come to me if I just let my mind wander.'

'Certainly,' I said. 'I'll see you for elevenses?'

'Of course. Can't miss coffee and cake. Oh, and if Zelda or Cheetham surface, please send them in here. I ought to be the one to tell them.'

◆　◆　◆

I returned to the kitchen so as to be on hand when the Grange contingent arrived. Miss Jones, trooper that she was, agreed that the kitchen shouldn't be used until it had been thoroughly examined by the inspector and then thoroughly scrubbed. Preferably more than once. And with the strongest soap she could find.

Edna offered to help, and they had just started on the task when Dora and Dewi let themselves in through the side door. I agreed with Edna's prediction that Dora would attempt to use the shock and distress occasioned by the death of another houseguest to swing the lead, and I had prepared a little speech intended to convey sympathy for her feelings while leaving her in no doubt that she'd be expected to press on regardless. As it turned out, Edna had things well under control.

'What's goin' on?' asked Dora, after she had hung her coat in the boot room. 'What's everyone doin' in here?'

'Please, sit down, Dora,' I said. 'You, too, Dewi. I'm afraid we have some more bad news.'

They did as they were asked.

'When I came down this morning,' I continued, 'I found Miss Euphemia Selwood lying on the kitchen floor. Dead.'

Dora let out a little squeal. 'Oh my good gracious,' she said. And then began to wail.

'Pull yourself together, girl,' said Edna sharply. 'You barely knew the woman.'

'Yes . . . but . . .' sobbed Dora.

'Yes but nothin',' said Edna. 'We's all sad – she was a lovely young lady – but there i'n't no good'll come of you carryin' on like that.'

'I don't think I *can* carry on.'

'Oh, do be quiet,' said Edna. 'I've known you since you was a babber and you was always a lazy little beggar. You've spent your whole life tryin' to avoid doin' what you ought, and it's about time you stopped gettin' away with it. We'll have a nice cup of tea to calm us all down, and then we're goin' to buckle down and get on with it.'

Dora sniffed. 'How did she die?' she said.

'We think it was a poisoned apple,' I said.

This brought forth fresh howls of anguish.

'What on earth's the matter now?' said Edna, whose tone had left 'sharp' some way behind and was now sailing in the direction of 'downright irritated'.

'I brought them apples,' said Dora.

'I beg your pardon?' I said. This was fresh news.

'There wasn't no apples in the house so I brought 'em down from The Grange. I loves apples. I could've eaten the poisoned one. It could've been me lyin' there dead.'

'We can but dream,' said Miss Jones quietly.

Dora affected not to have heard.

'I'd like you to speak to Inspector Sunderland when he gets here,' I said. 'He'll want to know where they came from.'

Dora was thunderstruck. 'You don't mean you reckons I done it?'

I suppressed a smile and decided to torment her a little. 'Well,' I said, 'it does look a little suspicious, doesn't it? We had no apples in the house, you bring them, and then poor Euphemia takes a bite and falls down dead.'

'But . . . you can't really think . . .' She began wailing again.

Miss Jones rolled her eyes. 'Well,' she said, 'I can't be hangin' around here all mornin' if the kitchen's out of commission. We'll need to see what Mr Holman can do for us.'

'You have that venison pie,' I said.

'I do,' she said. 'So we shouldn't need much. I can't wait for it to be delivered, though, so I shall have to go into the village to fetch it.'

'Perhaps you could take Dora with you if you has a lot to carry,' said Edna with more than a trace of hopefulness in her voice. 'Keep an eye on her, mind – she's likely to scarper now she knows the rozzers are on to her.' She winked, but the joke was lost on Dora, who let out a fresh wail.

Throughout all of this, Dewi had maintained a stoic silence. It wasn't until the two huntresses had set out in search of food that he finally said, 'I'm sorry to hear about Miss Euphemia. I liked her. She was kind.'

'And pretty,' I said.

He blushed. 'Beautiful.'

I patted his hand.

'I'd better go and see to Mr Cheetham,' he said. 'He'll be upset, an' all, I shouldn't wonder.'

Edna, too, left to set about some important task or other, leaving me alone with my now-cold tea. Time to see if the remaining film folk had risen.

◆ ◆ ◆

They had. They were full of bubbling enthusiasm, falling over each other to tell us about the massive audience for the second screening of *The Witch's Downfall*. Against our expectations, it had proven even more popular and successful than before. We let them talk themselves out and then I excused myself and left Lady Hardcastle to the difficult task of breaking the bad news.

While I put together a light breakfast for Mr Cheetham and Miss Drayton, Lady Hardcastle explained the morning's grisly discovery. As predicted, they took it very badly indeed, with Zelda letting out an anguished shriek that I heard from the kitchen. Once again, they retreated to the sanctuary of the morning room together. I took in their food and left them to their grief.

Skins and Barty were the last to rise and were equally shocked by the news.

'You should have woken us,' said Skins.

'I'm sorry,' I said. 'But what would you have done?'

'I s'pose you're right,' he conceded. 'You all right, mate?'

'Eh?' said Barty.

'Are you all right? You took a shine to young Phemie, didn't you? I know that look.'

'I did, yes. It's a bit of a blow, to be honest. I've been told to sling my hook many a time, but no girl's ever got herself murdered just to avoid me.'

The distress and tearfulness that had pervaded the house must have had more of an effect on me than I imagined – that's the only reason I can give for my sudden fit of giggles.

'You're a breath of fresh . . . something or other, Mr Dunn,' I said. 'Thank you.'

'Think nothing of it,' he said. 'Is there anything else we can do before we leave?'

'No, but you've brightened my day. Miss Jones has been out scouring the village for comestibles if you have time to stay for lunch.'

'Not sure we do,' said Skins. 'There's a Gloucester train at one forty-four and I told the bloke with the cart to come and pick us up . . . well, about now, actually.'

It would have been wonderful to report that the doorbell rang at that precise moment but, sadly, it didn't. We had time to get Dewi to retrieve the boys' instruments from storage and say our goodbyes before 'the bloke with the cart' rang the doorbell and took them off to Chipping Bevington and points north. I was sad to see them go.

We weren't without additional visitors for long, though. While Lady Hardcastle and I were sitting down to a surprisingly delicious lunch in the dining room – Zelda and Cheetham had declined the invitation to join us – the doorbell rang again. This time it was Inspector Sunderland. I showed him through to the dining room.

'Ah, Inspector,' said Lady Hardcastle. 'Do come in and sit down. Have some lunch – there's plenty.'

'Thank you, my lady,' he said. 'I wouldn't normally, but I've been on the go all morning and I confess to being more than a little peckish.'

'Help yourself,' she said. 'Try the venison pie. It's one of Miss Jones's finer creations.'

He took the proffered slice of pie and helped himself to a few of the other delights that Miss Jones had managed to procure.

'It's a joy to see you, as always,' said Lady Hardcastle, 'but I'm beginning to wish we could meet more often under less distressing circumstances.'

'I'm beginning to feel the same.'

'Would you like to examine the "scene of the crime"?'

'There's no rush. I'll have a quick glance before I go, but I don't think it will tell me anything that isn't already in Constable Hancock's report. He's a plodder, but a reliable one.'

'He's a poppet,' she said. 'How are the rest of your enquiries proceeding? Has Simeon found anything?'

'Poor old Gosling. He's having no luck with this case at all. There was a delay in getting the body to the mortuary yesterday – I gather the van broke down – and by the time it arrived, he was out on another matter. He was planning to start work on Newhouse today, but there was an outbreak of something nasty at the police station out in St George so he had to minister to the sick.'

'"Something nasty"?'

'I'm not certain you'd want details while we're eating,' he said.

'Ah, right you are. A touch of the colly-wobbles, as Nanny used to say?'

'More than a touch, and more than a slight wobble. I don't envy Gosling at all. But it means that we're no closer to a precise cause of death for Mr Newhouse, and young Miss Selwood will have to remain a mystery for a little while longer as well.'

'Surely, "being stabbed through the heart" is widely accepted as a potentially terminal event,' I said.

'You'd be right to think so,' he said. 'But without a police surgeon's report we can't be certain. "I"s have to be dotted and "t"s crossed. I've seen more than one case where a man was poisoned in one street, stabbed in another, and his body dumped in the next. Only a thorough post-mortem examination can tell us for certain.'

'He's not wrong, Flo,' said Lady Hardcastle. 'And we know he was stabbed before he was dressed in those clothes – no hole in his jacket or waistcoat, remember? – so there's no way to know for sure whether he was already dead by the time his chest was pierced.'

'If those blasted mortuary men hadn't been so officiously efficient, Gosling would have seen the body in situ,' said the inspector. 'That would surely have told him something.'

'They arrived here promptly this morning, too,' I said.

'If only they were as good at delivering bodies to the mortuary as they are at picking them up from the murder scene,' he said, 'we'd have more than half our answers by now, I'm sure of it. Ah, well, it can't be helped, I don't suppose.' He drew his notebook from his jacket pocket and flicked through it, looking for an empty page. 'What were your thoughts on the death of Miss Selwood?'

'It looked for all the world as though it were another kinematograph killing,' I said.

'I'll wager that's what the newspapers will be calling it by tomorrow. I gather you've got Dinah Caudle staying in the village so there's little chance of keeping any of this quiet.'

'She seems very keen to cover the story and to make it as sensational as possible,' I said. 'But back to the body. She was sprawled on the floor with a half-eaten apple in her hand. It might be that she wasn't killed by a poisoned apple just like her character in the moving picture, but we were certainly supposed to think she was.'

'There were no other marks or wounds on her body?' he said. 'No signs of a struggle?'

'None that I could see. Her head and face were unmarked and the kitchen was very much as we'd left it.'

'How was she dressed?'

'What do you mean?' I said.

'Was she in her night attire?'

'Ah, I see. No, she was wearing the same clothes as when she and the other "film folk" went out for the evening.'

'Do you know when they returned?'

'Not before we'd gone to bed, certainly.'

'And when was that?'

'What would you say, my lady?' I said. 'Midnight?'

'Then or then-abouts,' she said. 'We had some overnight guests and we were up yarning, but I don't think it was much past midnight.'

'More guests?' said the inspector.

'Yes. You might remember them: Skins Maloney and Barty Dunn.'

'The musicians from Clarissa Farley-Stroud's engagement party,' he said. 'Charming rogues. Or roguish charmers. I could never fathom quite which.'

'A little of both, I think,' she said. 'They were stranded nearby when their train broke down, or so they said, so we invited them to stay the night.'

'Most convivial,' said the inspector as he made a note. 'So you retired at around midnight and didn't hear the . . . What did you call them? The film folk?'

'That's them.'

'Thank you. You didn't hear the film folk return. So shall we allow, perhaps, an hour for you to ready yourself for bed and fall into a deep enough sleep that you'd not hear three people let themselves in?'

'That sounds reasonable,' she said.

'Which means that they probably didn't come home before one in the morning. We should give Mr Cheetham and Miss Drayton at least the same amount of time to raid your decanter for a nightcap and get off to bed, leaving Miss Selwood alone in the kitchen with a hankering for a late-night snack. She eats a poisoned apple and dies on the kitchen floor sometime between, let's say, two and three.'

'Why not later?' I asked.

'She was in her clothes,' said Lady Hardcastle. 'If it were any later, the chances are that she would be in her nightgown. She went looking for her snack before bed.'

'Quite so,' said the inspector. 'And then Miss Armstrong found the body at about six o'clock.'

'I did,' I said.

'With the apple in her hand?'

'Yes,' I said. 'Is that significant?'

'Possibly. One would expect it to have rolled away as she fell. She wouldn't have a tight enough hold on it once she was dead.'

'Unless the poison caused some manner of spasm,' suggested Lady Hardcastle.

'Perhaps,' he said.

'It was still tightly in her grasp when I pried it out to give it to Simeon,' she said. She looked thoughtful for a moment. 'But that can't be right. I presumed it was rigor mortis, but we're guessing that she died no earlier than two o'clock. I removed the apple at around . . . What would you say, dear? Eight?'

'A little earlier, I think,' I said.

'I telephoned shortly after seven,' said the inspector. 'If that's any guide.'

'Let's call it half-past seven, then, just for the sake of argument. She'd been dead no more than five hours by our current reckoning, and she was stiff as a board.'

'Rigor mortis,' I said.

'No, full rigor mortis takes about twelve hours. After less than five, only the small muscles would be affected.'

'You're right,' said the inspector. 'I'm impressed. How did you . . . ?'

'One picks these things up, dear. You know how it is,' she said offhandedly.

'No,' he said. 'Most people don't pick these things up. I'm most definitely impressed. This certainly is a queer one. We need Dr Gosling's report more than ever.'

'He'll get the job done, Inspector, don't worry. I've known Simeon for many, many years. He likes to play the bumbling duffer – he imagines it to be charming, which I suppose it is, up to a point – but he's as sharp as anyone you've ever worked with. He'll not let you down.'

'I'd rather formed that impression myself, actually. He's a good man.'

'He is.'

'How's your "crime board" coming along?' he said.

'I thought you'd never ask,' she said. 'Carry on with your sandwich – I believe it's one of Old Joe's famous doorstops from the Dog and Duck – and we'll take you through it.'

For the next half an hour, she and I did just that.

◆ ◆ ◆

'I knew I could rely on you two,' said the inspector when we had finished listing the runners and riders. 'Since I'm here for the afternoon, I'd like to speak to a few people. And I have my own transport, too, so there's no need to rush.'

'You managed to borrow Dr Gosling's motor car, then?' I said.

'Actually, no. We sent Gosling out to St George in a Black Maria in case they needed to move any of the prisoners, but I didn't need his motor car after all. We have one at the station now for CID's exclusive use. Arrived yesterday. I was surprised by how fast one can get here.'

'Poor Simeon,' said Lady Hardcastle. 'He was never the adventurous type. We shouldn't rag him too much about it.'

The inspector made a face that rather eloquently conveyed, 'Just you wait until you're in a hurry to get somewhere and you have Gosling driving you,' without his actually having to say anything. What he did say, as he consulted his ever-present notebook, was, 'I'll need a few words with the surviving film folk. I'm very interested to meet this Aaron Orum character. And I suppose I ought to speak to Dinah Caudle, though I know from previous encounters that she'll probably just irritate me.'

'You're not an admirer?' I said.

'She has plenty of those without needing an old fogey like me,' he said. 'It's her manner that grates on me. I can't put my finger on it.'

'She didn't impress me much, if it's any consolation,' said Lady Hardcastle.

'It doesn't do to talk about people behind their backs, I know, but she gets on my nerves. And her infatuation with Orum does her no favours at all. It seems a bit grubby for someone in her position to be fawning over an old roué like that.'

'What about the Hugheses?' I asked.

'Those two get on my nerves as well,' he said.

'Understandably,' I said. 'But will you be speaking to them?'

'I shall have to speak to them in case they witnessed anything,' he said. 'Though I strongly doubt that they had anything to do with it. They are, as the phrase has it, "known to the police", but for the most part they're just a confounded nuisance. I'd hound them off the streets if it were up to me. The trouble is that one of an Englishman's most treasured freedoms is the freedom to make a confounded nuisance of himself, so we're obliged to let them get on with it.'

'The vicar said the same thing,' I said. 'But they can't be as simplistic and simple-minded as they make out, surely. And even if all they want really is to save us all from our own sins, they can't have been happy to find that the second showing of *The Witch's Downfall* was even more popular than the first. Would that drive them to serve up another warning?'

'You might have to track them to their lair in Bristol,' said Lady Hardcastle.

'Might they have decamped?' he asked.

'They had a bit of a run-in with the vicar's wife's dog earlier,' she said.

'The vicar set the dog on them?'

'Heavens, no. He was just playing. He's an adorable creature – the dog, I mean, although the vicar is quite charming in his own way – but he has a tendency to become overexcited. He's not fully aware of the effects of his size and strength. And. Well . . .'

'He knocked the Hugheses and their claque on their bums,' I said. 'It was like a giant game of skittles.'

'I wish I'd seen it,' he said with a vengeful smile. 'I doubt the new King's Police Medal can be awarded to dogs, and especially not civilian ones, but I'm tempted to buy the hound a nice bit of steak. Many's the time I've wanted to knock that lot down. He's done the Force a great service.'

'Is there anything you'd like us to do while you're carrying out all these interviews?' asked Lady Hardcastle.

'You're welcome to accompany me if you wish,' he said. 'I always appreciate your insights. I'll set Dobson and Hancock to work speaking to witnesses. Anyone in the village who went to these moving picture shows or who was at the local pub might have seen something. It's boring work but that's what they're paid for. Oh, actually, you might be able to help there a little. Are you still good friends with Lady Farley-Stroud?'

'I am, yes.'

'If I might prevail upon you to try to get an account of the two evenings from her, that would be most helpful. I think she'd be more forthcoming if you were to speak to her.'

'Of course,' she said. 'Now?'

'No, she can wait. I want to speak to Cheetham first.'

I set about clearing the dining table.

Chapter Ten

Mr Cheetham and Miss Drayton were sitting in silence in the morning room. He was poring over a chaotic array of typewritten sheets of foolscap, while she was crocheting what looked like a shawl. Or a blanket. Or possibly part of a waistcoat. Her movements were jerkily anxious and she dropped more than one stitch in the few moments I was there.

'Mr Cheetham?' I said quietly.

He glanced up from his work. He looked pale and drawn. 'Please, call me Nolan. I think we're long past stuffy formalities by now.'

'Certainly, Mr Cheetham. Inspector Sunderland is here from the Bristol CID. He would like a word with you in the dining room.'

'Just give me a moment to tidy this lot away,' he said, indicating the jumble of papers. 'I'll be with you presently.'

We were sitting around the dining table when he finally poked his head round the door. Luckily, Edna had brought in the coffee tray and I was busy pouring us all a cup, so we didn't look too much as though we were staging a tableau of that Yeames painting.

'Please come in and sit down,' said Lady Hardcastle. 'Inspector, this is Mr – or do you prefer Colonel? – Cheetham. Mr Cheetham, this is Inspector Sunderland of the Bristol CID.'

'Colonel is more of an honorary title these days,' said Cheetham. 'How do you do, Inspector?'

'How do you do, Mr Cheetham?' said the inspector. 'You have my condolences on the deaths of your two friends.'

'Thank you,' said Cheetham.

'I don't wish to cause any further distress, but would you mind recounting the events of the past couple of evenings for me, please? I'm trying to build as detailed a picture as I can.'

'Certainly, Inspector,' said Cheetham. 'Where would you like me to start?'

'Lady Hardcastle and Miss Armstrong have given me a clear account of Tuesday evening as they saw it. They arrived at the hall after you'd been there for a while.'

'We were setting up our equipment, yes.'

'Did you have any trouble on the way in?'

'From the protesters? We were treated to a small amount of ill-informed abuse but nothing serious.'

'What sort of abuse?'

'Oh, the usual. Ungodly this, satanic that, thou shalt not . . . You know the sort of thing.'

'I'm afraid I do,' said the inspector as he carried on making his customarily thorough notes. 'Did anyone make any specific threats?'

'Other than eternal damnation, you mean?'

'Other than that, yes.'

'No. There was some snarling and a little pushing and shoving, but no one said they would kill any of us.'

'Who pushed and shoved?'

'Hughes,' said Cheetham. 'I've encountered him before. He likes to portray himself as doing God's work, but he's a nasty little thug at heart.'

'I can't disagree with you,' said the inspector. 'The show went well, I hear.'

'Very well indeed. You know, a lot of people have given up on the idea of taking this sort of show to the villages. There are dedicated picture houses in the cities now, and anyone who wants to tour tends to stick to the larger towns. But I think this is where you get to meet the real audience, the real people of England.'

It's where you meet the yokels who don't get out much and will lap up any mediocre fare, I thought, but his friends had been killed so I kept it to myself.

'And after the show,' said the inspector, 'you retired to the Dog and Duck, is that correct? That's where Lady Hardcastle's account ends.'

'Ah, yes, you came home, didn't you, my lady? Well, we were all but dragged to the local pub by an exuberant crowd, who insisted on treating us all night. The place was packed to the rafters.'

'No one stood out? No one seemed suspicious?'

Cheetham laughed. 'There was no one skulking about in the background, twirling his moustaches, you mean?'

'Or stroking his beard,' said the inspector.

'Ah, you mean my nemesis, the evil Aaron Orum?'

'He was there?'

'With his latest paramour, we assumed. I caught a glimpse of them in the other bar.'

'Who's this paramour?' asked the inspector. 'Is she on our list?'

'The newspaper girl,' said Cheetham. 'Came here yesterday with her prim little notebook and her insinuations.'

'Ah,' said the inspector. 'Dinah Caudle of the *Bristol News*. Is there a romantic link?'

'Difficult to say, sir,' I said. 'They were sitting together in the snug when I saw them earlier that day, but they're fellow residents of the pub. It might be improper in some circles for a man and a woman to be drinking together in a public house, but they could scarcely ignore each other, either.'

'I know that roué of old, though,' said Cheetham. 'If he's not tupping her, he's tried to.'

'Steady on,' said the inspector. 'No need for that.'

'I do beg your pardon, my lady,' said Cheetham. 'But, no, I didn't speak to Orum. He raised his glass to me in what you might call an ironic salute, but I ignored him.'

'I see. And you left the pub when?'

'About one in the morning, I should say.'

'All of you together?'

'No,' said Cheetham. 'To my eternal regret, we left Basil in the company of some of the villagers. He was in his element – free booze, a fat cigar, and spinning yarns to a captive audience. We couldn't drag him from that. But I wish we had.'

'And was there anyone abroad as you returned to the house?'

'A few revellers came out with us, but they all went back towards the heart of the village.'

'I see,' said the inspector. 'That does leave us with a troublingly large gap in our story. Hancock found the body at . . .' He riffled through the pages of his notebook. 'At, or around, five in the morning. That leaves us with four hours unaccounted for. We'll need to find out when Newhouse left the pub. Ah well, that's for another time. Are you happy to continue, Mr Cheetham?'

'Certainly,' said Cheetham. 'Though I fear my account of last night will be boringly familiar. Another very successful evening. An even bigger audience. A more excited reaction to the picture—'

'You showed . . . *The Witch's Downfall* again, I understand.'

'That's right. We're all very proud of the piece. We're not going to let the actions of one degenerate take anything away from that. So, yes, we showed the picture again. We brought the cast – it's not often that happens – and we wanted to show off our masterpiece.'

The inspector continued with his note-taking. 'And you went to the Dog and Duck again after the show?'

'Exactly as before, Inspector. We were treated all night and we left at around one o'clock.'

'And came straight back here?'

'Straight back, yes.'

'And straight to bed?'

'We yarned for a little longer in the kitchen, and then Zelda and I retired, leaving Phemie to look for a snack.'

'Thank you, sir,' said the inspector. 'I think that'll be all for now. You've certainly filled in quite a few missing details. Is there anything you'd like to add? Anything that might help us find out who did this?'

'Nothing I can think of, Inspector, no.' Cheetham stood to leave.

'Just one more thing before you go, then,' said the inspector, looking up. 'Who do you think is responsible? Who do you think killed Basil and Euphemia?'

The question seemed to have completely blindsided Mr Cheetham, who said, 'Orum,' before he could stop himself.

'Thank you, sir. Would you mind asking Miss Drayton to join us, please?'

Cheetham left without closing the door.

◆ ◆ ◆

The house was well built and pleasingly appointed in the modern style but, for reasons which baffled everyone, it hadn't been fitted with servants' bells. For the most part this wasn't a problem – there were few of us in the household and a spirited shout was usually sufficient. But uncouth yelling wasn't really the done thing when there were guests present and so it fell to Yours Truly to walk to the kitchen to order more refreshment. Tea this time.

I was cornered by Edna for an exposition of the ancient art of floor scrubbing – something she was expressly forbidden from doing until the inspector had . . . inspected. Miss Jones then invested a few moments in restating her objection to working in a room that had so recently contained a dead person. I decided to say nothing about the dismembered forequarters of the dead sheep in the larder, nor the corpses of the mackerel she had disembowelled in the sink the week before. Instead, I listened patiently, tutted and 'Oh, I know'-ed in the right places, and offered my reassurances that everything would be back to normal soon.

By the time I returned to the dining room, Zelda Drayton was already ensconced at the table and introductions had been made. I sat in my usual seat next to Lady Hardcastle and listened.

Zelda's account of the events of the two previous evenings added little to what we already knew. She was somewhat more generous on the subject of Aaron Orum, though it was clear that she still harboured some resentment over the way he and Cheetham had fallen out. The only serious divergence from the 'official' story was her own reaction to the deaths.

'I mean,' she said, breathily, 'it makes you wonder, doesn't it. Who's next? It's the witch, that's who. Burned alive. I'm not at all sure I ought to be hanging about round here waiting for that.'

The inspector let her voice her fears for a few moments more and, eventually, she subsided into nervous silence.

'Thank you, Miss Drayton,' he said when she had finished. 'I'm sure you have nothing to worry about. We'll have this cleared up in no time.' He looked back through his notes. 'Oh, there was one more thing. I didn't want to interrupt the flow. You said you saw Mr Orum getting up from his table as you left the pub on Tuesday night.'

'That's right,' she said.

'I wondered why you mentioned it. Did you attach any significance to it?'

She sat for a moment in thought. 'I don't know. I was just aware of it, that's all. And obviously he was the only other person in the pub that I knew, so I must have noticed.'

'Did you see where he went? To the bar, perhaps?'

She thought for a moment longer. 'Now I come to think of it,' she said, 'he was coming towards the public bar. We were heading out the door and it looked like he was coming towards us, but he veered off.'

'Did you notice where he veered off to?'

Another pause. 'Towards Basil, I suppose. The little crowd round him, at any rate.'

'But you didn't actually see him approach Mr Newhouse?'

'No, we were out the door and into the cold. I couldn't say for sure.'

'Thank you,' said the inspector. 'You've been most helpful.'

'Right you are,' she said, already standing. 'If you need me for anything else, you know where to find me.'

She was out in the hall with the door closed behind her before any of us could say another word.

'That was very illuminating,' said Lady Hardcastle.

'You mean the fact that her story was exactly the same as Mr Cheetham's?' I said.

'So, you both noticed, too,' said the inspector.

'Word for word in some places,' I said.

'They've definitely agreed on their version of events,' said Lady Hardcastle.

'They've spent hours together in the morning room,' I said. 'They've had a lot of time to get it straight. And what about all that stuff about "it's me next"? She's terrified one minute and sticking to a perfectly rehearsed version of events the next.'

'It happens more than you'd imagine,' said the inspector. 'Oddly, it's more often the innocent folk who go to such lengths. They want to make sure they're not falsely implicated in any wrongdoing, so they make certain that they tell a consistent story.'

'Oh dear,' said Lady Hardcastle. 'I thought we were on to something there.'

'Most likely not,' he said. 'But it's intriguing nonetheless.'

'They've both got it in for Aaron Orum,' I said. 'That bit about him going into the public bar sounded like a bit of lily gilding to me.'

'I agree,' he said. 'But we can't discount it just yet.'

'We often found that in our previous line, didn't we, Flo?' said Lady Hardcastle. 'It sometimes happens that people know things they're not prepared to give up, but they'll concoct a way of pointing you in the right direction so you can work it out for yourself.'

'True,' I said. 'Although just as often they were simply trying to settle old scores by dropping someone in it.'

'A policeman's lot is not a happy one,' said the inspector. 'Nor ever a particularly straightforward one. Shall we go to the pub?'

'I thought you'd never ask,' said Lady Hardcastle.

'To speak to Orum and Caudle.'

'Oh,' she said. 'How frightfully disappointing. Surely we could just have a swift one. Since we're there.'

'I'm not allowed to drink on duty, my lady,' he said.

'No, dear, I know. But Flo and I aren't on duty, are we? Get the coats, Flo – this has been a trying time and it is my considered opinion that the mainbrace is in urgent need of splicing.'

'Aye aye, m'lady,' I said, offering a sloppy salute and setting sail for the coat stand in the hall.

◆ ◆ ◆

As usual, Aaron Orum was sitting in the snug with a tankard of cider and a newspaper. If it hadn't been for the fact that it was Thursday's paper, I'd have been hard put to tell whether he'd moved from the spot at all since I'd first seen him there on Monday. And back in her own spot from Monday – indecorously close to Mr Orum – was the *Bristol News*'s eagerest reporter, Miss Dinah Caudle.

They both looked over as we entered. Mr Orum seemed a little nonplussed, but Miss Caudle knew all three of us. While Mr Orum favoured us with a puzzled frown, her glare was quickly replaced by an insincere smile.

'Lady Hardcastle,' she said. 'How do you do? And Inspector Sunderland, what an honour to receive an actual visit from one of the Bristol CID's finest. I thought you were too important to mix with witnesses these days. I thought you had uniformed lackeys to do that sort of thing for you.'

Lady Hardcastle offered a curt, 'How do you do?'

Inspector Sunderland smiled. 'Good afternoon, Miss Caudle,' he said. 'Am I to take it that you've given a statement to Sergeant Dobson?'

'Oh, no, Inspector. Nothing so grand as a sergeant. We had to make do with Constable Bumpkin, didn't we, Aaron?'

Mr Orum smiled at her and nodded his agreement.

'His name is Hancock,' said the inspector, 'and he's a very fine young officer. I hope you answered his questions fully, frankly . . . and politely.'

'He's an impertinent yokel,' she said.

'You think it an impertinence to work towards catching a murderer? A murderer who has killed twice already and may yet kill again?'

'It's an impertinence for an oaf like that to question innocent citizens as though they were common criminals.'

'Then I'm most terribly sorry, but I'm afraid I'm going to offend you further,' said the inspector equably. 'I should like to hear your account of the last two evenings for myself.'

'Then you shall be disappointed, Inspector. I have urgent business elsewhere.' Her manner softened as she said to Mr Orum, 'Shall I see you later?'

Orum smiled again. 'Of course. We've nowhere else to go, after all.'

She returned his smile before rising from the table and walking through into the public bar. We heard the clack of her heels on the flagstone floor as she strode briskly towards the stairs leading up to her room.

'I don't have any urgent business anywhere,' said Mr Orum. 'I'd be more than happy to answer your questions, Inspector . . . Sunderland, was it?'

'Yes, sir, that's right.'

'How do you do? Aaron Orum. Artist, innovator, businessman, bon viveur . . .'

'. . . buffoon,' I added silently. At least I hope I didn't say it out loud. Lady Hardcastle's sudden smile made me doubt myself.

'Please, sit down,' continued Orum. 'All of you.'

'Thank you, sir,' said the inspector. He placed his neatly brushed bowler hat on the table in front of him and drew his notebook and pencil from the inside pocket of his jacket. 'Did you attend either of the moving picture shows?'

'Both,' said Orum.

'Both of them? Really?'

'Really and truly. I was expecting a different programme for the second night – and for the most part I got it – but it was still touching to see my picture for the second time in a week as a tribute to poor dear Basil.'

'Your picture?'

'Yes, Inspector, my picture. Surely you've heard the story by now. Everyone else seems to know.'

'Indulge me, sir. Explain to me how the moving picture made by Mr Cheetham's company can be "your" picture.'

'I really shouldn't have to keep explaining this.'

'It's obviously very important to you,' said the inspector. 'I should have thought you'd be pleased to explain it to as many people as would listen. You seem to be implying some sort of theft, after all. Surely you wish recompense. Or retribution?'

'Now look here!' said Orum, half rising to his feet. 'I'm not above doing a few weeks in chokey for thumping a policeman, you know.'

'Then please save yourself a gaol sentence by sitting down and telling me what you're talking about.'

'And implicate myself further?'

'Further, sir?'

'You've as good as said you think I killed Basil and Euphemia.'

'I certainly didn't wish to suggest that,' said the inspector. 'I merely wish to learn all the facts of the case so that we can track down their killer.'

Orum resumed his seat with a sigh.

'Very well,' he said, wearily. 'A long time since,' he began portentously, 'veiled in the swirling mists of time, Nolan Cheetham and I were friends. Childhood pals. Boon companions. Our friendship survived the trials of adolescence, rivalries over girls, the exhaustion of working long days at the mill. We shared a passion, you see, a passion for the theatre. And we worked at it together. Became famous in our way. And opportunity stretched out before us like a diamond-cobbled road.'

'I see,' said the inspector. 'Though if you don't mind my clumping over your metaphor, diamond cobbles sound a tad slippery to me.'

'Clump away, my dear sir,' said Orum. 'Slippery and treacherous, they were. We soon fell from the glittering path.'

'What caused this . . . fall?'

'What always causes men to fall from the path of ambition and greatness, my dear inspector? A woman.'

'You ended a lifelong friendship over a woman?' said the inspector.

'Alas and alack, would that it were not true,' said Orum. 'Elsie Butterworth was her name. Lovely lass. We were to be wed, she and I. But Cheetham turned her head. He didn't want her. He didn't love her. He just didn't want me to be with her. She broke off our engagement and began walking out with him. Within a month he'd broken up with her. I could have taken it if they were really in love, I think, but when that happened, when I found out he'd only done it to split us asunder,

I couldn't bear it. I punched him on the nose and left the business. We barely speak now.'

'I don't mean to make light of your experiences,' said the inspector, 'and I'm sure they've had a profound effect on your life, but I'm struggling to see how any of this makes *The Witch's Downfall* your property.'

'You're not a patient man, Inspector, are you? I merely thought a little background would help to underline the completeness of our falling out. While we were still pals we would talk about all manner of things. Ideas fizzed around us like Bonfire Night fireworks. One evening, the whisky was flowing and we took off on a flight of fancy about seventeenth-century witchcraft. There were famous trials in the early 1600s, you know. The Pendle Witches. I concocted this story for a play about a witch who falls in love with a lad from the village but has to get rid of her rival, a beautiful young girl. I think that might sound a little familiar?'

The inspector looked to Lady Hardcastle and me for confirmation.

'It's the story of *The Witch's Downfall*,' I said. 'The core of it, at least.'

'I didn't just come up with the core,' said Orum. 'I thought up killing the girl with a poisoned apple, the suitor going insane and throwing himself from the church tower, the Witchfinder . . . everything. The whole thing was my idea. Cheetham began drawing sketches of the props we'd need on stage, of the scenery we'd have to build. "Special effects", he called it. We planned through the night.'

'But you never produced this play?' said the inspector.

'No, his betrayal put an end to our partnership before we could even begin.'

'I can well understand how you might feel aggrieved to see that same story made into a moving picture.'

'You have no idea, Inspector. No idea.'

'Has this sense of grievance ever spilled over into acts of retribution or vengeance?'

Orum laughed. 'I am a man of words and ideas, Inspector, not "acts of retribution or vengeance".'

'You said you punched your dearest friend on the nose.'

'Oh, yes, but that was in the heat of the moment. I prefer to exact my vengeance by doing what I'm doing now – I play the ghost at the feast. It is my fervent hope that that tiresomely toilsome little weasel chokes on his guilt every time he sees me. I've tried a more direct approach in the past. I've sent him letters, you know, explaining the situation in proper legal terms, but he ignores them. I thought of confronting him, too, taking him to task in public, but that would do no good, either. No one thinks of themselves as a wrong'un, do they? Everyone has some self-serving justification for their actions. But now I know how much it rattles him, I think that lurking about the place, being an irritating thorn in his proverbial side, as it were, might get the job done just as well.'

'And you've made certain that he sees you, I gather,' said the inspector.

'As often as possible.'

'In here on the night of the first performance, for instance?'

'And the second,' said Orum. 'Lurking, smiling, raising my glass – but never approaching him. Never giving him the satisfaction of a confrontation. Never giving him the chance to spin his lies and play the innocent party.'

'But you did approach Basil Newhouse once Cheetham had gone?'

'Of course. Basil and I were old pals. He'd worked with us since our earliest days in the theatre. I fell out with Cheetham, not the whole company. I wanted to congratulate him on the superb performance he gave in my story.'

'Was he pleased to see you?'

'Basil Newhouse was the very spirit of bonhomie. He was pleased to see everyone.'

'When did he leave the pub?'

'I'm afraid I have no idea, Inspector. I congratulated him, we reminisced briefly about the old days, and we assured one another that we should like to work together again in the future. Then I left him to his adoring public and took myself off to Bedfordshire.'

'Do you recall what time that was?'

'Two-ish?'

'And what about the next evening?'

'Much the same, but without dear Basil. I . . . ah . . . went to bed shortly after Cheetham and his ladies departed.'

'At around one o'clock, then,' said the inspector, still making his meticulous notes.

'If you say so,' said Orum. 'I confess I didn't trouble to look at the clock.'

'Did anyone see you go up?'

'Did anyone . . . ? Are you suggesting I might not be telling you the truth, Inspector?'

'No, sir, but corroboration would be helpful.'

'Dinah might have noticed.'

The inspector looked up from a brief re-examination of his notes. 'You seemed a little uncertain a moment ago.'

'I did? When?'

'When you mentioned retiring for the night.'

'Oh,' said Orum. 'Yes. I was trying to make up my mind whether it was worth the bother of telling you about my small misadventure. I decided it was too insignificant to trouble you with. Not germane to the case.'

'I should appreciate being given the opportunity to judge its pertinence for myself, sir, if you wouldn't mind.'

'Of course, of course. It was merely something that didn't happen. It had actually been my intention to take a walk before retiring last night. I find it clears my mind and helps me to sleep sometimes. I didn't go straight upstairs, you see. I left the pub by the side door and made to stride out into the chill night air, but I clattered into something in the dark and barked my shins. I was so annoyed that it quite spoiled the mood I was hoping to create within myself. I turned on my heel and limped back indoors.'

'And went straight to bed,' said the inspector.

'In high dudgeon.'

I filled the ensuing pause with a question of my own. 'What did you fall over?' I asked.

'Some damn fool had left a bi—' Orum paused for a moment, looking perplexed. 'A bicycle lying in the yard,' he concluded.

The inspector finished his note-taking and looked around.

'Thank you for your time, sir. I think I have everything I need now,' he said. 'There doesn't seem to be much chance of Miss Caudle returning. Would you be kind enough to let her know that I shall still wish to speak to her, please, sir?'

'Of course, Inspector. I'm happy to help in any way I can.'

'Thank you. I shall bid you good day. Will you be staying here at the pub?'

'I've booked my room until Saturday,' said Orum with a smile. 'The village's Bonfire Night celebrations are something to behold, so they say. I should like to experience the joy and excitement of a country Samhain before I return to the city.'

'Very good, sir,' said the inspector. 'I might call upon you again if I need any further clarification of events.'

'It would be my pleasure to see you.'

We stood to leave.

Outside, the inspector turned to Lady Hardcastle. 'Sarwin?'

She nodded towards me. 'I defer in all matters Celtic to my tiny Welsh associate,' she said.

'Samhain is the Irish festival to mark the beginning of winter,' I said. 'It actually falls on the first day of November – Lady Hardcastle and I were talking about *Nos Galan Gaeaf* only the other day.'

He looked blankly at me. 'I get the feeling you're teasing me, Miss Armstrong,' he said.

'It's the Welsh version,' I said. 'An ancient festival to mark the end of the light and the coming of the darkness. In our modern world it's All Hallows' Eve.'

'So why did he say it was tomorrow?'

'Because, my dear inspector,' said Lady Hardcastle, 'he's a pretentious old fool who doesn't know what he's talking about. He's playing a role.'

'He does seem a little . . . affected in his manner,' he said.

'Doesn't he just. And he forgets to do it sometimes. He wasn't nearly so flowery when we spoke to him yesterday. It's an act. A sham. Mummery and artifice, Inspector.'

'And all that nonsense about being reluctant to tell me anything before trotting it out like a music hall monologue. There's something not quite right about that fellow.'

'He's a cold-blooded one,' I said, 'for all his flowery pretension. It's one thing biffing your pal on the conk in the heat of the moment, but there's something altogether more sinister about the way he's following Mr Cheetham around and taunting him.'

We walked in contemplative silence back to the house, but not before the inspector had taken a good look around the yard at the side of the pub.

◆ ◆ ◆

Back at the house, the film folk were still closeted, Edna was still scrubbing the floor, and Miss Jones was reluctantly starting preparations for dinner in the 'contaminated kitchen'. Dewi and Dora had been recalled to The Grange to help the staff there deal with an undisclosed domestic emergency resulting from the rebuilding of the burned-out kitchen.

I made a pot of tea.

In the dining room, Lady Hardcastle was standing at the crime board, making notes on the 'timeline' at the bottom of the blackboard. '. . . and we still have these huge gaps here . . .' She pointed to the empty space between two and five in the early hours of Wednesday morning. 'And here . . .' She indicated a similarly blank space between two and six today.

'We do,' said the inspector. 'Then again, if we knew precisely what had happened between those times, we'd not be making notes on your blackboard; we'd be arresting the killer.'

'True, true,' she said. 'I can't get away from the idea that it was one of the film folk, though, you know.'

'Why's that?'

'Euphemia was killed in the house. In a locked kitchen. The only people who had access to her were here in the house with her.'

The inspector thought for a moment. 'But if it's poisoned apples, they wouldn't have had to get to her. Where do you get your apples?'

'Ah, yes,' I said, 'I've been meaning to mention that. We don't usually have apples in the house. We used to, but Miss Jones got fed up with no one eating them and cancelled the order.'

'So how did you come to have a bowlful?'

'It seems Dora Kendrick is partial to apples and was disappointed that we had none. She brought some from The Grange.'

'I see,' he said, and made a note. 'I don't suppose you know where they get their apples?'

'I couldn't say for certain,' I said. 'They have a few apple trees in the grounds, but they might just as easily have bought them from Weakley's in the village.'

'What's this Dora Kendrick like?' he asked.

'You would have spoken to her at The Grange when the trumpeter died at Clarissa Farley-Stroud's engagement party.'

'Ah, yes, I remember her. Impudent girl. Given to affected displays of emotion when she thought it might be to her advantage.'

'That's the one,' I said.

'Wasn't she carrying on with one of the musicians?'

'I congratulate you on your powers of recall, Inspector,' I said.

'I have my moments,' he said. 'Do you think this Kendrick girl capable of murder?'

I paused for a moment. 'I teased her about it when I found out that she was the source of the apples,' I said. 'But I can't say I was being serious.'

'Did she have anything against Euphemia Selwood?'

I paused again. 'Well . . .' I said 'Perhaps . . .'

'Go on.'

'The musician she was "carrying on with" at the party has been one of our houseguests. Barty Dunn. They ignored each other at dinner last night while Barty was flirting with Euphemia.'

'I've known men and women kill for less,' he said.

'True,' I said. 'And she did supply the deadly fruit.' Then a sudden realization hit me. 'Oh, but it could have been anybody – the door wasn't locked.'

'How do you know?' said Lady Hardcastle.

'Before I came up to wake you, I threw the bolt to make sure Edna and Miss Jones didn't blunder in on the body. When I let Edna in later, she said that she thought the lock was broken because she couldn't unlock the door. I didn't check it – I assumed it was simply that the door hadn't been locked in the first place. But that would mean that it had been unlocked all night. Anyone could have got in.'

'Or out,' she said. 'It's a big house. There are plenty of places to hide. Someone could have been lying in wait. Or was trapped when the film folk came home and hung around in the kitchen for so long. The murderer might have been doctoring the apples when they arrived and then, oh, I don't know, stolen into the larder to hide until they'd gone to bed and he could sneak back out through the side door. Well, there goes my hypothesis.'

'We should keep an open mind,' said the inspector. 'Very little can be ruled out at this stage. For myself, I'd put a small wager on Orum at the moment. There's something about that fellow that I don't trust.'

'Oh, he's definitely a cad,' she said. 'But if that were a crime, half the chaps I've ever met would be in chokey.'

'I dare say you're right, my lady,' he said. 'I was just—'

The ringing of the telephone derailed his train of thought.

'Excuse me,' I said. 'I'd better answer that.'

I returned a moment later.

'It's a call for you, Inspector,' I said. 'A Sergeant Williams. He says it's most urgent.'

'He's the duty sergeant back at Bristol. Steady chap. If he says it's urgent, then it must be urgent. Excuse me, ladies.'

He went through to the hall.

'Do you know what I wish?' said Lady Hardcastle while we awaited his return.

'Do you . . . Do you still wish you were a polar bear?'

She laughed. 'No.'

'Do you wish someone would invent a self-fitting corset? One day those laces will do for you.'

'I wish someone would decide that the wretched things had suddenly gone out of fashion, certainly. But no. I wish someone would invent some sort of truth drug. Oh, oh, or a mind-reading device. Does your man Jules Verne have anything like that? I find questioning these people so wearisome. I've had a lifetime of people lying to me. It would be lovely to talk to someone and know for certain whether they were telling the truth. And what the truth really was if they weren't.'

'That would be rather splendid, wouldn't it,' I said. 'Although we usually managed to get at the truth rather effectively in the old days.'

'In the end, yes. I always suspected it was a combination of things, you know. First there was the shock. Imagine yourself a foreign agent, captured out of the blue by who knows who, on information from who knows where. You're sitting there in some dank cellar, awaiting interrogation. You steel yourself, but you know you'll prevail. You've been questioned by the shrewdest of men. You've endured beatings from the toughest. And in walks a tall, staggeringly beautiful English lady—'

'You?'

'Of course it's me, silly. All elegance and charm and cheerful politeness. "This is going to be a piece of cake," you say to yourself. "This idiot woman doesn't stand a chance." And then her assistant arrives – a tiny little Welsh woman with a cheeky smile – and you say, "Well, if this is all they can muster, I'll be out of here in no time and all my secrets with me." But then crash-bang-wallop, a flurry of fists and elbows and you're lying face-down on the table with your arm in some fiendish Chinese hold. You feel as though it might be torn from its socket.'

I laughed. 'And that was the moment when you switched on the charm,' I said. 'You won their trust and they all but fell over themselves in their eagerness to tell you all about it.'

'Exactly so. Torture is overrated, I feel. It helps to be able to offer a credible threat of physical unpleasantness, but people do love to talk. Most especially about themselves and how clever they are.'

'True. But perhaps I should give Mr Orum a bit of a tickle. You know, just to let him know we mean business.'

'Perhaps you should.'

Our musings were cut short by the return of Inspector Sunderland. 'I'm so sorry,' he said, 'but I have to return to the city.'

'Oh dear,' said Lady Hardcastle. 'Nothing terrible, I hope.'

'Nothing "terrible", no, but one of my other cases is getting a bit lively. It looks like we might be able to nab a gang of counterfeiters if we're nimble. We've been working on this one for a couple of months and we've got word they're setting up their presses in an abandoned warehouse down by the docks.'

'Then we shall detain you no longer,' she said. 'You must be away. Although if you happen upon a couple of convincing-looking fivers while you're there, it's Armstrong's payday soon . . .'

'A tenner a week?' said the inspector with a laugh. 'I'm in the wrong game.'

'One can afford to be generous when it's fake money,' she said.

I gave a sarcastic smile. 'They'll never find your body, you know,' I said.

The inspector took a final sip of his tea. 'Well,' he said. 'I ought to be on my way. I'm sure they can collar the gang on their own, but I do like to be in at the kill, as it were.'

'Of course, Inspector,' said Lady Hardcastle. 'We quite understand. Is there anything we can do to help in the meantime?'

'Just carry on as you are, my lady,' he said. 'I know I can rely on you two.'

'Thank you, you're most kind.'

'There's one more thing, though,' he said with a smile.

'Name it, dear,' she said.

'Do you mind if I help myself to another slice of that cake?'

Chapter Eleven

Inspector Sunderland left with an extra piece of cake – '. . . for my wife, you understand; she's partial to fruit cake' – and our good wishes. Lady Hardcastle remained in the dining room to ruminate. I tidied away the tea tray and went to the kitchen to see if there was anything I could do to help there.

'Not really,' said Miss Jones when I made my offer. 'I reckon I has it all under control. I can't say as I'm not a little worried about our safety, mind.'

'Because of the murders?' I said.

'Of course. Two dead already. It could be any of us next.'

'If there is a "next",' I said. 'But so far it's been the two actors dying like their characters in the moving picture.'

'I knows what you're sayin', but we's all been in a movin' picture now, a'n't we? What if the murderer doesn't just hold a grudge against *The Witch's Downfall*, but against everythin' to do with the kinematograph? Lady Hardcastle filmed me guttin' a fish on Tuesday. What if you all wakes up tomorrow to find me hollowed out and stuffed with thyme and bay leaves? With my head on a dish for our ma's cat.'

'We'll find whoever's responsible long before your mother's cat eats your head for supper,' I said.

'Just see you do,' she said. 'I don't go in for none of that superstitious nonsense, but if there's a madman on the loose with a thing in his head about movin' pictures, we've all got to watch out.'

'I hadn't thought of it like that,' I said. 'I'll mention it to Lady Hardcastle. And what about you, Edna? Are you concerned?'

'Me, dear? No. I i'n't nearly interestin' enough to attract the attentions of no murderers. And she filmed me dustin' the bannisters. So unless you finds me stabbed through the heart with a feather duster, I reckons I'll be all right.'

'Right you are, then,' I said. 'We'll cross you off the list of possible victims. And what about work? Are you coping well enough without your assistants?'

''T i'n't so bad now we's only got two guests,' she said. 'We'll do just fine without they two from The Grange. I could live a long and happy life without either of 'em clutterin' up the place, to be truthful. Dewi's a nice enough lad, but he's mostly only any use for fetchin' things off high shelves. And that Dora. Well. Useless article. And so rude with it. 'T wouldn't break my heart if I never saw her again.'

'Shall I get Lady Hardcastle to pass word to The Grange that we have no further need of them?'

'It's up to you, Miss Armstrong, of course. But don't keep 'em on on my account.'

'Right you are,' I said. 'I'll see what Lady Hardcastle thinks. Our guests are leaving on . . . on . . . Actually I'm not sure if it's Saturday or Sunday now I come to say it out loud, but it's not long, anyway.'

'They's no trouble. Keeps their rooms tidy. I can cope.'

'Splendid. And how's your Dan? How's he coping?'

'There's another useless article. Let's just say it's not just the extra few bob a week that's makin' me grateful for the extra hours workin' y'ere.'

'He's a trial?' I suggested.

'He's a pain in the bloomin' backside, is what he is. All he does is moan and complain. It's a relief to be out of the house. Although he don't make that no easier. You'd think a man of his age would know how to boil a ham, or even push a broom round, wouldn't you? I works here all day – I'm not sayin' I minds, mind – and I get home to find . . . What do you think I finds?'

'That he's done the laundry, cleaned the house, and made you a delicious supper?'

She laughed. 'Ar, that'd be right. More likely I finds him sittin' in our front parlour suppin' cider with his mates and complainin' as how his dinner's not ready.'

It was my turn to laugh.

'If I didn't love the stupid great lump so much, I'd never put up with it,' she said. 'He still won't say how he come to break his leg in the first place, mind. I've given up askin'.'

'I thought you said he did it at work,' I said. 'He works on the Lock-Caradine farm, doesn't he?'

'It's just "Lock" now, m'dear. Noah and Audrey got wed.'

'That's right,' I said. 'I did know that. Sorry.'

'He works for them some of the time, but he's doin' odd jobs for Toby Thompson at the moment. Or he was.'

'I'm so sorry, you did say. Mr Thompson keeps dairy cattle, doesn't he? Dangerous things, cows.' I wasn't going to make much of it in front of Edna and Miss Jones, but I'm deathly afraid of cows.

'Trample you to death soon as bat their soppy great eyes at you,' she confirmed. 'But they's pretty much all brought in for the winter by now. No need for him to have anythin' to do with the cattle. No, I reckon he fell over doin' sommat foolhardy and he's too embarrassed to say what 't is. I'll get it out of him, mind, you'll see.'

'And what of you, young Miss Jones?' I said, turning to the cook. 'Are you coping?'

'I'm copin' just fine, Miss Armstrong,' she said. 'It's been no trouble feedin' the guests. They's got simple tastes. I could stand to be a bit more adventurous, to tell the truth, but I don't think they'd care for it much.'

'No, I don't think they would. And how's your mother? Is she getting along all right without you?'

'I know I shouldn't say it – on account of how it sounds selfish, like – but I'm almost disappointed by how well she's gettin' along without me. Part of me sort of hoped she'd be all of a tizzy, like, not havin' me around to fetch and carry for her, but it's almost like she don't need me.'

'I'm sure she does,' I said. 'I'm sure she's making a special effort to help you in your job. You'll be back to normal in no time.'

'Perhaps,' she said. 'Although if you decides you needs me here a little more even when the guests are gone, I'm not sure I'd say no.'

'I see. Well, I'll mention that to Lady Hardcastle, too.'

'What about you, my lover?' said Edna. 'How are you and Lady Hardcastle holdin' up? Are you any closer to findin' out who done these terrible things?'

'Sadly not,' I said. 'As usual we've got plenty of suspects but no real evidence. We were hoping that Dr Gosling's post-mortem examinations of the bodies would help but that all keeps getting delayed.'

'Can they tell much from a dead body, then?' asked Edna.

'They can usually find out what caused the person to die,' I said. 'Sometimes they can get a clearer idea of when they died, and what happened to them before and after.'

'After?' she said. 'Who'd want to know that?'

'They can sometimes tell if a body was moved. The way the bruises form is different after death.'

'Well I never. Who'd 'ave thought that? Did you know that, Miss Jones? Fascinatin', i'n't it?'

Miss Jones seemed less comfortable. 'I dare say,' she said uneasily. 'But they knows what happened, don't they? Mr Newhouse was stabbed through the heart and Miss Selwood was poisoned with an apple. You don't need to go cuttin' up no one's body to know that.'

I decided not to explain how you could find out when Mr Newhouse had been stabbed, and whether that was actually what had killed him or whether he had been killed by other means. The chest wound might have been inflicted after death to throw us off the scent.

And Euphemia, too. What poison was it? And was it really in the apple? Poisoning an apple in a basketful where it could be eaten by anyone seemed like a very poor plan. If it weren't for the fact that death-by-apple fitted Mr Newhouse's murder so perfectly – both of them dying the same way as their characters from the moving picture – it could have been that the apple was just a coincidence. Even if it were deliberate, though, there was no telling when and how she had been poisoned without a body to examine. The apple could just be a prop, the body staged – as we suspected Mr Newhouse's had been – for maximum impact. And we knew that the side door had been unlocked all night, so anyone could have arranged the murderous tableau.

'Did either of you buy the apples?' I asked.

'No,' said Miss Jones. 'You and me decided there weren't no point, seein' as no one was eatin' 'em.'

'I remember,' I said.

'Weren't me, neither,' said Edna. 'I can't abide apples. It's the texture. And that sour taste. They i'n't right.'

'Hmm,' I said. 'Well, will you excuse me, please, ladies?' I said. 'I need to speak to Lady Hardcastle.'

'Is everythin' all right?' said Edna.

'Fine, I think,' I said. 'I won't forget to mention what we talked about.'

I left them to their work and returned to the dining room, careful to close the door behind me.

'What's wrong, dear?' said Lady Hardcastle as I sat down opposite her.

'Wrong?' I said.

'You closed the door. Always a sign of impending wrong.'

'Or a draught.'

'It is a bit nippy,' she said. 'But I don't think it's draughts. You have something on your mind. It's a tiny head, but a mighty mind. Tell Emily all. Get it off your chest.'

'Is it on my mind or my chest?' I said.

'For all I know it might be large enough to cover your entire top half.'

'It's nothing profound,' I said. 'I was just thinking about the apple, that's all.'

'What about it?'

'Well, there's always the possibility that it might not even have been an apple that killed Euphemia . . .' I began.

'Great minds seem to be thinking alike again. I had a similar thought just before you returned.'

'Are any of the common poisons instantaneous?' I asked.

'Not really,' she said. 'In high enough doses, potassium cyanide works reasonably swiftly – a minute or so, perhaps – but twenty minutes is more likely. And if it were a high dose, we'd have smelled it. Almonds.'

'And the others?'

'As we found once before, they all take a while.'

'So if she were poisoned, it could have happened, say, at the pub?' I said.

'It could, indeed.'

'I'll talk to Daisy. She might have seen something.'

'That's not a bad idea,' she said. 'She's flighty, but observant.'

'She is.'

'On a more mundane domestic note, is everything in hand in the world of the serfs?'

'Miss Jones and Edna have everything under control. And stop calling them "the serfs".'

'Of course, dear. Whatever you say. And you have my permission to return to the pub and seek information from your pal.'

I turned to leave, but hesitated for a moment. Lady Hardcastle noticed.

'Is something wrong, dear?' she asked.

'Not "wrong" as such,' I said. 'But aren't you even just a little bit worried about this Günther Ehrlichmann business?'

'I can't deny that it's been on my mind, but it's all so dashed improbable. Impossible, even. Günther Ehrlichmann was shot through the head in front of a very reliable witness: you. He's dead. Whatever is going on in London, it doesn't involve him. I shall contact Harry once all this business is over and ask him what on earth he thinks he's playing at, sending our friends down here with ghost stories.'

'But shouldn't we—'

'Shouldn't we what, dear? Barricade the doors against some imagined Teutonic spectre?'

I smiled and took my leave. She was clearly in no mood to be argued with.

◆ ◆ ◆

I'd been itching to talk to Daisy ever since Wednesday morning, when Mr Newhouse's body was found. If anyone would know what had gone on in the pub on either night, it would be the World's Nosiest Barmaid. Especially if that same barmaid were also obsessed with the kinematograph. Frustratingly, though, I'd not yet had an opportunity for even the briefest chat.

It was five o'clock and already quite dark as I walked back around the green. It was none too warm, either, and I was glad of the blast of comparatively hot air as I opened the door to the public bar.

It was a tricky choice. I'd have more of an opportunity for a private chat with Daisy if I went into the snug, but I might run into Orum or Caudle in there. Out here in the public, the fire was bigger and brighter, the babble of conversation louder and more raucous, and the barmaid much busier. She was talking to one of the young farmhands who seemed to spend more time in the pub than in the fields.

I made my way to the bar and leaned across to attract her attention. She didn't see me.

I cleared my throat loudly and theatrically. 'Miss Spratt,' I said. 'Might I have a word?'

She turned from the young lad who was chatting her up, her face set in a glare and her lungs already filling in preparation for the rebuke she was about to deliver. And then she saw who had interrupted her flirting.

'Oh,' she said as her face brightened into a smile. 'It's you. Lovely to see you. How are you holdin' up? Must have been a shock findin' Euphemia Selwood like that.'

'Lovely to see you, too,' I said. 'And I'm fine, thank you. It seems to be the way of the world these days. For us, at least.'

'Trouble does seem to follow you, don't it?' she said. 'Anyway, what can I get you?'

'I'll have a brandy, please. And one for yourself.'

'I'll have a small cider, if that's all right. Anything else?'

'A few moments of your time?' I said.

She looked over at the handsome young labourer. 'Oh, go on, then,' she said after a few moments' thought. 'He'll be back.'

'Of course he will,' I said. 'You're a barmaid, and your dad's the local butcher. What more could any young man want?'

'I gots good looks and charm, an' all,' she said, striking a coquettish pose.

'In abundance. But that's not what I'm after.'

'No one ever is,' she said sadly.

'Oh, shush. I need your other great skill.'

'Which is?'

'You're . . . observant.'

'"Nosy", our ma says.'

'If I wasn't trying to butter you up, I would, too. But I need your help and so today you shall be observant; a seer of important things and a source of great knowledge.'

'As long as I can still be pretty and charmin', I can be as nosy as you likes,' she said.

'You're a goddess made flesh. And not one of the crusty old ones, either. So? What have you seen?'

'I seen everythin',' she said. 'I'n't nothin' goes on in here as I don't notice. What do you need?'

'You were working in here after both kinematograph shows, weren't you?' I asked.

'I was. Old Joe give me a couple of hours off both nights, seein' as how most of the village was goin' to be in the hall anyway. So long as I come back when it finished – to take care of the rush, like – he didn't mind. He's a good sort, Old Joe.'

'That he is,' I agreed. 'We're trying to piece the events of both evenings together. Everyone who was anyone seems to have come in here after the shows, so I thought, "Who's most likely to have seen all the comings and goings? That'll be my pal Daisy." So here I am.'

'You interested in anyone in particular?' she said, leaning forwards conspiratorially.

'Aaron Orum,' I said.

She stood up straight. 'I *knew* it,' she said. 'I've never trusted him. You reckon it was him, then?'

'We reckon we don't know what he was up to, that's all. On Tuesday night he says he waited till Cheetham and the others had gone before going over and speaking to Basil Newhouse.'

''S right. I seen him come through from the snug just after they left. It was packed in here so we had the door open between the bars. He must 'ave seen 'em leavin'. Been waitin' for his chance, like.'

'Did you hear what he said?'

'Not from over y'ere. It was heavin', like I said. Our ma would know, mind. She was there moonin' over Mr Newhouse. Our dad's been teasin' her sommat rotten.'

'Will she be in the shop?'

'Should be. He'll be closin' up soon, but she stays and finishes the books for him so she'll be there a while. Just bang on the door – they'll let you in.'

'Thank you. The next night he says he went up to bed earlier.'

'He did. Sloped off out the back once Cheetham had gone.'

'He says he started to go for a walk, but turned back when he fell over a bicycle in the yard.'

'He's a liar, then,' she said confidently. 'Ain't never been no bicycles in our yard. I know they's popular, but I don't reckon I knows anyone round y'ere who owns a bicycle. Mrs Bland might. Come to think of it, yes, I seen her ridin' a bicycle round the village. But she never brings it here. Why would she? They only lives round the corner. Not that she ever comes in, mind. Are vicars allowed to drink? I was surprised they was even allowed to get wed, but our ma told me that was just the Catholic ones.'

'She's right,' I said. 'And I believe there are no restrictions on drinking in moderation.'

'That's not what that shower outside the village hall reckons,' she said. 'They said we all needed to repent for seein' the movin' pictures, and that we was only compoundin' our sins by finishin' the evenin' takin' strong drink and carousin' till all hours.'

'They didn't join you, then?' I asked.

She laughed. 'You're kiddin'.'

'I suppose so. I just remembered they were gone by the time we left the village hall on Tuesday. No idea where they went?'

'They's all stayin' at the old Seddon place on the way to Chippin'. Some rich bloke from the city bought it when the Seddons moved out. He's got somethin' to do with their group. They all decamps up there of a night-time afore it gets too cold.'

'Do any of them have a bicycle?' I asked.

'Not so far as I've seen,' she said. 'They just marches on to their charabanc in orderly fashion and clanks off up the road. Don't seem to need no bicycles.'

'I wonder what Orum was on about, then.'

'Just makin' it up. He wanted to make out he'd had to come straight back in in case anyone saw him goin' out. Really, he was comin' over to your house to poison Miss Selwood.'

'Steady on,' I said with a laugh. 'We can't jump to conclusions. But it does seem like an odd thing to lie about. Makes you wonder what he was really up to.'

'Murderin' Miss Selwood,' she insisted. 'Like I said.'

'All right, let's say he was. Why?'

'Why do any murderers do what they do?' she said. 'They're mad. No sane person would kill someone.'

'You'd be surprised,' I said. 'Did you notice anything else, though? Any other suspicious goings-on?'

'I noticed that my best pal and her mistress didn't bother to come in and see me.'

'That's not all that suspicious, though. We often don't come and see you.'

'No,' she said sadly. 'I know. Oh, tell you what. You mentioned the crowd over by the village hall with their placards and that—'

'*You* did.'

'Did I? Well, now I come to think of it, I reckon I saw one of 'em peerin' in the window Tuesday night. The head bloke.'

189

'Hughes?' I suggested.

'Is that his name?' she asked. 'Him and his wife seem to be in charge.'

'Yes, that's Hughes. When was this?'

'After midnight, I reckon.'

'We all left the village hall by ten,' I mused. 'And they were all gone by then. And if the rest of them went to the old Seddon house in the charabanc, why was Hughes still hanging around in the village? And was he alone?'

'He's in it with Orum,' declared Daisy. 'They teamed up. Solves both their problems, don't it? Orum gets rid of his rival and Hughes gets rid of the "pedlars of filth", or whatever it is he calls 'em.'

'Maybe,' I said slowly. 'Except Cheetham is alive and well, and tucking in to Miss Jones's finest culinary creations at our house. And the filth is still being peddled. More so than ever now that the story is coming to life in our own village.'

'Well, I give up, then,' she said.

The impatient tapping on the bar of an empty tankard made her suddenly aware of her duties.

'I'd better see to that,' she said. 'Sorry, my lover.' She stopped and turned back towards me. 'We're safe, i'n't we?'

'Safe?' I said.

'From murder. There's two down and no one knows who's responsible. Any of us could be next.'

'Miss Jones said much the same thing a little while ago. It seems to be connected to the moving picture, though. I think you're fine.'

She pursed her lips pensively. ''Cept we've all been in a movin' picture now your mistress has been out with her camera,' she said.

'Yes, Miss Jones made that observation as well. But, really, I think we're all fine.'

'You might be,' she said. 'You and your Oriental fisticuffs and whatnot would be safe from anyone. But what about the rest of us?'

'Go and serve your customer,' I said. 'I'm off to see your mother.'
I left her to the attentions of the handsome farmhand and his
empty glass.

◆ ◆ ◆

The butcher's shop was, as I had been warned, already shut by the time
I got there. There was light peeping round the blinds, though, so I
took Daisy's advice and rapped sharply on the door. After a short delay,
the blind was pulled aside, and an angry face peered out at me. Either
it was an inherited trait or Eunice Spratt had taught her daughter the
'you'd better have a good reason for interrupting me' scowl because the
face looking through the glass of the shop door was nearly identical to
the one that had glared at me across the bar a few minutes earlier. It
softened just as quickly into the same welcoming smile when she realized it was me.

She fussed with the bolts and opened the door.

'Evenin' m'dear,' she said warmly. 'We've packed up for the day but
I dare say we could find a little sommat, seein' as it's you.'

'Don't worry, Mrs Spratt,' I said. 'I wasn't after meat.'

'Oh, that's all right, then. Our Daisy's up the pub.'

'I wasn't after her, either. Actually, I've just been talking to her. It
was you I wanted to see. May I come in?'

She opened the door and stood aside. 'Come on in, my lover. Me
and Fred's just doin' the books. I wants to get 'em done early so's we can
go to the picture show again. We a'n't 'ad this much fun in the village
since I don't know when. Even with the tragedies, an' all. I mean, I don't
want to sound callous nor nothin', but I do love a kinematograph show.
What is it they say? The show must go on? And it's been so popular since
the murders. Loads more people is comin' now than they did when it
started. I wonder if we should have a collection or sommat? You know,
raise a few bob for their families and that. What do you reckon, my

lover? Is that a good idea? I don't know what sort of people they was. Do they do that sort of thing? We usually does round y'ere, don't we, Fred?' She paused momentarily, as though gathering breath for another bombardment but seemed to be overcome by an uncharacteristic moment of self-awareness. 'But listen to me gabblin' on,' she said. 'What can we do for you? More meat, is it?'

'Oh,' I said. 'No, thank you. I think we have enough to be getting on with. I just wanted to ask you a couple of questions.'

'You're no trouble. Is she, Fred?'

Fred looked up from scrubbing the heavy wooden block behind the counter. 'Eh?' he said.

'I said, Miss Armstrong i'n't no trouble.'

'No trouble at all,' he said. 'Can we get you anythin'? I made some lovely sausages today, if I do say so myself.'

'She don't want no meat,' said Mrs Spratt impatiently. She turned to me. 'I'm sure he's goin' a bit deaf, you know.' And then louder. 'She wants to talk to me.'

I could have sworn that they'd all been concerned that she was the one who was going deaf. Perhaps I'd misremembered.

He returned to his scrubbing. 'I'll let you get on with it, then, my little apple blossom.'

'What is it you wanted to ask?' she said as she settled back to her bookkeeping. 'You don't mind me carryin' on with this, do you?'

'Not at all,' I said. 'I was just in the Dog and Duck talking to Daisy—'

'She could talk the hind legs off a donkey, that one. Chatters on nineteen to the dozen for hours on end, she does.'

I could see where she got it from. 'Yes,' I said, 'she does like to talk. We're trying to help Inspector Sunderland with the murders—'

'Terrible business, that,' she interrupted. 'Mind, I can't say as I'm surprised. I mean, I likes a good scary story as much as the next woman, but when you messes with the supernatural like that, well, sommat bad's goin' to 'appen, i'n't it?'

I frowned.

'It were witchcraft what done for him,' she said, as though this constituted a complete explanation. 'And for poor Euphemia Selwood. Dark forces was summoned. And so close to All Hallows' Eve. That's when they's at their most powerful, see?'

'I think we ought to keep an open mind about the cause of death,' I said. 'At least until the police have completed their investigation.'

'You keep your open mind, m'dear,' she said. 'But I's tellin' you it's witchcraft. You mark my words.'

'Consider them marked, Mrs S,' I said with a wink.

'You just be sure to tell your Inspector Whatshisname. He might be goin' off on entirely the wrong track.'

'He might at that,' I said.

Mr Sprat looked up and rolled his eyes – his seemed to be selective deafness. It also seemed that the supernatural was clearly a recurring theme in the Spratt household, and one which he had no great patience with.

I decided to try to return us to less occult ground. 'Daisy said you were talking to Basil Newhouse on Tuesday night after the show.'

Mr Spratt gave a little snort of laughter.

'I was,' said Mrs Spratt. 'And you can shut your gob, Frederick Spratt. He's been teasin' I sommat rotten. I was only chattin'. He was a lovely bloke, that Basil, God rest his soul. Charmin', he was.'

'"Basil", eh?' said Mr Spratt, still amused.

'You show a bit of respect,' she snapped.

'And you were still talking to him when Aaron Orum came over?' I asked.

'I was, yes. He's a nasty piece of work, that one.'

'Orum?' I said. 'How so?'

'Basil told us all about how he fell out with that nice Mr Cheetham, and then he comes over, bold as brass, as if they'd never had a cross word, and starts chattin' to Basil like they was still best pals.'

'It was a cordial conversation, then?'

'As cordial as you please,' she said. 'They talked about some mutual friends from the old days, about the kinematograph – Orum was very complimentary about that. Then Orum asks him where they's all stayin', and was it far, and was it nice? And then he asks him what time he was plannin' to head back to Lady Hardcastle's and maybe . . . they . . . should . . .' Her voice trailed off.

'What is it, Mrs Spratt?' I said.

'It was him, weren't it?' she said. 'He read all they books on witchcraft when he was workin' with Cheetham. He knows the spells as good as anyone. He was tryin' to make sure Basil would be on his own so he could lure him to the old rowan and murder him. Powerful magic, they are, rowan trees. And in the churchyard, an' all. Magnifies the power, it does.'

I was happy to let her have her witchcraft fantasy, but she had managed to make Orum's actions sound very suspicious. If she'd remembered correctly, then he'd gone to a great deal of trouble to find out about Basil Newhouse's movements. At best it was a little impertinent, even for an old friend. At worst it was downright sinister.

'I'm sure we'll get to the bottom of it,' I said. 'And I'm sure there'll be no more witchcraft to worry about. Do you remember anything else?'

'No, my lover,' she said. 'That was it. Fred and I left soon after that and we never saw poor Basil again.'

'Righto,' I said cheerily. 'I'll leave you to your work. Thank you.'

'My pleasure,' she said. 'Always happy to help Lady Hardcastle.'

I left the shop and walked back up the lane to the house. I briefly wondered how someone who was so convinced that the moving picture had unleashed a terrible evil could be contemplating going back to the village hall to see it again. But that was a fool's errand. If people were easy to fathom, there'd be nothing for the likes of us to do.

◆ ◆ ◆

Back at the house, Lady Hardcastle was still in the dining room, staring at the crime board.

'That was quick,' she said as I entered.

'I've been gone an hour,' I replied, slightly puzzled.

'Have you, by jingo? Well I never. How time flies when you're . . .'

'Completely baffled?' I suggested.

'Like His Majesty's Mediterranean Fleet on manoeuvres.'

'All at sea?'

'All, as you so perspicaciously say, at sea. Two bodies in two days and no earthly idea what's going on.'

'Apart from witchcraft,' I said.

'Well, there's that, of course.'

'Eunice Spratt is convinced of it.'

'I yield to no man in my admiration of dear Eunice Spratt. Fred might have mastered the arcane arts of butchery, but everyone knows that his shop would have floundered decades ago without Eunice's guiding hand upon the tiller. But while I am in awe of her business acumen, I'm less than impressed by her . . . How shall I put this without sounding like a thoroughgoing snob?'

I shrugged.

'When it comes to matters of science, her wits seem to fail her,' she continued. 'If an unscrupulous trader should try to swindle her husband with sub-standard beef, she'd see through him in an instant and send him packing. But one mention of ghosties, ghoulies, or long-leggedy beasties and she turns into the very worst sort of credulous ninny. Look how she fell for the nonsense that medium was peddling in the spring.'

'Credulous, yes, but reliable when it comes to the mundane. She says that Newhouse and Orum got on like old pals, and that Orum was especially interested in Newhouse's movements – where he was staying, when he was coming back here, that sort of thing.'

'And she thinks he was trying to fathom where and when best to attack him with witchcraft?'

'It is a little fishy,' I said.

'It's also the perfectly ordinary curiosity of an old friend. I don't think we can draw any conclusions from it.'

'Actually, I agree. But it does make me want to go to the show again this evening to see if we can keep an eye on him and find out what he's up to.'

'Oh, I say, what a wheeze,' she said. 'Shall we dog him like in the old days? I've not forgotten the old tricks, you know. I quite fancy a bit of cloak and dagger.'

'Well . . .' I said slowly, '. . . we can if you wish. But I had it in mind that we'd just go to the show, watch the pictures, and then tag along when everyone went to the pub afterwards. I'm not sure we'll need any advanced espionage techniques.'

'I suspect you're right, as always,' she said. 'It means we'll have to dine early, though.'

'Or late.'

'That may be preferable. To tell the truth, I'm still rather stuffed from lunch. Can you alert Miss Jones to our new plans, please? I'll consult the film folk.'

'What's left of them,' I said.

'I know. One feels partly responsible. They were staying under our roof, after all. We offered them our hospitality and two of them ended up dead as doornails.'

'We offered them a room for the night and a few meals, not a body-guard and around-the-clock protection from footpads and brigands.'

'Or witches,' she said.

'Especially not witches,' I agreed. 'I don't have the training.'

'I think you'd make a rather splendid little witch.'

I frowned.

'You're wily. Cunning. Agile . . .'

'Sounds more like a fox than a witch,' I said.

'Ooh, yes. With a big bushy tail. I think you should abandon your witchy ambitions and consider a career as a fox. Or a badger. I do love badgers.'

'I'll make the arrangements for supper, shall I?'

'Right you are, dear,' she said. 'I'll be upstairs. I think I ought to change.'

'If I were a witch,' I said as I left the room, 'I could change you into a sane woman.'

'Now where would be the fun in that?' she called. 'You'd tire of me in no time.'

I think I probably would, too.

Chapter Twelve

Miss Jones agreed to lay on a help-yourself supper for our return so I went up to help Lady Hardcastle get ready for an evening at the 'cinema show'.

'Ah, there you are,' she said as I entered the bedroom. 'Just in time. Do you think you might be able to work some of your magic on my hair, my little witch? It looks simply frightful.'

'It does look a little . . . nestlike,' I said. 'I fear that nestiness may well be its natural state, though. We seem to be fighting a constant battle to maintain it in a presentable condition.' I took up a hairbrush and began to 'work my magic'.

'Have you ever considered,' I said as I tugged at a particularly obdurate knot, 'simply embracing the chaos? You could cultivate your "batty old biddy" persona and allow your barnet to grow wild and free. It would save us hours.'

'It's not so much of a problem in the daytime when one can wear a hat,' she said. 'I used to wonder about cutting it all off and buying a selection of wigs to suit all evening occasions, but there's a degree of maintenance required there, too. No, for now I think I shall rely upon my faithful handmaid.'

'Very good, my lady,' I said, and continued brushing.

'Is Miss Jones amenable to our dining plans?'

'She is,' I said. 'And the film folk?'

'I knocked upon the morning room door, but answer came there none. When I opened the door, I found the room empty and our guests flown. They must have gone out while I was pondering.'

'You do get lost in your ponderings.'

'It takes a great deal of mental energy to ponder with such intensity,' she said. 'There's none to spare to pay attention to the comings and goings of houseguests. But no matter. We shall take their departure as an indication that they had no desire for an early dinner. We can give them the good news about Miss Jones's late supper when we see them at the village hall.'

By this time, my work was almost done. 'There,' I said as I pinned up the last loose lock. 'That's the best I can do without the aid of scaffolding and heavy machinery.'

She regarded herself in the glass. 'It looks marvellous, dear, thank you. The green dress with the embroidered skirt, I think.'

'Or the blue with the Chinese collar?'

'Whichever you think best, dear,' she said.

'Blue it is, then.'

Fifteen minutes later we were both dressed and ready for an evening out. Edna and Miss Jones had already set off for the village hall so I locked the doors and we made our way down the lane to the village green.

It was another crisp, cloudless evening. There was a huge full moon high in the sky, which bathed the village in a pleasing pale-blue light. Dirtier, yellowish light seeped from the pub's grubby windows on the eastern side of the green, and another pool of it spilled from the open doors of the village hall to the north.

'You were out earlier, dear,' said Lady Hardcastle as we approached the green. 'Is it still too muddy to walk on the grass?'

'I should say so, yes. The going is soft-to-heavy.'

'We should save our boots, then,' she said, and began to follow the road.

As we neared the Dog and Duck, we heard a commotion from within. Loud shouts and at least one scream were accompanied by the sound of furniture being hastily shoved aside and more than one glass breaking. We stopped on the pavement as the door ahead of us flew open and Aaron Orum came haring out.

'Help me!' he screamed. 'The demons! Demons from Hell!' He took off towards the church at the sort of pace that indicated that he really did believe he was being pursued by demons. A gaggle of bemused pub-goers followed him out on to the pavement, still clutching their drinks. They did not give chase.

'I say!' called Lady Hardcastle. 'Mr Arnold?'

'Old' Joe Arnold, the toothless landlord, had accompanied his bewildered clientele through the door. "Ow do, m'lady,' he said.

'What on earth's going on?' she asked.

'Couldn't rightly say,' he replied. 'One minute he's eatin' his pie in the snug, next thing we know he goes roarin' out through the public, screamin' as how the demons is gonna get 'im.'

Dinah Caudle, dressed far too glamorously for a pie and a pint in a village pub, barged her way through the throng. The diamonds at her throat twinkled in the lantern light.

'Out of my way, you useless articles,' she said. 'Why didn't any of you try to help him? Where's he gone?'

By this time, Orum had reached the church and we could hear him hammering at the huge oak doors.

'We ought to get after him,' said Lady Hardcastle. 'Come on, Armstrong, before he does himself a mischief. You'd better come with us, Miss Caudle. You might be able to help.'

With that, she hoisted her skirt and set off at a brisk trot towards the church on the other side of the green. I sighed and followed, with Miss Caudle not far behind me.

Orum's hammering had got him nowhere and he belatedly thought to try the door handle instead. The church door opened and he disappeared quickly inside.

The commotion had attracted the attention of the Hugheses and their gaggle of protesters, who had no audience for their protest anyway – the few early-arriving moving picture lovers were diverting from the village hall towards the church gate.

By the skilful deployment of her loud, commanding voice, and some of the rucking techniques she had learned from the Littleton Cotterell rugby team earlier in the year, Lady Hardcastle managed to get past the gathering throng, through the lych gate, and up to the door before any of them had a chance to object. She tried the handle.

'It's locked,' she panted. 'He's bolted the door.'

'I'd lock the door if demons were after me,' I said, somewhat less breathlessly.

'How is it that we've run the same distance but you're not puffed?' she said.

'Because I'm ten years younger than you and don't spend all day sitting on my ever-expanding backside?'

'That'll be it,' she said distractedly as she stepped back for a better look at the church. 'As long as there's a satisfactory explanation.'

Miss Caudle, similarly winded, had finally caught up with us.

'Are you two just going to stand there chattering?' she panted. 'Or are you going to take this seriously?'

Lady Hardcastle ignored her. 'How do you suppose we get in now?' she said. 'The vestry door, perhaps?'

'Perhaps,' I said. 'Although I'd keep it locked if I were the vicar.'

'You could never be a vicar, dear. You're too short to see over the lectern.'

'I would stand on a box.'

Miss Caudle let out an exasperated 'Argh', and pushed her way back into the crowd to try to get a better view.

Lady Hardcastle made to set off in the other direction towards what I always thought of as the 'rear' of the church, where the vestry door might afford entry. She drew up short when we heard a collective gasp from the small group of onlookers who were still outside the gate and could see more of the church building than we could.

Looking up, we just about managed a glimpse of Aaron Orum at the top of the church tower, silhouetted against the full moon. We went back out of the gate and on to the road with the others to get a better view.

Orum leaned over the parapet and paused for a moment, apparently scanning for signs of his Mephistophelian pursuers. It seemed as though he had calmed down and that he finally thought himself safe from whatever hellish beasts had chased him from the pub.

And then, with a sudden, soul-wrenching scream, he lurched away from the parapet and launched himself towards the other side of the tower. Out of sight now, he screamed again, but this time the sound was behind the church. Abruptly, it stopped.

We stood for a moment, transfixed by the shock of what we all knew had just happened. The spell was broken by a scream from one of Hughes's retinue. As one, we all took a step towards the church gate, but once again our progress was halted, this time by a blast from a police whistle.

'Stay where you are, please, ladies and gentlemen,' barked Sergeant Dobson in his most commanding parade ground voice. 'Constable Hancock and I will deal with this.'

There were mutinous mutterings from some in the small crowd, but, despite the understandable urge to find out what had happened, they seemed inclined to obey the authoritative voice of the policeman. Or perhaps it was the dawning realization of what they might find were they to go round to the other side of the church. I doubted many of them had seen a body broken by a fall, but I credited them with enough imagination to know that it wasn't something they would want to witness first-hand.

Sergeant Dobson, with Constable Hancock trailing obediently behind, pushed his way through the crowd and took up position in front of the lych gate.

'Go on, lad,' he said quietly to the constable. 'Take a look and report back.'

I couldn't make out the constable's expression in the dim moonlight, but from the sound of his timorous 'Right you are, Sarge', I guessed it wasn't a happy one. Nevertheless, he pushed open the gate and cautiously disappeared from view behind the church.

'I say! Sergeant?' Lady Hardcastle had to raise her voice above the growing hubbub.

'Lady 'ardcastle?' replied the sergeant. 'Are you here?'

'Yes, Sergeant,' she said. 'And Armstrong, too.'

He turned towards us. 'Make way there, if you please,' he said. 'Let them through.'

The crowd parted obediently and we made our way forwards to where he stood under the cover of the church gate.

'Thank goodness you got here so quickly, Sergeant,' said Lady Hardcastle. 'I shouldn't have liked to try to control even this small a mob on my own.'

'We was . . . nearby when the commotion started,' he said. I took this to mean that he and his colleague had been celebrating the end of their shift with a swift one in the Dog and Duck.

'Were you near enough to see what set him off?' I asked.

'As far as I know, he was eatin' his supper in the snug and then just went doolally. Screamin' and shoutin', wild-eyed and rantin'.'

'About demons,' said Lady Hardcastle.

'Sommat like that,' said the sergeant.

'What was he eating?' I asked. 'I believe Old Joe said it was a pie. Do you know what sort?'

'Joe was servin' his famous chicken and mushroom pie this evenin'. Lovely bit of grub, that. I was lookin' forward to a bit of pie meself, later.'

'Mushrooms again?' I said.

'You don't think . . . ?' said Lady Hardcastle.

'Well, he wasn't being chased by actual demons, was he?' I said. 'Something drove him over the edge. Aren't there mushrooms that make you hallucinate?'

She thought for a while. 'I think so,' she said at length. 'Though not round here. I recall reading accounts of religious ceremonies among the Indian tribes in America. I'm sure they use some sort of mushroom in their rituals. But that's in the southwestern United States, I think. The . . . No, it's no good, I can't remember the tribe. But it can't be that – I think we've just got mushrooms on the brain.'

'It might be worth letting Dr Gosling examine the pie, though,' I said. 'We lose nothing by being thorough.'

'If Joe hasn't thrown it away already,' said the sergeant, 'I'll lock it up as evidence.'

'Good man,' said Lady Hardcastle.

Constable Hancock reappeared from behind the church.

'You'd better come and look, Sarge,' he said.

'Is he . . . ?' said Dobson.

The constable nodded weakly. 'I didn't want to get up too close, like. I . . . umm . . . I didn't want to disturb the body. I threw my great-coat over it to save anyone from 'avin' to see.'

To save himself from having to see, more like, I thought. Not that he'd have been able to see much in the pitch dark without a lantern.

'I don't want nothin' goin' wrong with this one,' said the sergeant. 'You keep guard over the body and I'll take care of this lot here.'

Constable Hancock retreated reluctantly to his new post.

There was a kerfuffle at the front of the crowd and Dinah Caudle pressed her way through.

'Is he . . .' she said, her voice barely above a whisper.

The sergeant regarded her kindly. 'I'm afraid so, miss,' he said. 'But it would have been instant. If it's any comfort, he wouldn't have suffered.'

'It isn't,' she said.

I heard her sniff quietly, but she said no more. When I looked back towards where she'd been standing, she was gone, melted back into the crowd.

Sergeant Dobson returned to practical matters.

'Might I beg a favour of you, m'lady?' he said.

'Anything, Sergeant, you know that.'

'It's just that there's only the two of us and we'd both better stay here to keep things under control. I know you gets on well with Inspector Sunderland – would it be too much trouble for you to telephone him and let him know what's happened, please? I think this might well be somethin' that would interest him, given the circumstances.'

'It's no trouble at all,' she said.

'Thank you, m'lady. The station's unlocked and the telephone . . . Well, you knows how to use the telephone.'

'Leave it to us, Sergeant. Come on, Armstrong. Let's give the inspector the bad news.'

We set off towards the small village police station.

◆ ◆ ◆

Inspector Sunderland wasn't available. The desk sergeant who answered the telephone told Lady Hardcastle that he had left the station on 'important business' and wasn't expected back before morning. She left a message outlining the evening's events and we returned to the church.

With the village policemen on guard and preventing access to the churchyard, there was nothing to see. With nothing to see, there was little for the small crowd to do but speculate wildly about what might have driven the flamboyant visitor to jump to his death from the top of the church tower. And wild speculation was just as easy in the warmth and comparative comfort of the Dog and Duck. Easier, perhaps, with Old Joe's finest beer and cider to loosen the speculation muscles.

We arrived to find no one but Sergeant Dobson at the church gate.

'Where did everyone go?' asked Lady Hardcastle.

'To the pub,' said the sergeant wistfully.

'Even Hughes and the protesters?'

'I'n't nothin' to protest about,' he said. 'The picture show's been cancelled. Whatshisname . . . that Cheetham fella . . . He came out and told 'em it was all off. Didn't take 'em all long to work out they'd be better off over the road with a roarin' fire at their back and a pint in their hand.'

'Where did Mr Cheetham go?' I asked.

'Back to your place, far as I could make out. Him and that lovely Zelda woman. I lost sight of 'em in the gloom but they was headin' that way.'

'We'll catch up with them in a moment,' said Lady Hardcastle. 'I'm afraid Inspector Sunderland wasn't in the office but I left a message with the sergeant there. I suggested we take the body to Dr Fitzsimmons's surgery for safekeeping, but he was insistent that the new mortuary was the only place for it and that he'd send the wagon without delay. You shouldn't have to wait too long.'

'Right you are, m'lady,' said the sergeant. 'I reckon I'll leave it to young Hancock. Don't seem much point in my hangin' about now that everyone's dispersed. I'll give him the good news about the mortuary wagon and then . . .'

'Back to the Dog and Duck?' I suggested.

'Just for a quick one,' he said. 'Medicinal purposes.'

'Very well, then,' said Lady Hardcastle. 'We'll get back to the house and make sure that Mr Cheetham and Miss Drayton are being looked after. I'm sure we'll see you tomorrow. This is a bad business and I aim to get to the bottom of it.'

The sergeant touched his fingertip to the brim of his police helmet in a loose salute and we left him to his duties.

◆ ◆ ◆

We found Nolan Cheetham and Zelda Drayton in the kitchen, silently eating some of the cold supper left for us by Miss Jones.

'I hope you don't mind us starting without you,' said Zelda. 'For all the shock, it turned out we were starving hungry.'

'Not at all,' said Lady Hardcastle as we joined them at the kitchen table. 'I'm just sorry that we can't eat together in happier circumstances. I know you had all fallen out with Mr Orum, but the loss of a friend, even a former friend, must come hard after losing two even closer friends. You have our deepest sympathy.'

'Thank you,' said Cheetham. 'But we soldier on.'

'You do seem to,' said Lady Hardcastle. 'I'm not certain I could find the strength.'

'It shames me to have to admit it,' said Zelda, 'but I'm actually sort of relieved it wasn't me. I fully expected to be next. Burned alive, I thought.' She shuddered. 'But we're show business folk, I suppose, and the show must go on.'

'We lived by that in the circus,' I said.

'You're from the circus?' she said.

'My family,' I replied. 'My father was a knife thrower. My sister and I were born on the road.'

'I thought I'd heard you say you were from Wales.'

'I usually say it like that. It's easier to explain. My mother was from Aberdare and we left the circus and returned to her home when my grandmother fell ill.'

'Well I never,' she said. 'I did a stint with a circus show, you know.'

'Did you really?' said Lady Hardcastle. 'I sometimes envy you show business types, you know. There are so many exciting opportunities. One would think it was just the stage, but here you are working in moving pictures and now we learn that you once worked in a circus. It's all so glamorous.'

'I worked in a circus,' I said.

'And it was as glamorous as can be,' she said. 'I often wonder how you put up with the mundanities of normal life.'

'I enjoy looking after you,' I said, without thinking. We were in danger of becoming far too mawkish if we carried on down that road, so I quickly brought us back to the original path. 'What did you do in the circus, Miss Drayton?'

'My sisters and me used to do a humorous tumbling act in the music halls. You know, pratfalls and the like. The set-up was that we were a straight act but we kept getting it wrong. It was all carefully worked out. One night a bloke comes up to us backstage and asks if we fancy doubling our money working in his travelling circus. So we gave the theatre a week's notice and went off to seek our fortune.'

'The freedom of the open road,' said Lady Hardcastle. 'The romance of the travelling showman. Show-woman.'

'Something like that, yes.'

'I take it from your disconsolate tone that things did not turn out quite the way you had hoped.'

'Sadly not,' said Zelda. 'There are wonderful circuses out there. I'm sure your memories are much fonder than ours, Flo. But "tawdry", "shambles", and "penniless" would be three good words for Harry Hopwood's Cavalcade of Wonders. We stuck it for two weeks before running back to the music halls as fast as our legs could carry us.'

'What a shame,' said Lady Hardcastle. 'Still, no experience is wasted. I'm sure you gained something from it.'

'Unfortunately, yes. I said we ran back to the halls, but in actual fact I hobbled. I caught my ankle funny one night when we were trying out a new bit for the act. What we did was fine for the theatre, but it needed to be bigger for the circus. I overdid it and haven't been the same since. That was how I got into acting, see? Our tumbling trio became a daring duo and I picked up work here and there in comic skits and the like. Then one day, I just said, "Zelda, my girl, you can spend your days picking up crumbs from other acts' tables, or you can make something of yourself." So I auditioned for a repertory company down on the south coast, and never looked back.'

'I say. Well done, you,' said Lady Hardcastle.

'And that's when I saw her,' said Cheetham. 'I'd been ill and my doctor said as how a bit of sea air would work wonders. He recommended Blackpool but I've always been one for travel, so I went south. As it happened, Aaron and I were looking for a leading lady for one of our shows and when I saw this one in that little seaside theatre . . . well . . .'

'How very splendid,' said Lady Hardcastle delightedly. 'I rather miss travelling, you know. We should take a trip, Flo.'

'I've not seen nearly so much of the world as you seem to have,' he said.

'I don't know about that. I've mostly travelled eastwards. With the exception of a few months at the embassy in Washington with Roddy, half the planet remains entirely Emily-free.'

'Whereas I've only really been westwards,' he said. 'I was lucky enough to be able to visit America.'

'How exciting. Did your work take you there?'

'It did, yes. I wanted to see how they made moving pictures out there. It was an eye-opener, I can tell you, and New Jersey is going to be the moving picture capital of the world.'

'New Jersey, you say? I should have thought New York City would be the place.'

'No,' he said with an indulgent smile. 'Mr Thomas Edison's company controls the moving picture patents and they're based in New Jersey. It's going to become the richest place in the whole of the country once cinema really takes off, you mark my words.'

'Then we shall most certainly add it to our itinerary. Did you visit anywhere else?'

'No. Sadly, I didn't have the funds. But the cinema industry is attracting storytellers from all over the country. I met people there from California, from New Orleans, from Chicago . . . everywhere. You can sit in a bar in Fort Lee, New Jersey and hear tales that will make it feel like you've seen all forty-six states.'

'It sounds marvellous. We must definitely go.'

'If you're interested in moving pictures, you most definitely must,' he said.

'But, in the meantime, I promise we shall get to the bottom of the dreadful things that have happened to your friends.'

'Until tonight I was sure it was Aaron trying to discredit us,' said Zelda.

'It certainly looks like someone is,' I said. 'All the deaths have been taken straight from your moving picture.'

'Which means that I'm next,' she said. 'Burned at the stake.'

I frowned. That would be the next death in the sequence, certainly, but with Aaron Orum's death, the victim could no longer be certain. In the picture it had been George, the handsome young lad from the village, who had run mad and thrown himself from the church tower. I said nothing, though.

Instead, Lady Hardcastle switched effortlessly into the role of 'charming hostess' and diverted the conversation to cheerier topics. It seemed the others were as keen as I to escape from the horrors of the past couple of days and we passed a pleasant hour discussing everything from village life to the best way to remove soup stains from a dinner jacket.

She offered the film folk brandy and a chance to relax in the drawing room while she played for us, but they declined. We all retired early, glad for the chance to bring yet another dreadful day to a close.

◆ ◆ ◆

Wherever we had lived in the world for any appreciable time, Lady Hardcastle always took the local newspaper as well as *The Times*. The *Bristol News* was published twice a week, on Tuesday and Friday, and so it was delivered in time for breakfast the next morning.

Since we had guests, I toyed with the idea of ironing the newspapers to dry the ink, but I decided that that would simply be showing off. Instead, I placed both *The Times* and the *Bristol News* on the table in the morning room so that they might be available for everyone's perusal. I noticed as I did so that recent events in the village were being reported on the front page of the local paper under the headline 'Supernatural Murders in Gloucestershire Village'.

There followed several paragraphs of sensationalist prose 'From Our Society Correspondent' outlining the broad details of the three murders and their links with the events in *The Witch's Downfall*. Dinah Caudle had her front page, and from the tone of the piece she was revelling in it.

Miss Jones arrived and set to work on breakfast at once while I went up with Lady Hardcastle's tea.

She was awake when I entered the bedroom, but only barely.

'Good morning, my lady,' I said. 'I bring tea.'

'Florence of the family Armstrong, you're a lifesaver. Tea-bringer and harbinger of the glorious new day.'

'Not so sure about the "glorious" part today, I'm afraid. We've made the paper.'

'*The Times*? How glamorous.'

'No,' I said. 'The *Bristol News*. It doesn't paint a flattering picture of the village.'

'It's only to be expected. We do seem to be host to three dead entertainers.'

'She saves some of her more imaginative invective for you.'

'She? Oh, the Caudle woman. That's only to be expected, too. I didn't much take to her and I don't suppose she was greatly impressed by me.'

'Well, we know where she's staying if you want her to suffer a little . . . accident,' I said.

'You can be quite scary at times,' she said. 'I'm glad you're on my side.'

'Always,' I said, and turned to leave. 'Breakfast is in about half an hour.'

'I shall endeavour to bestir myself. Thank you for the tea.'

Back downstairs, I was surprised to find that both Zelda and Mr Cheetham were already in the morning room.

'Good morning, Miss Armstrong,' said Mr Cheetham. 'Is this tea fresh, do you know?' He indicated the teapot on the table.

'Good morning, sir,' I said. 'And madam.' I smiled at Zelda. 'It was made within the last ten minutes, I should say.'

'Grand,' he said.

'Would you like me to pour you a cup?'

'Thank you, no. We can manage.'

'As you wish,' I said. 'Miss Jones is making breakfast. I'm afraid we weren't expecting everyone to be up quite this early so it'll be at least another half an hour.'

'Sounds like perfect timing to me,' he said. 'Gives us time to have a brew and read the paper.'

'Don't take it too much to heart,' I said.

He looked puzzled. I indicated the front page of the *Bristol News*.

'Oh, that,' he said, picking up the newspaper. 'Water off a duck's back, chuck. I've been called worse than . . . "A blasphemous peddler of corrupting filth" in my time. You should have seen the reviews of our production of *Romeo and Juliet*. And d'you remember that time we were chased out of that theatre in Hull, Zel? What was that?'

'*The Heart of the Troubadour*,' said Zelda.

'Aye, that's right,' he said with a chuckle. 'Basil's pet project. He was a fine character actor, but it turned out he was a dreadful playwright.'

Zelda smiled fondly at the memory of her friend.

'I'll be in the kitchen if you need anything,' I said. 'I'm afraid we never got round to installing bells, but a shout or a whistle usually does the trick.'

'I'm sure we'll be fine, dear,' said Zelda.

I left them to it.

After breakfast, Lady Hardcastle retreated to her study with the stated intention of 'catching up with correspondence', though I suspected she would actually be engaged in some solitary pondering. With three dead and no firm idea who was responsible, she was certain to be feeling more than a little frustrated.

My own immediate concerns were altogether more prosaic: I had some mending to do. I was preparing to settle in the kitchen and catch up on gossip with Edna over a cup of tea and some darning when the doorbell rang.

'Morning, Miss Armstrong,' said Inspector Sunderland, for it was he.

'And good morning to you, too, Inspector,' I said. 'Please come in.'

'Thank you,' he said, and handed me his hat.

'Make yourself comfortable in the drawing room and I'll tell Lady Hardcastle you're here.'

'Is her "crime board" still in the dining room?' he asked.

'It is, yes. I haven't the energy to keep moving it about so we leave it in there with a dust sheet over it. I like to pretend it's an abstract sculpture.'

'In that case, might I be impertinent enough to ask to meet her in the dining room? I feel the presence of her sketch-strewn blackboard might help.'

'Certainly, Inspector. I'll bring tea, too. We were just about to have a pot.'

I showed him to the dining room and then alerted Lady Hardcastle to his presence on my way to the kitchen. By the time I returned with the tray, they were both seated at the dining table, engaged in small talk. The crime board was uncovered.

The board had changed a great deal since we had first started to investigate. Two of the potential suspects, Euphemia Selwood and Aaron Orum, had been pinned next to Basil Newhouse under 'Deceased'. The note under Dinah Caudle's sketch, indicating her flirtatious link to Aaron Orum, had been double-underlined. Clearly, they thought there was something significant there, though I thought her genuine distress at Orum's death spoke in her favour somewhat.

The Hugheses, too, were now double-underlined, with a new note saying, 'No one taking them seriously enough?'

We had always had to be circumspect about leaving notes concerning the film folk – it doesn't do to openly suspect one's houseguests of murder, after all – but I could tell from the many fingerprints in the chalk dust under the sketches of both Nolan Cheetham and Zelda Drayton that they had been much discussed.

The conversation now, though, had clearly moved on.

'The inspector tells me that he and Mrs Sunderland will be singing together at the cathedral next week,' said Lady Hardcastle.

'As part of a choir, I hasten to add,' he said.

'May we come? We'd love to see you under less investigatory circumstances, wouldn't we, Flo?'

'If you don't mind,' I said.

'I'm sure I should be most honoured,' he said. 'And Mrs Sunderland would love to meet you. She's always on at me to invite you to dine with us, as you know.'

'And yet you never do anything about it. We still haven't met the woman who manages to put up with you with such patient indulgence,' said Lady Hardcastle. 'Perhaps we could take you for a bite afterwards?'

'I shall pass on your invitation, my lady. Thank you.'

'Splendid,' she said. 'And now that Flo's here, I feel we should proceed to business. I couldn't help noticing that as you came in, Inspector dear, you looked "all of a pother", as Sergeant Dobson might say. Is there something the matter?'

'I'm so sorry,' said the inspector as he stirred his tea. 'I thought I'd managed to put it behind me as I drove up here. But you're right. I have been pothered to perdition.'

'Oh dear,' she said. 'Whatever is it?'

'The new mortuary has burned down,' he said.

'Good heavens. Was anyone hurt?'

'Thankfully the only people inside were beyond further injury. Which is lucky, because they were all fed into the incinerator before the blackguards opened up the gas pipes and set the place ablaze.'

'Oh, I say. Who would burn a mortuary?'

'There are some strange people about,' said the inspector wearily. 'It's set us back, though. Dr Gosling hadn't yet started on his autopsies and all three of our bodies were in the store.'

'Do you think it's related to our case?' I asked.

'I'd say it's related to *a* case,' he said. 'We had several bodies there for examination in relation to murder cases. I wouldn't put it past some of the city's more imaginative villains to get rid of incriminating evidence that way. One of the corpses had formerly made his living as muscle for one of the gangs trying to control the area down by the new tobacco warehouses. Ordinarily these things are done "publicly" as a show of strength, but there was something shady about this one. I'm beginning to wonder if the corpse might have had secrets to reveal.'

'And it doesn't now,' I said.

'Quite. But nor do any of the others. It's most frustrating.'

'Can you even secure a conviction for murder with no bodies?'

'We should be fine in this case,' he said. 'We have plenty of reliable witnesses who saw Mr Newhouse, Miss Selwood, and Mr Orum dead. It does complicate matters, though.'

'Simeon must be beside himself. He's not been in the job more than a few weeks and his office has been burned down.'

'He's not best pleased. He'd been looking forward to showing off for you, I think, my lady.'

'The poor dear.'

'He'll be joining me here later,' he said. 'You can pass on your commiserations in person.'

'I shall rag him mercilessly, of course. But poor you as well. What will you do now?'

'I'll carry on as normal,' he said. 'I've actually come up to speak to the *Bristol News*'s "Society Correspondent" about her piece in today's newspaper, but I thought I'd pass on the mortuary news on my way.'

'And cadge a cup of tea,' I said.

'It's part of our training. The entire police force is fuelled by tea and we're taught how to seek out the best in every town.'

'I'm honoured that we're considered the source of the finest tea,' said Lady Hardcastle. 'Would you like us to do anything else? We can accompany you to the Dog and Duck, if that would help.'

'Thank you,' he said, 'but in this instance I think I might do better without you. To judge from the way she writes about you, she's not one of your greatest admirers.'

'I fear you may be right. I'm not sure what I've done to upset her, but she definitely seems to have taken against me. Would we be interfering if we were to look around the churchyard? Sergeant Dobson barred the way last night but I'm really rather keen to examine the scene for myself.'

'Not at all, my lady. I know I can rely on you two not to damage any evidence. I shall be over there myself presently, but it never hurts to have another couple of pairs of eyes.'

'Splendid,' she said. 'Then that's our morning sorted out. Does that suit you, Flo?'

'Of course, my lady,' I said. 'I'll fetch our coats.'

'Thank you, dear. I'll pop out to the orangery to get my sketch pad.'

Chapter Thirteen

It was another bright, crisp autumn day in Littleton Cotterell. There was a light frost on the green and we left footprints as we walked across it to the church. Despite the terrible events of the past few days, village life carried on as usual. Shops were open and people were going about their business as though the murders of three strangers were an everyday occurrence. Sadly, in Littleton Cotterell it actually was an everyday occurrence.

The lych gate was shut and there were no disturbances in the frost. No one had been to the churchyard since the frost had formed. We followed the path around the west end of the building to the churchyard.

There was nothing to mark the point at the base of the tower where Aaron Orum had met his premature end. Almost as one, we looked up at the parapet of the tower and tried to track the path his terrified body would have taken.

'He must have landed here,' said Lady Hardcastle, waving in the general direction of the grass beside the path. 'Not much to show for a life lost.'

She was right. The ground had been disturbed by many boots since the tragedy and it was apparent that something had happened there, but there was no specific indication as to what. I'm not sure that I expected to see the imprint of his body in the ground, but it seemed wrong, somehow, that there was nothing more to mark the sudden snuffing out of a man's life.

'It's a good thing we don't need to fathom out what happened last night based on the footprints,' I said. 'This is a mess.'

'It is rather, isn't it?' she said. 'A few pairs of government-issue boots can create a bewildering muddle just by going about their business. Still, it tells a tale of its own. I shall make a few sketches so that we can ponder the scene at our leisure.'

'Have you ever thought about simply taking photographs?' I said.

'I have, as a matter of fact. But I got myself tangled up in a philosophical argument about the difference between what I see and what's actually there.'

'And they're different?' I asked.

'Quite different, don't you think? A sketch is an interpretation of what I see but a photograph is no more than a chemical record of the light reflected from the scene. For reasons I can't explain, I prefer to record my impressions.'

'You could form your impressions at any time from a well-taken photograph,' I said. 'And your first impressions might miss a crucial detail.'

'Yes, I argued those points, too. But no matter how many times I went back and forth, I never managed to get away from the fact that I really rather enjoy making sketches.'

'I wasn't trying to stop you,' I said. 'Just offering a more modern alternative.'

'And I appreciate the thought,' she said. 'Thank you.'

'Would you like me to leave you in peace?'

'I'm always delighted to have your company, but I do understand it must be frightfully dull watching a woman sketching a murder scene. If you wish to wander, I shall be fine on my own for a while.'

'I might explore the churchyard if I become too bored.'

219

'Please do,' she said as she began the mystical, magical work of rendering an image of the scene using only pencil and paper. Absently, she said, 'It's a terrible thing when anyone dies, but I confess to being especially disappointed that it was Orum.'

'He was definitely my front runner in the Top Suspect Stakes,' I said. 'His death rather inconveniently opens the field again.'

'Doesn't it just?' she said. 'On the other hand, we're in the old familiar position when it comes to multiple murders.'

'We could just sit tight and wait?' I suggested. 'Whoever's left standing at the end must be the killer.'

'Quite so. It's a gruesome way of going about things, but it involves much less effort than actually trying to figure it out.'

'Whom do you favour now?' I asked.

'Well, there's Nolan Cheetham,' she said.

'That would be very boring. With Orum gone and only Zelda left alive from the troupe, he's the only one familiar enough with the plot of the moving picture to want to mimic the murder methods so closely.'

'Yes, that would be very mundane, wouldn't it? Not to mention rather foolish in the long term. Morbid fascination might make his picture a success, but he'd not be able to repeat that success if he'd killed off all his stars.'

'You once told me never to underestimate the murderer's capacity for foolishness,' I said.

'Did I? How very wise of me. Brava, Emily. But foolish or not, it seems altogether far too desperate.'

'Agreed. Zelda, then?'

'There's no reason she couldn't have killed all three,' she said. 'It would be getting trickier by the day to keep her activities hidden, though. Cheetham would know by now.'

'And she'd have even less reason to murder her friends for the sake of a modicum of notoriety.'

'Well, quite. Notoriety . . . notoriety . . . What about the Caudle woman? Lord knows it's hard enough for a woman to be taken seriously at anything. But here she is with her story on the front page of the *Bristol News*.'

'Do you think she'd kill three people just to get her story on the front page?' I said.

'I've quite taken against the woman,' she said. 'I could easily be persuaded that she would kill three people just to get a decent cup of tea.'

I laughed. 'And we still haven't ruled out the Hugheses,' I said.

'The Righteous Hugheses, yes. But we don't know anything about them.'

'We don't,' I agreed. 'But how would three murders benefit them?'

'By reinforcing their claim that Cheetham's moving picture is a corrupting influence. You saw the quotes in the newspaper.' She flipped open her notebook. '"Someone has been turned into a vicious murderer as a result of watching that vile piece of so-called entertainment",' she read. '"An otherwise decent person has been turned from the light and on to the path of wickedness and damnation by these flickering shadows from Hell itself." It's attention-grabbing stuff, but only once there have been murders.'

'So why wait for someone to be corrupted when it's easy enough to do the killing yourself? Is that what you're saying?'

'We've seen less rational reasons for murder.'

'True,' I said. 'You know, I was wrong about the whole troupe being killed off.'

'You were?'

'Yes. What about the chap who played George?'

'George?' she said, trying to place him. 'Oh, the chap in the village who was sweet on the beautiful girl? The one who went mad and threw himself . . .' She looked around at the muddy churchyard.

'Yes, him. Why isn't he on this publicity tour? Perhaps he's enraged at being left out so he's killing off the cast one by one.'

'But why Orum?' she said.

'An old grudge,' I said confidently. 'They must have had a falling out in the past.'

She looked up from her sketch and smiled. 'Well, I'm always the one who says we shouldn't rule anything out until we have all the facts,' she said. 'And it's as likely as anything else at the moment.'

'It could be Lady Farley-Stroud trying to drum up business for the travelling picture show.'

'Now I know you're bored,' she said with a chuckle. 'Run along and play. I'll not be long.'

I went for a wander around the churchyard.

In the daylight, I saw that the churchyard was a good deal larger than I had thought. From the ancient rowan tree where we had found Basil Newhouse on Wednesday, I had only been able to make out a few head-stones and memorials in the pre-dawn gloom. But here in the autumn sunshine I could see a great deal more.

The graves, of which there were many, were neat and well tended. The older headstones were darkened with lichen, and some of them leaned haphazardly as though bumped by a clumsy giant. There was no wall, but the churchyard boundary was marked by a hedgerow and more trees, most of which seemed at least as old as the 'ancient rowan' but which I, as always, was unable to identify. A weathered old cart stood beside a gap in the hedge, which provided an entrance of sorts. The cart was piled high with hay, which seemed odd until I noticed that there was a donkey tethered within reach, helping herself to the feast. I was contemplating the oddness of there being a donkey in a churchyard when I was hailed.

'Armstrong!' It was Lady Hardcastle. It was bound to be. No sooner had I ambled off to be with my own thoughts for a few moments than she was calling me back.

'On my way, my lady,' I shouted. 'Quick as I can,' I said more quietly. 'See me run.'

When I turned, though, I saw that I wasn't being summoned on a whim, but because Inspector Sunderland had joined her, accompanied by her old friend Dr Gosling. I quickened my pace.

'Simeon and the inspector are here,' said Lady Hardcastle.

'So it would appear,' I said. 'Good morning, gentlemen.'

They both 'How do you do?'-ed and tipped their hats.

'What news from our local representative of the fourth estate?' asked Lady Hardcastle.

The inspector frowned. 'I take my duties and responsibilities as servant of the Crown and as an upholder of the public peace very seriously indeed. I am professionally bound to treat all my fellow citizens equally, without fear or favour . . . but that blasted woman gives me the pip.'

Lady Hardcastle laughed. 'I, too, am a patient and indulgent soul, but I confess she does the same to me. It's her manner, I think.'

'I've seldom met someone so rude, arrogant . . . and . . . supercilious as that wretched reporter,' he said.

It was Dr Gosling's turn to laugh. 'I say, old chap, steady on. Nice word, though. Must use it more often myself. I've met a few senior chaps in the medical world who could have that engraved on their calling cards. "Mr J Fitzherbert Fotherington-Smythe, surgeon at large and supercilious old buffer".'

'Well,' said the inspector, still exasperated. 'I mean. Really. She completely ignored my questions about her movements and whereabouts at the times of the murders and instead began to badger me about the failings of the Bristol CID in apprehending "The Littleton Cotterell Witch"—'

'To be fair,' interrupted Dr Gosling, 'you haven't actually managed to catch the witch yet, have you? She has a point.'

'I'm not above getting Sergeant Dobson to "accidentally" lock you in the cell for the afternoon, you know,' said the inspector. 'Unfortunately, when she finally saw reason and acceded to my polite and patient requests for information, it turned out that she went nowhere, saw nothing, and has witnesses to prove the thoroughness of her inertia.'

'"Unfortunately"?' I said.

'"Unfortunately", indeed,' he said. 'I should very much have liked an excuse to lock *her* in the cells for a few hours after all that.'

'We had speculated that she might have committed the murders herself in order to be first on the scene with the "scoop", as I believe they call it,' said Lady Hardcastle.

'The thought crossed my mind, too, my lady,' he said. 'But she has alibis for all three deaths.'

'She might have an accomplice,' I suggested.

'That crossed my mind as well,' he said. 'But then I had such a devil of a job trying to imagine anyone actually working with her that I had to rule that one out, too. No, she's an aggravation, but that's all.'

'Still,' said Lady Hardcastle, 'that's one more we can cross off the list. And this one didn't even have to die.'

'More's the pity,' said Inspector Sunderland.

She smiled. 'And what of you, friend Simeon?' she said. 'What news from the laboratory?'

'Apart from losing all my bodies?' said Dr Gosling. 'I'm going to be a laughing stock at the Police Surgeons' Annual Dinner.'

'Do they have such a thing?' she asked.

'I'm sure they'll convene one specially,' he said. 'Just so they can laugh at me.'

'It's not your fault, dear. The underworld tittle-tattle is that your premises were merely caught up in a spat among the dockside gangs.'

'Since when have you been privy to underworld tittle-tattle?'

'You'd be surprised, dear,' she said. 'But, in truth, the inspector told us.'

'Whatever the reason for it, it does make investigating murders rather tricky. You know, having no bodies and all that. But I do have some news.' He reached into the briefcase he was carrying and handed a manila file to Inspector Sunderland.

He carried on speaking while the inspector leafed through the papers. 'The apple you prised from the vice-like grip of the dead actress's hand – actually, Emily, remind me to talk to you about that later. Sorry, where was I. Oh, the apple. Yes. There was a small puncture in the skin and the apple itself contained quite an astonishing amount of potassium cyanide. Enough to kill her outright in seconds. Well, enough to kill her, her family, all her friends, and a passing herd of elephants, if truth be told. And still have some left over.'

'So it would seem,' said the inspector as he read the report for himself.

'Either the killer really, really, really wanted to make certain she was dead, or had absolutely no idea what he was doing and just kept squirting the stuff in until he thought there was enough.'

'What about the pie?' asked Lady Hardcastle.

'The pie?' said Dr Gosling.

'Yes, the pie. Was it filled with strange mushrooms?'

'It was a chicken and mushroom pie, certainly,' he said, looking slightly puzzled.

'But was there anything odd about the mushrooms? Might they be from the Americas? Of the sort used in certain religious ceremonies?'

'I've not had a chance to look yet,' he said. 'I don't see you nearly as often as I'd like to, old thing, and whenever I do, you bring me a pie filled with poisonous mushrooms.'

'Please look into it,' she said. 'I have a hypothesis. There are mushrooms native to the southwest of America which are used to induce trances and visions by some of the ancient tribes of the Americas.'

'Well, if they are . . .' he said slowly. 'Actually, I have no idea how I'd check. How do you know about them?'

'Oh,' she said airily, 'one reads about these things.'

'Oh, one does, does one?' he said. 'Well, I doubt there's anything in the standard medical texts that would help me. I could ask around and see if anyone knows a mycologist. Or even an anthropologist specializing in the Americas.'

'That would be splendid,' said Lady Hardcastle. 'Thank you. You see, if Orum had ingested these mushrooms, that would explain the hallucination that he was being pursued by demons.'

'I suppose so,' he said. 'Well, I can but try.'

'It's just that we know someone who has recently been to New Jersey.'

Dr Gosling laughed. 'New Jersey? I thought you said these things grew in the southwestern territories.'

'And central America,' she said.

'Thousands of miles from New Jersey, then, old thing,' he said. 'It's not enough to convict your putative suspect, whoever it is.'

'We shall see,' she said. 'We shall see.'

◆ ◆ ◆

Lady Hardcastle invited the gentlemen back to the house for coffee. They were extremely senior men who were frightfully busy with terribly important work that simply couldn't wait, and so, of course, they accepted immediately.

I left them in the dining room with the crime board while I went through to the kitchen to fetch coffee and see how things were progressing.

'Good morning, ladies,' I said as I entered.

'Mornin', Miss Armstrong,' said Miss Jones.

'Mornin', my lover,' said Edna. ''Ow bist?'

'I'm in the finest fettle, thank you, Edna. How about you?'

'Mustn't grumble,' she said.

'She mustn't, but she will anyway, if you gives her half a chance,' said Miss Jones.

'Better out than in, our ma always used to say,' said Edna. 'You shouldn't bottle things up.'

'You could give it a go once in a while,' said Miss Jones quietly.

'And what is it that you're not bottling up at the moment?' I asked. 'Dan still on the crocked list?'

'He is, the daft old beggar. Do you know, he finally told me how he come to break his stupid leg in the first place? Tripped over a bicycle. A bicycle, if you please.'

'Gracious,' I said. 'How on earth . . . ?'

'That's exactly what I said. "Daniel Gibson," I says. "How did a man of your age come to fall over a bicycle in broad daylight? Have you been drinkin' with that Toby Thompson again?" And he says, "I don't know, my sweet—" – I'll give him "my sweet" – he says, "I don't know, my sweet, I just didn't see it, like." So I says, "How could you not see a flamin' great bicycle?" and he says, "It was in the long grass. Just lyin' there. I swear."'

'Whatever was a bicycle doing lying in the long grass?' I said. 'And where was it?'

'I asked him both those questions myself,' she said, 'but he just mumbled about "winter pasture", "this year's heifers", and "old cottage" so I never did get to the bottom of it.'

'But you're a step closer,' I said. 'At least now you know that a bicycle was to blame.'

'And if I ever finds out what blitherin' nincompoop left their bicycle lyin' in a field I shall have words. Stern ones.'

'I'd not like to be the owner of that particular bicycle,' I said.

'I never could get on with 'em,' said Miss Jones. 'My cousin is mad keen. She brought it round one day to show us. She kept goin' on and on about how wonderful it was but I couldn't see it, myself. Once you get the hang of not fallin' flat on your face every few yards, you get a sore bum from the saddle.'

'You're not wrong,' I said. 'Now, then. Aside from clumsy husbands and sore bums, is everything else in order? Are Mr Cheetham and Miss Drayton being looked after?'

'It's all in hand,' said Edna. 'We made them some fresh tea shortly after you went out and they've shut themselves in the mornin' room again. Miss Drayton seems a mite nervous, though, I must say. She was witterin' on about window locks or sommat. I just smiled politely and played the know-nothin' servant. Locks on the windows, indeed. Whoever heard of such a thing? They might need 'em in the city, but there i'n't no one round here with more than a catch on their windows.'

'I might have to try to reassure her if she says anything further,' I said. 'Have you any idea what they do in there all day?'

'Haven't got the foggiest,' she said. 'Miss Drayton comes out periodically and asks for tea – ever so polite, she is – but I never goes in there till they've gone out. And when I does, the room's always spick and span like no one's been in there.'

'Most odd,' I said. 'Still, it's a distressing time for them, and everyone reacts differently to these things, don't they?'

'I reckon they should have a good old-fashioned wake,' said Edna. 'Everyone gets roarin' drunk and has a good sing-song round the piano. That's the proper way to say goodbye.'

'I dare say you're right,' I agreed. 'Each to their own, though. I think we should leave them be and I'll just take this coffee tray through to the dining room.'

'Will the gentlemen from the police be stayin' for lunch?' asked Miss Jones.

'A good question,' I said. 'I'll let you know.'

'. . . and he said he was in the United States.' Lady Hardcastle was standing before the crime board like a lecturer explaining her latest theory.

'I agree that it might have given him access to your mystical mushrooms,' said Dr Gosling. 'If that's what was in the pie. But New Jersey is as far from the Arizona Territory as we are from Constantinople.'

'And I have a perfectly splendid pair of Turkish slippers,' she replied. 'These things travel. Who's to say that some enterprising young businessman isn't selling these "vision mushrooms" from a corner shop in Fort Lee, New Jersey?'

'To be fair, my lady,' I said, 'you did pick up those slippers in a bazaar at Stamboul, not from a corner shop in Knightsbridge.'

'Your encyclopaedic memory will be the death of me,' she said.

'The stall holder was a voluble little chap with a gold tooth who kept calling you "malady", which I found pleasingly appropriate.'

'Be that as it may,' she said with exaggerated patience, 'Nolan Cheetham spent some time on the very continent whence those mushrooms originate.'

'I know you've always thought me something of a duffer when it comes to chaps and their motivations—' began Dr Gosling.

'You've always seemed to find people so baffling,' said Lady Hardcastle. 'You understand how the machinery works, but not the mind controlling it.'

'Quite so, old thing,' he agreed. 'Quite so. But, you see, even a duffer like me – a chap who is never surprised by anyone's actions because he long since resigned himself to the sad truth that he'd never be able to predict anyone's next move – even a duffer like me is completely thunderstruck by the notion that Cheetham would murder his pals to further his ambitions. It doesn't seem to make any sense. He'd have no friends left with whom to share his triumph, not to mention that he'd be killing off the proverbial goose.'

'I made the same anserine observation early on,' I said. 'It really does seem foolish to kill his own staff. What if he has a hit with the picture as a result of all the publicity? How does he compound his success with no actors to play in the follow-up?'

'From what I gather, he already has something of a hit on his hands. He asked if he could use the telephone earlier and I accidentally overheard him talking about increased bookings and box office takings and whatnot. I don't think the murders have done his business anything but good.'

'It still seems odd, though,' I said. 'Dead actors can't act.'

'I'm sure he'd be able to hire more,' said Lady Hardcastle. 'If he's callous enough to do away with them, he's not going to think twice about replacing them.'

'Perhaps,' I said. 'Although actors are a superstitious lot. He'd know how difficult it could be to persuade them to work for the "Company of Death". There are so many reasons not to go through with it, even for someone inclined to commit murder.'

'Who, then?' she said. 'Dinah Caudle?'

'She's little more than a spoilt child,' said the inspector.

'Spoilt children can do a lot of harm,' she said.

'She was genuinely upset at the church. And she's not an actress so it's less likely that she could have been putting it on so convincingly.'

'Perhaps,' she said. 'Have you checked her alibis for the other two nights, Inspector? We know she was dining with Orum when he ran mad and shot out of the pub.'

'Truth be told,' he said, 'hardly anyone has a watertight alibi. Not even you two.'

'We're paragons of virtue,' she said. 'It can't possibly be us.'

'And I remember telling you once before that if I ever choose to bump anyone off, you'll never find the body,' I said.

'I recall that myself, yes,' he said. 'You're quite a frightening woman, you know.'

'People keep saying that,' I said. 'I always thought of myself as winsome and charming.'

'You are, dear. Take no notice of them,' said Lady Hardcastle.

'It was you who said I was scary earlier,' I said.

'Did I? I'm sure I didn't mean it.'

I harrumphed.

'Be that as it may,' said Inspector Sunderland, 'I'm afraid that very few people have verifiable alibis. Two of the murders were committed in the middle of the night when all the suspects claim – quite reasonably in my opinion – to have been asleep in their beds, and there's no one to support or to gainsay them. The last – and I think we can safely say that Mr Orum's death was manslaughter at the very least – the last happened in a pub full of people.'

'None of whom,' I said, 'were Mr Cheetham.'

'Actually, she's right, you know,' said Lady Hardcastle. 'Cheetham was at the village hall setting up his projector.'

The inspector looked thoughtful for a moment. 'I'll give you that,' he said. 'Although dodgy mushrooms can be introduced into a pie at any time.'

'Shall you be speaking to Hughes?' asked Lady Hardcastle.

'I've been trying to put it off,' said the inspector. 'But I think the time has come.'

'Put it off?' I said.

'I find him very wearisome,' he said. 'I'd fight to the death to protect his right to hold any opinion he wishes, and for his right to express that opinion openly. But I'd also fight to the death not to have to listen to him while he's doing so. But I fear that I must reacquaint myself with him and his charming wife if I'm to do my own job thoroughly and well.'

'May we come?' asked Lady Hardcastle.

'I should be glad of some sane company,' he replied. 'Though I beg you to remember that it was you who asked to come. I'll not take the blame for any frustration or annoyance you might feel.'

'Agreed,' she said. 'Flo, would you be a poppet and tell Miss Jones we shall be six for lunch? You'll be staying, gentlemen?'

'I'm afraid I need to nip back into town,' said Dr Gosling. 'Some other time, perhaps.'

◆ ◆ ◆

Miss Jones was brushing some pastry with beaten egg when I popped my head into the kitchen.

'Five for lunch, Miss Jones,' I said. 'I'm not sure when we'll be back but it shouldn't be too long after twelve.'

'Are we invited, then?' said Edna with a mischievous twinkle in her eye.

'No,' I said. 'Inspector Sunderland will be joining us.'

'Oh, I guessed that, my lover,' she said. 'Never known a policeman to pass up a chance for some free food. I was meanin' that the other two, Mr Cheetham and Miss Drayton, has gone out.'

'Oh,' I said. 'I wonder how they . . . Never mind. Three it is, then.'

'Right you are, Miss Armstrong,' said Miss Jones. 'Anythin' else?'

'Not for the moment. Thank you, ladies.'

I rejoined the interrogation party and we set off once more across the village green.

Chapter Fourteen

The charabanc had already dropped off its passengers, and the protest was in full swing by the time we emerged from the end of the lane and looked out across the green. The placards were looking a little the worse for wear after three full days of angry waving, but their bearers were no less agitated and no less keen to see an end to the filth being projected into the minds of the impressionable. The kinematograph had to be stopped.

'We're doing nothing illegal,' said the leader, Mr Hughes, as we approached.

'Nothing illegal at all, sir,' said Inspector Sunderland. 'You're wasting your time, certainly, but you're doing nothing wrong.'

'Doing the Lord's work is never wasting time,' said Mrs Hughes.

'I can't argue with that,' said the inspector. 'But in this instance, the Lord might be prepared to let you have a day off. There's no picture show this evening. It's Bonfire Night.'

'Another pagan festival,' said Mr Hughes.

'Is it?' said Lady Hardcastle. 'I thought it was a celebration of the thwarting of a plot to blow up Parliament.'

'Yes. Well,' he mumbled. 'That's not how it's celebrated now. It's returned to its pagan roots.'

'Be that as it may,' said the inspector, 'I'm sure your comrades can spare you for a few moments now that you know there's no show for you to stop today. I should like to ask you some questions.'

'About what?'

The inspector raised his eyebrows, but said nothing.

'No one from our group had anything to do with those dreadful deaths,' said Hughes.

'No one has suggested yet that you did,' said the inspector. 'But I would be neglecting my duty if I were to fail to seek information from all possible witnesses. We should be able to find a nice quiet table at the Dog and Duck.'

'I don't drink.'

'I persuaded Mr Arnold that he could earn a few extra coppers if he were to serve tea and coffee,' said Lady Hardcastle. 'In the absence of a tea shop, I felt that he would be able to fill a gap in the market. He agreed.'

'I shall not set foot in that house of sin and debauchery,' said Hughes.

'The police station, then?' suggested the inspector. His tone was still courteous, but we could all see that his patience was wearing thin.

Hughes thought for a moment. Entering the pub would represent a minor betrayal of his principles, but a trip to the police station was still seen by many as a mark of disgrace. Who, other than criminals and their victims, ever visited such a place? And since he wasn't the victim of a crime, that would mean . . .

'Very well,' he said. 'The Dog and Duck. But I'll not linger a moment longer than necessary. And I shall definitely not partake of any alcoholic drink.'

'That's understood, sir,' said Inspector Sunderland. 'I shall order a pot of tea and you may drink it or not, as you prefer.'

Hughes handed his placard to his wife and walked with us across the green to the village pub. Daisy left her father's butcher's shop as we approached and gave me an inquisitive look. I mouthed, 'I'll tell you later,' and she hurried along the pavement to the pub to begin her second job.

We followed her in. Lady Hardcastle and the inspector settled their 'guest' at an out-of-the-way table while I went to order a pot of tea. Daisy had hurriedly removed her coat and was smoothing down her apron as she bustled towards her station behind the bar.

'Was it him?' she asked in a whisper. 'Our ma said it was. She don't trust that lot.'

'She was sure it was Aaron Orum when I last spoke to her,' I said.

'He's dead now, though, i'n't he?'

'It might have been guilt that drove him to take his own life.'

She paused. 'Oh,' she said. 'Oh, it might, mightn't it? So it's not Hughes, then? It really was Orum all along?'

I laughed. 'We still don't know. The inspector is just speaking to as many witnesses as he can find. Can we discuss it later, though? For now we need a pot of tea for four.'

'Not four pints of scrumpy, then? That would be much easier.'

'Before lunch? Goodness me, no. Hughes is a teetotaller and even we draw the line at booze for elevenses. Put the kettle on, there's a poppet.'

'I'll bring it over,' she said.

I rejoined the others mid-conversation. Inspector Sunderland was looking at his notebook as he spoke.

'. . . spotted looking in through the pub window after midnight on the night Basil Newhouse was killed.'

'It might have been me,' said Hughes. 'I was . . . out for a walk.'

'Out for a walk? In Littleton Cotterell? After midnight?' said the inspector. 'You're staying at the old Seddon house on the way to Chipping Bevington, aren't you? The rest of your group left the village before ten o'clock according to our witnesses.'

'I was with them. We took the charabanc back to the house.'

'And then you came back?'

'I couldn't sleep so I went out.'

'It's a good five miles to the Seddon house. That's a fair distance for a late-night stroll.'

'There's a bicycle at the house,' said Hughes. 'I rode back to the village. I wanted to see for myself the effect that the moving picture had had on the village.'

'And what did you see?'

'Debauchery. Carousing. Drinking.'

'The good people of Littleton Cotterell enjoying a lively evening in the pub, in other words,' said the inspector calmly.

'They'd clearly been riled up and inflamed by that dreadful moving picture.'

'That's beyond my area of expertise, I'm afraid. What did you do then?'

'I'd seen all I cared to see, so I cycled back to the house.'

'Did you see anything unusual on your return journey?'

'Nothing especially unusual, no,' said Hughes. 'A couple of drunkards staggering home and another bloke on a bicycle, but nothing out of the ordinary.'

'Did anyone see you when you returned to the house?'

'No, they were all asleep.'

Lady Hardcastle had been listening intently during all this. She smiled warmly at Hughes and said, 'You take your mission very seriously, don't you, Mr Hughes?'

'Of course,' he said. 'We're doing God's work.'

'It must sometimes feel terribly lonely, though,' she continued. 'Just you and your wife standing against a godless world.'

'You imagine that we're alone? You've seen how many we were able to gather to fight Cheetham's filth. They're but a small number of the followers we have in Bristol. There are like-minded all over the country. All over the world, in fact.'

'I never knew,' she said. 'You're an international organization, then?'

'A brotherhood,' he said proudly.

'How exciting.'

Inspector Sunderland was clearly unsure where this line of questioning was going and gave me an enquiring glance: should we stop her? I shook my head: she knows what she's doing.

Hughes hadn't seen us. 'We spread our message throughout the Empire, across Europe, and even to the United States,' he said.

'It would be wonderful for you to get a chance to meet them, I should imagine,' said Lady Hardcastle. 'Have you ever thought about getting together with your colleagues from around the world?'

'We've already had such a gathering,' he said, proudly. 'We gathered in El Paso.'

'Goodness me,' said Lady Hardcastle. 'How exotic. Spain?'

He laughed. 'You might think so, but no. It's in Texas. In America.'

'Well I never,' she said. 'That's a great deal more exotic even than Spain. What an adventure. It must have taken simply weeks to get there.'

'It was quite a journey,' he said. 'But it was worth it.'

'I should imagine it was. I'm quite envious, to tell you the truth. I've only ever been to Washington.'

He smiled indulgently.

'I'm so sorry, Inspector,' said Lady Hardcastle. 'I seem to have expropriated your interview. I do apologize.'

'Think nothing of it, my lady,' said the inspector. 'It's always helpful to have a little colour. But if I may . . . ?'

'Of course,' she said.

'Thank you. So you returned to the old Seddon house—'

'I do wish you'd stop calling it that,' said Hughes. 'It's owned by Mr Nathaniel Biddiscombe now. He has nothing to do with those godless Seddons.'

'The Biddiscombe house, then,' said the inspector. 'What did you do when you arrived?'

'I went straight to bed. The exertions of the bicycle ride were exactly what I needed. I dropped off to sleep almost at once.'

'And you were up bright and early to return to your vigil?'

'That's right,' said Hughes. 'I shared a plain breakfast with the group. We prayed for the success of our venture and for the downfall of Cheetham and his heathens, then we were ready and waiting on the drive when the charabanc pulled up in the lane.'

'And the next night?'

'I returned to the house as usual, but I didn't venture out again.'

'And last night?'

'We joined the gathering crowd when Orum fell from the tower, but as soon as it was clear that there was nothing we could do to help, we left the village and returned to the house once more.'

'Thank you, Mr Hughes,' said the inspector as he closed his note-book. 'You've been most helpful.'

'I'm free to go?' said Hughes.

'You were always free to go,' said the inspector. 'But, yes, I have everything I need. You're welcome to stay and finish your tea, of course.'

'Thank you, no. I shall get back to my work and out of this den of iniquity and vice.'

'As you wish. Good day.'

Hughes left without looking back.

'Where did you learn your interrogation techniques, my lady?' asked the inspector once we were back in the dining room. We were reviewing the crime board.

'My what?' she said. She was writing some notes on the board and wasn't giving the inspector her full attention. 'Oh, the America thing?'

'Yes,' he said. 'That was very accomplished.'

'Just a little idea we developed in a past life. We were talking about it only the other day, as a matter of fact. It turns out that people are happy to tell you everything they know – you just have to create the right mood and they'll chatter away without a care. Intimidation has its uses, of course, but mostly for bringing chaps to heel. Torture is so medieval, don't you think?'

'Some of my colleagues would disagree with you,' he said, 'and I've seen more than one confession beaten out of a hard man. But I've always favoured a less brutal approach. You should give lectures for the Force.'

'I hardly think the more brutal among your fellow officers would pay any attention to a dotty lady with a weakness for sentimental tunes and brandy.'

He smiled. 'Still, he'd not have told me about his trip to America if I'd asked him.'

'No, I don't think he would. But I don't think he would have told me if I'd asked him directly, either. One simply has to find a way of letting them talk about it for themselves.'

'And now we know that he might have had access to your mystical mushrooms,' he said. 'I'm not certain if it helps us at all, mind you.'

'To tell you the truth,' she said, still examining the crime board, 'I'm not certain it does, either. It makes him a possible suspect for the Orum killing, but he has alibis for the other two murders. Weak and uncorroborated alibis, I'll grant you, but he's able to make a claim to having been elsewhere both times.'

'I can't quite see why he would kill Mr Orum,' I said. 'Very few people knew of his link to the moving picture.'

'That might not be important,' said the inspector. 'If we assume that Hughes wanted to stir up controversy to get the moving picture banned, then it wouldn't actually make any difference who was killed as long as it was done in a way reminiscent of the story.'

'True,' said Lady Hardcastle. 'And the young chap who played Gormless George isn't part of the tour so it would have to be someone else. I think Gertie told me he was abroad in a touring production of *Lady Windermere's Fan*.'

'I suppose so,' I said. 'Someone definitely wanted to complete the set.' A thought struck me and I paused for a moment before slowly saying, 'Except . . .'

'Except what?' said Lady Hardcastle.

'Well, let's say your version is correct. Mr Orum was given his dodgy mushrooms in the pub and his demonic visions began there in the snug. He ran out, pursued by those demons, and hurried towards the church. He locked himself in and then threw himself from the tower to escape them. Just like in the moving picture.'

'That's it, as I understand it,' said the inspector.

'But what if the mushrooms had brought on a vision of fluffy baa-lambs gambolling in a spring meadow? He wouldn't have fled in terror then, would he? And how could the poisoner guarantee that he'd seek sanctuary in St Arild's even if he or she did manage to influence the vision somehow? And once there, how could he be persuaded to jump off the tower? There are too many . . . What is it you say, my lady?'

'Too many variables?' she suggested.

'Exactly,' I said. 'Too many variables, too many moving parts. It's a thoroughly unreliable way of killing someone if you also have something specific to say about the wickedness of moving pictures.'

'You make a good point,' said Lady Hardcastle. 'A very good point indeed.'

'You mentioned influencing the vision,' said the inspector. 'Do these mushrooms make one suggestible? Like hypnosis?'

'We'll have to wait for Simeon to do the research,' said Lady Hardcastle. 'He'll be the one to know. If they do work that way, our suspect would have to have been in the pub that evening, whispering in his ear.'

'That's a lot of people,' I said. 'It was busy in there – we saw them all tumbling out of the door to watch him go.'

'But it puts Dinah Caudle back in the running,' she said.

'Let's not jump to any conclusions until we've heard a little more from Gosling,' said the inspector. 'In the meantime, I need to check that all is well back at the station. Might I impose on your hospitality a little further and use your telephone?'

'Of course, Inspector,' she said. 'It's no imposition. You'll still stay for lunch?'

'Thank you,' he said. 'That would be most agreeable.'

I went to the kitchen to check on progress. Miss Jones had been hard at work and had done us proud.

'I see a bonus in your future,' I said. 'And for you, too, Edna. You've both gone above and beyond this week and I know that Lady Hardcastle appreciates your efforts. As do I. Thank you.'

'Just doin' our jobs,' said Miss Jones.

'She's right,' said Edna. 'What else would anyone do? I'd not say no to a bonus – every penny counts round our house while Dan's laid up – but I'd never expect one.'

'Nevertheless,' I said, 'I shall see that your wonderfulness doesn't go unacknowledged.'

'I tell you what you could do,' said Edna, 'and it won't cost the mistress a penny.'

'Go on,' I said, intrigued.

'Our Dan does love a cigar,' she said. 'And Mr Newhouse smoked such lovely ones. He has a . . . a whatchamacallit . . . a Thermidor in his room.'

'A humidor?' I suggested.

'That's the fella,' she said. 'And it's not like he's goin' to be smokin' 'em no more.'

'I can't see anything wrong with that,' I said. 'Mr Newhouse was a generous man in life. I'm sure he would be delighted to know that his cigars were bringing someone pleasure after his passing.'

'I'll just take a couple, mind,' she said hurriedly. 'It don't do no good spoilin' Dan. He'd just get accustomed to 'em and start complainin' when they ran out.'

'Take as many or as few as you wish,' I said.

I left them to their work and returned to Lady Hardcastle and Inspector Sunderland, who were still staring at the crime board in the dining room.

I recounted my recent conversation with Edna.

'Good idea,' said Lady Hardcastle. 'It will save them going to waste. Do you enjoy a cigar, Inspector?'

'I can't say I ever developed a taste for them,' he said. 'I used to smoke a pipe in my younger days, but Mrs Sunderland doesn't like the smell of the tobacco on my clothes so I stopped. I still carry my empty pipe, mind you.' He produced his familiar briar pipe. 'People seem to trust a pipe smoker, even when he's not smoking.' He held it by its bowl and pointed the stem at one of the sketches on the crime board. 'Handy for pointing at things, too,' he said.

'I say,' said Lady Hardcastle. 'It is, rather, isn't it? What do you think, Flo? Should I get a pipe?'

'An old-fashioned, long-stemmed clay pipe, my lady,' I said. 'Although, if all you're going to do is point at things, wouldn't a pencil be just as much use?'

'Where's the fun in that?' she said. 'I have a reputation as a batty eccentric to foster.'

'I don't think you've met anyone yet who has left the encounter doubting your batty eccentricity,' I said.

'Well, that's all right, then,' she said.

The conversation soon returned to the murders, but as far as I could make out we were just rehashing the same observations and arguments. There are only so many times one can hear the phrase 'But why on earth would he do such a thing?' before the mind begins to wander towards thoughts of lunch.

I was saved by the arrival of Edna bearing a sturdy pot of stew and dumplings.

'Thank you, Edna,' said Lady Hardcastle. 'Just what the doctor ordered.'

'My pleasure, m'lady. Though it was Miss Jones what did all the work – I just carried it through.'

'Nonetheless,' said Lady Hardcastle, 'your hard work is always appreciated. Oh, and Miss Armstrong told me about the cigars. Do take as many as you'd like.'

'That's very kind of you, m'lady,' said Edna. 'Though I'm havin' trouble findin' the Ther . . . the "humidor". I thought it was on Mr Newhouse's nightstand, with his cufflinks and collar studs, but I'm beggared if I can find it now.'

'How odd,' said Lady Hardcastle. 'You had a jolly good look, I take it?'

'I searched the room from top to bottom,' said Edna. 'But it i'n't there. There's not much else in there, and it's a big old box, so there's nowhere for it to hide.'

'Perhaps Mr Cheetham removed it,' I suggested. 'Or even Zelda Drayton. She was very fond of Mr Newhouse – perhaps the smell of the cigars is a comforting reminder.'

'It's possible, I suppose,' said Edna slowly. 'But don't forget I cleans their rooms as well and I a'n't seen the box in neither of them.'

'Most peculiar, indeed,' said Lady Hardcastle. 'Have you noticed anything else missing?'

'No, m'lady, just that. But I don't want to take up your time. I'm sure it will sort itself out. I just thought you'd like to know, that's all.'

'Of course, Edna, of course,' said Lady Hardcastle. 'Thank you for letting us know.'

Edna bobbed a curtsey and left.

'If it were any other household, I'd tell you one of the servants had pinched it,' said the inspector. 'Then again, in my experience there's usually a perfectly mundane explanation. I can't count the number of times I've been called upon to investigate the theft of some treasured possession only to find it had fallen behind a tallboy or been buried beneath a carelessly discarded coat.'

'You're almost certainly right,' said Lady Hardcastle. 'Let's not worry about it for now, though. Let's tuck in to this stew. I'm famished.'

◆ ◆ ◆

Immediately after lunch, Inspector Sunderland received a telephone call from the Bristol CID requesting his urgent attendance at the interview of a suspect in another case. Lady Hardcastle and I were left, once more, to our own devices.

'What now, my lady?' I said as I began to tidy the dining table.

She sighed. 'I do feel as though we ought to go hunting for clues, or questioning more witnesses, but I confess to being more than a little stumped. I wonder if a change of mental focus might give my poor addled brain a chance to regroup and come at the matter afresh in due course. Perhaps from a different angle.'

'It often helps,' I said. 'What will you do?'

'I still haven't reviewed that film we shot for the villagers. I thought I might go into the orangery and see what gems we ended up with. I'm sure I shall be able to show something at the village hall to lift everyone's spirits and remind them that moving pictures aren't all bad.'

'That sounds like a splendid plan,' I said. 'I'll get on with some mending.'

'Right you are, dear. See you back here at . . .' She consulted her wristwatch. 'Shall we say half-past two for a cup of tea?'

'Half-past two it is,' I said, and carried the dishes out to the kitchen.

I fetched my mending basket and yet another unaccountably ripped skirt – I had long suspected that Lady Hardcastle damaged her clothes on purpose just to keep me out of mischief – and settled at the kitchen table. The light was good, the room was warm, and I had Miss Jones to chat to while I worked.

We covered the disappointingly poor availability of fresh fish in the village – it always felt like a terrible risk to order it sight-unseen from the fishmonger in Chipping Bevington. We moved on to how much her mother's spirits seemed to have been lifted by having to fend for herself a lot more – Miss Jones didn't know whether to be pleased about this, but certainly felt that it brought her own ambitions within reach. And then we discussed her ambitions. There was no doubt that she was a marvellously talented cook, and I was delighted to find that she had no intentions of hiding her light under a bushel.

'I wants to study at the Ritz,' she said earnestly. 'Or the Carlton. With someone who's been taught by Escoffier. Or Escoffier hisself. Can you imagine that? The things I could learn. And then I'd find a hotel and turn it into the place where everyone wanted to eat.'

'I've never met a female *chef de cuisine*,' I said. 'That would be wonderful.'

'Yes, well,' she said sadly, 'that's where my plan falls down, isn't it? You a'n't never met one cause women i'n't allowed in the big kitchens. Not to cook, leastways. We're good enough to wash pots and chop onions, I shouldn't wonder, but no one's going to let me cook.'

'You'll have to dress as a boy,' I said. 'Sneak into their citadel in disguise.'

The back door opened abruptly and Lady Hardcastle hurried in.

'Who's in disguise?' she said.

'Miss Jones is going to dress as a boy to get a job in the kitchens at the Ritz.'

'Oh, I say, how thoroughly splendid. Good for you.'

'I i'n't goin' to do it really,' said Miss Jones. 'It was one of Miss Armstrong's flights of fancy.'

'Ah,' said Lady Hardcastle. 'She's prone to those. But if you need any tips, she's your girl. She's disguised herself as a boy on more than one occasion.'

'You've never!' said Miss Jones.

'No, she's right,' I said. 'It got me out of many a tricky situation.'

'And into a good many more,' said Lady Hardcastle.

'What's life without a bit of jeopardy?' I said. 'But the trick is baggy clothes to hide your shape and a big cap to hide your hair. Then you just make a few lewd comments to passing girls and challenge someone to a fight. There's really nothing to it.'

'Well, I reckons I'm going to have to become a great chef some other way,' said Miss Jones.

Lady Hardcastle thought for a moment. 'I think I might know one or two people who could help,' she said. 'If you're serious. I'd hate to lose you, but I'd hate to trap you here when you could be mistress of your own kitchen with the world beating a path to your door.'

'You're very kind, my lady,' said Miss Jones. 'But I's happy enough here, really.'

'For now, dear,' said Lady Hardcastle. 'For now. But when those feet start to itch, you just let me know. We'll sort something out for you.'

Miss Jones smiled.

'Well,' I said, 'now that you've seen to your cook's career, what can we do for you? It's not time for tea yet – you said half-past two.'

'I know I did,' she said, 'but I want you to come and see something on that film we shot. We really do need bells in this place.'

'Or some sort of internal telephone system,' I said.

'Even better,' she said. 'I shall look into it when we've got the current mess sorted out. But for now there is film to be examined. Chop-chop.'

I put down my sewing and stood up.

'Is that my skirt?' she asked.

'It is,' I said. 'How did you manage to . . . ?'

'There was a pair of fire tongs, as I recall. And a poker. And a recalcitrant fire. One thing led to another and the results are as you see them.'

I sighed. 'Let's go and look at your film,' I said.

◆ ◆ ◆

Lady Hardcastle had very few household rules. She made very little fuss about routine matters and simply expected that, between us, Edna, Miss Jones, and I would keep everything running smoothly. I'd had fifteen years to get used to it, but it came as a bit of a surprise to the other two, who had both worked in strictly regimented houses where their every move was controlled and monitored. Edna had initially been very disdainful of Lady Hardcastle and her laissez-faire approach to running a home, and I overheard her complaining to Miss Jones more than once in the early days. After a while, though, they both found that they rather enjoyed being trusted with the responsibility of doing whatever needed to be done to keep things jogging along smoothly. The quality of their work improved noticeably. Neither of them had ever been shirkers, but once they realized that they were being treated as competent, experienced staff, they began to take pride in doing their jobs to the very highest standard.

Though the rules were few, there was one which could never be broken. No one was to tidy or clean the orangery. At first glance, this made a certain amount of sense. There was expensive equipment in the studio that might be damaged. There were half-finished projects that, should any of the parts be knocked or moved, would be ruined. There were dangerous chemicals for developing film. It was only when one considered Lady Hardcastle's personality and habits that the rule began to seem somewhat foolhardy.

Lady Hardcastle was untidy. She moved about the world surrounded by an invisible cloud of disorder and disarray. She could walk into a room, have a conversation with someone, and then leave without apparently having touched anything. Once she was gone, the room would be in a state of chaos, as though a storm had passed through.

The combination of these two things – the no-tidying rule and Lady Hardcastle's innate talent for mayhem – meant that the orangery resembled the site of a recently ended, and extremely violent, battle. The blinds were drawn and the room lit with two oil lamps, but the state of bedlam was still evident. Every available surface was piled high with . . . things. Some things were unidentifiable, some things were clearly rubbish, some things could be grouped with other things and be put away in a drawer or cupboard where they could be more easily found when needed.

She went to the projector and fussed about with the film.

'Sit down, dear,' she said. 'This is going to take a couple of moments. The blessed thing keeps getting stuck.'

'I'd love to,' I said. 'But where . . . ?'

She turned to see me gesturing at the chair and stool, both of which were stacked with boxes and papers.

'Either,' she said, as though I had asked the most dunderheaded question ever uttered.

'And where should I put the . . . things?'

'On the floor will be fine. Just be sure to put them back where you found them when we leave. I have a system.'

I bit my tongue and did as I was bidden. Having decided on the stool, I moved a surprisingly heavy wooden box, a quantity of felt, some twine, two meat skewers, and a tin of moustache wax on to the floor. I perched on the stool and waited.

'There we are,' she said at last. 'Shutter those lamps for me, and let's have a look.'

With the room in darkness, she lit the lamp in the projector and began cranking the handle.

'I can't help but feel that some sort of properly regulated clockwork mechanism would be a better solution,' she said as the images twitched and stuttered on the screen.

'What am I looking for?' I asked.

'It's just coming up in a few moments,' she said. 'I'd have left the film in the right place, but this lamp is hot enough to set the film ablaze even when it's doused . . . Ah, here we are. What do you see there?'

'It looks like a bicycle leaning against the churchyard wall,' I said.

'Yes, so it does. That's not what I was thinking of, but remember that you saw it . . . Blast, it's gone now – I'll have to wind it back.'

I was treated to the comical sight of villagers walking backwards as she found the part she wanted to show me. 'There,' she said as the camera rotated towards the church again. 'Just disappearing up the hill beside the butcher's.'

It was a small cart, laden with hay. It appeared to be being pulled by a donkey, which was led by a hunched man wearing a short, dark coat.

'That looks like the cart we saw in the churchyard. If it carries on up the hill and turns left, that will take it to the lane that runs past the back of the church.'

'My thoughts exactly. I'd assumed that the cart and donkey were part of the fixtures and fittings, but it seems they only arrived on Tuesday morning, before the first show. Keep watching.'

There was a jump where the camera had stopped and we had moved it for another shot. The bicycle was still visible against the churchyard wall. The cheeky little lad whom Lady Hardcastle had persuaded to pose for us by the church looked awkwardly towards the camera. The Hugheses' charabanc came into the picture from the right, filled with their followers. They all began to debus.

'Ignore the protesters and keep your eye on the bicycle,' said Lady Hardcastle.

I did as I was asked. A few seconds later, a hunched figure wearing a naval peacoat and a cap came into view from behind the bus. He mounted the bicycle and rode off.

'That's the chap with the donkey,' I said.

'It certainly looks like the same man,' she said. She began to wind the film backwards on to its spool. 'Unshutter the lamps for me, would you? I'll just get this packed away.'

'You see some significance in the hunched bloke?' I asked as the room came back to life.

'I wouldn't have thought anything of him,' she said. 'But when I saw that he was connected with both the donkey and the bicycle, I began to wonder. There could be a perfectly mundane reason for there being a donkey in the churchyard, and bicycles are extremely commonplace. But bicycles do seem to keep cropping up, and now they're niggling at me.'

I thought for a moment. 'Dan Gibson broke his leg falling over a bicycle out on Toby Thompson's top field,' I said. 'And didn't Aaron Orum say he tripped over one outside the pub?'

'Exactly,' she said. 'Orum seemed a little embarrassed by it, but he definitely mentioned a bicycle.'

'So did Hughes,' I said. 'He rode back from the Seddon house on one, and he mentioned seeing someone else riding one as he went home.'

'Just so. I feel an idea forming. Just the tiniest seedling of a notion at the moment, but an idea nonetheless. How do you fancy a drive out to Toby Thompson's top field?'

'I'll fetch our driving togs,' I said.

Chapter Fifteen

As we made our way along the lanes in Lady Hardcastle's little red Rover 6, I was glad of the protection afforded by the heavy driving coat, gauntlets, hat, scarf, and goggles I had put on before we left home. It wasn't at all warm out.

'I really rather think,' I shouted above the noise of the engine, the wind, and the whooshing of the tyres on the road, 'that our next motor car ought to have some sort of enclosed cabin for us to sit in.'

'It is a bit parky, isn't it?' shouted Lady Hardcastle. 'I'll have a word with Fishy – see if he can design us one.'

As we rounded a corner on two wheels, I began to doubt the wisdom of owning a car designed by her friend Lord Riddlethorpe, the racing driver. She was bad enough in the little Rover with its top speed of twenty-four miles per hour. I could scarcely imagine the danger she would pose to the citizens and wildlife of Gloucestershire in a more powerful machine.

I was saved from having to make further comment by our arrival at our apparent destination. We had pulled up alongside a gate leading into a steeply sloping field. Down the hill to our left were the rich pastures farmed by Toby Thompson. Up the slope to the right was a patch of rough ground leading to a stand of trees. Lady Hardcastle pointed to the dried mud beneath the gate.

'As I suspected,' she said.

I looked at the spot indicated and saw the narrow tracks of bicycle tyres.

'Up towards the trees, I think,' she said, and led the way.

The small copse seemed to form a natural boundary to Toby Thompson's top field. It could scarcely be described as a 'wood', but the trees still grew several deep, making it impossible to see what was on the other side.

Lady Hardcastle pointed to the ground again. 'Ha!' she said triumphantly. 'I'll wager that's where Edna's husband tripped over the bicycle and injured himself.' A broad circle of the long grass was trampled flat. There were faint traces of tyre tracks in the exposed mud. 'I'd say he comes up here to hop the wag. He can sit among the trees, have a smoke, perhaps read the paper. He has a perfect view down across the fields in case his boss is about. If he were careful, he could be out the gate and back down the hill before he was spotted. No one would have tumbled to his scrimshanking if he hadn't tripped over the bicycle and broken his leg.'

It seemed a reasonable assessment. Most of the farm was laid out below us and Dan would have had a great vantage point from the tree line, while remaining out of view himself.

'That much we gleaned from his confession to Edna,' I said. 'But what's got you all hot and bothered? Why have we traipsed all the way up here?'

'Patience, tiny servant. If I'm right, all will be revealed on the other side of the trees.'

We trudged up the hill and my opinion of the heavy driving coat began to change. In the motor car it had been a welcome bulwark against the bitter wind as we sped along the lanes. Here it was a bulky encumbrance, and was starting to make me perspire in a most unlady-like way.

Breathing heavily, we cleared the tree line and walked for another minute through the small, but dense, stand of trees. As we progressed, we caught glimpses of what lay beyond.

'Ha!' said Lady Hardcastle again. It was a day for small triumphs. 'What do you see?'

'It's a cottage,' I said as the building came more clearly into view. 'Long abandoned, by the look of it.'

'But not, I suspect, unused,' she said. 'Let's have a little poke about.'

◆ ◆ ◆

'Are you armed?' murmured Lady Hardcastle as we trod stealthily through the grass leading towards the old cottage.

'You didn't say anything about needing to be armed,' I said.

'Oh, sorry, did I not? I brought this.' She produced a tiny automatic pistol from her coat. 'It's a Browning pocket pistol. It's pretty, isn't it?'

'It's adorable,' I said. 'You've had it for ages and you demand that I admire it every time you whip it out. But you didn't mention the pos-sibility of violence when you suggested this little trip.'

'I thought you always carried something deadly,' she said.

'Oh, I've got an antique musket concealed under my skirts,' I said tetchily, 'but I'd struggle to get it out in a hurry if things cut up rough.'

'There's no need to be like that, dear. Just cower behind me. I'll protect you.'

The small cottage had once been whitewashed but was now a dirty grey. Some of the window frames had rotted, some lacked glass, and the white paint that had once brightened them all was flaked and peeling. Where there was still glass, it was grimy and uncared for. But where glass panes were missing, someone had put up brown paper on the inside to keep out the worst of the wind. Someone was living there.

I stood back and allowed Lady Hardcastle to peer cautiously in through the nearest ground floor window – she was the one with the gun, after all.

'Someone's definitely been here recently,' she said. 'There are enamelled mugs and plates on the table – half a loaf of bread, too.'

'Any signs of life?' I asked. I was keeping an eye on the track through the trees so that no one could take us unawares.

'None that I can see. It's quiet, too. I count five plates. Five people make quite a racket just going about their daily lives. I'd say there was no one at home.'

'Shall we look inside?' I said. 'We've come all this way, after all.'

'You read my mind. I imagine the door will be locked.'

She was right. The old door had no visible keyhole, but someone had fitted a shiny new hasp and staple, and had secured it with a substantial padlock. I unclipped my brooch and removed the picklocks concealed within.

'My employer might have neglected to tell me that our outing might place us in peril of our lives,' I said, 'and for future reference I would have slipped a knife up my sleeve if she had, but I don't go anywhere without my picklocks.'

'Which I bought for you,' she said.

'For my birthday, yes. I'm profoundly grateful. Now get out of my light.'

I always loved big padlocks. They were heavy and sturdy. They gave the impression of invulnerability and protection. And I could open them in seconds.

'Once we're inside,' I said as I lifted the lock from the hasp, 'there's no way for us to re-lock this. If anyone comes along while we're inside, they'll know something's up.'

'There's not a great deal we could do to escape if that happens anyway. Let's just hang the lock on the staple and hope they think they forgot to lock up.'

'Unless . . .' I said slowly. 'Do you think any of these windows will open?'

'That kitchen window looks as though it might,' she said.

'In that case, you nip inside and open it. I'll re-lock the door and hop in through the window.'

'We'll still be stuck inside if someone comes back.'

'We will, but we'll get an extra few seconds while they fiddle about opening the door. That'll give us time to . . .'

'To what, dear?' she said.

'To think of something,' I replied. 'Perhaps there's somewhere in there to hide. If we leave the door unlocked, they'll tumble us as soon as they arrive. At least this way we give ourselves a chance of remaining undiscovered.'

'You make a good case,' she said. 'Let's hope it doesn't come to it, though. I don't fancy our chances either way.'

A few moments later we were both inside the cottage with the door securely locked.

To the left of the front door was the kitchen. As Lady Hardcastle had already attested, it contained evidence of recent occupation. As well as the bread and cheap tableware, the trestle table also held a chunk of cheese, a jug of milk, a handful of apples, and a tin of tea.

To the right of the door was a parlour. There were two army cots leaning against the wall, with their bedding rolled up neatly beneath them. Three folding chairs like the ones around the table in the kitchen were set up facing the fireplace.

There was a body on the floor.

'Well, that's unexpected,' said Lady Hardcastle, crossing the floor to examine the corpse.

'She is dead, I take it,' I said.

'Yes and no,' she said. 'She's certainly not alive, but then again, she never was. It's a dummy.'

She turned the dummy's head towards me and I saw its wax face for the first time.

'Zelda Drayton,' I said.

'I would say so, yes,' said Lady Hardcastle. 'That's even more unexpected.'

She put the dummy back as we had found it and we scouted around.

There was nothing much of any interest in the parlour, and an examination of the kitchen table provided only evidence that mice had been at the bread, fruit, and cheese.

There were two rooms upstairs, each being used as a bedroom. Each room contained two more army cots, though only three of the four beds appeared to be in use. We split up.

I went into the room above the kitchen. Two people had been sleeping here, and from the clothes lying in untidy heaps on the floor I could tell that it was two men. At least one of them enjoyed cigars, which he kept in a travelling humidor bearing a brass plate engraved with the initials BN.

'You ought to come and take a look at this,' I said.

'I probably ought,' replied Lady Hardcastle as she crossed the landing. 'There's little to remark upon in there. There are two sets of ladies' clothes, though only one of the beds is in use. Other than that, it's as neat as a pin. What have you . . . ?'

I held up the humidor.

'That's most unexpected,' she said. 'What's in the wardrobe?'

I opened the door and looked inside. It contained two suits of different sizes, a hat, and two wigs.

'A couple of suits,' I said. 'A couple of wigs.'

'A couple of what?'

I stood aside to let her look. 'See for yourself.'

'I'd say it was unexpected, but with quite so many surprises I'm beginning to expect them.'

'That probably sounded better in your head,' I said.

'I talk a lot, dear – you can't expect every utterance to be a perfectly crafted work of genius. What's that on the nightstand?'

I stepped over to where she was pointing. On the nightstand was a jar labelled MADAME THIBODEAUX'S PUFFERFISH POWDER, a small bottle labelled POTASSIUM CYANIDE, and an empty syringe with a hypodermic needle attached.

'Nothing good,' I said. I lifted the jar of 'Pufferfish Powder' to examine the papers it was standing on. 'Although these look interesting.'

Lady Hardcastle joined me and we looked at the documents together.

Our reading was interrupted by the sound of an approaching motor vehicle.

'Damn and blast,' said Lady Hardcastle. 'Time to hide. Put that back and come with me to the other bedroom. There's space enough for us both in the wardrobe in there – it's bigger than this one.'

Within moments I had replaced everything as I had found it and we had silently crammed ourselves into the nearly empty wardrobe.

We waited.

With no rugs or curtains to deaden the sound, we could hear everything quite clearly, even from our cramped hiding place. Van doors slammed and two men chatted cheerfully. We heard the clatter of the padlock being lifted and unlocked.

Once they were inside, we heard the clump of their boots on the stone floor. They continued talking. They sounded familiar, but I couldn't quite place them.

'I'll be glad when this lot's over,' said Voice One. 'I've stayed in some lousy drums in my time, but they usually come with a landlady and a fresh pot of tea in the morning. This place ain't fit for human habitation.'

'We'll be out by tonight,' said Voice Two. 'Just one more show and we can clear out.'

'Won't come a moment too soon, as far as I'm concerned,' said Voice One.

'Is this cable long enough?'

'Not a clue, mate. Just don't forget that bag – it's got all his clobber in it.'

Some thuds and thumps followed as they heaved something outside. A van door opened and, a few moments later, closed again. The men returned to the parlour.

'Where's the whatsitsname?' asked Voice Two.

'The stuff?' said Voice One with a chuckle.

'Don't mess about. The jar. I can't remember its stupid name.'

'It's upstairs. Himself wanted to keep it safe once he got here. I'll fetch it.'

Heavy boots clumped up the wooden stairs and into the other bedroom. 'Do we need anything else?' called the boots' owner. He sounded frighteningly close.

'No, that's the lot,' came the more distant reply. 'Come on, we can't hang about. We've got to get this lot set up.'

The boots clumped back down the stairs and the two men left, locking the door behind them. We waited until we heard the van clatter to life and drive away before we tumbled out of the wardrobe and straightened ourselves out.

'Most—'

'—unexpected.' I finished her sentence for her. 'Yes, wasn't it just?'

We got out of the cottage by reversing the procedure for getting in – I hopped out the kitchen window and unlocked the front door while Lady Hardcastle closed the window and checked that we'd not left any traces.

'If all goes well,' she said as I refastened the padlock, 'we'll have them banged up before night's end. But if it all goes cock-eyed, it'll be as well to leave things as we found them so as not to tip our hand. Then again, I'm not sure they'd notice anything out of place,' she said. 'If they're doing a bunk tonight, they're going to stumble around by candlelight picking up everything they can find and packing it into their van.'

We set off back through the trees and down the field.

'They're well funded if they have a van,' I said. 'Who on earth has a van? Our shopkeepers are all doing well and they send out a lad on a bike with deliveries.'

'Who, indeed?' she said. 'Who has a van?'

'The mortuary men,' I said suddenly. 'They've been backwards and forwards with a van all week. We'd have noticed if there were any other.'

'Would we, though?'

'Of course. We very often draw a crowd of children shouting, "Poop-poop!" and calling you Mrs Toad when we drive by in the Rover. Imagine the effect another van would have.'

'But the mortuary van?'

'I thought I recognized the voices. I'll lay ten to one it's because we've twice met the men from the mortuary.'

'You're certain?'

'As certain as I can be.'

'Well, that's—'

'Please don't say it. But you're right, it is unexpected.'

'I was going to say, "That's good enough for me", Miss Clever Clogs. Come on, don't dawdle. We need to get back to the village.'

'My turn to drive?' I said hopefully.

'Not on your puff. We're in a hurry. We haven't got time for you to peer cautiously round every bend in case there's a cow in the road.'

'In case there's a person in the road,' I corrected her. 'Although cows are always a worry. Terrifying creatures.'

'Moo!' she said, and tried to race me to the gate.

I beat her easily but held the gate for her and allowed her to board the Rover. I cranked the starting handle and jumped in beside her.

'What were you expecting to find out here?' I asked as we set off.

'Evidence that Hughes hadn't been staying at the Seddon house at all, and that he'd been hiding out up here.'

'To what end?'

'To make it easier for him to get in and out of the village to murder Basil Newhouse and Euphemia Selwood. And to poison Aaron Orum with those mushrooms. We've no actual proof that he was staying at the Seddon house, after all. He admitted he went about by bicycle, and Dan Gibson was injured by just such a machine up there in Toby Thompson's top field. I simply put two and two together.'

'To get three,' I said.

'Well,' she said, 'perhaps three and a half. I was right that there's something going on up there. And I've an idea I know what. But we need to get to a telephone, and then we need to get to the Bonfire Night celebrations before there's another murder.'

We sped on.

Having only terrified one old lady, two horses, and a pheasant, we arrived at the house relatively unscathed. Lady Hardcastle left me to manoeuvre the little Rover into its stable while she dashed in to make her telephone call.

'What news from the forces of law and order?' I said as I divested myself of the heavy driving coat.

'The desk sergeant at Bristol says that Inspector Sunderland is out but that he'd be sure to pass on my message at the earliest opportunity. It was the surly one, so I don't hold out much hope. He did tell me that Simeon is on his way out to see us, though. A social call, I think. Evidently, he said something about wanting to see a proper country fireworks party and set off about an hour ago.'

'It's probably more appropriate that we see him if the mortuary men are involved,' I said. 'Should we call Sergeant Dobson?'

'That was to be my very next task,' she said. 'Yours is to see if Cheetham and Zelda are still here.'

I checked their habitual lair – the morning room – but they weren't in residence. I ran upstairs to check their bedrooms. When I found both rooms empty, I went to the kitchen.

'When did Mr Cheetham and Miss Drayton leave?' I asked Miss Jones.

'I couldn't rightly say. Mr Cheetham came in the kitchen not long after you and the mistress went out. He asked if I'd seen Miss Drayton. When I said I hadn't seen her since before lunch, he got all agitated. Said she was missin'. I offered to call the Sergeant but he said he'd deal with it and then went out.'

'He left the house?' I asked.

'I certainly heard the front door slam.'

I swore colourfully.

'Sorry, miss,' she said, sheepishly.

'No, no, it's nothing you've done. I'm just worried that we might be too late. Thank you, Miss Jones.'

I hurried to sort out our overcoats.

In days gone by, the Guy Fawkes Night celebrations had been held on the village green. Following the rise in the fortunes of the village cricket team at the turn of the century, the club secretary had managed to persuade the Bonfire Committee that the damage they caused to the cricket pitch was unacceptable. The bonfire was now built in a small field at the bottom of the hill that led to The Grange, the home of Sir Hector and Lady Farley-Stroud.

Bundled up in winter coats and woollen scarves, with our sturdiest boots on our feet, we hurried over to the field. A decent number of villagers were already there, chatting merrily in the chill air. Old Joe from the Dog and Duck had set up a makeshift stall and was selling mulled cider, which was being warmed over a small fire in something that resembled a witch's cauldron. Mr Holman was doing a roaring trade in hot pies, while Mr Weakley, the greengrocer, was selling toffee apples from a trestle table. All were lit by lanterns and the site had a cheerfully festive air. But we were in too much of a hurry to be able to enjoy it.

Lady Farley-Stroud spotted us and carved a path through the small crowd to reach us.

'Evening, Emily,' she said, warmly. 'Wasn't sure you were going to make it. Not seen much of you these past few days.'

'Hello, Gertie,' said Lady Hardcastle distractedly. 'I'm so sorry about that. Our plates have been somewhat full, what with one thing and another.'

'Quite so, quite so,' said Lady Farley-Stroud. 'Feeling a bit guilty about that, to be honest. Feels as though I dropped you in it a while. You wouldn't have had nearly so much to worry about if our kitchen hadn't burned down.'

'Nonsense, dear. You weren't to know that all this would happen.'

'Suppose not. Still, things could have gone better. Not certain I'll be inviting any more kinematograph shows to the village.'

'I'm sure this week isn't typical of moving picture festivals,' said Lady Hardcastle.

Lady Farley-Stroud harrumphed.

'Look, I'm sorry to cut things short,' said Lady Hardcastle, 'but time is not our friend this evening. When do you light the bonfire?'

'Seven o'clock sharp, dear. Why?'

'Thank you. It's just that I rather think something alarming will happen and I shouldn't want to miss it.'

Lady Farley-Stroud already looked alarmed. 'Shouldn't we stop it?' she said.

'I'm not sure that would help us, to be truthful. I think things will go a lot easier if we let them unfold.'

'As you wish, dear. You've never steered us wrong in the past.'

'Thank you,' said Lady Hardcastle, and we hurried away together.

Once we were clear of the crowd that had gathered round the food stalls we had a better view of the bonfire, a stack of timber that stood about fifteen feet high. There were logs, fallen branches, carpenters' offcuts, and even a couple of broken chairs.

'Can you see what's on the top of the bonfire?' she asked.

'Not in this light,' I said. 'I was expecting a Guy Fawkes figure, but I see just a black lump.'

'So, do we suppose it's a Guy Fawkes dummy covered with a black cloth? That's a little theatrical for a village Bonfire Night display, don't you think?'

'Theatrical is probably exactly the right word,' I said. 'Do you not think we ought to do something about it?'

'Not quite yet,' she said. 'Let's see what transpires, shall we? I wonder where Simeon has got to.'

'Did someone mention my name?'

We turned to see Dr Simeon Gosling striding towards us. He was barely recognizable with his muffler up to his nose and a heavy cap pulled down almost to his ears, but there was no mistaking his voice or his manner.

'Simeon, darling, how lovely to see you,' said Lady Hardcastle.

'Wouldn't have missed it for the world,' he said. 'I can't wait to see what you yokels get up to on Bonfire Night.'

'I think you'll be surprised tonight,' she said. 'Did you see Sergeant Dobson on your way in?'

'I did. He asked me to tell you that "Me and Hancock will be ready and waitin'." Doughty chap, that sergeant. Ex-military?'

'I've always assumed so,' she said. 'One doesn't like to pry.'

'You rotten fibber,' I said. 'You like nothing better than prying.'

'Armstrong's not wrong, old girl,' he said. 'You've always been partial to poking your nose in.'

'You're both right, of course. Unpardonably rude, the pair of you, but unquestionably right. I shall endeavour to uncover the story of Sergeant Walter Dobson's life in due course. But for now we should keep our eyes open for something out of the ordinary. My money's on that black shape on top of the bonfire.'

I caught sight of some movement to our right. I nudged Lady Hardcastle and pointed out what I'd seen. 'Cheetham's here,' I said.

'So he is.' She gave him a wave but wasn't to be distracted. 'Eyes on the bonfire,' she said. 'I think we're under starter's orders.'

As we turned again towards the bonfire, we saw Lady Farley-Stroud, flanked by two burly men from the rugby club, each holding a flaming torch.

'Ladies and gentlemen of Littleton Cotterell,' boomed Lady Farley-Stroud in her best parade-ground voice. 'Thank you for coming to our little celebration. The fireworks will begin in just a few moments, but first we must light the bonfire. Gentlemen? If you please . . .'

The two torch bearers turned and marched towards the base of the bonfire. In perfect unison, they bent forwards and applied their torches to bundles of straw piled on either side of the huge stack of wood. The straw caught at once and the flames spread quickly. To judge from the smell that wafted back to us on the warm breeze, it had been soaked in paraffin oil to avoid the embarrassing spectacle of a Bonfire Night bonfire that wouldn't light.

There was an appreciative murmur from the crowd as the field filled with light and warmth.

The flames climbed higher until they caught the edge of the black cloth covering the object at the top. It disappeared with a flash of light and another gust of heat.

The sudden intake of breath as every villager gasped in shock seemed to pull even more heat towards us. Standing atop the burning pyre, bound to a sturdy stake, was Zelda Drayton.

The crowd was momentarily stunned into silence and inaction, but one voice rang out.

'Zelda!'

Nolan Cheetham started to run towards the fire.

As he took his first step, Zelda also moved. Her right arm raised and she pointed directly at him. He took two more steps before clutching his throat and pitching forwards. He lay flat on his face, completely still. There was another flash from the top of the fire and Zelda was entirely engulfed in flame.

Chapter Sixteen

There were screams and shouts. The crowd began to surge forwards. Lady Farley-Stroud was still standing between us and the fire. She had turned to face us when Zelda pointed, and now raised her hands commandingly.

'Stay back!' she bellowed.

We were jostled a little, but such was the force of Lady Farley-Stroud's will that most obeyed. Lady Hardcastle caught Lady Farley-Stroud's attention and we were beckoned forwards.

Dr Gosling examined the prostrate form of Nolan Cheetham.

'He's dead,' he said after a moment. 'I can feel no pulse, see no breathing. The body is unusually rigid, as if all the muscles had spasmed at once. If I hadn't just seen him fall, I might have assumed that rigor mortis had set in.'

'Like Euphemia Selwood's body,' I said. 'She was stiff as a board when we found her. Lady Hardcastle had to lever the apple from her hand with a spoon.'

'I wish I'd had a chance to examine her body,' he said.

Volunteers from the Guy Fawkes Night Committee had already started to try to extinguish the bonfire, but it was too well established by now. They managed to throw half a dozen buckets of water on it, but the only result was steam and a scattering of ash. After a brief confab with Lady Farley-Stroud, they turned their attention to controlling the crowd instead.

Lady Hardcastle, meanwhile, was no longer calm.

'I never saw this coming,' she said. 'I thought I had it fathomed out when we found the dummy. I never expected her to kill Cheetham.'

'Her who?' said Dr Gosling.

'Zelda Drayton.'

'She's behind all this? But she's dead now – we just saw the poor woman go up in flames,' he said.

'No, sir,' I said. 'That was a dummy. We saw it this afternoon while we were snooping.'

'A damned realistic one,' he said.

'It's her job,' said Lady Hardcastle. 'Making false things look real, I mean. She's an actress, after all. We completely fell for her "terrified" act.'

'But why?' he said. 'Why burn a dummy of herself?'

'So that we'd all think she was dead. She could get away with murder if we all believed she had died in a fire.'

'But we'd find the dummy in the ashes,' he said, still very much unconvinced.

'I believe she thought of that,' I said. 'You noticed how the dummy's black cloth cover disappeared? I believe it was a variation of something that stage magicians use. Have you heard of flash paper?'

'I don't get to the music hall nearly as much as I'd like,' he said.

'It's a flimsy material made from—'

'Nitrocellulose,' interrupted Lady Hardcastle. 'The same stuff they make photographic film from, actually.'

'Thank you, my lady,' I said. 'Nitrocellulose. It burns with a bright flash and leaves no ash. Magicians use it as a special effect in some of their tricks. I'd be willing to bet that she found a way to rig the dummy with something similar. The face was wax so that would melt. If the clothes and all the parts that made it look like a person went up in a flash, all that would be left would be some charred pieces of the wooden frame. And who's going to think it unusual to find charred wood in the remnants of a village bonfire?'

'You paint a convincing picture,' he said, 'though I confess to being at a loss to work out why she would kill all her friends.'

'You're not alone in that,' said Lady Hardcastle. 'I was planning to ask her when we caught up with her.'

'And how did you plan to do that?' he asked.

'She has some accomplices. They brought the dummy here and I was going to follow them. I reasoned that they'd want to hang around to make sure that everything went according to plan and they'd head back to their lair once the show was over. They left themselves a bit of work to do back at their hideout – tidying and whatnot – so I intended to follow them and see where they led me.'

'How will you know them?' he asked.

'I was hoping you would,' she said. 'They're your mortuary men.'

Before he could say anything, two members of the crowd pressed their way past Lady Farley-Stroud's volunteers and approached us.

'I do beg your pardon,' said the elderly gentleman, 'but did I hear someone say that this poor fellow is Nolan Cheetham?'

Dr Gosling stood. 'It is. And you are . . . ?'

'My apologies, sir,' said the man. His protruding front teeth made him whistle slightly on the 's's. He produced a calling card from his coat pocket. 'Dr Wilfred Peneger, at your service. This is my daughter, Ellen.'

'How do you do? I'm Dr Gosling, the Bristol police surgeon. And, yes, Lady Hardcastle has identified this as the body of Nolan Cheetham.'

'The body?' said Dr Peneger. 'He's dead?'

The young woman gave a yelp of shock.

'Yes, I'm afraid so,' said Dr Gosling.

'The cause?'

'To be determined. I shall have to conduct a post-mortem examination.'

'Well, I fear there's nothing I can do. I saw that he had collapsed and I came to offer my services. It seems I'm too late.'

'Sadly, yes,' said Dr Gosling. 'But thank you for taking the trouble.'

'It was no trouble, sir, I can assure you. One does what one can. Come along, Ellen. We should leave this to the police.'

And with that, they left.

'Someone you know?' asked Dr Gosling once they were out of earshot.

'Never laid eyes on him until just now,' said Lady Hardcastle.

'I thought you country types knew everyone in your little villages,' he said.

'We do, dear, but they're not from the village. They could be visitors from Chipping, or perhaps even further afield.'

'Well, it was jolly good of him to come and offer to help.'

'It was, dear,' she said. 'We're like that in the countryside. Helpful.'

'There's nothing more we can learn from leaving the body in situ,' said Dr Gosling. 'Do you think you can get some of your helpful countryside pals to move him to the police station for safekeeping while we wait for the mortuary van?'

'I don't think you'll have long to wait,' she said. 'Look over yonder.' She pointed towards two uniformed men who were walking towards us.

'What the devil?' said Dr Gosling.

'Your mortuary men seem to be very efficient.'

'My mortuary men?' he said in some surprise. 'Those aren't my chaps. Never seen them before. And how on earth did they know to come here?'

'We shall find out in due course, I expect,' said Lady Hardcastle. 'Don't challenge them. Just keep mum and let's see how this unfolds.'

'I'm not about to let two strangers carry off a body,' he said.

'Trust me, Simeon,' she said. 'Just trust me.'

He frowned his disapproval, but said nothing.

The two men finally reached us. One of them was carrying a stretcher.

'Good evening, gentlemen,' said Lady Hardcastle.

They took in the tableau. They'd seen Lady Hardcastle and me before, but from the panicked glances they shared, it seemed that they had no idea who Dr Gosling was.

'Evenin', m'lady,' said the one I knew as the driver.

'Dr Gosling has confirmed death.'

The driver looked relieved at having had the stranger identified to him.

'Dr Gosling,' he said affably. 'Pleasure to meet you at last, sir. Lewis and Jenner, sir. We keep missing you back at the mortuary.'

'What happened to the other two chaps?' asked Dr Gosling. 'And why on earth are you here of all places?'

'Both off sick, sir. We was drafted in from Stroud to cover. And as for being here, we might be sort of skiving . . . as it were. We've been up here a few times this week and we saw the signs for the bonfire so we thought we'd come along, like.'

Dr Gosling's look of disapproval was unchanged, but at least now it seemed to be directed at the two 'mortuary men'.

'Well, since you're here you might as well make yourselves useful,' he said. 'You have your van?'

'Of course, sir.'

'Then get this chap back to the mortuary. I'll . . . deal with him in the morning.' He glanced towards Lady Hardcastle for confirmation. She gave him the tiniest of nods.

'Right you are, sir,' said the driver. 'Come on, Jenner. If we hurry, we'll have time for a pint in the Eglington.'

With unhurried efficiency, they put Mr Cheetham's body on the stretcher and carried him off towards the gate.

'What now, then?' asked Dr Gosling. 'I've just lost another body. This isn't going to make an impressive entry in my record.'

'Your motor car is nearby?' asked Lady Hardcastle.

'A little way down the lane,' he said. 'But they'll have a couple of minutes' head start on us and we've no idea where they're going. They're certainly not taking him to the mortuary.'

'We know exactly where they're going,' she said. 'And if you let me drive, we can be there before them. I know a shortcut.'

Not only did Lady Hardcastle know a shortcut, but she was also prepared to drive it at considerable speed. Dr Gosling's motor car was a good deal more powerful than our own, and she was making the most of its capabilities.

'I say, old girl,' said Dr Gosling. 'Steady on.'

'We need to get there before they do. It always helps to have the drop on the other chap in situations like this.'

He was clinging nervously to the dashboard and I thought a distraction might be in order.

'I've been meaning to ask,' I said. 'What exactly is a pufferfish?'

'A fish from the tropics,' said Lady Hardcastle. I had hoped Dr Gosling might answer, to be honest. 'Ugly little fellow. Inflates himself with water when threatened. Do you remember we had some *hétún* in Shanghai that time?'

'The poisonous one that had to be prepared by an expert in case we died?'

'That's the chap,' she said. 'Eat the wrong part and it's all over but the shouting.'

'So a jar labelled "Madame Thibodeaux's Pufferfish Powder" isn't likely to be a patent, nostrum, or specific for scrofula, ague, and pains of certain areas?'

'Hardly,' she said. 'It's more likely to be a poison.'

Dr Simeon's grip loosened as he thought about what we were saying.

'When I was training in London,' he said at length, 'we treated a chap who had been in the West Indies. Dipsomaniac. Poor chap's liver was done for. Nothing we could do for him but treat him kindly and let him die with a little dignity. I sat with him one night. It was quiet and there was nothing else for me to do. By jingo but the man had some stories. That night he was full of tales of voodoo. He said he'd spent some time on Haiti, where he'd met practitioners of their local religion, d'you see? Voodoo. Have you heard of "zombies", either of you?'

'I can't say I have,' I said.

'They're the slaves of dark sorcerers, made from the reanimated corpses of the dead. He told some chilling stories about the dead rising from the grave after a day and a night and roaming the island, sowing terror and panic. Sent chills through me, I can tell you. When I was obviously good and hooked, the chap started laughing. Told me it was all nonsense. Said voodoo was descended from an old African religion and had nothing to do with dark sorcery. But he said something interesting about zombies. The chap reckoned there might be some truth in it, and was convinced it had something to do with pufferfish poison.'

'What sort of something?' asked Lady Hardcastle.

'He said that a low enough dose of the poison could make a chap appear dead without actually killing them. Pulse slows and weakens. Respiration, too. Even the most attentive physician might presume death. After "some hours" – he was a bit vague on the details – the poison wears off and the dead chap miraculously returns to life.'

'Well I never,' said Lady Hardcastle. 'Haiti, you say?'

'That's where he saw it,' said Dr Gosling. 'Though he said that there were voodoo practitioners all over the place. Some even in America. Louisiana, for instance. Quite a thriving voodoo community in New Orleans, he said.'

Lady Hardcastle was silent for a moment. 'I think that explains it all,' she said eventually. 'We've been terribly dense.'

The pieces were definitely falling into place.

With a squeal of brakes, Lady Hardcastle pulled in beside the gate we had used earlier.

'Everybody out,' she said. 'Up the hill towards the trees as fast as we can.'

With Dr Gosling to hold us back, we made stumblingly slow progress in the moonlit gloom. He was not a man of action. Thanks to Lady Hardcastle's terrifying driving, we had a few minutes' advantage over our quarry, which meant that there was no one there to hear his intemperate swearing as he managed to fall over every lump and bump in the field.

We made it to the stand of trees just as the mortuary van sputtered its way to the cottage's front door, its feeble headlights barely illuminating the rutted track in front of it. There was time for one more thud, and a winded 'Oof!' as Dr Gosling walked into a tree before we fell silent and peered towards the van to try to see what was going on.

The driver and his mate jumped down from the front of the van. While the driver unlocked the padlock on the cottage door, his mate opened up the back of the van. Four people climbed out, then the driver's mate and one of the passengers manhandled the stretcher out of the van and in through the front door. The others followed, and the last one in shut the door.

Lamps were lit inside, and with one final entreaty to Dr Gosling to please, for the love of all that's holy, look where he was going and not make a sound, we crept stealthily across the open ground to the cottage. I risked a careful look through the kitchen window.

Two of the party were there. I had only seen them before by the light of the Littleton Cotterell bonfire but I was ready to swear that they were Dr and Miss Peneger. He bustled about putting a kettle on the range while she spooned tea into the teapot. Once the enamelled mugs were lined up to her satisfaction, she unpinned her hat and took it off, letting her long blonde hair fall loose. She set the hat on the table and then pulled two more pins from her hair. She grabbed a handful of hair above her forehead and pulled upwards. The wig came free, revealing her own jet-black hair underneath.

Meanwhile, the older gentleman was undergoing a similar transformation. He peeled off a false beard, leaving behind just an impressive military moustache. Next came a putty nose and a set of false teeth.

'Well, that was unexpected,' I mouthed.

'The film folk?' mouthed Lady Hardcastle.

I nodded. Not quite as unexpected as all that, then.

She mouthed, 'Check the other window,' and pointed to the parlour window on the opposite side of the door.

I crept across and took a careful peek. The two mortuary men had manhandled Mr Cheetham's body on to one of the cots, watched by Zelda Drayton and Aaron Orum.

As I retreated from the window, I slipped on some loose gravel.

'What was that?' Orum's voice carried loud and clear through the broken panes and rotten frames.

'Probably just a badger or sommat,' said one of the mortuary men.

'Check it,' said Orum. 'We've had too good a run to have it all messed up on closing night.'

I gave Lady Hardcastle one of our old signals, the one that meant 'the game's up, let's get out of here'. She nodded to show that she understood, but chose not to scarper. Instead, she stood up, brushed the dust from her coat, and pulled the tiny Browning from her pocket. She stepped back a few feet from the door. I moved quickly to her side. Dr Gosling chose – wisely given his performance so far – to stand behind us.

The door opened and there stood the van driver's mate, brandishing a short wooden club.

'Good evening, dear,' said Lady Hardcastle cheerfully. 'Is the master of the house at home?'

'What? Sling your hook.'

Lady Hardcastle took a step forwards into the dim light that spilled from the open door.

'What?' he said again, this time slightly less sure of himself. He turned and looked over his shoulder. 'Mr Orum,' he called. 'There's . . . there's . . . umm . . . someone at the door for you.'

Aaron Orum appeared behind him, looking none too impressed by the younger man's efforts so far.

'What the . . . ? Oh,' he said, his voice trailing off. 'You.' Then his manner changed and he said chidingly, 'Where are your manners, Trevor? Let Lady Hardcastle in.'

Lady Hardcastle had been holding the tiny pistol behind her back. As she stepped in front of me to accept their invitation, she slipped it discreetly back into her pocket. She turned to make sure we were following her.

I, meanwhile, kept my eyes on Orum and the mortuary man. I saw Orum bend forwards and whisper something in the other man's ear, then step back out of sight. This didn't look good. I tapped Lady Hardcastle on the back using another of our signals. 'Cave! Something's not right here.' Her hand returned to her pocket.

They waited until we were all three through the door, and then jumped us.

Under other circumstances it wouldn't have been a fair fight. I'd have dropped the two mortuary men and Lady Hardcastle would have pulled her gun on Orum – it would have been over in seconds.

Unfortunately, we had an unfair disadvantage. We had Dr Simeon Gosling with us.

The one I now knew to be called Trevor came at me, waving the wooden club in a manner that demonstrated his inexperience and ineptitude perfectly. I felt a slight twinge of guilt at the ease with which I disarmed him and dropped him to the deck – it didn't seem entirely fair.

I turned to see Lady Hardcastle levelling the Browning at Aaron Orum. He put his hands up and stepped back. Basil, Euphemia, and Zelda hadn't entered the fray, but raised their hands anyway to make sure there was no misunderstanding.

Which left only the other mortuary man to be dealt with before we could go home to brandy and a warm fire. He wasn't a powerfully built man so Dr Gosling should have him well under control. I span quickly towards the front door to check.

'Nobody move,' said the mortuary man, 'or I'll stick the good doctor with this.' He twitched his right hand to draw our attention to the syringe it held. The needle was pointed at Dr Gosling's neck. 'Despite my uniform, I don't have any medical experience myself,' he continued, 'but my understanding is that a large dose of potassium cyanide isn't recommended for anyone who wants to live a long and happy life.'

Lady Hardcastle put her pistol on the ground. 'There's no need for that, dear,' she said calmly. 'You've harmed no one until now. You don't want to risk a visit to the hangman. Not now you've come so far.'

'Oh, do shut up,' said a newly emboldened Aaron Orum. 'We've had to listen to quite enough from you over the past week, thank you.' He bent down to pick up the pistol. 'Trevor? Trevor, you idiot. Get up.'

Trevor groaned and struggled to his feet.

'Tie these three up. By the time they're found – if they're found – we'll be on our way to N—'

'Good idea, Aaron,' said a croaky voice from the cot in the parlour. 'Tell them where we're going, why don't you?'

'Nice to have you back with us, Nolan, old pal,' said Orum.

'Nice to be here,' said Cheetham, who was now sitting up. He sipped at the water that Zelda had given him. 'Treat the ladies gently,' he said. 'They're interfering busybodies but they were generous and gracious hosts. No need for rough stuff.'

Trevor looked disappointed. It has always been my experience that men really rather resent being bested by a diminutive lady's maid – he had clearly been hoping for the chance of a little retribution.

While Orum kept us covered with the pistol, Trevor had the three of us sit on the floor where he tied our wrists and ankles with lengths of cord. Though he was a poor fighter, he seemed to be a reasonably proficient knotsmith. The skills he needed for stage fighting weren't much use in the real world, but I presumed he had also spent some time rigging scenery in the theatre. Those skills would be useful anywhere.

Once we were secure, they ignored us while they swiftly and efficiently packed up. In less than an hour they had cleared the old cottage of every trace of their occupancy. Without another word to us, they took the lamps and left.

◆ ◆ ◆

'I suppose you're used to this sort of thing,' said Dr Gosling forlornly. 'But I have to say that I'm really not having a lovely time.'

'Chin up, Sim, dear,' said Lady Hardcastle. 'We'll be out of here in a jiffy.'

'How?' he asked, plainly not much cheered or convinced by her assertion. 'That Trevor chap wasn't messing about when he tied us up. I can barely move.'

'Well,' I said as I wriggled my arms into a more useful position, 'while I grant you that Clever Trevor is well versed in the art of tying knots, bends, and hitches, he's really not that good with prisoners.' I wriggled my arms a bit more and was soon rewarded with the clatter of wood and steel on the stone floor. 'He entirely failed to search us for weapons.'

I took the knife and began to shuffle towards Lady Hardcastle.

'You told me you weren't armed,' she said as we sat back to back and I set to work on the cord securing her wrists.

'That was this afternoon,' I said. 'Once I knew you were going about the place with a pistol in your pocket, I thought I ought to slip a sticker up my sleeve.'

'Well done, you,' she said. 'And not so well done, Trevor. Ow! Steady on, there.'

'You know how you tend to gesture with your hands while you're talking,' I said. 'You're doing it now. Sit still or you'll get hurt.'

'I am hurt, dear.'

'Sit still or you'll get hurt again, then.'

It took me another few seconds to slice through the cord, at which point she was able to take the knife and set about freeing first her own ankles, then Dr Gosling and me.

'Is everyone fit?' she asked as we massaged life back into our hands and feet.

'As we'll ever be,' I said.

'Then let's get to the motor car and see if we can't catch the blighters.'

We hurried out of the cottage and back through the trees.

'They've got a head start again,' said Dr Gosling after bumping into yet another tree. 'And this time we don't know where they're going.'

'Of course we do,' she said. 'Orum all but told us.'

'Did he? I thought that Cheetham chap stopped him.'

'New Jersey,' I said.

'You got that from "N—"?' he said.

'It's the moving picture capital of the world,' I said. 'It's bound to be where Cheetham wants to end up.'

'So they'll be driving to Liverpool?' he said.

'Hardly,' said Lady Hardcastle. 'They're in a stolen mortuary van. They'll want to get rid of that as soon as they can. They'll have worked it so that they can ditch the van somewhere secluded, get to a railway station, and be on the last train north. Then even if anyone does find the van, they'll have a head start – no one will know where to look, and even if they do, they'll have no way to follow them until morning.'

'We could wire ahead,' said Dr Gosling. 'The Liverpool police can round them up at the station.'

'We should certainly do that as well,' she said. 'But we know how good they are at disguises – any description we send would be meaningless if they've had a few hours on a train to get themselves into makeup again.'

'Then . . . ?' said Dr Gosling.

'The nearest station is Chipping Bevington,' she said. 'But they'd be recognized there. If they don't know the area well, I'd say they'd head for Camsfield. There are enough places to stash a stolen van without making it obvious one is heading for the railway station.'

We reached Dr Gosling's motor car just as Constable Hancock arrived on his bicycle. The steep hill had left him winded and he struggled to speak.

'Got . . . here as . . . quick . . . as . . . I could . . . m'lady,' he wheezed.

'Well done, Constable,' said Lady Hardcastle. 'I'm afraid our birds have flown, but we have a plan to catch them. If you could be a good chap and get back to the village as fast as you can, we'd appreciate the help of the police at Camsfield. Telephone them and tell them we need to stop a party of five men and two women – the four people who were staying at our house, Aaron Orum, and the two mortuary men. They might split up, but that's the total we should end up with.'

The poor constable was still blowing hard, and a rivulet of sweat ran down from under his helmet and into his eye. He blinked it clear.

'But they're . . .' he said, clearly puzzled.

'Yes, we thought they were dead, too. But we have been hood-winked. And now we need to stop them.'

'Right you are, m'lady,' he said.

'Don't worry, Constable,' she said. 'It's downhill all the way back.'

The thought didn't seem to comfort him much as he wearily turned his bicycle and set off the way he had just come.

◆ ◆ ◆

Familiarity with Lady Hardcastle's driving style didn't make Dr Gosling a more confident passenger. If anything, knowing what was to come, and being able to anticipate the feeling of terror and helplessness, made it worse for him. Having been tied up at gunpoint hadn't done his nerves much good, either.

'Are you all right there, Sim, dear?' asked Lady Hardcastle as she took a bend slightly too quickly and scraped the side of his motor car against the hedgerow.

His reply was to open the window beside him and be violently and copiously sick down the side of the car.

'Better out than in, dear,' she said, and pressed on.

Once we were on the main road, the ride was a little less choppy but we had something new to be worried about.

'We've not seen them yet,' I said. 'How confident are you that they're going to catch their train at Camsfield?'

'Not confident at all,' she said. 'They have so many options, and the chances of our picking the same station as them are tiny. And that's if we assume that they're sailing from Liverpool to New York. They might just as easily take a ship from Southampton. Or not travel to New York at all and start a laundry business in Coventry.'

'But we'll go to Camsfield anyway.'

'Occam's Razor,' she said. 'The solution with the fewest assumptions is most likely to be correct. We assume they want to get to New

Jersey to start their life anew. We assume they want to get there as quickly as possible. We assume they don't wish to be caught.'

'Three very reasonable assumptions,' I said.

'Indeed,' she said. 'Ships from Liverpool to New York make one stop in Ireland. Ships from Southampton sail first to Cherbourg, then to Ireland, then to New York. So Liverpool is the best choice for speed.'

'Agreed.'

'And, as we said in the cottage, avoiding capture means leaving as few clues as possible to their intended ultimate destination. The mortuary van is very distinctive, so ditching it near an isolated railway station is a bit of a giveaway. But if it's found in a busy town, no one would have the first idea what their intentions were – they might have done anything next.'

'You make a good case,' I said.

'It's the best one I could come up with at short notice,' she said. 'But it comes with no guarantees. I could easily be so wide of the mark that poor Simeon's motor car will be scratched and puke-stained for nothing.'

'There's one thing I don't understand,' said Dr Gosling weakly.

'Just the one, dear?' said Lady Hardcastle.

'For now,' he said. 'What on earth's going on? Who are those people? Why were some of them dead for a couple of days? Why are they going to New Jersey?'

'All in good time,' she said. 'All in good time. I'm going to have to explain all this to the inspector in the morning – you'll just have to wait. I don't want to have to do it all twi—'

'Slow down,' I said.

'Not you as well?' she said. 'We don't have time to slow down.'

'Look ahead. Lights. How many vehicles do you imagine are out on the road at this time of night? If you don't slow down, we'll go clattering into them.'

'Don't we want to catch them?' asked Dr Gosling.

'Ultimately, yes,' I said. 'But we'll stand a better chance of rounding them up if we take them by surprise at the railway station, where we'll have a couple of burly coppers to help us. If we give ourselves away now, they'll have time to work out a new plan.'

'Oh,' he said. 'Sorry.'

'Don't feel too badly, dear. She's had a lot more experience of tactics and stratagems than you have. I'm sure she couldn't conduct a post-mortem or diagnose a case of the galloping quinsy.'

'I shall sit quietly while you go about your business,' he said.

Lady Hardcastle slackened her speed and we followed the van at what we considered to be a safe distance. I confess to being ever so slightly relieved when we saw it take the turning towards Camsfield, but I kept my feelings to myself. I didn't want to let on that I had harboured any doubts about the plan.

Lady Hardcastle felt no similar need. 'Thank heavens for that,' she said. 'It seems we were right after all. Shall we continue our gamble, do you think? Shall we stop following them and just head straight for the railway station?'

'You've been right so far,' I said. 'And I see no other reason for them being here.'

We were familiar by now with the back streets of Camsfield, having visited the town several times when Chipping Bevington was unable to meet Lady Hardcastle's shopping needs. She turned off the main road that ran through the town and took a less direct, but more discreet, route to the railway station.

I was further relieved as we drew up outside to see that the two local policemen were waiting by the main door. Lady Hardcastle parked the motor car and approached them.

'Good evening, Sergeant,' she said. 'I'm Lady Hardcastle. I asked Constable Hancock from Littleton Cotterell to call you. Our quarry will be arriving any minute so I think we might be better off concealing ourselves inside.'

'Right you are, m'lady. Come along, Perkins.'

'I hope it hasn't been too awful being out here in the cold,' she said as we went in.

'So long as it's not a fool's errand, m'lady,' said the sergeant. 'But if you're right, and we do end up catching a gang of murderers, I'd say it was worth any amount of discomfort.'

Dr Gosling drew breath as though he was about to set the man straight, but I shook my head. Now was not the time for a full explanation. We'd get more cooperation from the local bobbies if they thought they were helping to nab a gang of desperate villains rather than . . . My train of thought was derailed.

'Might I have a word in private, my lady,' I said.

'Of course, dear.'

We stepped away from the policemen, who were chatting with a much-revived Dr Gosling.

'It's just,' I said once we were alone, 'I'm not entirely certain why we're planning to arrest the film folk. Now that we know no one's dead, what crime have they actually committed?'

'There's the burning down of the mortuary at the very least. And if I'm right, there's conspiracy to defraud. They definitely need to be hauled before the beak.'

'I await your explanation with interest,' I said.

◆ ◆ ◆

The two policemen hid themselves in the ticket office by the simple expedient of standing behind an ornamental pillar. Lady Hardcastle, Dr Gosling, and I loitered by the door that led out on to the platform, our backs to the station entrance.

Sensibly, the fugitives had split up. First to arrive were Basil Newhouse and Zelda Drayton, who were supporting a very poorly looking Nolan Cheetham between them. They approached the ticket counter, where Basil Newhouse asked for three First Class single tickets to Liverpool. Hearing his familiar voice, Lady Hardcastle and I both turned to face them. They made to leave, but the two Camsfield policemen blocked the main door.

'It's over,' said Lady Hardcastle. 'Come with us into the waiting room.'

They meekly allowed us to lead them into the waiting room, where we secured them with handcuffs supplied by the boys from Camsfield. We returned to our post.

Next to breeze confidently into the ticket office were Aaron Orum and Euphemia Selwood. They were similarly acquiescent once they realized the game was up and followed just as obediently.

That left only the two men who had played the role of mortuary men all week. We didn't have long to wait. In truth, we didn't have long enough.

We were on our way back to our position by the platform entrance when they strolled in through the door, deep in conversation. Dr Gosling panicked and let out a loud 'Oh!', which attracted their attention at once. The older of the two knew they had reached the end of the line and held up his hands to indicate his surrender.

Clever Trevor wasn't nearly so eager to give in. Previous experience notwithstanding, he appeared to fancy his chances. He charged towards me.

Trevor wasn't one of Nature's fighters. He seemed to imagine that his earlier humiliation at my hands had been a fluke, or that I had somehow cheated and taken him by surprise. If he were to use his masculine strength and charge at me head-on, surely I would be flattened and he would be free.

I spent many hours on our trek across China in the company of a monk named Chen Ping Bo. He taught me the fighting arts of his order and as a result I know many interesting methods of attack and defence. One of the most important things he taught me was to allow my opponent to do all the work wherever possible.

Clever Trevor first began to wonder if his own optimism might be misplaced when, instead of fleeing from his terrifying charge, I took a step towards him. Further realization dawned when I grabbed the lapels of his jacket and began to fall backwards. Now completely off balance, he had the briefest moment of hope as he tumbled forwards and imagined that I had made a mistake. Surely he was about to land on me and pin me down.

Poor chap. Still rolling, I landed on my back and got my feet under his hips, flipping him over my head. Once his centre of mass was safely past the midpoint I let go of his jacket and jumped to my feet. I turned to face him just as he thudded on to his back and let out a mighty 'Oof!'

He lay motionless for a few moments, and then snarled some abuse as he tried to struggle upright.

'Really?' I said. 'I've put you down twice already without really trying. Are you really going to have another go?'

After a few more choice oaths, the fight left him and he flopped back down on to his back. The police constable fitted him with his very own pair of handcuffs.

We waited in silence while the sergeant went out to fetch the mortuary van from its hiding place in the town. When he returned, the prisoners were loaded aboard for transport to the local police station. We assured them that they would be collected by the Bristol force in the morning, and set off for home.

Chapter Seventeen

I was the first to wake on Saturday. I thought I had done well to be up so early after the previous night's escapades, but by the time I stumbled, bleary-eyed, into the kitchen, Edna and Miss Jones were already hard at work.

'Good morning, ladies,' I said. 'Are you early or am I terribly late?'

'It's a quarter to nine, miss,' said Miss Jones, pointing at the kitchen clock.

'Gracious,' I said. 'We'll be three for breakfast. It was late by the time we got back so we offered Dr Gosling a room for the night. Zelda and Mr Cheetham are in chokey.'

'But they're both dead,' said Miss Jones. 'I was at the Guy Fawkes party last night. I saw them. They hasn't been . . . ?'

'Haven't been what?' I said with a smile.

'You know . . . raised from the grave. Like that Dracula fella.'

'I think we're safe from vampires,' I said. 'It was all just a bit of fakery and humbug.'

'Well I never,' said Edna. 'We was all so shocked. They cancelled the fireworks. We had to go to the pub to settle our nerves.'

'Basil Newhouse and Euphemia Selwood are in the gaol with them. And Aaron Orum,' I said.

'But . . .' said Miss Jones. 'I saw . . .'

'We all did,' I said. 'But we were all the victims of an extravagantly elaborate hoax. I'm sure Lady Hardcastle will explain everything in due course, but we'll have to tell Inspector Sunderland first.'

The telephone rang and I excused myself to answer it.

'Chipping Bevington two-three,' I said. 'Hello.'

'Good morning, Miss Armstrong,' said a familiar voice. 'Sunderland here.'

'Good morning to you, too, Inspector,' I said. 'I was just talking about you. Would you like to speak to Lady Hardcastle?'

'Nothing too defamatory, I hope,' he said. 'I'm always happy to speak to Lady Hardcastle but you're just as much a part of this. I gather I have you two to thank for filling the cells with dead people.'

'Dead-ish,' I said. 'Although, to paraphrase Mr Twain, I think the reports of their deaths were an exaggeration.'

'So it would appear. Might I trouble the two of you to come down to Bridewell Lane and make a statement?'

'I'm sure that's already part of the plan,' I said. 'She's really rather pleased with herself so I think that trying to stop her from making a full statement might be the challenge.'

His familiar chuckle crackled through the earpiece. 'And do you know the whereabouts of our police surgeon?' he said. 'We seem to have misplaced him.'

'He's here with us,' I said. 'I'm afraid he got caught up in some unpleasantness.'

'Good lord. Is he all right? Are you?'

'We're all fine,' I reassured him. 'It was all in a day's work for us, but I think it took Dr Gosling a little by surprise. We thought he ought to stay here for the night rather than drive home.'

'I await your full report with interest,' he said. 'When do you imagine you might be able to get into town?'

'I'm not sure, sir. There are still . . . one or two things to arrange.'

'They're not up yet, are they?'

'I couldn't possibly comment,' I said. 'I've not been back upstairs yet and we have no male servants to check Dr Gosling's room. Let's just say that I wouldn't be willing to contradict you. I'll make every effort to ensure that we're there by midday, though. Does that suit you?'

'Under the circumstances, I'm more than happy to accommodate whatever you propose. I'm sure a couple of additional hours in the cells will do our recently undeceased residents a bit of good.'

'Thank you,' I said. 'We'll be as quick as we can.'

◆ ◆ ◆

Breakfast was a lively affair. Lady Hardcastle was still full of herself, and still infuriatingly refusing to fill in the missing details. Long experience had taught me not to fuel the fire and to ignore her until she was ready, but she had a new person to torture. Dr Gosling naively fired questions at her, becoming visibly more and more frustrated by her refusal to answer. I let it run on for a few minutes – I felt I owed her that since I refused to play along any more – before I interrupted Dr Gosling.

'You know that she gets a cruel pleasure from seeing our frustration, don't you?' I said.

'I was beginning to suspect as much,' he replied. 'I'd forgotten how infuriating she can be.'

'I find the best thing is to keep mum,' I said. 'She's dying to tell us, really, so in the end she'll have to give in before she bursts.'

'You're a rotten spoilsport, Florence Armstrong,' said Lady Hardcastle. 'I was enjoying myself.'

'I'm glad I provided some small entertainment,' said Dr Gosling. 'I feel I've given you a little something in return for your generous hospitality.'

'You're very kind,' she said. 'Now, then. We should get togged up for a drive into town.'

'You're not coming in my motor?' he said.

'No, I think we ought to bring the Rover,' she said. 'That way we can make our own way home when our civic duties have been discharged.'

'Right you are,' he said. 'In that case I might push off now so I can pick up a clean shirt from my flat. See you at the station later?'

'Where all will be revealed,' she said.

Not long later, Dr Gosling, Lady Hardcastle, Inspector Sunderland, and I were sitting in an interview room in the Bristol Police headquarters on Bridewell Lane. A uniformed constable had brought us a pot of tea and four scratched enamel mugs of the sort we had found in the cottage.

'I believe this is yours, my lady,' said Inspector Sunderland as he handed the Browning to Lady Hardcastle. 'We found it in the mortuary van and one of the recently un-deceased mentioned that it belonged to you.'

'Thank you, Inspector,' she said. 'I thought I'd seen the last of it once Orum had picked it up.'

'My pleasure,' he said. 'But other than their names and addresses, it was the only piece of information we managed to get out of any of them.'

'Then it's a good thing we're here. I think we can supply enough of the missing pieces to enable you to complete the picture.'

'About time, too,' said Dr Gosling.

'You didn't ask her to tell you before she'd wrung the greatest possible entertainment from keeping you on tenterhooks, did you, Gosling?' said the inspector.

'I stopped him before he'd suffered too much,' I said. 'But he was beginning to turn purple with the frustration of it. I feared for his health.'

'Schoolboy error,' said the inspector. 'You'll know better next time.'

'When you've quite finished besmirching my character,' said Lady Hardcastle, 'perhaps I could continue?'

'Please,' said the inspector, 'do go on.' He opened his notebook to a fresh page.

'I'm a little embarrassed that it took me so long to put it all together,' she said. 'We had the bare bones of the solution all along: no matter how many other possibilities presented themselves, we kept coming back to the idea that Cheetham was killing the cast of his picture to generate sensational publicity.'

'Why would he go to such lengths to promote his picture?' asked Dr Gosling. 'Why not simply place advertisements in the newspapers?'

'That would be fine if there weren't so much riding on its success. But Cheetham and his company were stony-broke. Flo's friend Daisy Spratt had lent Flo a magazine that contained an article about Cheetham. We knew the gist – that Cheetham's star was on the wane and that *The Witch's Downfall* was important for the company's future – but until I read the article for myself, I didn't realize how serious things were. According to the author of the piece, this was very much his last roll of the dice. Creditors were snapping at his heels.'

'Then why not sell off all his assets and come to some arrangement with them?' said Dr Gosling. 'I'd bet his cameras and whatnot would raise a good few bob.'

'They would, but then how would he continue to make moving pictures? Even a bankrupt is allowed a bed, a suit of clothes, and the tools of his trade.'

'Then why not allow himself to be declared bankrupt?'

'Reputation,' she said. 'Social standing. Cheetham had come from the humblest of beginnings and was very proud to be so highly regarded as a moving picture producer. He could never have coped with the ignominy of bankruptcy.'

'You're right, though,' said Inspector Sunderland. 'We did keep coming back to Cheetham during the investigation.'

'We did, indeed,' said Lady Hardcastle. 'But we were always pulled up short by the callousness of killing one's friends to promote a moving picture. Not to mention the impracticality of killing one's artistic collaborators – that seemed as self-defeating as flogging the cameras. And so we were stuck. It wasn't until Flo and I happened upon a mechanical dummy and a humidor in the cottage hideout that I began to have an inkling that we might have been simultaneously right and wrong.'

'I made a note to ask you about the cottage,' said the inspector. 'When my lads got there this morning, they found it locked and secure. And yet you're saying you saw it from the inside. Is this something I need to leave out of the official record?'

'There might have been a certain amount of breaking and entering,' she said. 'We were very professional about it.'

'I don't doubt it. I don't think we need to mention it, though.'

'As you wish,' she said with a smile.

'But I interrupted you. We were right and wrong, you say.'

'We were, yes. We had the right man, the right motive, and entirely the wrong crime. As you've seen, the "victims" weren't dead at all.'

'That much we know,' said the inspector. 'I'm somewhat in the dark as to how two experienced policemen, a police surgeon, and two ladies such as yourselves came to assert so confidently that five perfectly healthy people were dead.'

'I think I ought to lay out my hypotheses on the apparent "crimes",' she said. 'First there was Basil Newhouse. We've not managed to speak to any witnesses who saw him leave the Dog and Duck on Tuesday night, but we know from Daisy and her mother that he was still there at two o'clock on Wednesday morning. His body was discovered in the church-yard by Constable Hancock at around five. When we examined the body, we agreed with the village policemen that he had no pulse, and there was no sign of breathing. Flo and Simeon subsequently worked out why.'

'My word,' said Dr Gosling. 'We did, didn't we? You mean the powder Armstrong asked me about, don't you? Of course.'

'We seem to have skipped a few steps in the reasoning here,' said the inspector. 'What powder?'

'When we weren't upstairs in the cottage after not breaking in by expertly picking the lock,' I said, 'I came upon a glass jar labelled "Madame Thibodeaux's Pufferfish Powder". Cheetham must have picked it up in America. He did say something about meeting people from New Orleans when he was extolling the virtues of Fort Lee, New Jersey. When I asked Dr Gosling about it, he told me that some people believe it's possible to use it to fake death in voodoo rituals.'

'Like the apothecary's potion in *Romeo and Juliet*?' said the inspector.

'Just like that,' said Lady Hardcastle. 'Cheetham and Zelda Drayton even mentioned that play when we were chatting to them. I should have made the connection then.'

'I twice overheard Euphemia Selwood telling them that someone was going to get hurt and that it was too dangerous. At the time I wondered if they were threats, but I think she was having second thoughts about the safety of the drug.'

'Quite so,' said Lady Hardcastle. 'Who wouldn't? I don't think they knew too much about how it worked, either. We were always puzzled by the fact that Basil Newhouse wasn't wearing his overcoat on such a cold night, but my guess is that they gave him the powder back at our house, expecting him to have time to get to the churchyard and help them set up the scene before it took effect. When he conked out almost immediately, they had to carry him down there. In all the panic and struggle, none of them thought about the overcoat. Once they'd got him there, they arranged him by the rowan tree while they set up the fake blood stains and dropped the witch's doll where we could find it.'

'You say the powder was at the cottage, though.'

'Yes. They couldn't risk storing all their props at our house, so they used the abandoned cottage. They were always going to need somewhere for the "corpses" to hide out. Do you remember when we were interviewing Aaron Orum in the pub and he described going outside for a walk? He hesitated as he was saying that he fell over a bicycle, as though he suddenly realized he shouldn't mention it. I think Cheetham was cycling back and forth to the cottage with anything incriminating that needed to be hidden away.'

'And how did they know we'd not discover that the victim wasn't dead?' asked the inspector.

'I've been puzzling over this one all night,' said Dr Gosling. 'But it's quite simple, really: that's why they had two of their chaps playing mortuary men. They took the bodies back to the cottage instead of to my mortuary. As long as the paperwork was up to date, no one would double check that the bodies were actually present. I'll bet we find that the real men were paid handsomely to stay at home for the week and not answer the door.'

'It was a gamble,' said the inspector.

'Not really,' said Dr Gosling. 'There's always a bit of a backlog at mortuaries. They'd have been on safe ground in assuming that no one would get round to cutting anyone open until they'd had time to burn the place down and conceal the fact that the bodies had never been there in the first place.'

'That makes sense,' said the inspector.

'Who were the "mortuary men"?' I asked. 'I've been assuming they were members of the company but other than finding out that one was called Trevor, we've learned nothing new.'

The inspector flicked back a few pages in his notebook. 'They were members of the company, yes,' he said. 'Your man Trevor is Trevor Preston, a former music hall acrobat who fancies himself an actor and appeared as the lovelorn George in Cheetham's kinematograph. The van driver rejoices in the name of Léon McDuff, though I strongly suspect that to be his "stage name".'

'Thank you,' I said. 'Although we should have recognized "George". I suppose we weren't expecting to see him again, and he was an eminently forgettable character.'

'You'd be surprised by how often witnesses forget what people look like,' he replied. 'Now, then. Euphemia Selwood was the next "victim".'

'She was,' said Lady Hardcastle. 'That one was even easier. They just gave her the powder, posed her with an apple that they'd injected with cyanide and let us do the rest of the work. Cheetham must have planned to hide everything at the cottage and get back before we were up.'

'Planned?' asked the inspector.

'Yes, I presume that's why the side door was still unlocked when Flo let our servants in later on. He would have intended to come back, let himself in through the unlocked door, and lock it behind him before stealing upstairs to bed. The door remained unlocked, so I think he used his alternative entrance.'

'Which was?'

'The morning room window,' I said as the realization dawned. 'That explains why they were always closeted in there. He was in and out through the window whenever he needed to get to the cottage, and we were discreet enough to leave him to it. None of us actually saw him come downstairs that morning – he was just "there". I assumed he'd come from his bedroom rather than the morning room.'

'Just so,' said Lady Hardcastle. 'Anyway, the "mortuary men" arrived promptly and took Euphemia's unusually rigid body away. We should have noticed then that something was amiss.'

'The stiffness, you mean?' said Dr Gosling. 'I'd always wondered about that. I asked you to talk to me about it, as I recall. But, yes, it's probably a side effect of the fish toxin.'

'The next "death" needed all their theatrical skills,' said Lady Hardcastle. 'Aaron Orum was eating his pie and started screaming about demons. He ran out into the street in front of a dozen witnesses, including us, and tore across the green to the church. He let himself inside. This is speculation, of course, but my guess is that at that point they administered the powder and laid him out on the ground. Meanwhile, one of the others – I'm assuming one of the "mortuary men" – dressed in the same clothes and wearing a wig, made his way to the top of the tower. He put on a show so that we all saw him and then jumped, apparently to his death, but in reality on to an old cart filled with hay.'

'That's some jump,' said Dr Gosling. 'A foot out in any direction and they'd have had a real corpse on their hands.'

'I knew a chap in the circus who would dive from a high platform into a water barrel,' I said. 'Hitting a cart is nothing if you know what you're doing.'

'Exactly. They wheeled the cart out of the way and the chap changed back into his mortuary uniform in time to collect the body.'

'What about the mushrooms in the pie?' asked Dr Gosling. 'What was all that about?'

'I doubt the mushrooms were anything other than common or garden edible mushrooms, after all. When I thought the deaths were genuine, it made sense that Orum would have been dosed with something to make him hallucinate. But now we know it was an act, it's much more likely that he was just eating a tasty pie. He didn't need to be drugged if he were a conspirator.'

'We have to assume that the stories of the enmity between Cheetham and Orum were fabricated,' said the inspector.

'Our only sources were the two men themselves with some corroboration from other members of the troupe. They needed someone who appeared to be on the "outside" to reel in Dinah Caudle and the *Bristol News*. Someone who could make sure she was fed all the details to generate as much sensation as possible and who could become part of the story without being obviously part of the gang.'

'And that leaves the burning of the witch and the "death" of Nolan Cheetham,' said the inspector. 'You said you found a mechanical dummy in the cottage, so I presume that was the witch.'

'Yes,' I said. 'It was an ingenious thing. We saw the plans among some papers in the cottage. The arm was worked by a cable. Probably one of the gang round the back of the bonfire.'

'With nitrocellulose to make it burn,' said Dr Gosling. The inspector looked at him quizzically. 'Miss Armstrong told me,' he said. 'Stage trick. Apparently.'

'Right,' said the inspector. 'Then Cheetham collapses after taking a small dose of the powder and the "mortuary men" arrive as if from nowhere to take him away.'

'That was the only thing that nearly went wrong,' said Lady Hardcastle. 'Basil Newhouse and Euphemia Selwood were there disguised as a doctor and his daughter to make sure Cheetham was declared dead and taken away. They beat a hasty retreat when they realized that the police surgeon was already in attendance.'

'That seems to cover almost everything,' said the inspector. 'How did you know to look for the cottage?'

'Our housemaid's husband's broken leg,' she said.

'Of course,' he said. 'I feel foolish for asking. And the motive for all of this?'

'The publicity,' she said. 'I had that part entirely wrong. Or right but then wrong. We suspected that publicity might be at the heart of it, but we were assuming that the deaths were real so I discounted it. It never made any sense. I could see that with all those deaths associated with the moving picture, theatre attendances would be guaranteed but until I tumbled to the fakery I could never see it as a reasonable way to get increased business. But it's all falling into place now. They'll have some way of getting at the money, some holding company or something. Then, with everyone dead, they could flee their debtors and set up in America. A fresh start.'

'Using the picture's takings as starting capital.'

'Exactly so. And the takings from this week alone would cover their fares, not to mention the collection that the villagers took up. By the time all the company's affairs had been settled, they'd have been living in New Jersey making moving pictures under new names.'

'Well, well, well,' said the inspector, after taking a moment to consider this new version of events. 'It's certainly all very plausible. Let's see what they say when I put it to them that I know exactly what's been going on.'

◆ ◆ ◆

'Do, for heaven's sake, sit down, m'girl,' said Lady Farley-Stroud. 'You're making the place look untidy.'

'Sorry, my lady,' I said. 'Sitting now.'

I sat.

We were in the library at The Grange. We had arrived just as the Farley-Strouds were finishing their lunch. They had invited us to join them in the library for a 'post-prandial livener'.

'What'll you have?' asked Sir Hector as he waved a decanter at us. 'Scotch? Brandy? A pink gin, perhaps?'

'Oh, Hector, it's too early for that,' said Lady Farley-Stroud. 'You ought to sit down, too.'

'Nonsense, my little buttercup. The sun's over the yardarm somewhere in the Empire.' He waggled the decanter at her.

'Sit down,' she said again.

'Right you are, light of my life.'

He sat. He grinned at me, and winked.

'Well, then, m'dears, what brings you to our humble abode?' said Lady Farley-Stroud. 'It's not more bad news, I hope. Do please tell me that no one else is dead?'

'No one is dead at all, dear,' said Lady Hardcastle.

'We've had the vicar round here saying much the same thing,' said Lady Farley-Stroud. 'I know he was trying to be comforting, but I'm really not in the mood for metaphysics.'

'I mean it literally,' said Lady Hardcastle. 'Basil Newhouse, Euphemia Selwood, Aaron Orum, Zelda Drayton, and Nolan

Cheetham are all alive and well. They're being held in the cells by the Bristol police.'

'Well, I'll be blowed,' said Sir Hector. 'How the dickens . . . ?'

Lady Hardcastle told the story as she'd outlined it to Inspector Sunderland earlier. Together we added the details of our discoveries at the cottage. When we were done, our audience sat in thunderstruck silence for a few moments.

Eventually, Sir Hector said, 'Well, I'll be blowed,' again. And then, 'I think we really do need a drink after all that.'

'Make mine a large one,' said his wife.

'I'll have a brandy if you're offering,' said Lady Hardcastle.

'Certainly, m'dear,' said Sir Hector, who was already on his way to the drinks globe. 'What about you, Miss Armstrong?'

I was trying to decide between my usual brandy and the pink gin that Sir Hector had previously suggested. It seemed I hesitated for just a second too long.

'She'll have a brandy, of course,' said Lady Farley-Stroud. 'Always has a brandy, this one. Do pay attention, Hector.'

'As you command,' he said, and poured four generous measures of brandy.

'We must tell the village,' said Lady Farley-Stroud once the drinks had been served.

'I'd be very surprised if the news hasn't already spread,' said Lady Hardcastle. 'Inspector Sunderland will have wired or telephoned Sergeant Dobson by now. And while I have nothing but admiration and respect for our village sergeant, he's not the most tight-lipped of fellows, is he? He'll have told Constable Hancock first, of course, but only in as much detail as he could manage before he hurried to the Dog and Duck to tell 'Old' Joe Arnold. If Daisy Spratt were working behind the bar, the news would be all the way to Woodworthy before Wally Dobson had finished his first pint.'

'I don't doubt you're right,' said Lady Farley-Stroud with a chuckle. 'What do you suggest we do, then?'

'We do what the English always do, dear: we carry on. Did you let off the fireworks last night after we left?'

'No, there wasn't any appetite for it with two deaths on the field. We packed everything away and sent everyone home. Most of them went to the pub.'

'Then let's give them a Saturday night to remember,' said Lady Hardcastle.

We returned home via the pub, where I was dropped off to make further use of the village gossip network. I told Old Joe, Daisy, and Daisy's mother, Eunice, about the plans for the evening and asked them to spread the word. When I arrived home and let myself in through the front door, I was accosted by Edna.

'Is it true what they says about all them film folk not being dead?' she asked.

'They're alive and well and contemplating the failure of their plans,' I said.

'Well, carry me upstairs!' she said.

'It is rather astonishing, isn't it?'

'And you and the mistress fathomed it all out?'

'Mostly her,' I said. 'Though I suppose I helped a little. As did your Dan.'

'My Dan?'

'If he hadn't fallen over that bicycle in Toby Thompson's top field and broken his leg, we'd never have found their hideout.'

'I needs a cup of tea,' she said after spending a quiet moment trying to absorb all this. 'Want one?'

'I never say no, Edna. Can you bring a pot through to the dining room, please?'

'I'll be there in two shakes,' she said, and bustled off.

I confess to having been slightly disappointed that she hadn't followed up by requesting confirmation of that evening's festivities. But it would have taken real witchcraft for the news to get back to the house before I did.

I spent the rest of the afternoon tidying away the crime board. I transcribed the notes on to paper and carefully filed them, together with Lady Hardcastle's sketches, in a manila folder. I made a few notes of my own in case anyone ever wanted to refer to the case again. I had done the same with the notes from our previous investigations. One never knows when these things might come in useful.

While I busied myself with these administrative duties, Lady Hardcastle re-checked and packed the things she needed for the evening.

'I dreads to think what the cricket club will say,' said Constable Hancock as the first skyrocket went off.

'I imagine they'll be delighted,' I said. 'They'll say, "What a splendid use of the village green. How thoughtful of them not to let off the fireworks on the wicket." Don't you think?'

'I hopes you're right,' he said. 'Arthur Tressle don't even like people walkin' across it.'

'The esteemed captain of the cricket club can go to blazes,' I said. 'And the bicycle he rode in on.' I might have had a couple more drinks by this point.

'You're not the first to have said it,' he admitted. 'I must say I loves a firework.'

'Me too. Ooh, look. That was a pretty one.'

I felt a hand on my shoulder.

'There you are, dear,' said Lady Hardcastle. 'I wondered where you'd got to.'

'I've been here all along,' I said.

'Are you having fun?'

'More fun than gunpowder and assorted chemical whatnots ought to inspire,' I said. 'It might be the brandy, mind you.'

She laughed. 'It might well be,' she said. 'When you're done, can you come and give me a hand in the hall, please?'

'Of course,' I said.

The fireworks were finished all too quickly and I made my way to the village hall. The crowd that had assembled to watch was still milling about, chatting and drinking. The next part of the evening's entertainment wasn't due to start for a little while yet.

Mr and Mrs Hughes and their faithful band were still standing sentinel.

'Good evening, Hugheses and friends,' I said.

Mr Hughes reluctantly returned my greeting. His friends half-heartedly shook their placards.

'You know that we're not showing Mr Cheetham's moving picture this evening, don't you?' I said.

'You're not?' he said. 'Well . . . we still need to make people aware of the wickedness that caused so many deaths,' said Hughes.

'I can't believe you're the only ones who don't know,' I said. 'No one died. Cheetham and his friends are locked up in chokey.' I left them to mutter confusedly among themselves before I added, 'Why not come into the hall out of the cold tonight? We're showing some pictures that Lady Hardcastle took in the village.'

'Moving pictures?' asked one of the band.

'Moving pictures,' I said. 'You're in some of them. Come and join us and have a look. We'll be opening the doors soon.'

That was all it took. After another brief, muttered discussion, they carefully stacked their placards against the wall and formed an orderly queue by the door. They were going to be the first ones in.

Inside, I was delighted to see that there was nothing left for me to do. Dewi was in charge of the projector, Daisy was supervising the seating, and Ladies Hardcastle and Farley-Stroud were huddled conspiratorially in the corner. I approached.

'Hello, dear,' said Lady Hardcastle.

'Hello,' I said.

An awkward pause followed.

'Did you want me for something?' she said.

'No, my lady, you asked me to come and give you a hand.'

'Did I? Oh, yes, so I did. It's all taken care of.'

'So I'll just . . . ?'

'Do as you please, dear. The night is yours.'

So I did as I pleased.

I sought out Daisy and we sat together during the screening, making *sotto voce* comments about the antics of the villagers. So enthusiastic was the response from the audience that we had to watch it through twice more, and by the third time, no one's comments were *sotto voce* as everyone piped up to mock their friends and neighbours.

The evening ended with another screening of *Town Mouse and Country Mouse*, followed by a speech of thanks from Lady Farley-Stroud for everyone's help and support during the first ever Littleton Cotterell Moving Picture Festival.

First? I thought to myself. Surely there won't be another one.

Lady Hardcastle and I were chivvied out and told to leave the tidying up to the committee. We arrived back at the house to find two shivering vagabonds on the doorstep.

'You're a couple of idiots,' said Lady Hardcastle as I unlocked the door and ushered everyone inside. 'Why didn't you come to the village and find us?'

'We wouldn't know where to look,' said Skins. 'So we just sort of waited here.'

Chapter Eighteen

Barty Dunn and Skins Maloney had left their instruments on the train to London when they hopped off at Chipping Bevington.

'It was delayed,' said Skins. 'Leaves on the line or some such old tosh. We'd been sittin' there for ages waitin' for . . . Actually, I never worked out what we was waitin' for. Some bloke with a broom to clean the tracks, probably. So we said, "Why not go and cadge a bed for the night at Lady H's gaff?" And here we are.'

And there, indeed, they were.

I managed to put together some bread and a cold collation, and we polished off the evening with gossip and songs around the piano. Both men turned out to be able piano players and they took it in turns with Lady Hardcastle to hammer out a few popular tunes. Between songs, we filled them in on everything they'd missed since they left for Gloucester on Thursday afternoon.

'You two don't do things by halves, do you?' said Skins. 'Anyone else would be content to watch a few pictures and polish off the night with a swift half in the local pub. But not you two. You have to get mixed up in murders what ain't murders and get yourselves held prisoner at needle-point.'

'To be fair,' said Lady Hardcastle, 'we didn't invite Cheetham and his co-conspirators to the village, and we weren't held prisoner for long.'

'Although we were brought to heel by nothing more than a needle,' I said.

'Which we thought was on the end of a syringe loaded with cyanide,' she said defensively.

'Weren't it?' asked Skins.

'No,' I said. 'It was water. They weren't real murderers.'

'No, but we all thought they were,' said Barty. 'Because we all thought half of them were dead.'

'Not entirely unlike your news of Günther Ehrlichmann,' mused Lady Hardcastle. 'We all thought he was dead, too.'

'But he must be,' I said. 'You shot him. In the head.'

'And yet . . .' she said.

The ensuing silence was broken by Skins's cheerful voice.

'Still,' he said, 'it wasn't exactly your typical Friday night, was it?'

'It's dismayingly typical of our Friday nights,' I said. 'But what about you two? How was Gloucester?'

They went on to describe the horrors of sitting in for the rhythm section of a third-rate ragtime band 'in the middle of bleedin' nowhere'. I decided not to ask them where they thought they were now if a city like Gloucester could be dismissed as being in the middle of nowhere. The outer edges of nowhere, perhaps.

We retired well after midnight, but not before I had discreetly let the boys know that it was now Lady Hardcastle's birthday.

'You should have told us sooner,' said Barty. 'We could have got her something.'

'I could,' I said. 'But I had no idea you were both going to pitch up on our doorstep tonight, now did I?'

'Fair enough,' he said. 'We'll have to think of something.'

'Nonsense,' I said. 'Your good wishes will be more than sufficient. I just wanted to make sure you knew why we were making a fuss of her in the morning, that's all.'

I left them to 'kip down in the best doss-house in the West'.

◆ ◆ ◆

Breakfast in bed was most definitely called for on birthdays. I let the old girl sleep in (she was forty-two now, after all, and needed her rest, the poor thing) but by half-past eight I decided I couldn't wait any longer. With Miss Jones's help I put a pre-breakfast tray together, with soft-boiled eggs, buttered toast, coffee, more toast, and a pot of jam.

I knocked on the bedroom door and entered without waiting for a reply.

'Happy birthday,' I said excitedly as she stirred beneath the covers. A tangled cloud of dark hair emerged from the blanket cocoon she'd been nested in.

'Good morning,' she mumbled. 'Is that coffee I smell?'

'Birthday coffee for the birthday girl,' I said. I set the tray on the bed and threw open the curtains with a flourish, whose exuberance the thin wintry light dribbling in through the window entirely failed to live up to.

'Presents?' she said as she sat up.

'On the tray,' I said.

'Oh,' she said with the tiniest trace of a pout. 'An envelope. You shouldn't have.'

'Just open it, you miserable old biddy,' I said.

She lifted the flap and pulled out the contents. She set several pieces of paper aside and read the letter.

'"Dear Sis",' she said. 'Oh, it's from Harry, how lovely. "Dear Sis, Lavinia and I have been driven almost barmy by the ceaseless bickering between various branches of her illustrious family and have decided to give the old cathedral-and-baronial-hall-nosebag a miss. Instead, we plan to elope, and to the devil with the lot of them. Please find enclosed two tickets to Gretna Green. Strong-arm has all the details. Happy birthday, old girl. Love, as always, Harry." What a lovely treat. When is it?'

'We leave first thing tomorrow,' I said.

'"First thing"?' she said warily.

'The train leaves Chipping Bevington at nine-fifteen in the morning.'

She groaned.

'Buck up,' I said. 'It's the start of an adventure. We travel to Gretna Green, where we meet Harry and Lady Lavinia. Once they've done whatever it is they do in the blacksmith's shop at Gretna Green, we leave the happy couple to their honeymoon and we're off on another train to Edinburgh. We'll be staying at the North British Hotel, courtesy of the groom, who is also treating us to dinner in lieu of a posh wedding breakfast.'

'Actually, that does sound rather lovely,' she said.

'There's lots to do in Edinburgh,' I said. 'And we need a break.'

'We do. You're right.' She cracked her egg. 'But what did you get me?'

I reached into the pocket of my apron and produced a small box.

'I had this made for you,' I said.

She opened the box to find a brooch in the shape of two mice, one in a top hat and morning coat, the other in flat cap and tweeds.

By the time Lady Hardcastle made her way downstairs, the boys were up and doing . . . something or other in the morning room.

'I'm not sure we should let houseguests hide themselves away in the morning room any more,' said Lady Hardcastle. 'Who knows what they might be getting up to in there. We'll probably wake up tomorrow to find that they've been murdering local musicians in some sort of plot to become Gloucestershire's only ragtime rhythm section.'

'I think it's a good deal more innocent than that,' I said. 'I'll just check whether it's all right to go in there yet.'

'Have you two nearly finished?' I asked as I popped my head around the door.

'All done,' said Barty.

'You can send her in,' said Skins.

I stood aside and held the door open. 'Please, my lady, do go in. I'll get Edna to bring breakfast through.'

By the time I rejoined them, they were sitting around the table. Lady Hardcastle had yet more paper in front of her.

'It's a day for treats,' she said. 'They've not only made me this enchanting birthday card . . .' – she held up a piece of folded foolscap; they had drawn a caricature sketch of themselves with the caption *Happy Birthday to a regular ragtime gal* – '. . . but they've also given me this suspiciously unofficial-looking handwritten invitation to the Rag-a-Muffin club at a time of my choosing. There's even a promise of complimentary cocktails.'

'We know the management,' said Skins.

'It's all completely above board,' said Barty.

'It's a splendid gift,' said Lady Hardcastle. 'Thank you very much, boys.'

Edna arrived with yet more food.

I got Miss Jones to make the musicians some sandwiches for the train. I also managed to find a couple of bottles of beer in the larder, though I was glad I wasn't going to be around when they opened them – heaven alone knows when we bought them.

They'd thought ahead and had instructed the chap with the dog cart who plied his trade at Chipping Bevington station to pick them up at noon. We waved them off at the door and they loaded themselves on to the cart. I was about to close the door when I saw Skins trotting back down the path.

'Did you forget something?' I said.

'Well,' he said, 'you see . . . the thing is . . . well . . . what I mean to say . . .'

I smiled and raised my eyebrows, encouraging him to go on.

'I . . . umm . . . was sort of wondering . . .'

Barty was clearly growing impatient. 'Hurry up, Skins!' he shouted. 'We'll miss the bleedin' train.'

'Yes . . . well . . . you see . . .' Skins mumbled.

'Seriously, mate,' shouted Barty. 'We've got a job tonight.'

'Er . . . yes . . . well, I'd better go, then,' said Skins, and ran back down the path to the waiting dog cart.

'What was all that about?' asked Lady Hardcastle when I'd shut the door.

'I'm not entirely certain,' I said. 'I think I might have been paid court. To. Or however you might like to say it.'

'But you're not certain.'

'It was very hard to tell.'

'I'm sure we'll see them again.'

'I'm sure we will, my lady,' I said. 'But for now I have to pack for Scotland.'

Author's Note

In the early days of moving pictures, it was common for filmmakers or actors to stand to the side of the screen and narrate the action. By 1909 this had fallen out of fashion but I felt it would have been exactly the sort of thing Nolan Cheetham would have done, and I'm assured by my tame expert that it wouldn't have raised any eyebrows in a small village like the fictional Littleton Cotterell.

Similarly, the practice of filming local folk during the day and showing them the results for a fee in the evening had fallen out of fashion by 1905, but it would still have been possible to amuse villagers in this way, especially if the film were being shot by one of their own (in this case, Lady Hardcastle).

Speaking of Lady Hardcastle, she's quite the innovator. Stop-motion animation techniques had been around for quite a while, but they were far from commonplace, even in 1909. I thought it would be fun to have her as an amateur pioneer.

In case you were wondering, there is no Bishop of Rochdale.

On 4 November 1909, the moon was in its final quarter and didn't rise over the west of England until after 10 p.m. I know because I looked it up. Nevertheless, I needed a full moon to make the events of that evening visible so I wrote one and had it high in the sky by 7 p.m. I hope you don't mind.

Despite the way it's repeatedly used in fiction, tetrodotoxin (pufferfish venom) can't be used to fake death, it can only be used to kill you. Nevertheless, it persists in stories of voodoo rituals and there is some evidence that Haitian zombie powder contains small amounts of pufferfish venom; it is still suggested that it might account for the stories of people returning from apparent death.

Hamlet the Great Dane's appearance in the story is by way of being an affectionate nod to the memory of my mother's cousin Beryl, who died while I was writing the book. She played a strong and loving part in my childhood and I miss her. Almost as much, I miss one of her dogs, a 'blue' Great Dane who genuinely did rejoice in the name of Hamlet. He was boisterous, wilful, and clumsy (a congenital defect meant that the inner bones of his forelegs – the radius – grew faster than the outer – the ulna – leaving his front paws splayed out and difficult to control). One of his favourite pastimes was to stand with his wonky front legs on a high retaining wall at the end of the front garden and loom over passers-by, at whom he would joyously bark. He never – to my knowledge, at least – knocked down a small crowd of people, but I'm sure he would have loved to, had he ever had the opportunity.

Acknowledgments

I am indebted to Dr Peter Walsh for sharing his extensive expert knowledge of turn-of-the-twentieth-century British cinema. I probably owe him at least one more lunch.

I am also inordinately grateful to Jo Webster-Green, whose painstaking cataloguing of Lady Hardcastle's previous exploits has saved me from making many a mistake with characters and their histories.

And of course, a massive, heartfelt 'thank you' to the team at Thomas & Mercer. I'm most especially grateful to my two (count 'em, two) wonderful editors, Jane Snelgrove and Victoria Pepe, without whose professional and personal support during a trying year none of this would have been possible. And I can't leave out Hatty Stiles, either, because that would just be rude.

About the Author

Photo © 2018 Clifton Photographic Company

T E Kinsey grew up in London and read history at Bristol University. He worked for a number of years as a magazine features writer before falling into the glamorous world of the Internet, where he edited content for a very famous entertainment website for quite a few years more. After helping to raise three children, learning to scuba dive and to play the drums and the mandolin (though never, disappointingly, all at the same time), he decided the time was right to get back to writing. *A Picture of Murder* is the fourth novel in a series of mysteries starring Lady Hardcastle. There is also a short story, 'Christmas at The Grange'. His website is at tekinsey.uk and you can follow him on Twitter – @tekinsey – as well as on Facebook: www.facebook.com/tekinsey.

Made in the USA
Monee, IL
16 April 2024

56840834R00187